Shadow Flight

By John Harrison

Published by C. E. R. Ellwood
under the House of Harrison imprint

ISBN-13: 978-1-947061-12-5

Printed in the USA
Second trade paperback edition, November 2019
First trade paperback edition, 2014

This series is for those that love life... and all of its possibilities.

I also dedicate this book to my mom, Sue A. Harrison. You not only taught me how to live, you helped me learn that life is not what we find, it is what we make it of it. Thank you.

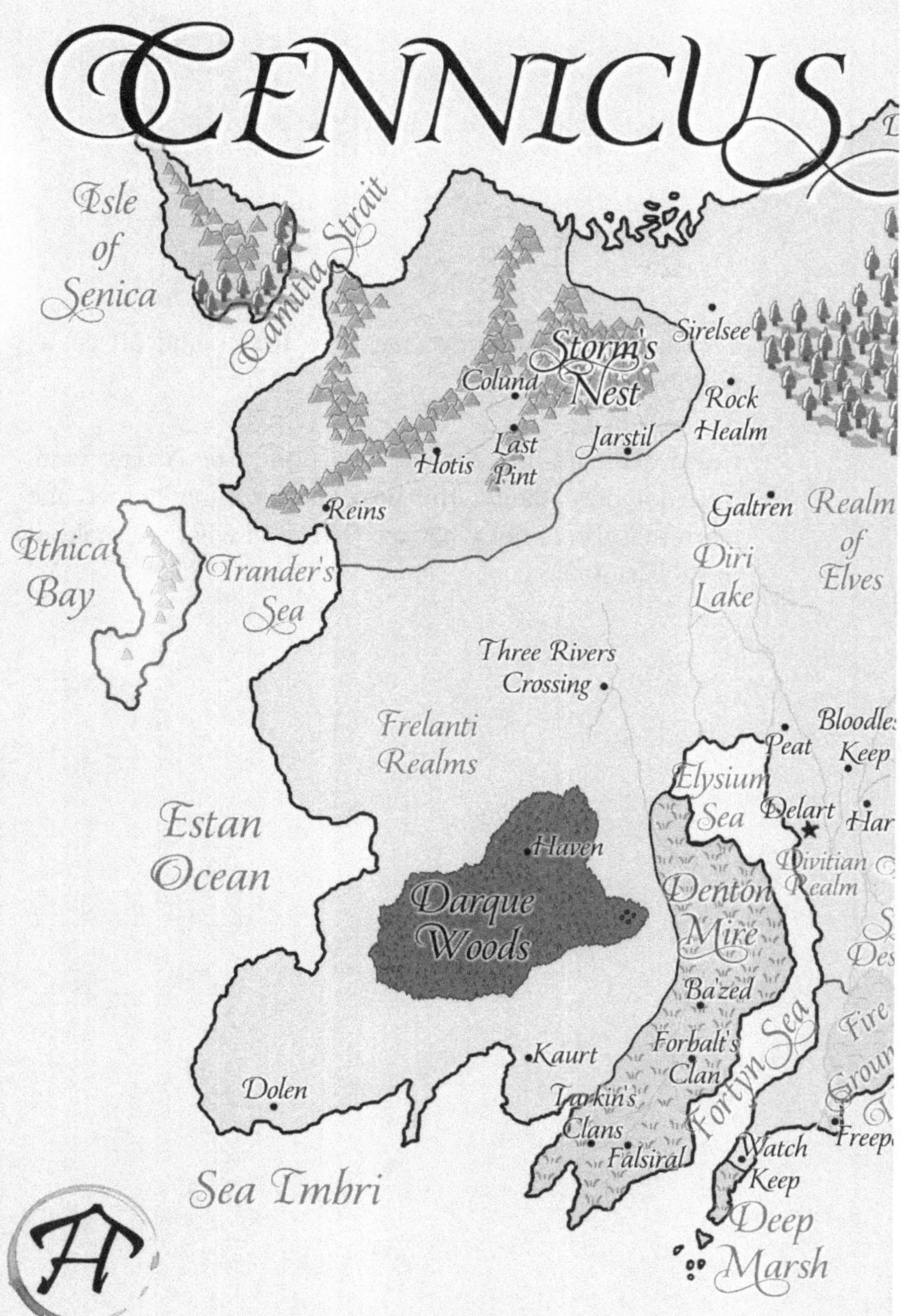

CENNICUS
Isle of Senica
Camitia Strait
Storm's Nest
Sirelsee
Coluna
Rock Healm
Last Pint
Jarstil
Hotis
Reins
Galtren
Realm of Elves
Ithica Bay
Trander's Sea
Diri Lake
Three Rivers Crossing
Frelanti Realms
Bloodles Keep
Peat
Elysium Sea
Delart
Har
Estan Ocean
Haven
Divitian Realm
Denton Mire
Darque Woods
Ba'zed
Fortyn Sea
Fire Groun
Des
Kaurt
Forbalt's Clan
Dolen
Tarkin's Clans
Falsiral
Watch Keep
Freep
Sea Imbri
Deep Marsh

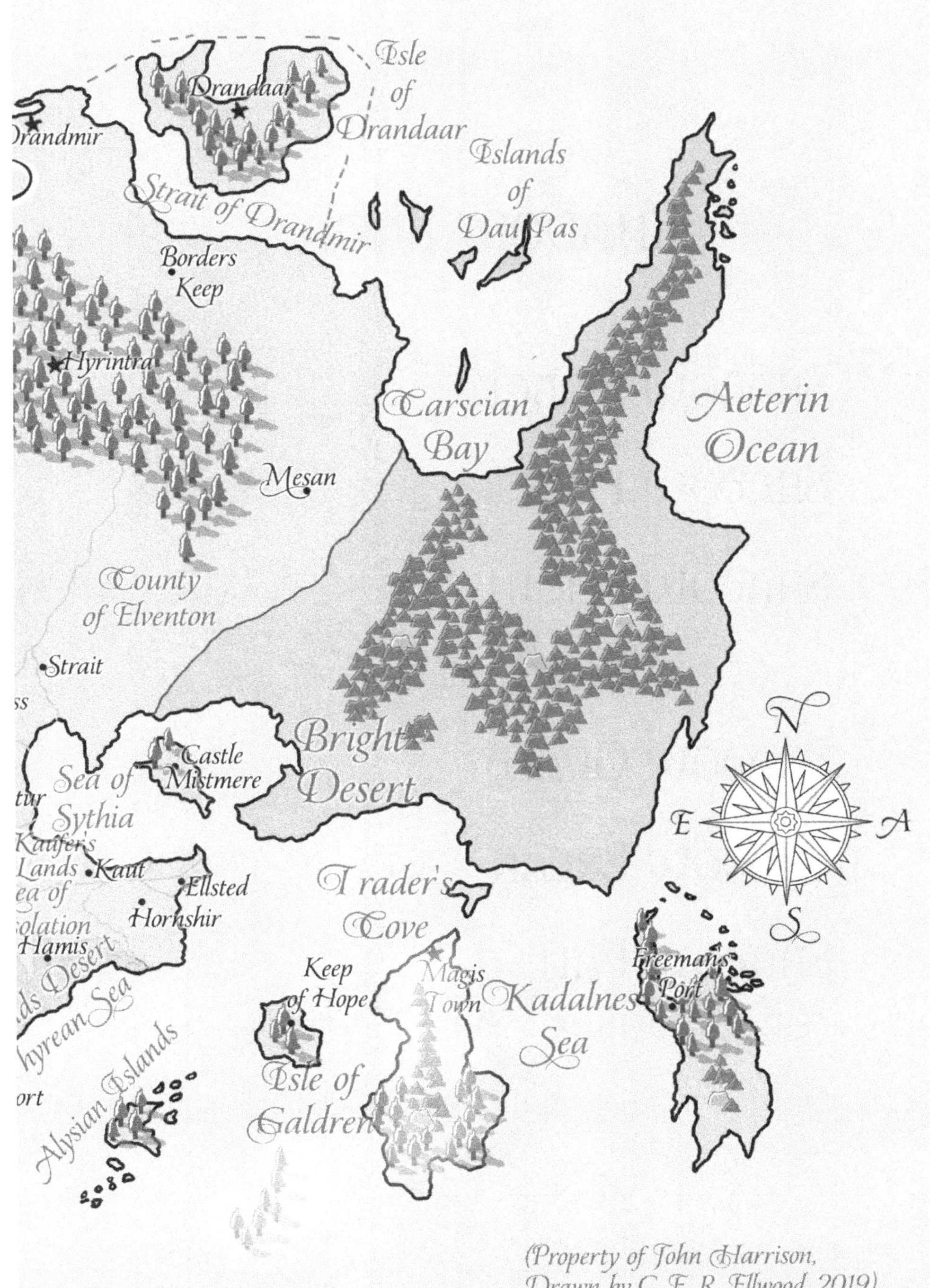

Isle
of
Drandaar
Drandaar
Drandmir
Islands
of
Dau Pas
Strait of Drandmir
Borders
Keep
Hyrintra
Aeterin
Ocean
Mesan
Carscian
Bay
County
of Elventon
Strait
Bright
Desert
Castle
Mistmere
Sea of
Sythia
Kaufer's
Lands
Kaut
Ellsted
Hornshir
Sea of
Desolation
Hamis
Trader's
Cove
N
E
A
S
Keep
of Hope
Magis
Town
Kadalnes
Sea
Freemans
Port
Thyrean Sea
Port
Alysian Islands
Isle of
Galdren

(Property of John Harrison,
Drawn by C. E. R. Ellwood, 2019)

Shadow Saga

Shadow Dance

Shadow Play

Shadow Flight

Forthcoming:

Shadow Guard

Shadow Break

Shadow Fall

Prologue

Some riddles are not meant to be solved!

Words written to hide the winds of truth
Dreams of time devoured by its serpentine grip
Yet the riddle remains…unchanged and
unchanging time and again…time out of mind

Clues, like history, ebb and flow,
lost and are found
like the answers we desperately seek…
elusive and just out of reach…
caught in the coils of time

Yet hope steels our resolve…
We refuse to give up and so,
are forced to persevere

Will they lead us to salvation?
Or deeper into the very darkness
we seek to escape?

What shall come of them then?

Indeed…

What shall come of us all?

Chapter One:
Sources

The elf pressed his keen ear flush to the cool stone in anticipation. He knew she had heard him, Landolin just wanted to make sure he could understand her response. They had spent far too long trying to track where his soldiers had explored and their safety was not guaranteed.

He shuddered involuntarily as he closed his garnet hued eyes in a futile attempt at removing the sight from his memory. Even the darkness of their surroundings did little to mask the gruesomeness of the scene. Pools of blood and gristle littered the floor and practically coated the walls. The memory of walking through the dripping tunnel was almost unbearable. Those ghastly images and the iron-laden scent in the air only made him want to find his people even more.

"He is dead," Farvais answered slowly. Her morbid response was muffled by the thick stone slab that separated them. "I heard him go. Something out there tortured him before he died. Can't you see the blood out there?"

"We can." Landolin practically yelled his response. "How did you get separated?" Landolin asked as he shot a skeptical glance to Gienna.

They had been in these tunnels for far too long and after their encounter with the nassarid, he wasn't sure about anything they came across. Even so, there was something lacking in her tone.

He knew how much Farvais had meant to Trainor. He hid this knowledge from either of them, of course. Landolin could not afford his subordinates to know everything he discovered. At the same time, he had always prided himself on knowing his soldiers better than they knew themselves. That way he knew how to get the most out of them when needed.

"We found this door and figured out how to open it." Her response seemed distant, more distant than muffled. "We traced the lightly carved symbols from left to right, top to bottom," a haunted quality seemed to transfix itself into Farvais's words as they floated through the solid rock. "Trainor told me to go in first, so I did. That's when the door closed. While he was trying to get it opened again, the thing attacked him. I can't seem to find any way to open this door from my side, so I was useless to him."

He watched Gienna trace the symbols in the pattern Farvais mentioned lightly with her fingers. They both watch visibly amazed at how noticeably silent the hidden door swiveled open. Not even the telltale noise of stone scraping across stone as it moved of its own volition. Not even the air was disturbed by the massive stone as it swung open.

"Come out here then, that is if you have nothing to hide," Gienna said evenly.

His sister's tone was flat, yet somehow managed to lend an ominous air to her words. The accompanying clatter as he saw his soldier's weapons skitter across the stone floor conveyed her understanding of Gienna's intent.

"Obviously, she doesn't want either of us attacking her," Landolin thought to himself as he quickly tugged a stray lock of hair back into place behind his ear. "I can't say as I blame her. Knowing how effectively we work as a team, it would be foolish to think she could beat us."

Several more moments passed before a white cloth

flashed from the dark shadows. He knew whoever waved it wore Farvais's armor. The bracers Trainor had designed for her were very distinctive. They were made from blackened leather with an intricate silver knotted pattern etched into their face. The design looked like either a dragon or a unicorn depending on how you viewed it.

Once he saw Gienna secure Farvais's weapons, he cleared his throat. "It's safe to show yourself. We will not attack you unless you give us cause."

Deep down Landolin knew Farvais had heard these words on several occasions, but they had never been directed at her. He knew it felt different when you were the one being addressed. Landolin's stomach knotted itself as he repressed unwanted memories from when he had been taken, prisoner.

Hesitantly Farvais's feet led her petite frame through the darkness's threshold. The inky blackness of the room slowly unwound its tendrils and allowed her out into the regular darkness of the passageway.

"Thank you for freeing me," her words sounded brittle as she spoke and Landolin noticed the subtle wince as harder consonants dropped from her lips. Farvais stepped clear from the doorway hurriedly as if to make sure she would not be trapped again before she added, "I have been locked in there for way too long." The air of playfulness in her words seemed a little too forced for his liking.

"At least you survived," Landolin said as he looked over his soldier's ebony haired head at his sister. "You are one of the last to have survived this mission." The solemnness of his baritone voice added emphasis to the heaviness that surrounded them.

"I know you and Trainor were close. Which is why I think he would want you to have this," he continued as he handed Farvais a dagger from his belt.

It was plain. The sheath was made from dark brown leather which mirrored the smooth chestnut color of the handle. Even the metal was a subdued gray hue and barely managed to catch any hint of the scarce light that surrounded them.

Farvais looked at the dagger with a confused look in her violet eyes as she accepted it carefully. "Thank you for your dagger, although I am not sure why Trainor would have wanted you to give it to me."

Landolin smiled at her apparent naivety. "You passed," Landolin said softly. "We had to be sure."

"I understand," Farvais said with a blank look on her face. Then, without any apparent thought, she added cautiously, "Are we finished here, sir? Have we found everything we came for?"

"We have," Gienna said from behind them.

His sister's fingers brushed the bottom of her new choker as she spoke. It was eerie, yet somewhat comforting. Somehow she had grown very attached to her souvenir; he just hoped her mind would pull through. Killing the beast affected her more than he had seen it impact any of his soldiers and it worried him a little.

"Good, when can we leave?" Farvais said. A hint of nervousness tugged at her words as she spoke and caused them to sound hollower than normal.

"Now," Landolin said as he motioned for his sister to hand Farvais her weapons.

"The sooner the better," Farvais shuddered as she glanced back into the inky blackness of the room she had been trapped in. "If you don't mind, I would like to bring up the rear, sir."

"I understand," Landolin replied coldly. "But I have to decline your request. I need you to stay in the middle. You have been in a darker place than either of us. Your eyes are more accustomed to seeing in it. But I will allow you to hang back a bit. Just stay close enough to be seen."

Landolin waited to move until he had seen both ladies

nod their understanding. Then, without another word, he motioned for Gienna to take the lead.

A slight smile played across his lips as his sister shot him a withering glare. He knew she had enjoyed following him. There is a certain feeling of security in the rear, a sense of exclusivity, which readily lends itself to sorting out your inner thoughts and turmoil. This more than anything is why he could not afford to let either of them be the silent sentinel.

"I need them vigilant," he thought to himself warily. "More so than they would be otherwise," his eyes followed his sister's fleeing form until she was out of sight. He waited for a few heartbeats before he cleared his throat again.

Farvais understood his intention and did not wait for him to speak before she followed Gienna into the darkness. He could tell her attention had been riveted on the room she had just vacated.

There was an odd air about his youthful captain as she tore her eyes from the space she had so recently been imprisoned in. It was almost as if she was looking at something or someone.

Without thinking, Landolin pressed on the door and watched it swivel back into place. He may have imagined it, but he thought he saw something stir in the room. It may have been a hand or maybe a leg. Either way, he was not sure, but it was too late. The door was securely in place before the thought of what it may have been could even register.

The weight in the air matched his mood. Even the muted conversations seemed to mirror the dark thoughts that claimed his mind. No matter how much he wanted it to be over, Namir knew it wasn't. Worse, he sensed the struggle that waited for him was even harder than he could imagine.

His steel blue eyes darted across the courtyard. Without thought, he marked where every person around him stood. As the wind tugged at his golden hair, he tallied professions and skills. Old training Namir thought he would never need slowly took over.

"IMPRESSIVE," Zelios's words played across his frontal lobe. "EVERY DAY YOUR SKILLS AND TALENTS SURPRISE ME, SA'OUVANT."

He felt each syllable tug at his resolve in different ways as if she tested his resolve. Namir wasn't sure what she played at, but he did not like it.

"Carness was a fierce teacher. He demanded only the best from us. His lessons are not easily forgotten," his words flew from his mind as his fingers absently counted what little coins he owned.

"The last meal took most of what was left," his mind raced as he tried to decipher how much he was going to need for the provisions to come. "Hopefully I can at least replace my boots." He thought ruefully as he scanned the snow-laden clouds.

"Not much for a king to live on," he thought to himself bitterly. He knew Haradine was also getting what she felt they needed, but this knowledge only added to his anxiousness.

Namir knew his face was flushed. He felt the burning sensation as it claimed every inch of skin. The only thing he knew to do was expel it with his words, so he did, "How am I supposed to be a good leader if I am always depending on others just to survive!"

It was going to be a rough and uphill fight to lay claim to his Crown and his heritage. Namir knew it, but there was nothing he could do. He had no real choice that is if he wanted to fulfill his destiny. His acceptance of this did little to ease the sting of its reality. Although Namir wished it could be little easier than this, he knew it wouldn't.

The tunic and breeches he wanted to buy for his announcement were a tempting expense, however, after he looked at the price, he decided against getting them. The price was too high. Even though he knew his claim would be better received if he could look the part, he couldn't risk spending the last of his few coins so trivially.

"Maybe next time," he muttered under his breath as he turned and left the shop.

The crisp afternoon air pulled at what little heat his cloak offered. His stride stuttered a little as he stepped into an unexpected drift of snow. Icy fingers of pain shot through the skin of his feet as some snow explored various holes in his boots he was unaware of. He knew drifts always seemed to gather near the buildings of town, but he always had been bad at gauging exactly where they would be.

"There you are," Haradine said from behind him. Her conspiratorial tone was not easy to miss. "I have been looking for you."

Out of the corner of his eye, Namir studied the elf as he turned. Something was odd. She seemed taller for some reason. He quickly glanced over her body again and realized why. She wasn't standing in the snow; she was on it.

"How do you do that?" Namir asked amazed.

"Do what?" Haradine asked. Even if he hadn't seen her right eyebrow slightly arch, he knew it had by the warble in her voice that betrayed her confusion perfectly. "Are you trying to change the subject?"

"How do you stand on the snow?" Namir asked, still oblivious to her second question. Although he knew it was rude, Namir could not stop staring at her feet.

The smooth soles of her soft gray doeskin boots seemed to glide across the surface of the snow. Somehow they displaced her weight instead of making her sink like his did. Namir even noticed how dry they were, it was as if her boots repelled the moisture from the snow.

"That must make traveling in the winter a lot warmer," he remarked under his breath. The practicality of it was as amazing as it was unbelievable to Namir and he was hypno tized by it.

Haradine giggled, "Sa'ouvant you are such a child at times. All elves walk on snow. The same goes for mud. We have learned how to disperse our weight across it and use the strength of the water instead of succumbing to its softness."

The jovial tone of her voice stung more than his inner voice that chided him for being so ignorant. Namir knew she wasn't trying to be mean, but that did little to ease the pain it caused him. It was comical. There was just so much he needed to know if he hoped to rule and he knew too little about most of it,

Namir also understood that he could not afford to let other's mock him for his lack of understanding. That is why he always made it an imperative to figure out how things worked differently for Haradine and others before he said something. This time his astonishment proved to be too great and he instantly regretted it.

He couldn't hide his scowl, so instead, he leveled the sternest stare he could manage at her as he asked, "How about just water, are you able to walk on that too?"

It was obvious to Namir that the elf realized she had overstepped her bounds with her response. The way Haradine's gaze shifted from his face to her feet mixed perfectly with the quivering lip that jutted out from her face. All the signs of regret mixed together in her gestures, both small and large.

Haradine slowly tilted her head and looked at her feet as she replied sullenly, "No, not unless there is enough debris in it to distribute our weight, we sink like most other races. Snow and ice seem to be the only exception."

"Interesting," Namir said as he slowly walked around her. "So you said you were looking for me?" He changed the subject as smoothly as he could, to ease the pressure he knew that she felt.

"Aye," Haradine agreed. "Tipin and Carness both asked

me to escort you to the council hall. They decided there are enough issues for them to deal with without needing to worry about the safety of the heir apparent. After a little debate, they figured by sending me to escort you, they could make sure you were safe and distract me from their other tasks."

"Tipin and Carness both asked you to escort me? What happened?" Namir asked.

His attention instantly diverted itself from the subtleties of her race and latched upon the meaning behind her words. Normally the two men kept to themselves. For both to work in unison was rare.

Namir attempted to recall what the few times were when they had cooperated and was hard-pressed to come up with many. The few rare occasions he remembered were the night his parents left Ellsted, a handful of times after that, even when they talked with him about his parent's disappearance. They always made sure to discuss it with him alone.

"It must have been some sort of attack," he reasoned to himself in a furtive whisper.

Namir could see a hint of amazement in her body language. The way her somewhat blank look coupled neatly with a slightly hesitated step was all he needed to see. Even the fact she turned toward him a little more than normal to get a good look at his face, only reaffirmed his assessment. She was astounded and he knew it.

"How did you know there was an attack?" She asked quietly.

Her words were hushed and halting. These two affirmations only proved his assessment was correct. She was genuinely astonished by his perceptiveness.

"A few years ago a wolf attacked one of the villagers. Carness and Tipin worked together to find and kill the beast. Last year we had a problem with a vagrant that attacked a few of our women. The two of them banded together again. The only other time I can think of is when Faris's men tried to restrain Daffer. Carness and Tipin came together again to save the soldiers from Daffer's wrath." Namir ticked off the incidents on his fingers as he turned and to walk toward the smithy.

"Where are you going?" Haradine asked as she purposefully stepped in his way.

"I have to collect my things," Namir said, a little confused by Haradine's lack of understanding. "You said we are going to stay in the council hall until I can address them. I need to get my belongings and your father's books from the smithy if I hope to be ready to meet with the council."

Namir was certain that if he explained it right, Haradine would let him go. Surely she could understand the logic he assured himself as he stepped around her.

"Sorry, sa'ouvant," Haradine's apologetic tone did little to soothe his nerves. Her hand pressed gently against his chest as her smooth footwork allowed her to step in his way before he could react. "I think you misunderstood me. I am to escort you there straight away. We are not supposed to go anywhere else."

"So I am a prisoner?" Namir ventured. He was taken aback by Haradine's straightforward approach.

"No, sa'ouvant, you are not. However, I have been charged with your safety and that is best achieved by going only to the Council Hall instead of traipsing around Ellsted. Once we get you into the safety of those secret rooms, I will gather your belongings."

Haradine's stable stance told him that she obviously waited for Namir to acknowledge her before she would move. He could also tell by the way she stood that she would not back down on this, so he nodded his agreement sullenly. As soon as he nodded his ascension, she motioned for him to head back into the heart of the town toward the Council Hall with her.

Aves smirked as she pulled the jerkin over her head. "So you think he is handsome?"

"I did not say that," Hessa replied quickly. She felt her blush make its way up her neck, so she looked away from her sister quickly. "I just said it might not be a bad thing if he happened upon us right now." She carefully laced up the leather breeches she had found in one of her mother's many chests.

"So you do think he is good looking!" Aves said. Hessa knew that her mistress loved watching her squirm about boys. "Why else would you want him to happen upon us right now'?"

Hessa's blush completely consumed her cheeks. "So what if I find him attractive? You do too and you know it." She dared Aves to respond and when she did not, Hessa continued. "I'm sure that you thought the same thing when he offered to take you to find me."

"I did," Aves admitted sheepishly. "He is very attractive and I just could not help but think about what might happen on the road with him."

"And what did happen on your way here?" Hessa asked. She liked it better when Aves had to answer her questions more than when she was forced to do the same.

"Nothing, he was a perfect gentleman," Aves pouted sullenly.

"Aww too bad," Hessa said sarcastically. A knowing grin had settled on her lips. "He may have been able to teach you a few things to impress your future husband with."

"Stop it," Aves giggled, "You are bad and you know it." She picked up the jacket that Hessa had set aside for herself and threw it at Hessa. "I can't help it! He is cute!"

"He is," Hessa agreed as she looked out of the window at Onas again, "even if he is a little older than us." She tried to banish the improper thoughts that started to swim through her mind as she saw Onas easily lift the saddles into place.

"Age really doesn't matter too much, does it?" Aves asked somewhat innocently. "I mean, older men know what they are doing more than boys do. At least that is what I have heard."

Hessa could tell Aves scrambled to regain her verbal footing and saw the telltale streak of red making its way across her chest and up her neck.

"You really are infatuated with him, aren't you?" Hessa dared.

"No!" Aves blurted out childishly. "I mean, not really." Her lie was obvious and the slight waver in her voice let Hessa know she was still trying to regain her mental balance.

"You're lying and I know it," Hessa teased. "It's alright if you are, though."

"Is it?" Aves asked. Her emotions played across her face. Her fidgeting broadcast that her feelings were still a little raw from their previous exchange. "I mean, when I look at him it is all that I can to focus on what he is saying." She confided with a whimsical smirk. "The whole way here he kept talking about where we were or things we had passed. I didn't really hear any of it. I was too busy watching how he moved on the back of the horse, so fluid and graceful. My mind wandered to how his arms felt around me as he lifted me into my saddle. So when he asked me a question, I just had a dumb smile on my face and nodded mostly." She twisted a lock of her hair as she spoke and the images practically played across her face.

Hessa could tell she had almost forgotten where they were. The sound of the house's door opening snapped Aves instantly back from her pleasant, if not embarrassing, thoughts. "You can't tell him any of this," she said to Hessa hurriedly as the sound of Onas's boots reverberated through the quiet house as he approached the room that they were in.

"Are you both almost ready?" Onas's baritone voice

could be heard easily through the closed door.

"Almost," Hessa replied as she motioned to Aves to move closer to the door. "It is fine if you want to come in, we are decent at least." A mischievous grin played along Hessa's delicate lips as she spoke.

"What are you doing?" Aves whispered worriedly to Hessa as she heard Onas turn the knob.

"Don't worry, it'll be fun. Hasia and I have done this a few times." Hessa playfully winked at Aves as the door started to swing open. She gracefully stepped forward and stopped it before it could open too far and in one effortless step, Hessa blocked Onas's view of the room by pressing up against him. "Are the horses ready?" She asked breathily against his chest.

"Aye," Onas gulped a little as he replied.

It was obvious he was taken off guard by Hessa's actions. Hessa enjoyed seeing the longing for her simmer deep in the depths of his pupils. She knew he was lost in the deep pools of her luxurious hazel eyes. It wasn't the first time she held someone at the brink of desire and she doubted it would be the last.

"Good," Hessa said again as she held his gaze with hers.

Her hands found his easily and pulled him into the room. She could tell he was a little uncomfortable and that made her heart race.

"This is the fun part," she thought to herself as she re-called her first time.

She had been in Aves's spot and Hasia had played this game with her. Then awkwardness Aves must be feeling mirrored what she had felt just a few years ago.

Hessa moved her head closer to Onas as she spun him into the room and backed toward the center of the room fluidly. There was an urge to kiss him that she fought. She knew that if she did, Aves would be destroyed. That was something Hessa knew she couldn't live with, so she fought the urge to let their lips touch.

His breath slid from between his narrowly parted lips and scalded hers with its heat. She let her lips part slightly as well and waited a few tantalizing moments. She saw his eyes dart down to her lips and back into the depths of her stare furtively. She timed his glance perfectly and licked her lips when his eyes had moved to them.

"I am glad to hear that we can leave as soon as we are ready," she breathed quietly.

Before he could respond, Hessa spun away and left him off-balanced and confused. She quickly stepped over to where Aves stood and easily pulled her in close as they spun from the wall.

She used the force of their spin to bring Aves into a tight embrace. Her breath played across Aves's ear as she whispered, "He is all yours to do as you please. I will be in the kitchen when you two are through. Try not to take too long with him; we do need to leave while there is still some light." Her voice was playful, yet filled with subtle innuendos.

Hessa cast a knowing glance at Aves as she spun her toward Onas. With a final twirl, Hessa passed through the open doorway and closed the door behind her as she left.

Chapter Two:
Onset

"You don't have to escort me the whole way," Namir rebuked Haradine as she quickly led him through the winding passages under the council hall.

"I have my orders, sa'ouvant, and I will not be swayed." Her tone was as fierce as her swagger and Namir felt intimidated it.

"I would rather find where the artifacts have been hidden, or even work on my speech for the council than being escorted to a place I know how to get to," he seethed inwardly as his words flew from his lips quickly.

Namir knew he was being defensive just like he knew if Haradine sensed his fear of her, he would lose her respect. None of this was easy, especially hiding his emotions. He hated how much he had to change, but there was nothing for it. While Namir secretly longed to have things go back the way they were, he was painfully aware of how much that could never happen. People needed him and he would not let them down, not this time.

Haradine's abrupt stop pulled at his soul and he froze a few paces behind her. Something was not right. His eyes darted around the empty street as he resisted the urge to walk past her.

"What is she doing?" Namir wondered.

He could feel his patience wearing thin. When her feet slowly moved down the alley, he was relieved. At least until she stopped after just three more steps. It was too much.

He ignored her left hand as she raised it in a slow attempt to signal him to wait. They were alone in the alley and he knew. The bewilderment that etched itself across her face was as annoying as it was amusing. He took smaller steps than he would have liked, but he didn't feel like completely disrespecting her caution.

Namir watched, somewhat detached from reality, as her right hand wrapped itself around the hilt of the short sword on her hip. The hairs on the back of his neck rose in anticipation as she nervously looked around them again.

Several long moments passed before he grew bored with her caution. Nothing moved. Not even the wind. Enough was enough. He decided to move past her. No more chances. Haradine's bewilderment quickly shifted to outrage as she realized he planned on walking past her. She quickly reached out to grab his wrist but froze.

The sudden blue flash from Zelios erupted from under his tunic and held her. An odd tug pulled at Namir's mind as he saw the amulet's light reflect in her blue eyes. He knew she was held in place by the feeling inside his mind. Her soul struggled against futilely against Zelios's power.

Aves and Hessa snickered amongst themselves as they followed Onas down the wide path on horseback. The way his hair seemed to float in the slight breeze held both girls' attention. The way his muscles moved under his shirt in response to the demands of his tasks only added heat to their gluttonous stares.

"Did he at least satisfy your curiosity?" Hessa inquired quietly. She skillfully allowed the creaking of their saddles hide her words as their horses trotted down the path.

"You are incorrigible," Aves hissed. The rosy color in

her cheeks expanded to her neck quickly.

"That doesn't answer my question," she pried once more.

"I know," Aves replied to her attempts aloofly. "I am still not sure how upset to be with you, that's why I am avoiding your question." Aves attempted to sound perturbed, but her ploy was far too obvious.

"I see," Hessa said with a sound of satisfaction in her voice, "and it has nothing to do with the fact you didn't even get so much as a kiss out of him then?"

Aves looked over at her longtime friend in shock. She was startled by Hessa's forwardness. "That shows how much you know. We kissed and then we…," Aves said defensively before she could catch herself and then blushed harder.

"Good, so there is some hope for you yet." Hessa gave Aves a quick wink as she continued, "So, how far did it get?" Her interest was obviously peaked and Aves knew it.

"We only kissed and held each other," Aves admitted somewhat ashamed for saying even that much. She felt like she had betrayed Onas's trust talking to Hessa like this. "Why do you care anyway?"

"You are my sister, I need to make sure you are being taken care of," Hessa responded with a sly smile. "Besides, I need to know if you can give me pointers or if I'm still more knowledgeable than you are about these things."

"You really *are* incorrigible. You know that, right?" Onas called back to the girls over his shoulder.

His response made both girls blush and Aves could not help but devour on every inch of his exposed skin with her gaze. Even his arrogant snicker only added to the building sexual tension.

"We are nearing the foothills, so the caverns you mentioned should be around here somewhere." He motioned toward the hills looming before them as he spoke.

"I will keep an eye out for it," Hessa offered.

Aves was glad the subject had changed and earnestly started to scan her surroundings for any sign of the caverns. "As will I," Aves said a little quieter than she had meant to.

Once Aves was certain Onas had turned his attention back to the path ahead of them, she closed her eyes and sighed. Too many things were happening too fast for the girl and she desperately hoped her life would return to the way it was. The way it should be.

Hessa's insistence on getting Aves attention ruined her peace. Between the slight noises and sound of her fingers rubbing together, Aves could not resist opening her eyes. The first sight that met her glance was Hessa's finger waggling at her.

"His ears are just as amazing as the rest of him seems to be," she mouthed.

Another giggle bubbled to the surface when Aves felt blood flood to her own cheeks. Hessa's only response to her unease was a bit of eye rolling mirth.

Namir walked around the corner and out of sight before Haradine could regain her senses. She felt shaky and confused. Something had stopped her. Held her there unable to move and when she could, her muscles felt weak. Haradine slowly started to follow her liege as feeling returned to her legs in electric jolts. She tried to hurry and almost stumbled.

"Tumere, help me," she prayed under her breath as she struggled to catch up to Namir.

The sounds of metal as it struck against stone hastened her step. Bright blue flashes erupted from the darkness ahead of her. A new sense of urgency rippled through her aching muscles as she struggled to close the distance between her and her liege.

Haradine practically flew around the corner. Although her feet barely touched the ground, she threw herself at it as she slipped around the corner. Both of her blades slipped free from their scabbards as she sprang free from her well-timed roll.

Without being able to see it, her blade collided with the sword of Namir's attackers. She parried it subconsciously and spun to attack. Arrows clattered against the stones of where she had been moments before and her second blade slid along the edge of yet another sword.

With a quick thrust, she ended one of their foes. The telltale ease of resistance as the tip of her sword pierced the thin metal his armor was made from was all the confirmation she needed. Another fluid spin and she easily pulled the blade from his corpse so she could face another attacker.

Scuffling boots and flashes of steel told her all she needed to know. There had been three of them. With this one dead, only two were left to worry about. Haradine did not need her keen elven sight to know one of the two was close to her, his breathing and the stench of his sweat made that all too apparent.

Another blinding flash erupted from Namir's neck and Haradine felt the searing pain that always seemed to accompany it wash over her skin. Screams erupted from both of their remaining assailants and, for a fleeting moment, Haradine thought her voice joined theirs in agony.

Between the scalding power and the pain in her sensitive eyes from the sudden blinding light, she was hard-pressed to remain conscious. The sudden spots swimming in her vision fought against her attempts to see where she had seen one of their attackers.

"Get behind me," Haradine screamed as she took a defensive stance reflexively.

Her vision was still clouded and she hated it. Only the slight scuffling of armored boots against the stone near her revealed her targets' locations to her. Haradine nearly jumped out of her skin as she felt Namir's light touch on her shoulder. Part of her was thankful he moved so quietly, but another part of her thought he had been an assailant, so she had to squelch her initial instincts.

An unusual tingle passed through her skin where his fingers settled against her shoulder. To Haradine's surprise, everything refocused sharper than before. Even the keen elven sight, a gift from her mother's lineage, usually took longer than this.

The novelty of the moment was quickly replaced by surprise as the tip of a dagger pierced the darkness in its arc toward her face. Reflexes forged from decades of training took over and, without any thought, the crossbar of her dagger found its way into the dagger's path.

The clatter of the missed throw rang loudly against the stone passageway as she thrust her blade into the darkness ahead of her. Another boon of her training, she thought somewhat amused. The weight of the blade pulled her through the lunge and into a parry, then a draw. Nothing slowed or stopped the blade. Her overly taut muscles allowed her to resume her ready stance.

Another flick of her wrist to her right as she turned slowly allowed her to probe the outer range of her vision without exposing herself. The familiar resistance of leather against the tip of her blade was a pleasant surprise for Haradine.

Iron mingled with humidity in her nostrils. The first draw of adrenaline shot through her veins in a rush and she flipped her grip on her dagger. Another quickly followed it as she punched its hilt into the darkness. She lunged just to the left of her target and she breathed a little easier when her strike did not connect with anything.

The subtle shift of a blade as it sliced the air, where her head would have been if she had not lunged, let her know target was where she expected him to be. Another flip, this time of her sword, as she shifted her weight onto her heels. This allowed her to redirect her attack and move into a more protected stance all in one fluid motion.

The jarring impact of boiled leather meeting the keen tip

of steel gave her more than a little satisfaction. She pressed her weight into her blade as much as she could while she whipped her hips for the extra power. Like an overly stretched band being released, Haradine rocked her weight back onto the balls of her feet and drove the tip of her sword through the breastplate. As she felt her sword pierce the leather, she slammed her dagger into the neck of her target.

Haradine's feet slid under her as she stepped into some brackish liquid and her emotions slid with them. Something wrapped itself around her left ankle so she let the force of her attack pull her down on top of her target instead of into her next one. Haradine prayed Namir could handle himself, at least until she managed to untangle herself from whatever it was that restrained her and regain her footing again. It was not until the familiar sound of steel against stone filled the hall that she realized her prayers had been answered.

"That was certainly unexpected," Namir grunted as he tugged unsuccessfully at the hilt of the sword in his hands.

He struggled to free the sword's blade that had somehow managed to wedge between the two battered metal plates of his assailant's armor. Haradine snickered to herself as she watched her liege struggle.

"His weight is going to hold the blade fast. Here," she said as she pulled the weapon out of the soldier's hand under her feet, "this one is more your style." Haradine offered the sleek looking short blade to Namir hilt first. "Now please stay here while I check the room for any more surprises."

"Thank you," Namir said as he closed his hand around the leather and metal wrapped hilt of the short black blade Haradine held in her outstretched hand.

"You're welcome, sa'ouvant." Haradine curtsied as she let go of the blade. She eyed Namir carefully and, as soon as she was certain he was safe; she darted through the open doorway separating them from their destination.

Jerine saw the sidelong glance Nurn leveled at him as

he approached. While he knew the massive boy was anxious to help his brother, the snow was building and, no matter how much the boy goaded, it did not change the fact. "Tell me again why we have to make camp so early?" Nurn's anger rolled behind his words like the rumble of distant thunder.

"If we don't, if we push until there is little light left, all of our hopes for catching anything fit to eat will dwindle down to nothing." Jerine's tone was pleasant and even. The last thing he needed was for Nurn to get too out of control with rage.

"The Calanari's rage is strong in him," the elf thought ruefully. "I just hope we can keep it in check, otherwise, we both might not survive."

"Fine," Nurn brooded. "But I don't have to like it," Jerine knew the Calanari hated asking questions, especially about things he had been told a few times. So instead of trying to figure out what bothered the boy, the elf watched helplessly as a silent war raged behind the youth's black eyes.

Something about the pensive silence that surrounded Nurn made Jerine think the boy always had someone clever available to help him understand things. Now that he was alone, without either Namir or his brother, Halin, provide him the skills he needed to figure things out, he felt lost.

Jerine touched Nurn's shoulder with a reassuring grasp. "We will find your brother. I promise." Jerine knew Nurn would not understand his certainty, but somehow he knew they would be able to locate Halin.

"How can you be so sure," the doubt in Nurn's voice stabbed at Jerine's heart. The pain it conveyed was almost overwhelming for the elf.

"I just am," Jerine explained. "There are some things I know to be true and this... this is one of them."

Jerine looked through Nurn's dark eyes and into his soul

as he spoke and was surprised by the void he found.

"He is lost," Jerine said silently and was amazed at the extent of Nurn's pain and doubt.

"Tumere will keep him safe." He quickly waved away Nurn's surprised look as he continued. "I know you pray to the god of your people, just as I do to mine every night. She will keep him safe. Tumere has never let any of her followers suffer needlessly." Jerine left his hand on Nurn's shoulder as they spoke and felt the rage seep out of the boy's muscles as they relaxed a little.

Nurn lowered his head as Jerine spoke and he fought back tears. Even though the youth was discreet, it was obvious to Jerine that is what he was doing. Once he was a little more composed, Nurn said quietly, "Thank you. You are a good friend."

There was no eye contact between the two of them as Nurn's words fell from his lips and Jerine did not need it to tell how much of the boy's inner strength it took for him to say these few words. The elf also knew this sa'trandon could not have kept his composure if they had.

"I am sorry for all my rash words. I just feel like we've already lost him. Everywhere we go, no matter how hard we look, there is never any sign of him." Fingers of despair clung to each word as he spoke, no matter how much the youth tried to dispel it.

"Think nothing of it," Jerine said reassuringly. "I am just proud to be numbered amongst your friends." Nurn stole a glance up at him and he could not help but smile.

"I promise I will not quit searching until we find your brother," Jerine squeezed the large boy's shoulders as he spoke. "Now let's see what we can catch to eat. I am starving."

∽——∽

Haradine looked out the window and gazed over the tranquility of the smithy's walled courtyard. "I will miss this solitude," she sighed to herself as she set about gathering Namir's books and papers.

Although she knew time was of the essence, she paced herself in order to be thorough. The last thing she wanted to do was leave an important piece of her father's puzzle behind. She fully understood how much these articles meant to Namir and she refused to be the one to have forgotten something.

She slowly shuffled the papers into neat stacks and slipped them into their respective leather satchels. Haradine stopped frequently to roll a map or sketch and stow them in the appropriate wooden case before placing them into the appropriate bag. Overall it took far longer than she wanted, but it was rewarding when the realization she was almost done dawned on her.

Haradine glanced glance the window quickly as she tried to gauge how much daylight she had left and her face fell. Three armed soldiers stood on the roof across from the smithy's walls. She could not stop the alarms from going off in her breast as she easily recognized them as Faris's men.

"Where is he?" Haradine wondered aloud as she moved around to the other windows.

She squinted against the glare of the late afternoon sun as it glinted off the white stone walls surrounding the smithy. The subtle movement of shadows across the canvas that backed the assorted shelves drew her attention to the forge.

"There he is," she whispered to herself.

Haradine frantically scooped the few remaining books into the final satchel and drew it shut. She quickly scanned the desk and floor to make sure everything had been returned to their proper places before she scooped up the two large bags and affixed them to her back. A few loose sheets of paper caught her attention as they bobbed against the subtle shifts of air caught in a crack between the floorboards. She easily freed them and folded them in one fluid motion. She neatly slid them into one of her belt pouches as she then she turned and stuffed one loose case she had almost forgotten in with it.

Once she was positive none of her liege's belongings had been missed, she made her way down the stairs. All of the escape routes both Namir and Tipin had taught to her flew through her head as she searched for her best option. To her dismay, all but one exited in, or near, the forge. The only one leading away from where Faris lurked was the one she really hoped to avoid.

A deep breath filled her lungs as she exited the stairwell near the bedrooms on the second floor. Haradine paused outside of Nurn's bedroom and said a silent prayer before she continued. With trembling hands, she slowly unlatched the door and opened it enough to slip through. Smoothly she fastened the lock on the door and slid Nurn's dresser against it. Opening the window silently, she leaned out to get a better look at her options. A brief sense of vertigo took over as her head swam at the thought of jumping. She took a few faltering steps away from the opening to clear her head.

The young elf steeled her nerves, closed her eyes, and moved closer to the open window again. The sound of creaking floorboards forced her to open her eyes and focus on the flimsy looking boards connecting Nurn's window to the building on the far side of the street. She shakily put her foot onto the swaying boards.

"Jia take my fears," she whispered as she attempted to steady her feet.

A slight metallic jingle floated from across the room and forced her to pause. In less time that it took her to breathe, she realized the noise came from the latch on the door. Her adrenaline surged and she leaped from the building and embraced the source of her fears wholeheartedly.

Chapter Three:
Effects

Skara paced carefully across the boards above Allair. She was confounded by the woman's actions. What little the cat knew of humans made no sense as she contemplated her prey.

Every action this woman made flew in the face of reason and believability. The felinoid's head cocked in wonder as she watched the diminutive lady search the same barrel for the third time.

"What is it that she is looking for?" Skara mused in wonder.

Without thinking, she stopped and crouched on a rope directly above her. Skara hoped to figure out what it was the woman searched for by peering around her shoulder from above. She squinted and strained her eyes to no avail.

The darkness, which normally would not pose a problem for her, was too impenetrable from where she crouched.

Skara cursed under her breath as she waited for Allair to continue her search. Unfortunately for Skara, her prey had been staying out in the open. It was thirsty work baking in the sun as she followed an apparently crazy lady around. She had hoped Allair might go down an alley or at least a deserted part of town, but she had no such luck. The lack of urgency her prey shown while lurking below her in the gathering gloom only added to her frustration.

As she waited, the erratic path played itself through her mind. At first, Skara thought the Chancellor of Ellsted was tailing the knife merchant, which was what drew the feline to her trail, to begin with. However, after a few missteps and obvious blunders, Allair made it readily apparent she was not following him. Skara was then forced to speculate on who else she could have been tailing. That is when the woman changed her tactic. She rummaged through the random crates and barrels lining the streets.

Her catish eyes carefully watched all of the departing merchants pack their wares from the booths into similar containers and place them on the side of the road. She assumed they would later return with carts or wagons and collect their discarded belongings.

In the meantime, her prey had taken it onto herself to rummage through them. She searched some of them more than once in her attempt to find something. It annoyed Skara to no end that she could not figure what it was that Allair searched for.

"It's almost as if Allair wants to keep both of us here," Skara thought gloomily.

An epiphany erupted in Skara's mind as the thought passed through it. An almost silent growl escaped from her throat as she refocused her attention on Allair to put her theory to the test.

She watched as her prey finished repacking the crate of pottery she had just finished searching. Skara's ear twitched as Allair glanced around the nearby crates.

"There," she thought as she saw a furtive, and almost imperceptible, glance right at her. Skara crept over to the top of a building near a different clump of crates. She snarled to herself as she saw Allair move over to the crates below her.

"She is stalking me," Skara screamed at herself mentally

in disbelief.

She quickly fell onto her back and rolled along the rooftop. It was getting darker and Skara knew she needed to find Faris. She hoped he had managed to have better luck with his mission than she had with hers. Either way, she needed to get back to him for support in case someone else was working with Allair.

All of the humor drained from their conversation as the three of them passed the silent statues of fallen soldiers. The air around them thickened as they passed. Even the rhythmic sound of their horses' hooves was devoured by the solemnity of the memorial garden.

The three of them breathed in unison as their path veered towards the statues. Before either of the girls knew it, they were in the middle of a small circle of statues commemorating heroes of the many long forgotten wars and battles. The silence grew weightier as it enveloped them slowly. The further they ventured into the clearing, the heavier it seemed.

"How much farther do you think the cavern might be?" Aves asked visibly shaken by the heavy oppressive feeling took its hold on her soul.

"It shouldn't be too much further," Onas offered. His tone betrayed his uncertainty better than his words could hope to.

"What is this place?" Aves asked, her words all but absorbed by the holy silence surrounding them.

"Have you never been here before? Onas asked. The way his words raised as he said them made his amazement at their innocence very obvious.

"No," Aves answered somewhat sheepishly.

A quick glance at Hessa was all she needed for reassurance after her statement. The way her friend shook her head mixed with a look that mirrored her own let Aves know she was not alone in her ignorance.

Onas chuckled to himself as he smiled at them. "It is a memorial, one of many." He added this bit of wisdom as if he forgot to mention it previously.

"A memorial of what, exactly?" Hessa asked.

He quickly glanced back and between the girls with an obvious look of astonishment. "Neither of you have ever been told about these shrines? They were made to honor Cennicus's fallen heroes and soldiers of the Great Wars?"

Every word that slipped from his lips carried disbelief with them. Their lost looks only made his apparent amazement deepen. Onas gently pulled his horse's reigns until his steed stopped smoothly as he sighed deeply.

Aves watched in amazement as she watched his horse. Although the horse had seemed docile before, it was more so now. It didn't even lower its head to graze any of the lush grass filling the glade.

She watched their horses as they followed the gypsy's lead and slowed to a stop smoothly. Their mares kept their heads high, just like Onas's had. Even though each of the girls stopped extremely close to his horse, their horses did not try to prance or move about nervously. Somehow this odd behavior only enhanced the silence that dampened their voices better than any room she had ever been in.

Onas cleared his throat as he unconsciously straightened his spine. "This is one of the thirteen memorials King Cendir decreed would be built in his kingdom. He wanted to make sure every one of his subjects understood the sacrifice these men and women had made to ensure that our great kingdom survives."

His words flowed out in a harsh whisper like a well-rehearsed river. Each syllable seemed laden with a secret message of intrigue. His delivery only made Aves want to hear more.

"The king, in his wisdom, hired the Dekkari to sculpt these memorials out of the landscape to ensure they would survive any natural disaster. You see, he knew the Dekkari understood natural magic well enough to make his dream a reality. That is why he approached our people." Onas added conspiratorially.

"These statues are that old?" Hessa said more than asked in obvious awe. "These are really from King Cendir's time?"

"Aye," Onas replied solemnly.

"How have they survived so well kept for so long?" Aves chimed in as she motioned toward the nearest statue.

The closest statue was a foot soldier. It was heavily decorated with pieces of armor and weapons. The attached possessions were accented by other paraphernalia gathered in small piles around the stone base on which it stood.

"If you two were not of Dekkari blood, I would say magic," Onas winked at each girl in turn before he continued. "However, since you are, I will reveal the secret to you both."

His hand motioned toward the same statue that they were sitting in front of as he spoke. "Look closely. There are telltale signs in the rock the statue is carved from." He waited as he saw the girls look at the statue futilely.

"Do not look at the arms or legs. Don't even look at the well-sculpted chest, you won't find what you seek there. Instead, look at the feet. Over here, at the base." Onas said as he pointed at the nearest one. "Do you see the wear lines from the wind? How about the little pits and dimples from the sand as it is blown across it?" His smile deepened as he saw the girls start to realize the truth behind his words. "The galanetri took great pains to ensure these memorials were as protected from the ravages of time, but in the end, they were only human."

"But if the gal-ne-trees are such powerful wizards, why wouldn't they be able to stop even these subtle damages from happening?" Aves asked ignorantly as she stumbled, somewhat purposefully, on the Dekkari pronunciation.

"Galanetri means gardener in our tongue," Onas explained patiently. "Please forgive me; I forgot you do not know all of the subtleties of it yet," Onas added before he finished answering Aves's question.

"The galanetri are not wizards, although many outsiders believe that they are. As their title says, they are gardeners." He motioned for them to hold their questions as if knew their thoughts. "Although it is amazing what they can accomplish through their skills. You see, they know the patterns of the world as well as you know how to breathe and think. To them, it's second nature. Did you notice there are no leaves or dirt near the bases of the statues?"

Onas waited until he saw them nod before he answered. "That is because the galanetri have ensured each statue's placement is perfect. The wind blows across them and places the debris into other areas. Places that are not as noticeable, like beneath a bush or in the cracks of those rocks over there." He directed the girls' attention over to the wall a few yards behind the statues. "By doing this, one galanetri can care for multiple memorials at once."

"Do you think we will see one of the galanetri?" Aves could not mask the amazement she felt as her question bubbled from her throat.

"It is possible," Onas said smugly. His tone mingled with his calculated movements made Aves think he knew more than he was sharing.

"Why do you say it like that?" Hessa asked as she studied the gypsy's movements.

"Our people are drifters. We like to roam and, as I mentioned, there are only thirteen memorials in the whole kingdom. This makes the likelihood of seeing a galanetri remote at best." He smiled at the girls as Aves felt her spirits fall.

Everything he said swam around in her mind as she struggled to make sense of it. She knew he was frustrated at their lack of understanding, but Aves could not help it. Hessa probably struggled with it as well, which only added to the tension.

Another deep sigh from the gypsy pulled a response from Aves's hesitant lips. "So why are the statues decorated like they are?" She really didn't care about the reason, she just needed to break the silence.

"People come and pay their tribute to the fallen. Everything you see here was left by other visitors." He motioned from the piles of armaments to the very statues themselves.

"People left the statues?" Aves asked with a confused tone in her voice.

"Not the actual statue, but everything not made of stone has been brought by those paying their respects. That includes the helms some of the statues wear down to the leather straps that adorn them."

"Wow," Hessa said. Her awe was almost overwhelming. "So the sword in this statue's hand was not planned by the sculptor?"

"No, not really," Onas agreed. "If you notice, the statues are all in different poses. These were the stances each warrior was known for in life. For example, this statue is of Jarin the Deft. He was known for his skills with the sword as well as his ability to learn fast. He was often seen with a sword in hand, so the sculptor carved his hand to hold a sword. That way, if someone decided to leave one, he could hold it."

"Interesting," Aves added when she noticed the subtle tension build between Hessa and Onas. "So any one of these items could be what we are looking for?"

"If the artifact is been hidden in here, yes," Onas nodded his agreement.

The gypsy's brow furled as he obviously pondered Aves's words. Aves was surprised that neither Hessa nor Onas had come to the same conclusion, but they hadn't. From what she could see of Hessa's face, she knew her friend was as surprised as Onas seemed to be.

"Hopefully it hasn't been," he said. His response came after a brief silence.

"Why?" Aves asked before Hessa had the chance to. "Gypsy magic," Onas responded as a slight grin played across his lips.

"What do you mean by that?" Hessa blurted out a little confused. "But you said the galanetri were not sorcerers."

"And they're not," his tone was flat and unreadable, "but they were not the only Dekkari approached by the king to create the memorials. Our seeresses were also tasked to protect the statues and the gifts left in their memory. Only the person, or a direct relative, that brought the souvenir in may take it out."

"So, no one can take something out from here?" Aves asked incredulously.

"Not alive," Onas's tone was as ominous as his words were.

"Thankfully my mother's journal says the artifact is in a cave," Hessa interjected. "Does the magic extend into the hills around us?"

"No, it does not," Onas answered a little hesitantly. "At least, not that I am aware of."

"Let's hope not," both girls said in unison. Their voices blended together so well that it was almost impossible to distinguish between them.

Halin looked at the water in silence. It careened down the face of the rock completely oblivious to his amazement. Freshwater was a luxury he had not been afforded for some time and he was in complete awe.

Unable to stop the tremor that stole control of his hand, Halin reached slowly toward the rock's glistening surface. The smooth water-worn face of the rock was as cold as the water that cascaded across it. The crisp mirror-like surface only added to the surrealness of the moment.

To Halin's surprise, the water pooling at the base of the rock face was deeper than he expected it to. He shuddered as his hand rested on the rough basin. Chilled water siphoned the heat of his forearm.

Aside from the coldness, the seemingly endless supply all but put him into shock. For the amount of water that flowed, the roar should have been deafening. Instead, it barely whispered as it coursed in front of him. What little sound he did hear was created more from his fingers interrupting the stream than from the force of the water itself. Before Halin disturbed it, there was no sound in the cave other than his breathing.

"This must be some sort of illusion," His voice hurt as much to hear as it did to speak.

Although he could not be certain of its purity, Halin could not resist the temptation to taste it. Even if it was half as refreshing as it looked, he knew it would help to scoop a little of the liquid into his mouth. Thankfully it was more refreshing than he expected.

Subconsciously he held his breath. His mind raced as he waited for something to go wrong. His imagination flooded with possibilities as the silence drowned him with its stillness.

"THE WATER IS NO MIRAGE OR ILLUSION," the words vibrated all around him and took Halin completely off guard. His mind filled with a blinding light as the disembodied voice continued, "IT IS A GIFT FROM THE GODS. WHEN YOU ARE READY FOR MORE, COME FIND ME."

Stunned, Halin glanced around him warily. Although he felt some of his recent paranoia lessen, the ominous voice unnerved him. Both the tone and the way in completely enveloped him made Halin want to melt into the floor to hide.

His eyes strained in the darkness as he struggled to find the voice's source. After several long unfruitful moments, he resigned himself to the fact he would never find it.

There was nothing around him. Nothing moved or breathed. Even the pooling water had vanished. He failed to find even a hole the sound could have emanated from.

"Where are you?" Halin asked with no expectation of a reply. "Where can I find you when I need more?"

"YOU WILL FIND ME WHEN YOU ARE READY," the response was almost instant and it startled Halin even more. "UNTIL THEN, YOU SHOULD REST. YOU WILL NEED THE PEACE THIS GIFT BRINGS IN THE COMING DAYS."

"What do you mean?" Halin barked into the darkness around him.

Despair closed its deathly grip on his thoughts and he mentally struggled to remain strong. Silence settled around him again as he waited for a response. But nothing came, not even the silent whisper from the water that had been in front of him a moment before.

Hessa studied the words carefully etched into the wall in front of her as if they would break down and tell her their hidden message. The tooling was smooth and clean. Nothing looked rough or hurried. Even the edges of the letters were smooth.

"Controlling your enemies is wise. Find the key, for in your heart it lies. The brave and decorated surmise how to snatch defeat when he spies. A man, who looks to his arms, dies. And his chest, his legs, his hands, his eyes. If his secret is your prize, go now and try it on for size."

Her fingers flowed along the impossibly smooth inscription as she recited the words. Even the jutting corners of the harder letters felt smooth as she traced each of the eight lines in turn.

"It's almost as if water has flowed over them for a long time," Hessa said more to herself in awe.

"But what does it mean?" Aves asked a little confused. "You said that your mother's journal said there was an item of power around here, but so far all we have found is an old monument and this weird riddle." She wrinkled her nose in contempt of their situation as her words fell from her soft lips harshly.

"It does," Hessa agreed. "I don't understand it either." The ache of despair pulled at her voice painfully as she spoke.

Her fingers reached toward the etched letters of their own accord. There was something serene about the setting that pulled at her soul. Something oddly familiar tickled the back of her mind as well, but Hessa could not quite place what. Strange memories tugged at the edges of her consciousness as she yielded against the urge to touch both the stone and the perfectly crafted letters set into it.

"There is nothing else any further in," Onas's voice echoed down the narrow passage. "It just ends at a wall with an odd carving."

"What?" Hessa asked only half cognizant of what he had said.

"I said the passage ends at a wall with an odd carving etched into it. There is nothing else in here. This is a dead end." The weariness in his voice betrayed his annoyance at the task he had been given as he added under his breath, "If I had known we would be chasing legends and fables, I wouldn't have agreed to help."

"What is the carving of?" Hessa asked a little more alert than she had been a moment ago.

"It is an oddly shaped circle with some small carvings inside." Onas's voice grew and filled more of the cave them the more he spoke. "I really don't see anything special about it.

"Could it possibly be a map of something?" Aves asked curiously.

Her sister's question cut through the oddly hypnotic effect Onas's voice carried with it. For some reason, Hessa was not sure if it was the sound of Aves's voice or the odd level of insight it held. She shot a quick glance toward the tunnel Onas was in and imagined that he was just as surprised by Aves's comment as she was.

"It could be," Onas replied hesitantly. "Why don't the two of you come here and see it for yourselves then?"

Chapter Four: Tactics

Namir paced the small room impatiently. "Where is she?" He shouted his question to no one.

He was alone in the darkened room and was too afraid to light a lantern. His most recent brush with the dangers of being the heir apparent wore heavily on his nerves. His new found solitude did little to ease them.

"SHE WILL RETURN," Zelios replied in his mind.

"I know," although Namir knew he could just think his responses to the soul of the amulet, he preferred to speak them. There was something comforting and more natural about verbally communicating for him. "I just hate not knowing."

"NO, YOU HATE NOT BEING ABLE TO DO AS YOU PLEASE," she replied soothingly.

The truth of the amulet's words rankled Namir's soul. "You may be right, but I still hate not knowing what's happening." He paced around the room a few more times before he continued his thought verbally. "You will always protect me, right?"

"THAT IS CORRECT," Zelios replied.

"So if I were to go somewhere less than safe, you will

keep me alive?" Although Namir asked the question verbally, he pictured his intentions in his mind to illustrate it better than he could speak it.

Images of him making his way across the rooftops in search of Haradine filled his head. For some reason, he could almost feel the palpable danger he expected to find as he searched.

"YES AND NO," the amulet's ambiguity did little to ease Namir's troubles. "I CANNOT STOP YOU FROM DYING IF YOU ARE BADLY WOUNDED OR IF YOU HAVE AGED TOO MUCH, BUT I CAN STOP YOU FROM BEING WOUNDED, MOST OF THE TIME."

"Most of the time?" Zelios's response only worried Namir more. "What do you mean by 'most of the time'?"

"ALTHOUGH I AM FROM THE GODS, I TOO AM LIMITED. IF I AM SHIELDING YOU FROM ONE TYPE OF ATTACK, ANOTHER TYPE MAY SLIP PAST. I AM SORRY IF THIS WORRIES YOU," SHE SAID SOOTHINGLY, "I JUST WANT YOU TO UNDERSTAND MY ABILITIES BETTER."

"I see," Namir said somewhat crestfallen.

The sound of distant thunder interrupted Namir's brooding. Minor tremors vibrated the floor and rattled the sparse shelves in the small room. Small bits of dirt and mortar freed themselves from the cracks between the stones in the ceiling as Namir glanced around the room.

"What was that?" His words flew from his lips before he could restrain them. The startled look on his face mirrored the dread lodged deeply in his tone.

"HARADINE WILL BE BACK SOON," Zelios offered as if what she said matched Namir's question.

"I don't understand," Namir said as he sat back down obviously confused.

"YOU WILL KNOW SOON ENOUGH," her words hung ominously in Namir's mind as he felt them resonate deep into his soul.

Jaconis squinted against the bright light of the morning sun. It had been days since he had been allowed out of his cell. Although he yearned for freedom of the small confines, he was unsure if he would have preferred its blessed darkness to the constant pain the incessant barrage of bright light the sun shot into his senses.

"This way young master," his companion said as she escorted him through the busy market. "We need to gather just the right ingredients for dinner tonight." Her voice was satiny and as smooth as velvet. It's musky tone held an alluring sensuality in its enthralling folds that made Jaconis almost hang on her every word.

"I am aware of this," Jaconis said dismissively.

He was unsure how he managed to live around all of the competing noises and scents of the city before he joined the church. Reflexively Jaconis grabbed the cuffs of his thin sleeves for comfort as they stepped into the semi-shadowed streets that signaled their entry into the meat markets.

The lady nodded her understanding of his pain. As if she wanted to make his situation worse, she deftly wound her way through the busiest parts of the street. Her ability to slip through the impossibly narrow gaps between people without bumping into them was very impressive.

Jaconis attempted to discern how she managed this without ever deviating from her course. Watching her in this way also forced him to notice her supple build and alluring features. The lady was magnificent and he knew she could read his thoughts about her by the look on his face.

What amazed him more was the way her coal black hair caught the slightest breeze and danced in it of its own volition. She was his type. From her playful green eyes down to her dance-like steps, she took when she walked. Silent, deadly and beautiful.

"Tali," Jaconis forced himself to remember his love's features.

He allowed the pain he felt at their separation seep into his heart as a balm to renew his conviction to Lotevilar. He knew his new Goddess's loved pain, especially when it was used for growth.

"I promised I will aid you in your goals no matter the cost. To be true and fearless for you and I shall." His thoughts burned through his mind as if they were on fire. "Lotevilar grant me pain so I may prove myself in Thy service," he muttered his prayer under his breath as he refocused his mind from his escort and back to their task at hand.

"I'm sorry, did you say something?" His companion slowed to a stop as she asked.

Jaconis forced himself to look away from her. Instead, he shook his head in denial as the only response he gave. He carefully withdrew the list of ingredients the deacon had given him from his pouch and acted like he was trying to recall something.

"I was just saying the fish merchant is the other way," his sardonic smile drove home the point that he knew she had let herself get distracted.

He allowed her to think he had somehow known they were going in the wrong direction as he met her confused glance with an icy stare.

"Of course, young master," she bowed her head submissively as she spoke. Her apology sent a thrilling shock down Jaconis's spine as he realized the opportunity she had just given him. "I'm sorry, it won't happen again." Her almost whispered apology was the sincerest he had ever heard. It felt like music to him as her softly spoken words teased at his ears.

"You might not be yet, but you will be," his well-rehearsed lines seemed to fall from his lips as if they were natural for him. Jaconis's malicious promise hung in the air between them and he savored it. "I expect to see you in the devotional at sunset," he instructed calmly.

It took every ounce of self-control he had to seem so calm. Inside he was buzzing with anticipation of finally being able to practice his teachings on one of the converted.

He felt her timid glance play across his handsome features as he spoke. The haunted look in his eyes and the sinister grin on his overly pale face sent a visible shiver of dread down her spine.

"Of course, young master," she acquiesced. "Your bidding is my command."

Aves, Hessa, and Onas stood around the crude carving etched into the wall in front of them. It bore none of the grace and elegance of the previous inscriptions. Instead, it seemed to be a roughly carved circle with little triangles and squares scattered throughout it. Down the middle of the circle snaked a lighter, almost imperceptible, crack in the stone.

"Is that a trail?" Aves asked as she tapped the crack gently with her finger.

"I think it is just crack," Onas said snarkily. "You know sometimes a crack is just that... a crack." A wry smile crossed his face as silently chuckled at his own jest.

"Not this time," Aves said matter-of-factly. "Here is the trail we came in on," Aves fingered a small divot in the face of the stone as she spoke, "and this is the cave we are in."

"It could be," Hessa squinted at the divot as she replied. "If that is the case, then these triangles and squares could be the monuments." She surmised as she tilted her head slightly in order to gain perspective. "Onas, how many monuments are there?"

"Twelve," his response was almost instant. "I already thought of that, but there are too many symbols for these to represent the monuments." Onas's voice was flat and distant. Not at all like either of the girls thought it would be.

"Is it possible the galanetri used this as their planning table?" Hessa's comment was more of a statement than a question.

Aves recognized the tone instantly as the same one Hessa had used in their negotiations in Hornshir and jumped in without any hesitation. "I would think it's possible. I mean, there are only twelve triangles."

"But there are easily three times that many squares!" Onas shot each of the girls a disgusted look as he spoke.

"True..." Hessa agreed. "How many small piles of offerings are there around each of the statues?"

A look of realization slowly settled in as he tilted his head the same way that both of the girls had. "If that is true, if," he conceded, "then what is this symbol around this triangle?"

"If it's true…" Hessa started to say.

"It is where the item is." Aves completed Hessa's sentence perfectly.

Onas rubbed his head as he glanced from girl to girl. "It is getting harder and harder to tell the two of you apart," he said abashedly. "Very well," he conceded, "we had best make a copy of this. That is if we hope to remember all of these details."

Onas stepped back a few paces and searched through the few pouches he wore. When it was apparent he could not find what he was looking for, he turned to leave.

"I will be back in a moment." He called over his shoulder and vanished into the cavern.

"What do you think the item is?" Aves asked with the excitement of a child.

"I have no idea, but based on what we saw around the statues, I am going to guess it is a weapon of some sort," Hessa responded.

Aves saw the slight twinkle in her sister's eyes as she spoke and chuckled silently to herself. "Although it is still odd to think of her as my sister, I hope she can contain her excitement better than I can," Aves thought as they waited for Onas to return.

Only a few brief moments passed before Onas stepped back into the circle of light cast by the sputtering torch on the cavern wall. Just seeing him pulled Aves away from her thoughts and drew her excitement to a crescendo.

She watched him intently as he skillfully pulled a scroll case loose from his belt and opened it with one hand. He deftly reached into the small pouch on his right hip and pulled out a dark piece of stone. Before Aves could voice her confusion at his actions, Onas stepped passed both of the girls and placed the page over the crude carving.

With broad fast movements, he rubbed the stone across the page he had pressed the stone's surface. The girls watched in amazement as the details of the etchings appeared slowly onto the page. The detail became clearer with each pass of the black stone.

"How did you do that?" Aves was the first to find her tongue.

"This?" Onas asked as he motioned to the map he now held.

"Aye," Hessa nodded in unison with her sister.

"Have neither of you made rubbings before?" he asked skeptically.

"What is a rubbing?" Hessa asked as she eyed the map.

Aves had never seen anyone draw a map so fast and so accurately. From the astonished look on Hessa's face, she could tell that her sister had not either. The fact that he copied every detail without even looking at the wall only added to her amazement.

"This is some sort of Dekkari magic, right?" Aves said a little unsure of her answer.

Onas chuckled lightly at her question. "I spent many hours, as a boy, making rubbings of almost everything. I can hardly believe that neither of you has ever done this. And no, it isn't magic of any sort." Onas's smile betrayed his mirth as they spoke.

"Tell me, when you were younger did you ever trace leaves onto paper or copy a pattern from lace?" His eyes darted from girl to girl as he asked.

"No," Aves admitted somewhat hesitantly.

"I copied lace patterns," Hessa admitted, "but not like this. I had to look closely at the lace and draw what I saw. It took quite a while and many mistakes." Her cheeks filled with a slight red hue as she spoke.

"Well, this is like that, but easier and it is so simple anyone can do it. All you need is a page and some coal." He held out the smoothed black rock he had rubbed against the parchment as he spoke. "Warming the coal a little first makes the process faster and, I have found, also helps get the finer details transferred onto your rubbing easier. To do this, I sometimes burn one end to soften it." He advised.

"Can we make a rubbing of the poem as well?" Hessa asked. The child-like enthusiasm in her voice mirrored Aves's excitement perfectly.

"We can," Onas nodded in agreement. "In fact, that is a great idea. It might help to decipher the riddle's meaning if we had it with us."

Nurn took a deep breath and choked back the pain the bitterly cold and icy air caused as he desperately filled his aching lungs. He was unsure how much longer he could go at this pace. "I need to stop," he hated to say it, after all, it was Halin's life that was on the line if they failed to find him.

Jerine nodded his understanding and slowed his pace. He quickly scanned their surroundings as he stopped. "I would hate for something to sneak up on us. How much farther do you think you can go?"

Nurn felt the elf's ice blue eyes on him and he knew Jerine was studying him in case he lied. While he hated to seem weak, he knew they needed to tell each other of their limitations if they hoped to find his brother.

"I have a little more strength, but not much" Nurn puffed. Another ice filled breath of air filled his lungs as he marshaled his reserves.

"The ridge is not far," the elf replied. "And then it is a short jaunt into the forest waiting on the other side of it."

Jerine's words hoisted Nurn's spirits from the depths he had been feeling. An odd warmth he had not expected built a little in his chest and it comforted him.

"There is plenty of safety in hiding," Nurn said sagely as he stretched his aching muscles. He hoped this simple movement would allow the blood to ease some of the warmth into his veins.

"That there is." Jerine nodded.

"How do you know about this place?" Nurn asked as he adjusted his pack and settled his thick cloak back into place.

"A few moons back Aras was exploring this area in his quest for more information to share with Namir," Jerine replied. "Landolin provided him with a few guards to protect him while he explored the old dwarven caverns."

"So you were one of his guards then?" Nurn asked much quieter than normal.

The shock at Nurn's insinuation was visible on both Jerine's face and demeanor. He slowed his step and turned to face the boy as they continued to move through the snow. "No, I was originally asked to guide him to Landolin's encampment. Which I did. Then I had to complete my mission, which was finding your friend in Hornshir."

There was unusually somber sound to Jerine's voice as he replied and it caught Nurn a little off guard. He also noticed Jerine's reluctance to use either Namir's name or title and he was a little surprised. Elves tended to use titles instead of names to refer to people, this subtle nuance only made Nurn even more leery to speak loudly.

"That still does not tell me how you knew of this place," Nurn all but whispered.

"Before I could make it back to Hornshir, I felt the urge to turn around and go back to Landolin's camp," Jerine said softly. I came back and found the camp in chaos. Landolin was gone and Aras's wife, Alequa, said her husband was missing. She told me where he had gone and that Aras had taken a small contingent of Landolin's forces. I had no choice to leave, but I promised to return as soon as I could."

"Is that why you decided to bring us here after you found him?" Nurn asked as he tried to make sense of what had happened.

"Aye. Originally I was tasked with finding him and keeping him at the manor until Aras could make his way there. But Aras's guards were killed to the man and he was gravely wounded." Jerine's voice took as lethal of a tone as his eyes held as he spoke. "I have now been asked, by his wife, to seek vengeance against the monster that attacked them."

"Do you know who it was?" Nurn was enthralled by the elf's story and almost forgot to keep his tone hushed. "It was Morcant and his pack of nassarid," Jerine's words sent a chill down Nurn's spine as they all but flew from his lips.

Nurn flinched unconsciously at the thought of a whole pack of creatures as foul and gruesome as Morcant. "How many nassarid do you think Morcant had with him?"

"Judging from the carnage, I think there are at least six, maybe twelve. It is hard to say for sure." Jerine's voice held a subtle sense anger in it, almost as if he drew each word from a hidden trove he dared not spend all at once.

"There are that many nassarid?" Nurn's eyes widened with both fear and wonder. "Is... is Morcant unique amongst his kind?" His deep voice, normally full of confidence, faltered as he spoke and betrayed the underlying fear he felt in his soul.

"Aye, he is."   Jerine nodded.   "His uniqueness that makes him so cunning and dangerous."

Haradine bolted around the corner at a full tilt. She knew Faris had seen her as she dove out of smithy's attic window. Although she was nimble, she could not restrain the screech that escaped her lips when she plummeted toward the ground. She had quickly grabbed the rope she leaped toward, but she was helpless in her fight against the phobia plaguing her mind when it came to heights.

She darted down the third alley she came across and sprinted toward the low wall at its end. In one fluid motion, the elf hurdled it as she twisted her body gracefully into a ball and allowed her momentum to roll her toward a stack of barrels. Haradine lost no time maneuvering safely behind the neatly stacked pyramid of crates and barrels.

After she was certain her pursuers were not overly close, she meticulously unstacked the outermost barrels and placed them strategically to block access to her hiding place. She hurriedly searched for a barrel just big enough to hold her. Once she had, she grabbed three larger empty ones.

Haradine took a ragged breath as she freed her knife from the inseam of her boot. Deftly placing its tip against the outer edge of the largest barrel's lid, the elf pried it open. She reached down and tore a small square of fabric off the bottom of one of her pant legs and wedged it inside of the barrel. She repeated this with both of the other barrels.

Without hesitating, she reached into the pouch firmly nestled against the small of her back. The elf easily pulled out three small vials. She carefully nestled each of them into the center of the barrels. Haradine spared no thought to what needed to be done as she unstopped the vials and securely sealed them up.

Haradine took a moment to look over her work before she used the pyramid of barrels to make her way to the nearest roof. Panting, she pressed herself tightly against the smooth clay singles beneath her. The cold bit at her skin through her thick leather jerkin.

"She went this way," a gruff voice called out from below her.

Haradine's heartbeat faltered as she heard the commotion. The rough voice was followed closely by the soft scuffling sounds of padded boots. Several men crowded into the alley she just left.

"I need to put some distance between us if I hope to live," Haradine thought as she silently crawled along the roof and then dropped down to a ledge on an adjacent building.

She quickly reached and pulled herself onto that building's roof. Haradine had just cleared the ridge of the next building's roof when the world shook all around her.

Chapter Five:
Chased

Skara rushed across another rooftop as she darted from shadow to shadow. Silently she cursed herself for a fool as she ran. "How could I have fallen for her ploy?" Skara seethed mentally. "Why was she trying to delay me?"

Skara pondered as she leaped over another of the many winding roads silently. Her feet made almost no sound as she gracefully landed on the rooftop of the bathhouse. Below her, a raucous party masked what little noise she made perfectly.

Gracefully she arced across one of the main roads leading to the council hall on her left as she absently grabbed a hold of a dangling rope that seemed to be waiting for her. Her eyes scanned her surroundings for any signs of danger as she swung across to the roof of the bakery.

Skara tucked into a roll to lessen her profile as the setting sun silhouetted the area around her. She allowed herself to easily slide against the eaves as she sprawled out fluidly allowing her momentum to dictate her direction.

"I wonder where Faris has gotten off to." Skara's words raced through her mind faster than her eyes could take in all of her surroundings.

She effortlessly peered over the edge of the roof and

absorbed the scene below her. A small smile pulled at the corner of her mouth when she saw Faris's men searching a pile of barrels below her.

"It looks like my tracking skills are better than even I knew," she thought happily to herself as she noticed Faris step out of the shadows across the street.

A whisper from somewhere behind her caught Skara's attention as she pushed away from the ledge. Skara cautiously rolled onto her back and then as she sat up. She sniffed the air around her and allowed her keen ears to find the source of the sound. The only sound that met her ears was the subtle whispers caused by the slight breeze as it tossed small bits of debris toward her.

An uneasy feeling settled in the pit of her stomach and forced Skara into action. She gave herself enough room for a running start and then, at the last minute, she balled into a crouch and leaped across the alley where Faris and his men searched. As she landed on the roof of the next building, Skara planted her hands and pushed herself enough to change her momentum. This allowed her to skillfully vault off the roof and land on her feet in the shadows behind Faris.

"How goes your search?" Skara purred as she rose to her feet and stepped close to her comrade.

"Not well," Faris grunted. "One of the boy's female companions was in the smithy and managed to give us the slip."

"Which one?" Skara attempted to hide her excitement. As she spoke, her tongue flicked across her teeth and lips in anticipation.

"I'm not sure; we didn't get a good look at her as she jumped out of the window." The annoyance in his voice betrayed his true aggravation at the situation. "She is fast whoever she is," Faris commented as he turned to face Skara.

"Well then," Skara purred a little quieter as she reached one clawed finger out to Faris's chest and lightly ran it up to his neck playfully, "your men need to be faster." She flicked her wrist and scratched his throat with just enough force to coerce a fleck of blood to well up to the surface.

"Careful what you wish for..." Faris's voice became deep and gravelly as his words oozed off of his tongue. "I have been known to... "

"We found something over here in a barrel," his lieutenant shouted to them from behind the stack of barrels. "It looks like she may be hiding in one."

"What are you waiting for then?" Faris half turned and glared at his lieutenant. "Open it and get her out!" He barked impatiently.

"Sometimes you have to take matters into your own hands," Skara cooed up at him.

Faris seemed a little shorter and broader in the chest than she recalled, which bothered her a little. However, she felt this concern seep away when he turned and locked her with his eyes. She could tell he was seething with a pent-up rage and desire, both of which made her all the more interested in him.

"I plan to," Faris said as he placed his hands gently on her shoulders.

Skara sigh deeply as she felt him pull her closer. She closed her eyes and licked her slowly parting lips in anticipation. The bone-jarring explosion caught her completely off guard.

Before she had a chance to react, Faris threw her down and landed on top of her forcefully. Skara's eyes flew open as she arched her back in desperation and managed to throw him off of her as she rolled to her feet.

"What is going on?" She screamed at Faris. Her emotions swirled together to form an out of control whirlwind and she wrestled with them in a futile attempt to unwind them.

Faris moaned as he rolled onto his back. "I have no idea,

but I aim to find out." He said as he rubbed his head and slowly stood up from the debris around them.

The wind howled through the darkening monument as the three of them stared up at the well-sculpted statue. The last of the sun's rays glinted brilliant shades of red and blue off of deep red metal of the helm that completely concealed the statue's features. His banded leather armor was pristine as were the three gold bands that encircled each arm at his bicep, forearm, and wrist. His hands were outstretched and reached reassuringly toward them as if the statue greeted them as friends.

Instead of the usual assortment of swords and shields they had found at previous statues, this one had only a wide variety of staves and clubs carefully placed in unique patterns and arrangements surrounding it.

"Is this the one?" Aves asked as she squinted against the reflected light.

"Aye," Onas said as he studied the statue completely lost in thought. "Dryan the Calm."

Hessa studied the map and then glanced from the statue ahead of them to the other statues just a short distance away. She was amazed by the accuracy of the sketching. It had all of the piles in the right places. It also indicated the correct distance separating each statue. When she looked close enough, Hessa was able to determine what each pile consisted of.

"Onas is right. The piles surrounding this statue match what the map shows," although she was a little exacerbated, Hessa was glad that they were so close to finding the item.

"I thought it was going to be a weapon that the statue held," Aves said in confusion. "This statue holds nothing. Are we going to have to look at each of these staves and clubs? If so, what are we looking for?" The whine in her voice was somewhat hidden, but it was still there.

"Well," Onas said calmly, "Dryan was known for his

soothing effect on friend and enemy alike. Maybe his greatest weapon was his charm."

"How can we take his charm?" Aves asked a little dumbfounded. "Are you saying we need to take the whole statue with us?"

"Controlling your enemies is wise." Hessa recited the poem from memory as she stood in front of the statue. The golden glow reflected off of the statue and perfectly bathed the spot where she stood motionless and serene.

"Find the key, for in your heart it lies. The brave and decorated surmise" she paused long enough to open her eyes and stare at the statue again with the first two verses rolling around in her mind.

"That's what he is doing. He is controlling those around him." She wanted to make sure Aves and Onas understood what she was saying. "Onas, is there any warrior more decorated in this memorial?"

Onas's brows furrowed as he obviously calculated the numbers of monuments for a few moments and shook his head as he responded. "Not from what I have seen. There are some with a few more decorations added, but none were more officially decorated by the Crown. Dryan was single-handedly responsible for ending the combined attacks against the Keep of Hope."

"You mean he had an army following his orders, right?" Aves asked skeptically.

"No," Onas said flatly. "I mean all alone."

"But both dragons and merfolk threatened to destroy the keep. No one person can stop that sort of threat alone." Hessa could not keep her incredulity to herself. What Onas said was far too fanciful to be true.

"I know. That is why he was the most decorated. I have heard tales from some of our brethren that had been there. They say the battle was fought amongst our enemies instead of against us." Onas's words held the solemnity of the grave in them,

"They fought each other?" Aves asked somewhat confused.

"Aye. The stories I heard say the morning of the battle, Dryan went to the main gates and asked for them to be opened. Dressed only in his helm, armor, and bands he walked out to face the armies alone. He called out to them and spoke words in their own tongues. When he was done the two armies faced each other and fought to the last man. When it was over one remaining dragon turned and face Dryan. He had been standing there watching the whole time. The dragon bowed deeply to him. Then, Dryan said something to it and it left."

"How is that possible?" Aves asked in awe.

"The gift of the Gods he had been given," Hessa said as realization dawned on her. "He had the gift back then as well."

"He must have," Onas agreed, with a somewhat distracted tone

"What are the next words of the riddle?" Aves asked. Her excitement was visceral and beamed out of her youthful hazel eyes as they spoke.

"It says something about spying I think," Hessa said as she stared at the statue.

"Onas, where is the paper?" Aves asked as she turned away from Hessa long enough to make eye contact with him.

"How to snatch defeat when he spies." Onas recited as he handed the page with the rubbing of the riddle to Aves. "Here, take it. There is something I must see to."

Hessa could tell he was distracted, but she did not care. Instead, she focused on the words. She quickly scanned the page as she turned to face Aves, "A man, who looks to his arms, dies."

Haradine staggered into the secret hallway winded and

confused. She knew Namir's secrets were important enough for her father to live a life of secrecy, but she did not realize how badly others wanted them.

"Whatever it is that my father knew, it was important," she muttered to herself under her breath as she paused against a wall.

"YOU DON'T KNOW THE HALF OF IT." The deep voice resonated through the stones around her with its unasked for response.

The words seemed to materialize around her and Haradine panicked. She felt the numbing cold start to settle into her exposed flesh and knew that one of the shadow races was upon her.

She skillfully drew her blade as she stepped away from the walls. Although she felt drained, a new surge of energy quickly filled her veins as she scanned the impossibly black shadows with her elven sight.

"I MEAN YOU NO HARM," Deracai whispered as he stepped free from the shadows. "YOUR FATHER AND I ARE, WERE, FRIENDS. I OWE HIM MY LIFE MANY TIMES OVER." He allowed his cloak to fall off of the back of his shoulder to let Haradine see that he was unarmed.

Her eyes scanned him from toe to head. Her gaze lingering only at the many places one could hide weapons to ensure his had been properly secured. She felt an odd pull as her eyes danced along the pommel of his sword.

Its black metal seemed alive with an inner light all its own. When Haradine was confident that he was not a threat, she nodded her approval and refocused her attention to his overly pale face.

"Why are you here shadow walker?" Haradine asked icily.

"TO HELP," a wry smile played across his handsome features as he spoke, "AND TO BE INTRODUCED TO THE HEIR

THAT WE HAVE BEEN WORKING SO VERY HARD TO KEEP ALIVE."

"What is your business with Namir?"Haradine's words carried her defensiveness about Namir too well and she was instantly aware of it.

"AGAIN, I MEAN NO HARM. HE IS THE CULMINATION OF ALL THAT YOUR FATHER AND I HAVE FOUGHT TO PROTECT THESE MANY LONG YEARS. I SIMPLY WISH TO MEET HIM AND OFFER HIM WHATEVER AID THAT I MIGHT." His eyes cajoled Haradine for her overt possessiveness of Namir as he spoke and she felt every veiled barb. "ALL I ASK FROM YOU IS A PROPER INTRO-DUCTION. CERTAINLY, YOU CAN PROVIDE THAT."

Haradine nodded as she asked, "And who am I supposed to say is making the request?"

"TELL HIM THAT A SHADOW HE ALMOST MET IN THE FOREST WISHES AN AUDIENCE," Deracai's smile broadened. This added bit of mystery only added to his allure.

"Can I not know your name?" Haradine asked a little breathless as she stared into his dark eyes. She fumbled for her belt as she used that act to pull her eyes from him long enough to sheath her blade.

"NOT YET, BUT YOU SHALL SOON ENOUGH," he replied as he shrugged his cloak back over his shoulder to conceal himself once more in its dark warmth.

Haradine stared at the mysterious figure for a few mo-ments as she gathered her breath and her composure. Once she was certain there was nothing else the shadow walker would tell her, she continued on her way.

Just before she rounded the corner and left the sightline of her visitor, she stopped and said, "I assume you will wait here until I can announce you."

"THEN YOU ASSUME WRONG," his voice was once again

behind her although she had turned to face the shadows he had just been in. "DO NOT WORRY; I WILL KNOW WHEN I HAVE BEEN ANNOUNCED. IT WOULD BEHOOVE YOU TO MAKE IT THE FIRST THING YOU DO."

Between the ominous tone of his voice and the chill that ran down her back as she spoke, Haradine understood his threat all too well. She nodded her understanding and then turned to face the darkness where she assumed he now stood.

"If you can please give me room, I will make sure to announce you." His silence was the only answer she received.

A few awkward moments passed as her elven sight adjusted to penetrate the darkness again. She suppressed her amazement at the emptiness that stood before her. Although she knew shadow walkers were aptly named, she had never experienced their movements quite like this. She found it unnerving.

Haradine resisted the urge to run and warn Namir of this visitor. Instead, she took metered steps and advanced cautiously. Haradine knew the shadow walker was watching her and she hated it. The last few steps seemed to take forever as she finally made it to the closed door and tapped twice with her fingertips on its cold stone surface.

"What kept you?" Namir asked as he opened the door. His irritation visibly faded as did the hardened look in his steely eyes as he saw how disheveled Haradine was.

"I had to make a slight detour," she lied as she easily stepped past him into the well-lit room.

Haradine breathed a sigh of relief as she heard him click the door in place. "This room is too well lit for the walker," she thought to herself as she set her liege's pack down on the bare table. "Now I know why he gave me the task that he did." Her thoughts flew through her mind faster than she could move.

The elf gently tugged her hair back into the loose queue that she had it in originally before she turned and faced Namir to deliver the shadow walker's message. "My liege, you have a visitor outside the door." She started to say and was a little surprised when she saw him wave her into silence.

"They can wait," Namir started as he looked her over. "I need a report from you first. What happened and why did you have to make a detour? What caused the shaking? Was it tied to your little tardiness?" Namir fired off his questions to her as if she were a general in an army and expected her to respond in what little gap he provided.

"I don't believe that your guest is accustomed to waiting," Haradine replied with a small smirk on her face. She was impressed by Namir's astuteness and delighted he was able to put together events so quickly.

"While in the forge, I noticed that there were some of Faris's men gathering outside. I hurried to collect your things and was surprised when I heard them enter the smith's house." She paused to let her words sink in enough to show on Namir's features before she continued.

"I took the paths that you showed me when I left, but they still managed to track me, so I created a distraction," Haradine replied. "To give a full report, the explosion was my doing. Hopefully, I managed to kill some of Faris's men in the process."

"Did you think about what it would do to this town?" Namir asked incredulously. "Not many from around here have ever heard, or experienced, anything like that." He admonished her as he regained control of the discussion.

"I did not," Haradine admitted as she dropped her gaze to her feet. "I am sorry for my lapse," she offered feebly.

Namir placed a hand on her shoulder reassuringly as he spoke, "Do a better job next time. We cannot fix the past or undo what has been done. Now tell me about the person you said is waiting to meet with me."

The easy air of leadership Namir displayed amazed Haradine. She was more used to seeing Namir as a confused boy and less of a ruler. "He is a shadow walker and he told me to say that a shadow you almost met while in the forest wants to be introduced to you."

Namir's eyes widened as he heard Haradine's words. He immediately walked over and dimmed the burning lanterns in order to make the room more habitable for his guest. "By all means, tell him to come in."

"THANK YOU MY LIEGE," the voice erupted from the darkest corner of the now dimly lit room. "I HAVE LONGED DREAMED OF THE DAY I WOULD FINALLY BE ABLE TO MEET THE MAN YOU WOULD BECOME." He smiled as Namir squirmed a little uncomfortable. "WE HAVE MUCH TO DISCUSS AND, IF I AM RIGHT, WE DO NOT MUCH TIME TO DO IT IN."

"Agreed, so let's begin," Namir nodded as the shadow walker stepped out from the shadows and opened his cloak.

Onas slipped away from the girls as Hessa's words hung in the air. He carefully made his way towards a set of bushes just outside the perimeter created by the staves.

"I know I saw something moving over here," Onas's thoughts rattled around his head as he cautiously reached forward and moved the light branches of the bush away from his path.

"And his chest, his legs, his hands, his eyes." Hessa's voice pulled at the back of Onas's consciousness as he pushed his way through a thicket of bushes.

The ground became softer as he moved further through the foliage. Onas heard the girls discussing what he assumed were the passages that Hessa had just read, although he could not hear what they said.

"Hopefully they can figure the riddle out before I get done here," Onas muttered to himself. He did not relish the idea of removing anything from the memorial, even if it was a relic from the gods.

"I hope so too," the reptilian sounding response was unexpected and forced Onas to reassess his surroundings and what might be in them.

"Who is there?" Onas challenged. He stopped just shy of the edge of the cover he had been pushing his way through. His senses seemed heightened as he attempted to discern where the voice had come from.

"Step out and see for yourself," the voice hissed at him from just beyond the few remaining branches separating them.

The distinct smell of wet steel helped him make up his mind to remain where he stood. Onas listened closely to the noises around him as he trained his eyes on the almost liquid quality that the ground under his feet had taken on. The soft almost velvety shuffling sounds of something sliding through the mud met his ears and worried him.

"Whoever it is, they are either very large or have a few friends." Onas tamped down the fear that filled his mind with his thoughts as he stood statuesquely.

"I will not kill you," the words seemed to slither through the leaves as they were spoken and sent a chill down Onas's spine. "In fact, I think that we both want the same thing. To protect those we love."

New sounds of leaves as they rustled from something moving through them forced Onas to rethink his strategy. He knew if he stayed where he was, the thing would find him. He slowly raised his eyes from his boots to the base-line of the foliage and noticed, for the first time, the floating bits of bone that bobbed amongst the leaves.

Onas quelled another upwell of fear as he realized that there was only one thing he could do to keep the girls safe. He took a deep breath as he stepped through the final layer of branches and into the clearing beyond.

Chapter Six:
Accords

Skara traded furtive glances with Faris as they looked over the twisted and mangled remains of his men. "How could one girl do this much damage?" She asked as if Faris had an answer. Her stomach churned as she glanced over the splintered husks of barrels and crates with all of their hidden stores burned or destroyed.

"I think I know which one of his companions it was," Faris said, more to himself than to Skara.

"Which one could have done this?" Skara felt her iron grasp on her emotions slip a little as she glared at Faris.

He was rock solid like she used to be. Something about her targets and this town was robbing her of that cool detachment and she detested Faris for his calm demeanor.

"Haradine," Faris seethed.

He reached into what was left of a barrel and pulled out the remains of a bottle. Just the oddly conical base remained, but it was enough for him to recognize the elf's handiwork.

"Her general, Landolin, once told me about some of the weapons they had developed. He called it fire from the gods. A liquid that would burn so hot and so fast it stole the very lives of everyone around it. I always thought it was a lie. Something one soldier says to another to either spread fear or gain an edge. I never really believed that they had such a thing," he marveled aloud.

"It looks like you were wrong," Skara scoffed. She felt some of her objectivity return as his story distracted her from the grizzly scene they stood in.

"That it does," Faris's voice held a hint of remorse as he slowly rose to his feet. "It seems I have misjudged quite a bit in the past and am now living long enough to see these mistakes come to haunt me."

The hollowness of Faris's voice stuck Skara oddly. "How many men do you have left?" Skara asked in an attempt to return the favor and distract him from his thoughts.

"None," his arms made a sweeping gesture as he spoke. "These were the last three I brought with me. Even the men that I sent ahead of our arrival are dead." Faris shook his head in a morbid sense of amazement. "I have taken some of these men into battle and they survived, but we couldn't even fulfill one little mission to kill a few children!" The disgust in his voice was palpable.

"The only thing we can do is report to our mistress then and ask her advice," Skara offered.

"Her advice will be to kill ourselves or not return," Faris said sarcastically.

"I doubt that," Skara said as she pulled the small orb from her pouch. "Make sure no one approaches me while I operate this."

"There is little fear of that," Faris mocked. "The smell of burnt flesh will keep people at bay for a few more minutes. Let's make this fast."

"Agreed," Skara nodded as she focused her mind's eye on the orb in the palm of her hand.

A warming sensation spread through her hand where it sat and within a few moments, the orb levitated a few inches from her palm. A light glow slowly emanated from its clear surface and within seconds the image of Tali's face floated within it.

"Report," Tali's disembodied voice rang out clearly in both of their minds.

"All of Faris's men were killed," Skara said somewhat hesitantly.

"And your targets, are they dead as well?" Tali queried impatiently.

"No," Faris said with metered disgust. "The girls have vanished and the boy is sequestered."

"What are your commands?" Skara cut Faris's report short in an attempt to regain her hold as the leader of their mission.

"Return to Hornshir, there is nothing more for you to do there." Tali's voice betrayed no emotion as she spoke her instructions. "I will take other, less subtle, actions to resolve our interests in Ellsted."

Skara stared at the glowing orb in disbelief. "You want us to do what?"

"Leave," her mistress's disembodied voice replied. "You two have failed!"

The edge of malice in Tali's voice forced Skara to shrink away from the skrying ball in fear. Her sudden movement almost forced her to lose her control of it entirely.

"Enough!" Tali exclaimed. "Just be free of Ellsted by nightfall."

"If his secret is your prize," Aves and Hessa said in unison as they surveyed the statue carefully. They had already decided to rule out the assortment of weapons that decorated the scenery around them. "Go now and try it on for size." Their final words seemed to echo ominously as each of the girls looked at different parts of the statue.

"Helmet, bands, or armor?" Aves asked as she stared at the statue's feet. "It looks like his shoes are a part of the initial carving. So we can rule those out."

"The passage said something about arms right?" Hessa asked as she looked as close as she could at the bands.

She dared not get too close for fear of triggering the gypsy magic Onas warned her about. One wrong thing touched might be the last thing Hessa did, so instead, she leaned over the base of the statue and examined what she could from her vantage point.

From what she could see, most of the bands were actually carved from a gold colored stone. The bands were seamless except where a solitaire palm-sized glimmered in the ever-receding light.

"I think so," Aves said as she turned her attention back to the rubbing. "A man, who looks to his arms, dies. And his chest, his legs, his hands, his eyes. If his secret is your prize, Go now and try it on for size." Aves read aloud.

She annunciated each word and Hessa knew it was for her benefit. That way she could hear them better, but not become distracted from her thoughts.

"So does that mean we can rule out the bands since they are around his arms?" Hessa asked as she tore her attention from the flawless craftsmanship of the gem in front of her.

"Why would it?" Aves asked pointedly. "I think it means what we said earlier. Arms can refer to his weapons."

"But what if it means that, as well as, more literally anything he wears or uses with his arms, chest, legs, hands, and eyes." Hessa's head cocked to the right slightly as she spoke.

"Okay, I'll bite," Aves replied seriously. "Let's say it does mean both, what are we left with?"

"The helmet," Hessa said a little defeatedly. "Really?" The shock in Aves's voice perfectly matched the disappointment Hessa felt.

"It seems that way." Hessa pointed to the bands as she continued, "The bands here are on the arms, the armor is on the chest and legs.   He has nothing in his hands, but the assorted weapons would be what he would have filled them with.   From what I can see, he has nothing in or around his eyes.   That leaves the helm resting on his head."   She thought it would have been harder to solve than this and Hessa knew Aves could hear it in her voice.

"Wouldn't the helm be ruled out since he has to see through it with his eyes in order to find his enemy?" Aves asked hesitantly.

Aves's logic was not as sound as hers, but Hessa was glad that Aves wanted to make sure they had thought about everything before they took a chance by grabbing the helm. Hessa walked back over to Aves and read the entire passage again.

"Controlling your enemies is wise.   Find the key, for in your heart it lies.   The brave and decorated surmise, How to snatch defeat when he spies. A man, who looks to his arms, dies.   And his chest, his legs, his hands, his eyes.   If his secret is your prize, Go now and try it on for size."   She crinkled her nose and pondered it as Aves reread it quietly to herself again.

"I think that since the helm rests on the head and not the eyes, it would be free from the restriction," Hessa said as she looked at the helm.   "Besides, it mentions spying just before that.   It has to be the helm.   There is nothing else that fits into the riddle."

"Some riddles are not meant to be solved," Aves offered. "I don't want to lose you this soon," her voice was filled with concern and it dripped from each tear-filled word.

Tali studied the deacon in front of her as they spoke. He was outwardly calm like all of them were, but the inner turmoil that haunted him took a little while to discern. Once she did, she knew his duties were weighing heavily upon him.

"What troubles you so, brother?" Her tone was pleasant

so as not to overly betray her curiosity.

"What makes you think there is something on my mind?" His response was a little too quick and she could tell by the way his brow furled that he knew it as soon as the words fell from his lips.

Tali took a deep breath and turned from the mirror and faced her subordinate. "Haran, we have known each other for far too long for me not to know when something is amiss. So, please, tell me what it is." Her stare conveyed the hidden threat her words veiled in their niceties better than anything else could.

Haran nodded as he submitted to Tali's will, "It is the new novice. He learns what he needs so fast and absorbs everything too well. Sometimes I fear that he is overly zealous and dismissive."

"It is in his nature to try and please those he cares about," Tali lied. She fought hard against her own emotions as she spoke. She did not dare betray her excitement at how well Jaconis was doing. "Besides I need him to be ready. The Dark Travelers have not had a new member in far too long and I have a mission they need to complete. This boy's talents are suited to this task in many ways."

"A Dark Traveler so soon?" The astonishment and contempt in his voice were unable to be masked in any way.

"Aye Haran, a Dark Traveler." She let her icy stare linger as her words slid between them. "Is there an issue with this?"

"No issue, your grace. I am just surprised. Many of us have toiled for decades before we were considered for that privilege. Surely there is someone that has been toiling in our goddess's name that may prove better suited for your needs." Haran said with a challenging tone.

Tali knew Haran did not question her authority and decision outright, but at the same point, she understood his reasoning. Many of Lotevilar's followers might see this unprecedented appointment as a travesty to their faith, so he could not let this pass unchallenged. No matter what she might do to him.

"Has the boy passed every test and challenge presented to him?" Tali asked offhandedly.

"Aye," Haran replied obediently.

"Doesn't he show ample promise in promoting Lotevilar's will amongst the chosen?" She continued as if Haran's response were unnecessary.

"Aye, as far as can be told," Haran bowed his head as she continued her questioning.

"Has he not progressed far enough in our faith to be granted the opportunity to cleanse one of our fold when the next opportunity arises?" She carefully studied her old advisor's mannerisms as she spoke. She searched for any sign of his resolve weakening but found none.

"He has. All you say is true," Haran answered unbidden. "That does not change my plea. What is it about this boy that makes him so essential to our mistress's plans?" Haran finally caved and asked the one question that plagued him.

Tali smiled as she felt Haran's will finally snap. The pride in his voice betrayed his contempt for her decision in choosing Jaconis for her plans. This was the point of weakness she had been waiting for.

"Are you questioning Lotevilar's will or my authority to enact it?"

Haran's silence was his only response.

"Are you implying that I am not fulfilling Her desires?" The silence only deepened between them as she spoke. "He is vital to the skein of things. More importantly, he needs to be ready to travel before this moon's passing. Have you arranged for him to receive the rest of his training?"

"Aye," Haran responded quietly. "His next level of training is contingent on the cleansing."

"Good, then all is proceeding as planned. That will be all." Her command sent Haran scrambling both mentally and physically.

Tali was relieved when she heard the door to her chambers close behind him as he departed. She hated to betray Haran's trust, but she had no choice.

With the extent Deracai had managed to harm her, she knew she needed to find another way to ferret out the location of Zelios. Without it, her liege would not be able to ascend to the throne and she would have failed in her duties to Lotevilar. Neither of which she was willing to accept.

Carness and Tipin stared at each other over the debris-ridden scene. It was as grizzly a sight as any they had witnessed in their service to the Crown and the first they had to bear since the end of the war.

"Allair and the rest of the council will be here momentarily," Tipin muttered to the constable.

"Good, then we can be done with this," Carness responded as he nudged a broken blade with his boot. "I know any number of things could be responsible for this, but I have my suspicions about the cause."

Tipin nodded silently. He knew better than to interrupt Carness when he was on a tirade. His eyes wandered over the bodies and the shattered remnants of the wooden casks and crates.

"It looks like most of these were yet to be filled," Tipin's bass voice filled their surroundings and resonated off of the silent flat surfaces evenly.

"They were," Carness agreed. He stretched his overly taut muscles before the resumed his search.

The constable moved purposely around each of the broken shards of pottery and glass. He diligently traced where each of the items would have been prior to the explosion that violently flung them from their homes. Carness placed a tick mark on the quick map he had sketched of the scene at each place a piece of shrapnel intersected one of the remains.

"Most of these were set aside for our local craftsmen to fill with trade items to be sent to Hornshir. All part of the new agreements your sons helped negotiate." Carness said as he completed his initial investigation of the scene.

"I see," Tipin mutter, more to himself than to the constable.

Carness glanced up at Tipin momentarily as he ensured their privacy. "Is Namir safe?"

"Why do you ask?" Tipin asked, a little unsure of Carness's reasons.

"I know his true purpose," Carness said in hushed tones reassuringly, "and, judging from the wreckage, these men were hired killers. Their only real goal in Ellsted, from what I can piece together, would be to assassinate someone of importance. I doubt if anyone in our town council would warrant such an attempt."

His wolfish eyes studied Tipin as he spoke as if he weighed the giant's reactions to his words as he continued. "A few nights ago the main square was consumed in flames and the gypsies lost their matron. One of these men were found dead not too far away from it."

"Are these Faris's men?" Tipin asked a little surprised he had not realized it sooner.

"They are," Carness nodded. "This one here," the constable nudged the most severely damaged corpse with his foot as he spoke, "was involved with the staged attack on Hessa outside of the inn a few nights back. Someone wanted to eliminate them as a threat and I can think of only a handful of people skilled enough to do something like this." His words bore a hard edge to them.

The smith felt Carness's eyes bore through him as he listened to his rant patiently. He understood perfectly well that Carness saw him as a suspect, but he did not allow his nervousness at the prospect show.

"I have a few suspicions about who did this as well. The

real question is going to be what will we do about it." Tipin said as silently as could.

"That is a question for the council, not a blacksmith!" Armani's voice erupted from the alleyway on the outside of the wreckage as the council members stepped clear of the debris.

"Good, you're here. Now we can get on with this." Carness said with mock relief.

Hessa wiped away a bead of sweat with her arm as it threatened to roll into her eye. She was delicately balanced on the statue's shoulders with a foot on each. Carefully, she bent over its head with an arm extended on each side. Hessa tried to keep her balance as she reached around the statue.

Hessa made sure she looked out over the memorial in the same direction the statue did. This way she could avoid any magical trap either Aves or her could think of dealing with the riddle. She also figured that by facing this way she had the best leverage for removing its helmet.

The tremors in her fingers would not stop as she slowly lowered them toward the bottom of the helm. Between her trembling fingers and her nervously twitching legs, Hessa was not sure if she would be able to complete her task. Another deep breath filled her lungs as the warm metal met her fingers softly.

"May Ea guide your hands," Aves called out as she noticed Hessa hesitation.

Hessa spared Aves a small grin as she glanced at her briefly. It was all the distraction she needed to steel her will to her task. Gently her fingers slid along the metal surface and coiled around the lip of the helm. There was something odd about how warm the metal was. It seemed to mirror her own heat, almost s if it warmed to her touch.

"That's right, now lift it off," the voice seemed to surround them and forced Hessa to stop.

Hessa frantically searched their surroundings in an attempt to locate its source. She let her fingers slowly slide off the helm as she scanned as much as she could. A modicum of relief swept through her when she noticed Aves doing the same.

"Where is Onas?" Hessa asked, now completely aware she had not seen their guide in quite a while.

"I'm not sure," Aves replied as she slowly moved toward the bushes on the far side of the statue. "He said something about needing to check on a few things and then left."

"How long ago was that?" Hessa wondered loud enough for Aves to hear her.

"Too long," Aves replied.

"Onas!" Hessa yelled as loud as she could. Her words echoed off of the stone cliffs that bordered them with an eerie tone.

"Do not worry, he is with me," the voice hissed out of the shrubbery Aves had been walking toward. "Focus on your task and let's be done with this game."

Hessa felt her blood freeze as she heard the voice again. The snakelike sound in its voice was unnerving and Hessa could not help but allow the feeling of panic sweep through her.

"Who are you?" Hessa fought back the wave of panic she felt sweeping through her.

"The guardian of the shrine," it hissed in response from the other side of the brush.

Aves slowly backed away from the bushes as she squinted in an attempt to see the thing. "How do we know that Onas is safe?"

"You don't," the deep lines of anguish let Hess know the creature's reply was more than Aves could bear. Tears started to flow down her face as she heard the creature speak. "You are just going to have to believe that he is."

"You could let him step forward so we can see for ourselves," Hessa offered.

She stood precariously on the statue's shoulders. Her body sprawled across its surface. The way her overly taut muscles pulled and stretched only added to her anxiety.

"I could," the creature agreed, "but then I would have allowed you a modicum of safety. I have already bested him once; I would hate to do it again."

"At least show yourself so we know who we are speaking with," Aves demanded through her tears.

"Very well, if you insist." Its reply caught them off guard and only managed to raise the level of their anxiety.

Both girls could somehow sense the thing smile as it responded. They held their breath as the long grass and the branches of the bushes parted slowly. An eternity seemed to pass as the thing moved ever closer to the edge of its cover and then into their view.

It was amazing. Beautiful and deadly all at once. The silver tip of the creature's tail as it moved sideways to clear a path for its large, yet sleek, body was the first thing they were able to see. The spear-like tip elegantly lashed from side to side.

The creature's smooth, almost liquid, silver head slide from behind the cover of brushes and it was breathtaking. Although neither of the ladies had ever seen a dragon, Hessa knew that is what this thing was almost instantly. The last few rays of the evening glistened off of its metallic hide and cast a halo around it. It was both unbelievable and beautiful.

As the dragon advanced, its long ivory claws gripped it the loose stones on the ground and pulled itself forward. A ruby colored tongue flicked out and tasted the air around them as it approached. Even though the creature was large, it somehow moved without leaving a mark on the soft soil.

"Wow," Hessa said breathlessly.

She struggled to keep her balance as she felt the world spin away from her. Hessa spared a glance at Aves and noticed her sister struggled as well. It was all she could do not to fall or to stare at the magnificent spectacle displayed before her.

"Where is Onas?" Aves's question was more of a squeak than a real question.

"He is here," the dragon hissed its response. Part of the dragon's back rippled like water and a wing seemed to extend from nowhere. Onas lay silently in the gap that had been created below it.

"See for yourself, I have not harmed him." The dragon's tongue flicked out again as it half spoke and half hissed at them.

Aves cringed at the size of the creature and it was apparent by the jerkiness of her movement that she could not force her legs to move. Hessa screamed inwardly at her own fears as she stared at the spot where Onas lay. He was not bound, yet he stayed exactly where they first saw him. No matter how hard she tried, she could not tell how he remained where he was at.

Seeing that neither girl moved, the dragon spoke again. "Now, child, please continue your task." Its voice shifted and became more melodic the longer it spoke. "Once we are done here, Onas will be returned to you." The dragon almost sang.

Hessa felt her body respond against her will. Silently she cursed her own weakness as her fingers moved of their own accord. The lukewarm surface where she had held the helm previously met her palm eagerly. It was alluring and sensual. The odd thrill of pleasure spread through her arms as she gently tugged the helm from its resting place.

"Now bring it down," the dragon instructed in its new sing-song voice.

"How can I climb down?" Hessa asked.

She could feel what little self-control she had as it slipped free from her mind. No matter how she mentally twisted her situation, she strained to think her actions through. After a few moments, she decided the best thing to do was to toss it to the ground. Again her arms moved of their own volition and she was powerless to stop them.

Tears well up in Hessa's eyes as she watched the one thing she searched for start to slip out of her fingers.

"No, do not drop it." The dragon's song held a tinge of panic in its tone as it sang, "Put it on, and then climb down."

"No!" Aves screamed. "It's a trick!"

"Do not listen to her, she is insignificant. Put the helm on, climb down and bring it to me." The subtle music of the dragon's words became more compelling as Hessa listened.

Hessa arms felt like lead as she struggled against the weight of the helm. Slowly she managed to tighten her grip on it and stop it from falling. After several more impossibly long moments, Hessa shifted her grip and raised it over her head.

She heard Aves's screams, but could not quite make out what it was that she said. Hessa felt as if her world were suddenly muted and meaningless. All that seemed to exist for her was the helm.

Its silvery hue amazed her. It was argent and black in the oddly reflected light cascading around her. Her arms grew tired of holding it, so she tilted it and slid it on. All at once her world exploded around her.

Chapter Seven:
Pacts

Alequa glanced at Allair and then to the council members as she knelt beside the wreckage. She knew her daughter had caused this mess. Somehow she had to hide this fact from them and her mind raced as she put a hasty plan together.

"I have seen this before," she admitted, "and so have Carness, Tipin, and Daffer. During the last great war, this kind of destructive magic was common."

"Do you have any idea who could have worked them here?" Saril's question rang out through the growing din of the crowd as it gathered to see what the council would decide.

"None," Alequa lied. She hoped her blind friend would not notice her increased heart rate and the elf held her breath as the words fell from her lips.

"That is too bad," Armani took control of the conversation back from the elven healer as he stepped up to her side.

She felt his eyes study her every move as he spoke. Carefully she picked through the debris surrounding them again. Her only response to the mayor's increased scrutiny was a slight shrug and a deep sigh.

After a few long moments waiting for her response, he

continued. "I'm sure the constable's investigation will be a thorough one, which is why I am certain the council will be able to make a decision about this by this evening's special meeting."

The last few words seemed to be more directed at the crowd than at her, so Alequa breathed a small sigh of relief. She knew this sort of thing was out of place in the small town and could only wonder at what forced Haradine to do this.

"Don't forget all of our previous engagements," Allair reminded the chancellor.

Armani wrinkled his brow in an attempt to hide his displeasure with Allair's interruption. "Don't worry. I have not forgotten all of the council's responsibilities, nor will I. I am just confident in both Carness's and the council's ability to push unnecessary aspects of the meeting to the side long enough to address a matter of public safety." His stare conveyed more meaning than his words could hope to and Allair shrank back reflexive from its withering intensity.

"Then there shouldn't be an issue if I were to assist the constable in his duties," Tipin challenged Armani more with his tone than actions.

"Well," Armani started to say in a somewhat broken tenor as Tipin cut in again.

"That is assuming Carness agrees to my aid," Tipin smiled at the visible increase in Armani's frustration level.

"Of course," Armani agreed hesitantly. "After all, who am I to tell the constable how to conduct his investigation? Just as long as it is resolved quickly."

Alequa could tell Armani was back peddling and she knew how much he hated being forced out of the decision-making process, especially when it was something as visible as this matter. She knew that as Mayor he could order Carness to disallow Tipin from helping. The problem was a political one.

If Armani did restrict Tipin, the public would find out and he could lose votes. From what Allair had shared with her earlier, she knew the margin from the last election was too slim to give him the sense of certainty he needed to do as he wished.

"Well mister mayor, if that is how you truly feel," Carness cut in, "then I would love to have the blacksmith's help. His skills would be invaluable." A lopsided wolfish grin made its way across his face.

From the smirk on his face and his more relaxed stance, Alequa could tell that Carness appreciated the opportunity to make Armani squirm. Especially now that some of the dealings they had found seemed to link the mayor to some of the shadiest dealings happening in Ellsted.

"I don't see why I have to be the one to deliver the message," Farvais pouted. "I want to stay here in the manor. Besides, too many of us have died trying to ensure this boy has his chance to ascend to the throne." She brushed a raven lock of hair away from her eyes as she spoke.

"Be that as it may, we need to mobilize our soldiers and get them ready for the next step," Landolin said exasperatedly.

"Besides, if you hurry you can get there, deliver the message and get back before anyone realizes you have been gone," Gienna jumped in.

She could tell her brother was getting irritated with Farvais and puzzled her. "Normally Landolin would not promote someone that acted this way to the position of Lieutenant. I wonder why he would make an exception for her." Her thoughts flowed through her mind like liquid as she refocused her attention back to the conversation.

"You do realize that you will be the sole emissary of your general. This means you will have everyone's attention. Even Karous would be beholden to you." The little sparkle that took hold in Farvais's eye as she mentioned the renowned elven trainer force Gienna to smile inwardly.

"Alright, I understand. This message needs to be delivered and I am the only one who can do it." Farvais nodded her head as if the idea had been hers from the beginning. "I will leave straight away." Her last few words slipped from her lips and occupied the space she left.

"It would be best if you waited until first light," Landolin Called after her. "We need to make sure if anyone, or anything, is watching the manor, they do not follow you."

"Sage advice," Gienna chimed in.

Farvais's footsteps halted just outside the doorway. She obviously heard Landolin and waited for his instructions. She traded secretive glances with her brother as she lent him some of her mental strength. Farvais set off way too many of her internal alarms. Gienna had not liked this particular lieutenant before, but now she outright distrusted her.

"Very well," Farvais said dejectedly from the hall. "I will wait until morning, but I will leave at the sun's first crest. Now if you will excuse me, I need to get my beauty rest. After all, a girl has to look her best when delivering a message of such importance."

Landolin and Gienna traded glances again as they waited until her footfalls faded. The subtle creak of the stairs as she ascended to her room. Both of them let out a joint sigh of relief as soon as they were alone.

Gienna motioned for her brother to sit still as she silently rose and stalked over to the hallway Farvais exited through. She cautiously crouched as low as she could before peering around the corner. It was empty.

She stood back up and paced back over to her chair and confided, "She has changed. There is something different about how she carries herself."

"I know," Landolin replied quietly. The relief in his voice did more to confirm her suspicions his words had. "She seems to know everyone Farvais does. She even knows the special procedures I taught to only my core leaders. But her attitude and personality are different. She is more careless and outgoing than she ever was before."

"Agreed," Gienna nodded. "She seems almost anxious for attention. The soldier I knew was more reserved and coy. Maybe losing Trainor was too much for her."

"Maybe, but I fear it is more than that." Landolin took a sip of his hot tea as he replied.

"HE iS RiGHt, SHE iS ПOt tHE SAПIE AS SHE OПCE WAS," the Maugutie's voice tugged at Gienna's mind as if it were taffy. "ПO OПE HAS EПtEREÐ tHAt ROOПI VПiПVitEÐ AПÐ SVRViVEÐ. THERE HAVE OПLY BEEП tWO PEOPLE I HAVE EVER KПOWП WHO EVEП ПIAÐE it OVt OF tHAt ROOПI. AS FAR AS I KПOW, ПEitHER FVLLY RECOVEREÐ FROПI WHAt tHEY SAW iП tHERE."

She shook the alien thoughts from her head discretely as she put her hands on her temples. "My mind hurts," she whispered to her brother.

"Mine too," Landolin confided. "I will be glad when our part in this is over."

"I fear that will be a long time in coming," Gienna's words were a little more than a whisper, yet they had the impacted both of them as if they were barbed arrows.

Alequa stared at the bodies dumped beside the road just outside of town. "These humans have no idea how to handle their dead," she thought disgustedly.

The chill of the evening breeze blew through the scarves she had created her makeshift jacket out of. She shivered as her eyes momentarily locked with the gaze of the nearest corpse involuntarily. The distant sightless eyes seemed fixated on her soul.

"I hate having to be so discrete," she thought to herself as she gingerly picked her way through the more overgrown section of the roadway. She continually glanced back at the pile of bodies and shivered each time she did. Alequa knew they were not following her, but she could not help but feel as if they did.

"Death haunts us all," she reminded herself as she recalled the verse of Tayant's teachings.

"Though it only lingers a moment, its permanence is revered for all time," the words fell smoothly from the shadows and startled the elf.

The correct completion of the verse threw her off guard. Alequa fought a wave of fear off as she squared her shoulders and started her prayers to Tayant, in case she needed them in defense.

"Calm yourself, I come in peace." Again the words came softly, yet had enough substance to be heard over Alequa's pounding heartbeat.

"Who are you," the elf said as she strained her already taxed elven sight to make out the person's image in the shadowy darkness that always seemed to accompany deserted roadways.

"An old friend that has finally found his way back from the brink of eternity," the words fell with more velocity than they had a few moments before.

The voice was familiar like it belonged to someone she knew a lifetime ago. There was more power in the voice now than there was a few moments ago. Although there was an uncanny familiarity to it, Alequa could not place it. She wracked her brain as she struggled to plumb her mystery guest's identity.

"What brings you here?" She asked defeatedly. "You do," the voice took on a more masculine air as the words pulled at Alequa's heart.

"How did you know I would be here?" Alequa asked. This man seemed more and more like Aras and that bothered her.

"History does not lie," he said quietly, "and neither do

old habits. You are heading to the cottage you usually seek refuge in when places like Ellsted are no longer safe for you." His deep voice was soothing.

His highly polished black boots were the first thing she saw as he moved out of the shadows and toward her. A wave of relief rushed over her when his profile began to separate itself from the darkness. The highly polished black metal armor was easy for Alequa to identify. There was only one man who wore armor like that, and he had served at Watchkeep with them.

"I thought you were dead!" Alequa exclaimed as her old friend stepped the rest of the way into her field of vision.

"As did I," he said as he removed his long-brimmed hat.

He masterfully bowed and took her hand. Before she realized it, his lips were pushed against the smooth skin of the back of her hand.

"It would seem the rumors of my demise have been long in the telling and have been dispelled at last. Now why such the long face?" There was a subtle hint of joviality to his voice and it eased her nerves.

"Aras is dead, the new heir is in danger, and I am unable to be near to him for fear of attracting the wrong kind of attention and endangering his life." Alequa did not want to say everything, but she could not stop herself

"Well then, it seems we have a lot of catching up to do," her friend said as he winked one of his aqua colored eyes at her playfully.

"It's time," Tipin's voice filled the room before he even had a chance to enter it.

A small smile creased Namir's lips as he saw Tipin's hulking form. He noticed the blacksmith wore his old war axe on his belt and carried the Calanari war helm he had mounted above the hearth.

"We are ready," Namir said quietly as he reached for his

tattered cloak.

"That will not be necessary sa'ouvant," Haradine responded as she placed her hand on Namir's to stay his hand. "It is not appropriate for you to wear something like that while you give your speech."

She motioned her free hand toward his cloak as she spoke. Namir could hear her disdain for his choice in apparel drip from each syllable she uttered and it aggravated him. He hated the preening he knew would be coming, but Namir knew there was little he could do about it.

"What would you have me wear then?" He was near exhaustion and everyone present could hear it in his voice. "I have selected the best clothes I own. I know it isn't good enough for what I must say, but it will have to do."

"We brought some better ones." Tipin's deep voice softened the blow to Namir's pride. "Allair insisted that I bring these. You know how she can be," Tipin smiled as he thrust a tightly wrapped bundle he concealed under his cloak into Namir's hands, "especially considering the news you are about to share with Ellsted's elders."

"Thank you," Namir replied quietly. He felt the words catch in his throat as he fought against his emotions. "I assume my message is why you are here in full regalia," Namir was a little surprised by the tone of his own voice as he directed his attention to Tipin.

"No," Tipin said with a wry smile. "Your message has little to do with my decision. You see, I am escorting the heir apparent to an official matter of the Crown. I should be dressed appropriately. Besides, Allair and I were attacked last night and I refuse to let the same thing happen to you. Not while I can do something to stop it. We haven't much time left, please get dressed my liege."

Tipin's tone froze Namir's blood as they locked gazes. He had never heard Tipin's voice hold such a somber air and it concerned him. Namir knew Tipin would not budge on this, so he unwrapped the package while they spoke.

The silver silk shit that met his gaze was impressive. The deep purple sash and black leather pants were just as impressive. No matter how elegant they were, his mind still fixated on Tipin's words.

"They were attacked." Namir thought as the waves of shock the idea created settled as he mouthed the words instinctively. Tipin and Allair were the only two people that were there when he needed someone, now this. The thought was almost too much for him.

"Who attacked you?" Namir struggled to control his emotions.

"I don't know," Tipin confided as he lowered himself to his knees. Namir recognized this position. It was the same one Nurn took anytime he prayed to Tumere. "The attacker came while we slept. Only Allair's hearing saved us."

"What do you mean?" Haradine asked as she finished the makeshift changing screen she created out of Namir's tattered cloak and the remnants of his table.

"My wife somehow knew that something was wrong." Tipin's face relaxed as he recalled the details. "She told me to get my dagger and check the forge, so I grabbed my axe and went straight to the courtyard." Tipin gave Namir a knowing smile as he continued. "That's when I saw the intruder. He was halfway up the wall and heading straight for Halin's window. I knew I needed to stop him before he could gain entrance, so I threw my axe in an attempt to slow him down. It worked."

"Who was it?" Namir asked. His interest was noticeably peaked, but he did not care if the others knew. "Was it anyone we know?" He asked as he pulled the silk shirt over his head.

"I didn't get the chance to find out." Tipin confided solemnly.

"But you just said that you knocked him down from the wall," Haradine added incredulously.

"I did, but he somehow managed to twist his body enough to kick off the wall and change the angle of his fall. I ran across the courtyard to where he landed, but he was quick. The intruder somehow managed recover from the fall and made his way to the small wall connected to my forge. By the time I reached him, he jumped to the forge's roof in one fluid motion." Tipin seemed embarrassed as he continued. "He was gone before I could get out of the forge."

"That does sound unusual," Namir commented as he stepped out from behind the screen. He felt their surprise stares settle on him as he turned to face Tipin. "How big was he?" Namir's tone held an air of authority as did his stance.

"He was small. Lithe, built a lot like Jaconis." Tipin replied.

His awe in the visible change Namir had undergone was apparent on his face as he spoke. Namir knew Tipin had always known about Namir's past, but he could tell by his reaction that the smith had not fully believed it until now. Namir shot a quick glance at Haradine and was surprised to see her standing with her head bowed.

"I was afraid that Morcant followed us here." Namir intoned as he looked from Tipin to Haradine and back. The matter of fact tone in Namir's voice completely hid his fear for Tipin and Allair's safety.

Tipin lowered his head as if in prayer, then breathed, "No, although I didn't think about it before. It may have been one of his brethren."

"What do you mean?" Namir walked over to Tipin and looked down at his hulking frame.

"I mean, it may have been a nassarid," Tipin said plainly.

"Really?" Namir asked a little surprised. The idea that a nassarid could be smaller than Morcant did not sit well with him. "I had assumed Morcant was a standard nassarid."

"No," Tipin's voice, though submissive, filled the chamber. "A nassarid's shape and size are determined by the task they are initially created for." Tipin's answer did little to ease Namir's mind.

Chapter Eight: Meetings

"I have to remain close to Namir," Alequa pleaded. She knew desperation had taken over both her voice and demeanor, but she did not care. The elf could not let this happen.

"How close are you now?" His voice was eerily calm.

Alequa fought the urge to scream at him. His passivity was irksome. The worst part of it was that she knew Valeron acted this way on purpose.

"You know what I mean." She begged.

Alequa hated many things about this man, just like she admired just as much. Although it was in the past, she hated that he was one of the men responsible for starting the last Great War. If he had not incited the humans to break from their rulers, then the wrong child would have been placed on the throne.

The thing she hated more than his misguided attempt to save his people was that she knew Aras would have done the same thing. That is if he had found himself in the Knight's shoes.

"That may be true, but I need you to realize the truth in my words. There is very little that you can do from here. So, you might as well be somewhere that you can be of use."

Valeron shot Alequa a sidelong glance as he continued, "We need you. The elves can only hold their boundaries for so long against the horde the Isle of Drandear has amassed.

"What do you expect me to do, single-handedly end the conflict?" Her scathing look was more than enough to express her true feelings about the subject.

"You know that is not what I was getting at," Valeron fumed. "We need your expertise in subversive tactics and maneuvers. Specifically the ones you and your late husband were known for using during the last great wars. Without you, we are as helpless as sheep. Hopefully, between these and your healing skills, we may have a real chance of surviving. We may even have a shot at winning."

"You know your words would be considered treason by your own kind. Why are you so invested in the defeat of the human regime?" Alequa tried to change the topic to one she was a little more invested in, his true intentions.

"All that matters is I am opposing them now," Valeron replied automatically. "At least that is all that should matter."

"But you were sworn to defend them from threats like these," Alequa repeated her argument again. "You are a Knight of the Realm or something like that. Am I right?"

"You are correct," Valeron replied coolly. "I am a Knight of the Realm. I have been sworn to protect the citizens of Drandear from any threat." His brown eyes held a lethal edge as he spoke. "The problem I face now is a unique one. The greatest threat to those I am honor bound to save comes from the people I helped to usurp the power of the throne. Now can we end this line of questioning and get to the point where you to accept my request and come to our aid in our time of need?"

Alequa blinked at Valeron's silent form in amazement and shock. "Why did you finally decide to tell me the truth?"

"You deserve to know," Valeron looked across the little

room as he stood. "That and the fact we are desperate." He locked glances with the elven healer for a few moments as if he weighed her intentions. "I will wait outside for your answer." He abruptly turned and took his leave.

Alequa was speechless. She understood the position this Knight was in, but she also knew she needed to help Namir. If she wished to put a true end to the next war of the races the current human leadership was steering them towards, Namir needed to ascend the throne.

She struggled with her morals and her desire to see her husband's quest through to its end. She hated knowing that so many would suffer, but she could not abandon Namir or countless more may suffer.

It was the panicked whinny of the horses that drew her from her inner struggle. It seemed like just a few moments had passed, but when she stepped outside, she noticed the remaining light of the day had given way to the bottomless shades of evening. Her elven eyes adjusted almost instantly and she leaped to Valeron's side as he struggled against both horses in a futile attempt to keep them both calm.

"Hold the reins tight," Alequa instructed as she placed her hands as gently as she could against the horses' neck. Her fingers traced and caressed up to the back of their jaw.

She closed her eyes as she struggled to stay in contact with these fabulous steeds. Within moments she felt her goddess's gift pass from her hands and into each of the horses. As the energy flowed, she smiled as the fight in the horses flowed away with it.

"The last time I saw my horse react like this, the king had just released a dragon for us to hunt," Valeron said to no one in particular.

"Me as well, but it was because I came across one unexpectedly." Alequa confided.

Silence now filled the tepid air between them as the two stood still and scanned their surroundings in perfect synchronicity. Alequa studied every leaf and branch. Nothing moved.   Both of them stood statue-still as her keen elven eyes probed the darkness.

She felt Valeron's sidelong glance pass across her waist before he cast his gaze to search the sky.   She knew he wanted to make sure that she had no weapons drawn.   As she was about to give up, he quickly pointed to a black spot in the sky.

"There," he whispered hoarsely.

Alequa's eyes immediately flew to the blackness he pointed at.   The quiet hiss of air as it was pulled from her lungs by some invisible source was all either of them could hear.   She fought off a wave of panic as she recognized the creature for what it was, a dragon of darqueness.

"How did one of those cross over to this side?" Her words fell heavily from her lips and with each utterance, her despair deepened.

"More importantly, what is it doing all the way out here?" Valeron stared at the dragon's fleeing silhouette in wonder as he spoke.

"It's here to kill a king," Alequa stated as if the answer should have been obvious.   She felt the electricity of desperation mix with adrenaline in her body and was instantly energized by it.   "That is what they are made for after all. Now grab your gear and come with me.   We have a king to save!"

"LET YOUR MIND GO," the voice was soft and sweet and its words felt like honey to Hessa's embattled mind.

"WHO ARE YOU?" Hessa thought in response.

"I AM THE HELM OF DURIUS AND I BRING YOU YOUR KEY TO SALVATION," the words echoed in Hessa's mind hollowly as she struggled to understand exactly what was happening.

She glanced around her past the armored slits in the helm and nothing seemed to move.   Even the leaves on the rush near the dragon hung as if caught in a stationary breeze.

"What is happening?" Hessa thought in an attempt to understand.

"I HAVE GIVEN YOU THE GIFT OF TIME. USE IT WISELY BECAUSE IT WILL NOT LAST LONG. ASK ME WHAT YOU WISH AND DURIUS SHALL GRANT IT IF HE CAN." The helm's words vibrated through the very fabric of her being as it spoke.

Hessa felt a strength she thought lost rekindle in her breast. "Thank you," her mind responded naturally as if this type of communication was second nature and this surprised her. "I don't know much about Durius, can you enlighten me?"

"NOW IS NOT THE TIME, BUT I SHALL AS WE GROW TO-GETHER. JUST KNOW HE IS THE GREAT NEGOTIATOR AND OTHERS FIND HIS WISHES HARD TO IGNORE." The silence following these words was far more complete than Hessa had ever heard.

A subtle shift in energy pulsed around and through her. Little things started to move across the sides of her eyes. Hessa thought quickly about her options as she saw the time ripple around her once more and take a hold of the things around her. It was like a slow moving wave that hit her from all sides at once. The closer it came, the more anxious and desperate Hessa felt herself become.

"Can you make the dragon let us go?" Hessa thought quickly to the helm as she saw the creature's tail twitch once more.

"I CAN MAKE YOU MORE PERSUASIVE, BUT I CANNOT FORCE IT TO DO ANYTHING IT IS AGAINST. CHOOSE YOUR WORDS WISELY AND THEIR IMPACT WILL BE GREAT." As the helm's final words chimed in her soul, Hessa saw the creature fully resume motion.

"Now climb down," the dragon cooed once more at

Hessa in its soothing sing-song way.

Unlike before, Hessa did not feel compelled to do what it asked. This time she remained in complete control of her limbs and, more importantly, her will.

A quick glance at Aves allowed her to make sure her sister was still controlled. She was safe, but of no real use to her. Hessa decided it was best to follow the creature's orders. That way she could keep her sister safe and possibly learn more about it.

Hessa clamored down the statue carefully so as not to disturb any of the other items still on the statue. She would hate to succumb to the gypsy spell now that she had finally obtained the artifact they had come for.

Once Hessa was down, she walked cautiously toward the dragon and stopped between Aves and the looming creature. It was quite a bit larger up close than it appeared while she was on the statue. Even while wearing the artifact, Hessa had to fight off a wave of incapacitating fear as she approached it.

"I have retrieved the helm and brought it to you. Just as you asked," Hessa attempted to sound less confident than she felt as she addressed it. "Please let Onas and Aves go, they are no longer a part of this." Hessa felt an odd vibration play across the front of her head as she issued her subtle command.

She watched in anticipation as the dragon considered her request. After several long moments, it nodded its head in agreement. It lowered its wing to the ground and shifted to allow Onas's stationary body to start its sliding descent.

As it did this, Hessa waved her hand at Aves in a gesture for her to get Onas. A grateful feeling spread through her when she saw Aves respond appropriately. Within a matter of moments, Aves had Onas's stationary body huddled against the base of the statue. After she was certain they were both unharmed, Hessa turned her attention to the dragon once more.

"Please remove whatever you have done to Onas. He needs to be able to lead Aves out of here." She struggled to keep her tone even. The last thing she wanted to do was make her sister think she was trying to command her.

She doubted the dragon would release them, but she had to try. Hessa felt more assured that it might when the same vibration she had felt a few moments before made its way across her forehead.

A new sense of understanding swept through her as she saw the dragon comply. It raised one of its large ivory claws and made a quick motion. As it did, a glimmer of light danced across Onas's head and his eyes lost the faraway look they once held.

"Thank you," Hessa said to the dragon in true appreciation for what it had done. "Onas, please take Aves to the horses and leave. I will follow shortly."

Hessa instructed once she was certain Onas could understand her. To Hessa's horror, her words were accompanied by the odd vibration she had felt while convincing the dragon to do her bidding.

"MY POWERS WORK ON ALL THAT WOULD DO OTHER THAN YOUR REQUEST. NO MATTER IF THEY ARE FRIEND OR FOE," the helm quickly answered her unspoken question.

"Madam Chancellor, please call the next party forward," Armani said from his seat in the council hall. He surveyed the crowd and was surprised to see that so many people had decided to attend.

"My Lord Mayor, aside from the Constable's report, the last matter before the council is a request from the Crown." Allair's voice rang out and clearly filled the hall. She made sure that everyone present could hear and understand her words.

"Let's hear from the Constable then," Armani directed with a wave of his hand.

"I understand there are reasons, my Lord Mayor, that you would not want to hear from the Crown. However, typically the needs of the Crown take precedence over local matters." Allair chastised Armani evenly.

Carness knew that she hated calling him out publicly. But for her to do it during an assembly and air the growing division in the council this way was a new level of animosity. The constable understood she must have felt that Armani had left her little choice, but he knew she could have handled it differently if she had wanted to. Something was off with both of them. Ever since the children returned from Hornshir, the Mayor had changed. But then again, so had the entire town.

"I just wish to give the Crown the longest uninterrupted time. That way none can claim we rushed anything here, as we promised to the townsfolk this afternoon." Armani snapped back. The tone in his voice carried his indignation at Allair better than the seething glare he offered with it.

"The Constable's report will have to wait until the next meeting," Carness cut in.

He wielded the edge in his voice like a sword to keep the two of them separated. The concern on Allair's face tore at his soul. Watching these two bicker was worse than dealing with thugs and criminals.   In the past, they had been in lockstep with one another.

"What happened to us? We once had the same goals and led this town it the same direction." Carness shook away his wayward thoughts. He refocused his attention on the demanding looks cast his way by the rest of the council.

"My investigations are ongoing and most of my suspects are dead. There is little I can do just yet, but I will get to the bottom of things shortly."

"Very well," Saril nodded his approval, "then, I feel, the only matter we have left is that of the Crown." Everyone knew he had directed his comments to the Mayor, but just in case he turned his sightless eyes to Armani's dais.

"Agreed," Armani admitted defeatedly. "Please escort the emissary to the platform to address this council."

"You mean escort them to our stage, correct?" Allair corrected.

"No, I said to the platform below us," Armani said louder in case he had not spoken loud enough to be heard.

"This is unusual. Normally matters of the Crown are to be addressed from our stage." This time it was Saril who voiced his concerns.

"Normally the Crown would have sent proper notice and divulged the nature of their request." Armani sent a scathing look at Saril as he continued, "Normally the Crown would have sent letters of verification so we could know that it was, in fact, from the Crown. But, as we all know, the Crown died in the Great War and there has been no one acknowledged as ruler for quite some time. So forgive me if I am hesitant to believe that this emissary is anything other than a fraud." Armani shot a withering glance at each of the council members to show them the extent of his authority and his will in this matter.

"Will the emissary from the Crown please make their way to the platform to address the council?" Allair called out, clearly defeated.

Rocks tore at Aves's feet as she stumbled through the darkness. Fear gripped at her mind as she struggled to put more distance between that thing and herself.

"This way," Onas's voice filled the void around them.

She had almost forgotten he was with her. The girl's mind was so jumbled with everything that had happened. It was too much for her in such a little time.

"Where are we going?" She managed to ask after she managed a few more shuffling steps.

"The cave just outside," Onas intoned.

His labored breathes were a few feet ahead of her in the

darkness. She could barely hear his footfalls. Aside from her stumbling, nothing else seemed to disturb the tomblike silence.

"Where are the horses?" Aves asked, finally finding enough air to voice the question tumbling inside her mind.

"They probably ran from the dragon," Onas spat in response. "We must hurry in case it changes its mind and decides to eat us!"

Aves could tell the gypsy was irritated, she just was not sure why. He seemed desperate, more so than she felt. Something was different with him. Aves hoped she could figure out why.

"I am hurrying," she gasped.

The distance to the cave did not seem that far when they were on horses. Now she wondered if they were even going to make it before her legs gave out. Shooting pain raced from her feet through her legs and it seemed like this pain was the only unspoken answer to her growing fear she would get.

Jaconis wrung his hands in anticipation. He stood in front of the mirror as he adjusted his robes one last time before he stepped across the room to make it ready for his visitor. Deftly his fingers flew over each of the metal lined tools. A sinister smile played over his lips as he recalled the torturous use of each in turn.

"This is going to be fun," he whispered to himself. "Thank you Lotevilar for giving me this opportunity to serve you." He bowed his head as he said this quick prayer.

An almost imperceptible knock drew Jaconis from his devotion. He took his time to become centered in the present before he rose. Carefully he tucked the tools of his trade under a large deep red velvet blanket before he straightened his clothing in front of the mirror one last time. The rapping became a little louder as his guest showed some of the impatience that people were known for. To Jaconis it was remarkable that the longer he lived, the more people wanted to have everything done immediately.

He also chuckled silently to himself that, until recently, he had once been numbered among them.

"There is just no pleasing people these days," he thought to himself wryly. This thought forced another one to bubble up almost as if his subconscious decided to answer him. "That is why there are people like me. We teach some of Lotevilar's grace and humility to those who need it."

Bang! The knock took on more of a frantic characteristic as his guest's impatience became more pronounced. Jaconis took a deep breath and finally crossed over to the door. In one fluid motion, he opened the door and drew his hood to enshroud his face in darkness.

A smile tried to force its way onto his lips as he looked down at the young lady. She was the same one that had previously accompanied him to the market. Her long brown hair was loose and flowed over her caramel colored shoulders. Her hair framed her face perfectly and made her deep brown eyes seem more pronounced and alluring.

Jaconis's eyes followed a bead of sweat as it formed along her scalp and slid delicately down the side of her neck. There was a little tantalization as he watched it meander across the top of her chest and came to rest on the edge of her chemise. Her breathing was ragged and her pupils were dilated as if she had just run a race.

"Come in, my dear," Jaconis said calmly as he motioned for her to step into his inner sanctum.

She bit her lip hesitantly as if she weighed her options before she took a faltering step into the room. Her eyes darted from shadow to shadow and only lingered long enough on any one thing to appraise its use and proximity to her.

"What shall I call you?" She asked as she heard the door

close solidly behind her.

"Call me whatever you'd like," Jaconis replied coolly. "Mine is a service I provide. A window, if you will, to view the divine. What you choose to call me matters little."

His demeanor held all of the graciousness of a wolf before it attacked. He knew she could feel the electric buzz that was building between them and Jaconis hoped she enjoyed it. He licked his lips quickly in anticipation for what is to come.

"Please, tell me your name." Her request held an urgency that Jaconis had not experienced before.

While he was aware that she would be his first cleansing without guidance, he was not new to the conversations that took place between the brethren and their devotees. Some of them needed assurances before they could fully allow Lotevilar's light to guide their lives.

"Jaconis," his voice deepened a little as he spoke his own name. It felt odd on his tongue after so long of disuse.

"Thank you, Jaconis," she said as she looked down to the floor. A light blush flooded her cheeks and settled on her partially exposed bosom. "Please call me Abid."

"Very well Abid, shall we get started then?" Jaconis asked as he watched her lithe body walk past him toward the center of the room.

"This is my first-time Jaconis, will it hurt?" Abid's voice was melodic yet playful.

Somehow her voice also held an air of innocence that only added to the veracity of her statement. Her admission sent a thrill through Jaconis's soul. He gets to be one of the first to induct this girl into the order's deeper mysteries. Such a boon and one far more than he expected to be given.

"It is fitting that she is my first then," Jaconis thought to himself as she stepped up behind her.

He reached up and ran his fingers through her hair gently until he had a handful of hair. Then, without warning, he closed his fist and he pulled her head back as hard as he could. Fear danced in her eyes as he looked down on her face.

He licked his lips lightly as he responded, "Oh yes, my dear. I'm afraid it is going to hurt quite a bit."

Chapter Nine: Ruins

Namir looked out across the empty hallway toward the awaiting platform. "Why are they making me address them from down here?" Namir asked Tipin perturbed. His vocal registry automatically fluctuated into a higher register as he attempted to calm himself.

"I'm not sure, but I don't care for it," Tipin said as he donned his helm. I will go speak with them and convince them of their error." The threat his words held balanced palpably between them.

Namir felt Haradine's eyes flit from Tipin to himself. He could tell by her arching eyebrows she was amazed by their conversation. He knew the council's decision to slight them in this way was a calculated one.

"Is there any hope of changing their minds without using violence?" She swallowed hard and physically shrank back a little when Tipin glared his response at her.

Namir put a hand on the giant Calanari's shoulder as he nodded his agreement to her words. "Haradine is correct. We cannot use force to show them the error of their ways. If we do, we lose all legitimacy of my claim."

"This is unheard of my liege," Tipin growled as he fumed. "They are trying to debase the Crown and you along with it!" He was so angry that his skin visibly turned red as he spoke.

"Easy my friend," Namir said calmly. A soft blue light peaked around the edge of his shirt as he spoke. "I will not give them the satisfaction of succumbing to their ploy and I definitely will not allow this treatment to remain unaddressed."

With that, Namir locked glances with both Tipin and Haradine, in turn, to ensure he was not missing anything. Once they confirmed this for him with their subtle nods, he turned and stepped through the door at the back of the room they were in.

He recalled the butterflies he had felt just a few months ago when he walked this same hallway before. All the fears he had held for the unknown were mostly forgotten. Now they were replaced by regrets.

"How can I be so bold as to demand this town defend itself when I have failed to keep its trust so many times before?" Namir asked himself mentally as he steadily kept his steady pace.

While Namir struggled with his failures, he moved ever closer to the platform that seemed to hold his entire fate in his hands. He took a deep breath as he neared the stairs up to the platform. Some of his anxiety eased as he felt more than saw the soft blue glow shine from under his shirt.

"Thank you for your help," Namir whispered to Zelios as he stepped up onto the platform.

"YOU ARE VERY WELCOME MY LIEGE," Zelios responded in his mind with a soothing tone.

A strange energy pulsed from the gem's surface as its words echoed through his brain. Namir could tell it relaxed him. It also bolstered his spirits. There was something about how it reacted to his very being that was deeply encouraging to him.

"My Lord Mayor," Namir started once he was in the

center of the platform.

He knew he had waited until Haradine and Tipin were in their correct places as his entourage and guardians, but he couldn't stop himself from looking to make sure one last time as he spoke. His eyes darted from Tipin to Haradine and back as he cleared his throat. Namir smiled a little as he realized they flanked him perfectly. His smile only broadened as he saw them scan the crowd for threats in unison.

"I have come to ask for two things from Ellsted. The first is a favor for your people and the second is for posterity." Namir's tone, though crisp, held none of the malice he felt for the council's decision to make him speak up to them.

"What drivel are you speaking about nephew?" Daffer spat, visibly irritated and bored.

"On the first matter, Ellsted needs better defenses. There should be walls to keep the populace safe. The second matter is to announce my lineage to the council and ask all present to be the first to offer your fealty." Namir explained readily.

There was a subtle edge to Namir's words and stance. The way his steel blue eyes locked gazes with each of the council members and finally fixated on Armani was daunting. Even his tone held an air of authority that dared anyone to challenge him.

"Who are you to claim to know more than the council about our people's defense?" Armani challenged. There was a hint of anger in his voice.

"I am Namir Merides, heir to the throne of Cennicus," Namir replied coolly.

Namir was well aware they would challenge his claim, especially since he took the royal name as his own. This was the moment he had been preparing for and braced himself mentally for their ridicule.

"You? Heir to the throne?" Daffer spat as he laughed.

"You are my nephew, not some lost and illegitimate heir!"

Namir felt the weight of Armani's stare as well as the heat in Daffer's. Both gazes were grueling and withering in their own right. Namir had been prepared for Daffer's response, but not the mayor's.

He could tell his uncle could not fathom Namir's claim. Even if he had known Kalta was not his real father, Daffer would never accept that the boy he had mistreated was anything other than a nuisance.

Armani, on the other hand, he had expected a better reaction from. To Namir, it seemed as if the mayor was more angry than shocked at the news and this surprised the boy. He was certain Armani would have found his claim to the throne interesting. But the anger surprised him. Even in the worst case, he assumed the mayor just wouldn't believe him.

Namir knew as a child he had never displayed any sign of nobility in him. And, aside from Aras, there had never been anyone from outside of the community that may have kept an eye on himself to ensure his safety.

"What happened to you in Hornshir?" Armani mumbled under his breath.

Although it was under his breath Namir heard the question clearly. Even this type of response was not what he had expected. His brow furled as Armani raised his hand as a sign he was about to speak.

"So, you now use the last name of kings as your own. Yet, while growing up here in Ellsted, you were only known as Namir Kaltason. What right do you claim your ascension to the throne with? Think this through carefully or we will have you tried for treason before this night's end." Although Armani's words were softly spoken, everyone in the chamber heard them clearly. The silence of the grave had taken residence in the council hall.

"I know it is hard to believe, but it is true!" Namir

replied easily.

Namir's voice hardened and took on an undeniable air of authority. He sounded regal and his words felt more like a decree, or royal edict, rather than just a statement of fact. Even the aloof stance he used to have a child was replaced by a more noble one as he spoke.

"I admit I left here filled with a burning desire to find out what happened to my parents. But when I did, I put Ellsted's needs above my own. I knew the best way for me to find my answers was to lead the expedition. I also knew that in leading it I would help the populace of this fair town that I have been honored to call home. As a whole our mission was successful. We raised a great amount of attention for the feast and managed to successfully negotiate a new trade agreement with Hornshir. I led the group there and back again with no casualties."

"You call the mission a success and only half of your party returned!" Daffer interrupted the youth caustically. "That statement is a mockery to this gathering. You claim that no one perished, yet you cannot prove any of this!" His uncle scowled so hard that most of the assembly shank back in their seats.

"Enough!" Tipin decried. "Both of my sons are amongst those that did not return, yet you will not see me wail and lament as if they were dead. Daffer, you are bitter because your son chose not to return to you and your inn. One of mine wandered off, the other stayed to find him. Although we do not know what happened, I bear no ill will toward Namir nor do I see his leadership as diminished in any way by my sons' actions. You should not either." His bass voice boomed louder than anything else and the silence following it was as almost deafening.

Tipin's tone was not the only thing that carried a threat. The Calanari's stance communicated both his intention to protect Namir in every way and his dedication to doing what is right for Ellsted. It was obvious to Namir that Tipin considered Daffer's words as an attack against both. Just as it was obvious Tipin was prepared to defend both against Daffer's machinations.

"Please keep your guards at bay," Armani stated bluntly as he cast a sidelong glance at Tipin.

It had always been obvious by his actions that Armani thought he was superior to most of the other council members. The affectionate disdain he held for most of the citizens was also a well-known fact. However, the way his eyes cast hate filled daggers at Tipin showed how little he cared for the blacksmith and his actions.

"You have asked for an audience and we granted it. Now that it is not going how you thought it might, your guard talks out of turn. We expect you to remain civil, as well as candid, and for your companions to remain silent." Armani took a slight pause to make sure Namir understood his words.

"While we currently tolerate your claims, assuming they can be proven, we will not tolerate interruptions from those you have chosen to adorn yourself with. Now then, I believe that I was the last to ask an official question," Armani's voice dripped with an odd mix of formality and malice. "Madame Chancellor, can you please verify from the record?"

"Aye, the last "official" question was indeed asked by you, my Lord Mayor," Allair said acidly.

As the mayor leveled an expectant gaze at him, several of the stories Namir had heard around Daffer's bar flooded back to him. From what he recalled, most of the Gathering Place's patrons saw Armani as an overreaching showman. Some of the stories went further, but Namir had never put much stock in them.

Now, Namir was certain the mayor was worse than he had believed. From the tone of his voice and the arrogant tilt of his head, the mayor looked more like a want-to-be despot than the head of a small town council. It seemed as if Armani had become a megalomaniac that would not stop until he held all of the power inEllsted.

In a way, Namir felt sorry for him. "Such small dreams for such a talented man. What a waste," Namir thought to himself as he shrugged. He noticed Allair steadied her pen and prepared to record his answer, so he refocused on giving the answers they needed to hear.

"Thank you, Madame Chancellor," Armani said off-handedly to Allair before he focused his attention again on Namir. "Namir, can you please help us understand why you claim to be of royal descent?"

The smugness in his voice grated on Namir's nerves. He did not need to look at either if his retainers to know bothered them as well. His connection to the jewel around his neck only amplified this feeling. Namir could sense Armani lean forward to hear anything they might say just as he could feel the mayor's disbelief.

Silence settled once more as all eyes shifted to the boy who stood on the small stage below them. Namir stepped back far enough to be within arm's reach of both Tipin and Haradine before he spoke.

His left hand carefully touched Tipin's massive forearm without turning. At the same time, Namir watched Haradine out of the corner of his eye. She slowly moved her hand from her sword's hilt back to her side.

He knew Armani was trying to goad him or his people into saying, or doing, something damning. Namir refused to fall into his trap. No matter what he did not want to give the mayor anything to use against him. Not answering the question was not an option, but Namir did not know how to answer it without sounding insane. Time was passing and Namir could hear the council and those attending getting restless.

Thoughts whirled around in his mind and forced his head to lower just to remain in control. A soft blue glow leaked through the seams of his shirt as he hung his head. It was different than it had been before. The light was harsher than it ever had been.

Namir squinted against the brightening light as he slowly opened the top of his shirt. To his surprise, the amulet was floating. Its weight decreased as the volume of light increased. Before Namir could blink, the entire chamber was filled with its white-blue rays.

An overly familiar warmth spread through Namir's veins and mind at the same time. He was weightless and it felt amazing. His eyes widened as he soared above the gathered townsfolk and revealed at their gasps. Namir regretted the fear he saw in the crowd's eyes, especially in Carness's wolfish ones, but he was happy Zelios had finally decided to help him convince them.

Namir's momentum carried him far above both the assembled citizens and the council's stage. He wanted to wait until he stopped moving before he addressed the council. Between his disorientation and nerves, Namir was unsure what he was going to say. His mouth opened and closed a few times cautiously, but nothing came out.

"IS THIS PROOF ENOUGH OR DO I NEED TO DO SOMETHING MORE?" Zelios timed her words to match Namir's pathetic attempt at speaking.

"The use of magic does not preclude royal heritage, I expect actual proof!" Armani boomed as he glared up at Namir floating above them.

"THEN PROOF YOU SHALL HAVE!" Zelios's voice rang from every surface in the room as she enveloped Namir in her heavenly glow.

"I AM ZELIOS, THE PROTECTOR OF THE CROWN AND THE KEEPER OF DRAGONS! MY GODDESS HAS TASKED ME WITH GUARDING THE ROYAL LINE OF CENNICUS AND I VOUCH FOR HIM." Zelios stated as her body spilled out of the light surrounding Namir and poured onto the dais with the council members to coalesce into her form just below him. "WHILE ΠAMIR IS THE HEIR TO THE THRONE, I HAVE BEEN TASKED TO KEEP HIM ALIVE SO HE CAN PURSUE HIS DESTINY!" Zelios rebutted as her gossamer gowns caught the breeze and floated around her as if even her clothing defied gravity.

"More magic and trickery!" Daffer bellowed as he rose to his feet. "How dare you defy the rules of this town by trying to exploit the fears of its people?" His hands clenched into ham hock sized fists and released multiple times as he spoke. It was almost as if he squeezed each word out of his own brain by the force of his muscles.

"Calm yourself Daffer," Carness said dismissively.

The constable stood slowly as he spoke.

He stretched his overly taut muscles as he held Daffer's gaze. Namir knew Carness was gauging his uncle's intentions. When the constable's attention shifted to Zelios's shimmering form he knew Carness no longer thought Daffer posed a threat.

With a wolfish grin, Carness set down his club beside his seat. Meticulously, the wiry man stripped off the rest of his weapons. A small and deadly pile slowly emerged on the floor in front of his dais. Once he was certain he had removed them all, he approached Zelios cautiously.

"If she was summoned by some sort of trickery, then she isn't real. That means my hand would pass right through her," Carness said aloofly over his shoulder. Namir noticed the constable's gaze never wavered from Zelios the whole time.

"I WARN YOU, I AM OF THE GODS. THOSE WHO TOUCH ME DO NOT FARE WELL." Namir could see that Zelios's warning fell on deaf ears by the determined look on his face.

Carness did not let the threats from their spectral visitor sway his actions. He visibly braced himself for the unknown as he slowly reached toward her. His hand moved mechanically forward, almost as if it moved on its own.

The constable swallowed hard and glanced at the bracelet he wore on his right wrist. It was a plain band, nondescript and black. Even the ample light that blazed before him did not mar or reflect off its surface.

"Tayant protect me," he whispered loudly in an obvious attempt to refocus his will.

His fingers inched forward and touched the exposed skin of the beautiful lady standing before him. As Carness touched her, the audible gasp of everyone in the hall made Namir's heart skip a beat.

To everyone's obvious surprise she was very solid. Carness licked his lips as pressed the rest of his calloused hand against her. His stunned expression was all Namir needed.

"You are real," his statement puffed from between his trembling lips.

"I AM," Zelios replied courteously, "AND I AM SORRY FOR WHAT IS ABOUT TO HAPPEN."

Namir felt her regret through their bond. He was not sure what was about to happen, but he worried for Carness. If the amount of sorrow she felt was any indication about what was to come, the constable was in more trouble than either of them anticipated.

Her words seemed sweet until Namir saw the suffering in Carness's eyes. The pain must have ripped through his soul. He crumpled. The constable's hand was still on her chest, but he dropped to his knees in front of her. Crimson tears coursed down his cheeks as he trembled in front of Zelios's angelic form.

"Enough!" Namir commanded.

He felt everyone's eyes land on him. The astonishment in the faces below him bothered Namir deeply. He could not tell if they were afraid of him or of Zelios, not that there was much of a difference.

"He is a good man," Namir continued, "he only meant to prove our claim. I will not have him tortured in this way."

Zelios averted her eyes from Namir as she nodded her acceptance of his command. She gently reached up and traced Carness's outstretched arm from his elbow down to his fingertips. Her lithe fingers ran over every ripple and valley of his well-muscled skin until they reached his hands. Then, she entwined her fingers in his and slowly pushed Carness's hand off of her exposed chest.

Carness all but collapsed as the building pressure inside of his body was suddenly released. His breath, though ragged, evened out as Zelios released his hand. The entire populace of Ellsted seemed to hold its breath as they waited for their constable to recover from his encounter.

"HE WILL BE FINE," Zelios stated as she turned her attention to Daffer and Armani. "I CANNOT SAY THE SAY FOR YOU."

"Are you threatening us?" Daffer's raised voice seemed out of place in the silence that claimed on the hall.

"NO, I AM NOT. I AM STATING A FACT. YOU HAVE DISRESPECTED THE HEIR AND DEFIED THE GODS. I AM BUT AN INSTRUMENT FOR THEIR USE. I WILL DO NOTHING I AM NOT INSTRUCTED BY MY GODDESS TO DO, BUT I NEED TO WARN YOU. SHE IS VENGEFUL AND DOES NOT HOLD FOR ILL-TREATMENT OF HER FOLLOWERS OR THOSE SHE HAS SWORN TO PROTECT." Zelios bowed her head as she spoke humbly.

Namir could tell the ramifications of her words were not lost on anyone. There was a genuine sense of fear in everyone present's eyes and Namir hated it. He did not want to be a king of slaves. Instead, he wanted to free them of the shackles they felt from the old ways. From what Namir could tell, Daffer was the only one not cowed by Zelios's actions.

Daffer met the glowing lady's response with the most confused look Namir had ever seen on his face. His eyes were wide and his brows furled together and apart. After a few moments his mouth quite moving up and down uselessly and he seemed to have made a decision.

"I think that is a threat... " Daffer started to say as Armani held his hand to stay Daffer's tongue.

"We only did as we needed to in order to ensure this child," Armani motioned to where Namir floated above them as he spoke, "was not an imposter who saw a chance to exploit our community. No true harm was meant unless he proved to be a fraud."

"AGAIN, HE IS NOT AN IMPOSTER." ZELIOS SAID WITH AN OBVIOUS EDGE IN HER VOICE. "THIS ASSEMBLY WOULD DO WELL TO HEED HIS WARNINGS. DARKNESS HAS SLOWLY CONSUMED THE REST OF CENNICUS AND IT HAS FINALLY COME TO ELLSTED. THE WORLD AS YOU KNEW IT IS GONE. AGENTS OF THE NEW HUMAN KING IN DRANDEAR HAVE MADE THEIR WAY AROUND THE ELVEN LANDS TO THE NORTH AND CROSSED THE BURNING DESERT. EVERYTHING LEFT OF THE OLD REGIME AND THE ORDER IT MAINTAINED WILL BE DESTROYED."

Her iridescent blue eyes scanned the audience as she spoke. By her demeanor, everyone could tell she found little solace in the panicked stares offered by the assembly. "THERE IS HOPE, BUT PRECIOUS LITTLE TIME. GO NOW AND SECURE YOUR HOMES AND YOUR BELONGINGS. DO NOT TARRY AND ALLOW THOSE THINGS YOU HOLD MOST DEAR TO BE TAKEN FROM YOU IN THE NIGHT!"

Zelios slowly rose as she spoke and her body emanated, even more, light until the brightness was too much to bear. Gasps from the gathered masses mirrored Namir's surprise and pain. The lack of control was unnerving for him and he desperately wanted to do more to help.

As if on cue, the stone walls behind the council exploded and rained debris on all present. Steely talons and glowing red eyes cut through the smoky darkness. Nothing else was visible through the wall of dust now occupying the place where the expertly carved stone once stood.

Chapter Ten: Sacrifices

"Now that my friends are safe," Hessa said to the dragon that looked hungrily at back at her, "what should I call you?" She knew curiosity had overruled her better judgment and she decided to see where it would lead her.

"Why would I give that to you?" The dragon's features shifted from a fierce glare to one of confusion as it spoke to her.

"Because it is only polite. I already told you my name. I would like to know what to call you during the few remaining moments before you eat me." The look she chose to give the dragon as she spoke would have melted almost any man's heart. She was truly pathetic looking.

"I do not intend to eat you. In fact," it stated coolly. "As long as you do what I ask, no harm will befall you whatsoever."

"I'm sorry, but I find that a bit hard to believe." Although she held onto the innocent little girl look, Hessa also allowed some of her sarcasm to show as she spoke. "I might believe you more if you were more amicable." Hessa felt the odd tug along her forehead as her last words slipped through the metal gap in the helm near her mouth. The effect was slightly dizzying.

"Galadril," the dragon replied. "My name is Galadril and I am a silvern dragon from the Allysian Isles." Its voice was calm, yet there was an odd metallic ring to it that Hessa had not noticed before.

"The Allysian Isles?" Hessa said surprised.

She recalled hearing Armani mention that some of his acquired belongings were from there. Most of them were bone or ivory. She remembered asking him about the place, but he was always vague or silent on the matter.

"Correct," Galadril answered easily. "Now give me the helm so I can take it and be on my way." The dragon cocked its head to one side as it spoke. Somehow Hessa knew it was bored of the exchange and would rather just leave.

"Tell me more about the Allysian Isles and yourself," Hessa instructed as she closed the distance between the dragon and her.

The smooth and metallic scales were amazing from where she had stood and Hessa desperately wanted to get a closer look. Another odd sensation pulled at her scalp and she mentally waved it away. She knew the helm was reacting to her words and direction. There was a part of her that wanted to take off the helm as soon as she could. There had to be something happening to her from its powerful effects and she wanted to figure out what it was before she used it too much.

A faraway look filled the dragon's eyes as she spoke. Hessa could feel it try to shake off the helm's effects and she knew it was unable to.

"She is using some kind of enchantment," Galadril thoughts filled the inside of the helm as it reflected the recent events. "I need to find a way to stop her."

Without another thought, Galadril lowered its head. He allowed Hessa to approach and cradle its massive head in her delicate hands. Its mercury snake-like eyes closed as it did so. Hessa felt its enjoyment at her touch and sensed its bewilderment at it.

"Please, Galadril," Hessa started," I would love to learn more about you and your kind. You see, I have never seen a dragon before and you are magnificent." Her words compelled its actions and she knew it and Hessa did not care.

She marveled at the fineness of the scales and their durability. The minuscule scales overlapped in such a way to make them appear liquid and did not exist at all. Hesitantly she reached a finger toward the fine scales of Galadril's neck and half expected them to feel like water. Instead, they felt as if she touched one of Armani's silver serving dishes. The dragon felt cold, hard and metallic.

"Where should I start," Galadril reflected more to himself than to Hessa.

She felt its interest and its confusion. Galadril struggled with its own need to have her close. Each time the dragon tried to come to terms with it, she felt the turmoil grow deeper instead of lessening.

"How about at the beginning," Hess offered.

Her fingers danced from the dragon's chin and along the underside of its neck. She was surprised to find the underside was a little rougher than the rest of the scales. Hessa smiled at this revelation as her hand slid along the neck down to the top of its chest.

Hessa delicately turned and sat in front of Galadril as its deep voice started its telling. The girl leaned happily against its heaving chest as she lost herself in its words.

Armani carefully dug himself out of the remains of his cloister. He silently praised himself for having the foresight to reinforce this section of the Council Hall in case something like this happened. The mayor's eyes scanned the building's remains for survivors meticulously.

"He has to be out there somewhere," Armani thought silently to himself.

A warm sense of relief spread through his limbs. He found his target. There, huddled behind the rail of the second-floor balcony.

"How did he get up there?" Armani wondered in amazement at the youth's luck. "He should have fallen down into the pit. At least then the crushing rubble would have buried him." His thoughts were as bitter as the pain he felt coursing through him.

Armani carefully pulled himself against the wall and into the nearby shadows. Now he knew where Namir had fallen, the mayor needed to know the whereabouts of everyone else. A quick glance around the room allayed his immediate fears.

"At least none of the other councilors were seriously injured," Armani's thoughts raced through his mind.

His overly taut muscles relaxed a little as relief washed over him. The mayor was relieved that no more of Ellsted's residents were killed. This constant barrage of attacks involving Namir and his friends was becoming tedious.

"There is still a chance to keep it that way." These last few words tumbled through Armani's head faster than ever.

Quietly, he reached down and gathered a handful of pebbles. He carefully lined up his shot and waited until the dragon's head moved closer to where Namir hid. With the aim of a skilled knife thrower, Armani let his first pebble fly.

Elation swept through his veins when he heard it skitter off of the wall next to Namir. He waited a couple of seconds to see if his ruse worked. Unfortunately, it failed.

"Why didn't the thing notice it," He muttered under his breath in frustration.

Another pebble flew from the darkness and hit the same spot. The mayor instantly threw his third pebble at the dragon's snout. The fourth stone winged its way to the wall near Namir.

"I'm glad we found the horses," Aves said over her shoulder as she carried in her bedroll.

"As am I," Onas replied.

His muscles heaved as he carried two chests on his shoulders. Very little light spilled into the cave around his hulking form. Aves set her things down just in time to see him enter.

The gypsy's musky scent filled her nostrils as she rose to her feet. She was about to brush past him to bring in more of their supplies when her knees started to buckle. Before she could breathe, Onas's arms were around her.

"Are you alright?" His baritone voice was filled with compassion and it made her legs weaker.

"I-I am," she lied. "I will be fine. We need to bring our things."

Aves did not want him to let her go. Her feelings whirled through her and she struggled for some semblance of control. Eddies of desire mingled with fear and Aves felt helpless against both.

"Rest a bit. I will bring in the rest of what we need," Onas assured her.

She could tell by his tone that he would not accept any resistance. She was grateful for his sense of chivalry. Although she regretted him leaving, her emotions eased a little as he carefully lowered her to the ground.

"Do not worry. I will not take too long." Onas whispered to her.

His face hovered less than a foot away as he spoke. Aves's heart was in her throat. There was nothing she wanted more than to have him stay where he was. Close enough to her so she could feel his heat.

"I will build a fire before I go," the gypsy said as if he read her mind.

She watched eagerly as he gathered little pieces of wood and stacked them. Within moments a neat little stick pyramid stood in a small ring of stones. Aves could not recall where he gathered them from, but she was amazed by his swiftness.

The glowing ember sprang up in the loose wood shavings he had placed inside the stick shrine. It lit Onas's face as he leaned over and gently blew it into a flame. All she noticed was how his pursed lips coaxed flames out of the wood. Aves wished it were her that his breath caressed instead of the fire and she felt ashamed.

Aves tore her eyes away from him and blushed deeply. She knew he saw her looks, but she could not think about it. Aves wanted him to know how she felt.

She licked her lips as she spoke, "Why me?"

"What do you mean?" Onas asked as he stood and stretched.

"I mean, why are you interested in me?" Her voice was hardly more than a whisper, but she could not coax any more volume. "You are older than I am…and a gypsy." She tried to look coyly at him, but she knew she failed.

"Please, quit using that word. We are both from a proud and noble race. We are not vagrants like that slur suggests." Aves heard the ire in his voice, but it was different than it had been before. It was softer and almost pleading.

"I'm sorry," she looked away from him again. This time her gaze shifted to the fire.

"No, I must apologize for my impatience. I know this is all new to you. I should not expect you to come to terms with your heritage so fast." His voice was soothing.

"But you still haven't answered me," she prodded delicately.

"You are right. I didn't," Onas replied with a haphazard grin. "Because I am afraid of what you will think if I answer."

"Oh?" Aves's eyebrow arched as she spoke. Her eyes lingered on the fire for a brief moment before she refocused on Onas's face. "Is that because you're afraid that I'll think it is for status?"

The shocked look on Onas's face seemed disingenuous. Whether it was the knowing twinkle in his hazel eyes or the nonchalant cock to his head Aves was not sure. Something seemed off.

"Why would you think that?" His reply seemed a little too quick to Aves.

"Because, according to you, my father was a chief. That means I am something like a princess to your people." Aves said flatly. A half breath was all she could take before he started to respond, so she cut him off. "I am used to that. I am the mayor's daughter after all."

"I see," Onas replied. His look of false shock gave way one of cunning. "So, what are you really asking me?" Onas asked as he gazed deeply into Aves's hazel eyes.

"Just tell me the truth. What is the real reason you are interested in me?" Aves asked a little coyly as she stepped closer to him.

Onas smiled as she approached him." We still have a few things to do." He said with a playful grin. "First we should get our blankets ready. If we lay them out near the fire they should warm up."

"You are still dodging the question," Aves replied a little disappointed.

"I may be. We can talk about anything you want after we get the bedding ready for the three of us." Onas said smarmily.

There was a hint of innuendo in both his words and his voice. Aves liked this side of the gypsy. Playful and inappropriate, two things she didn't know she liked.

Darkness settled in as they finished getting the cavern as ready as they could and the cold became more pronounced. The small fire in the center of the room offered little light and less heat. In the wavering light, the carved inscription took on a life of its own. It felt both ominous and alluring.

"What is taking her so long?" Aves asked Onas a little unnerved.

"I do not know. When the dragon had me completely under its spell, it was impossible for me to tell what was real and what wasn't." He confided quietly to Aves.

"That must have been scary," Aves said as she huddled closer to the fire.

"It was," Onas admitted.

Aves sat down on her bedding. She shuffled a little closer to the flames. Although Aves could not see her breath, she shivered as if she could.

"You look cold," Onas said softly as he offered her a piece of bread and his soft leather pouch.

Thank you," Aves said graciously as she took both. "And I am."

"It's going to get colder," his tone offered a hint of warmth, more than his words did. "It might be best to huddle closer to each other. Besides, being closer together will make sharing our food easier."

"Agreed," Aves smiled at him. "It will make it easier to talk about that other thing as well."

Aves took a handful of dried meat from the pouch before she handed it back to him. The flavor was tangy. Just enough spice to make her mouth water and enough sweetness to make her want more than just a bite.

"This is delicious," Aves said around the small piece still in her mouth. "Where did you get it?"

"Thank you. It's a recipe I learned as a boy." Onas confided. "I always make sure I dry some meat after marinating it. That way I can have some in case I need it."

"You made this? Well, you are a man of many hidden talents." Somehow Aves felt her playful tone was a little out of place, but she did not care. "I'm still cold," she said as she looked at him through her lashes.

"I can think of a way to help," Onas replied. Without another word, the gypsy stood and handed

Aves the leather pouch and one of his wineskins. While she was finding a place to put these, he grabbed his blanket and flung it over his shoulders. As it settled, he eased himself behind her and wrapped her in it.

"Is this better?" He asked as he pulled her closer to him.

"Much," she replied.

His arms felt great around her and his chest felt wonderful behind her head. Onas's warmth was consuming. Aves nestled against him and shifted until she was comfortable.

"So, are you going to tell me yet?" She said coyly looking up at him.

"Tell you what?" Onas replied mirthfully.

"The answer to my question, of course," Aves said breathily.

Aves forced herself to focus only on Onas. Everything else seemed to blur and shift. It felt as if she looked at everything through the heat of the fire. The effect was dizzying.

"You are pakvora miri rawnie," Onas replied wolfishly. "Why wouldn't I be interested?"

"I don't even know what you said," Aves snickered. "You know, it's not fair switching languages when answering questions."

"Forgive me, I forget you do not speak our tongue," Onas admitted. "I said you are beautiful."

She enjoyed feeling her softness against the hardness of his arms. Aves secretly hoped Hessa would be a little longer so Onas could hold her this way for a bit longer.

"Your pena, I mean your sister, should have been back by now." Onas's baritone voice, though soothing, disturbed the peacefulness of the moment. "I hate to say it, but I am beginning to worry."

"I am as well. Do you think that we should go look for

her?" Aves asked somewhat disappointedly.

She turned her head her head to look up at him better and pressed it firmly against his chest. Aves shifted just a little in his arms so she could look him in the eyes as they spoke. She was pleasantly surprised at how close his lips were to hers. Her heart almost skipped a beat as she stared into his eyes.

Onas whispered, "We may need to, but not just yet." His words danced along the soft skin of her cheeks and Aves closed her eyes momentarily.

The heat from his eyes played across the smooth skin of her eyelids and then down to her supple lips. She knew they were slightly parted and inviting. Aves hoped he would not be able to help himself.

His lips pressing against hers was more than exhilarating than she had expected. The tantalizing sensation as his lips explored hers forced Aves to lean into him harder. It was more pleasurable than she imagined it would be and she did not want it to end.

Aves shifted more as she threw herself into their kiss with wild abandon. She turned and pressed herself against him. Feeling his muscular chest as it pressed against her ample bosom made her head swim.

Onas let his lips dance off of hers and gently caressed her cheek as he moved his attention toward her ear. As they clung to each other passionately, he carefully swept her arm away from the ground and gingerly laid her back against her blankets on the floor of the cavern.

"Maybe we could wait a few more moments before we look for her." He whispered in her ear.

Aves nodded as she felt Onas's steamy breath play across her neck. "A few moments might be good," she replied breathlessly.

She writhed against him as she felt his fingers briefly trace the small of her back through her chemise. The only thing she could think about was Onas and how intoxicating his scent was.

Onas breathed in the scent of her hair and gently kissed the nape of her neck before he sat up and removed his shirt. A playful blush spread across Aves's face and her smile mirrored his. He reached down to take her hand in his for a moment before he skillfully guided it to his exposed chest.

"I do not want to do anything that you don't. Please explore so you can feel comfortable with this." Onas's smile shifted to more to the look a fox gets when it makes it into the rabbit's den.

"Thank you," Aves said looking up at him.

He was magnificent. His rippling muscles reminded her of Nurn. A slight pang in her heart twinged as she thought about him.

"I hope Nurn and Halin are alright," she thought guiltily.

Her fingers moved down along Onas's taut muscles. Part of her regretted what she was doing. Aves always figured her first time would be with Nurn, but he had never shown much real interest in her. She looked up playfully at Onas and met his steamy gaze.

Her hands rested on his belt involuntarily. Aves took a deep breath and arched slightly. She watched as Onas's gaze drifted from her eyes to her breasts in anticipation and smiled more.

Chapter Eleven:
Forebodings

Tipin carefully slid the large slab of rock that once was part of the council's dais off of him.   His motions were smooth and even.   The last thing he needed was for whatever it was that had attacked them to know he was still alive.

The cacophony of mingled screams and shrieks from the populace caught his attention first.   Those were closely followed by the little, quieter, noises.   Sounds of pebbles falling from the ceiling and others digging themselves out of the debris were distinctive, yet muted.   The one thing he stained to hear was some hint of what had attacked.

He needed to find a better vantage point.   The large Calanari quickly scanned his surroundings for somewhere to better assess the situation.   Tipin's hand reflexively closed around the haft of his axe as he slowly moved toward the doorway.   If he could make it back to the stairs, he could make it to higher ground and form a plan of action.

A pebble skittered from above him somewhere and he did not hesitate a moment.   He balled up and rolled to the nearest wall as if his life depended on it.   A silent sigh of relief escaped his lips when the monstrous foot, of what could only belong to a dragon, press down on where he had just been.

"A dragon here in Ellsted?" Tipin thought to himself silently. "How is this possible?" His mind balked at the improbability of it.

Frantically the smith searched the shadows above him for some sign of where the pebble had come from. After a few moments, he chalked it up to coincidence. He felt blessed that the pebble managed to warn him in time to react.

The beast's scaled hide was easily visible from where he crouched and it looked amazing. Although the overlapping scaling was fine, it was still thick enough to ward off most blades he could think of.

Most of them were blacker than the darkness around him, but there were a few charcoal grey ones intermixed. The edges were hard to see because they practically absorbed the light as it touched them. Not a single scale seemed to reflect any light whatsoever. Tipin's knowledge of dragons was limited, but he had never heard of a dragon without shiny scales.

He squinted in the darkness and the growing dust that slowly settled down to his level of the building. The Calanari warrior knew he needed to see the thing better. The more details about the creature he could make out, the better he could plan its defeat. The only thing he was certain of was that the scaling looked like dull unpolished metal.

"Nothing living can be made of metal," he thought to himself as he decided to test his theory.

Tipin carefully palmed one of his daggers and calculated the distance from where he stood across to the doorway. Once he was certain he knew how far he would have to sprint, he carefully moved away from the debris.

A deep breath filled his lungs and emptied slowly. With his exhalation, he threw his dagger at the dragon's foot. As the pommel slipped from his fingers, Tipin vaulted toward the doorway as fast as he could. A rolling dive allowed him to clear the doorframe and slide into the safety of the shadows.

The metallic ring of steel against stone competed with the thumping noise of his heart. He waited, crouched and ready in case the thing reacted to his attack. A few long moments passed before he dared to stand fully erect. Tipin steadied his breathing and paused long enough for the beating sound of his heart leave his ears before he dared move a muscle.

Complete silence was all that met his overly taut senses. A few more moments of nothingness passed. Tipin's eyes stayed fixed on the door he had just rolled through and his ears strained to hear the beast move against the ruined structure of the hall. He wanted to make sure the dragon would not follow his movements to his sanctuary.

Tipin's axe arm was heavy. It had been too long since he had manhandled this old friend and it showed through the dull aches he now felt. The smith knew needed to rest if he hoped to use the axe to his fullest ability.

Carefully he lowered the axe head to rest lightly on the ground. The accompanying stretch felt good and Tipin sighed a little in relief.

Once his stretch was done, and he was positive nothing followed him into the room, Tipin stepped free from the shadows. Without shuffling his feet, he meticulously crept up the sloped hallway toward the main entryway to the council hall.

"I might be able to get at this beast from a different angle," his mind raced with a series of tactics.

He knew he was outclassed. There was no way he could match the dragon's strength or fury alone. Hopefully, Namir, Haradine, Carness and the others survived the initial onslaught. He might have a fighting chance at survival if they did.

Tipin carefully pressed on the door's latch and eased it opened. Peering down the hallway was tedious, but necessary. His eyes strained to see through the darkness and grit.

Once he was certain he was alone, the smith stepped through the open portal.

The sounds of more pebbles skittered across the floor made him freeze in mid-stride. The noise came from behind him this time. Without thought, he spun and flattened himself against the wall.

Filled with dread, Tipin allowed his wartime training to guide him deeper into the darkness. His eyes stayed riveted on the cloud of dust looming ahead of him. Small steps were all he dared take in case he disturbed something or worse fell.

More pebbles arced nearby and skipped against the floor and wall. They were closely followed by more dust and dirt. With each stuttering tick, Tipin's heart threatened to skip a beat.

Minor tremors vibrated the wooden planks beneath his feet as he moved. Even the smallest step seemed to elicit some faint grumbling from either the wood or its stone moorings.

"How can I hope to evade this thing if the very building acts against me? I can't move until these things stop!" Tipin thought harshly to himself. "Tumere, keep me in Your austere hands," his lips followed his thoughts soundlessly.

The Calanari's breath, though slow, became easier as he felt the minor tremors slowly abate. His tension mirrored his breathing. Then, all at once, a deafening rumble filled his ears and Tipin's jaw fell.

A massive claw split the cloud in front of him and raked through several rows of seating. The dragon's arm reached through the darkness and into the room in search of its prey.

"How many of the others are still alive?" Tipin wondered silently to himself.

Splintering wood and falling stones dogged his steps as he retreated from the beast's relentless search for him. He hated how quickly he managed to cover the distance back to the main entrance. It meant he had been moving too slow, to begin with.

More debris cascaded through the open door as he struggled to close it. It took almost no time to slide the large wooden beam through the iron fixtures on the large doors and dive away from them. A jarring thump against the door was the only reward Tipin received and he was a little relieved.

"That should hold him for a bit," he muttered.

Sweat beaded along his scalp and ran in rivulets into his eyes. He quickly removed his helm so he could wipe it off as he slung his axe back into place across his shoulders. The smith took a few moments to clear his vision and his head.

Muttering darkly to himself, Tipin glanced back down the sloping hallway he had made his way from. Then he focused on the stairs leading up to the higher levels. Both seemed clear.

"Higher is always better," was his reply to another splintering thump against the door.

Scooping up his helm, he sprinted to the stairs. His axe shifted a little as his long strides carried him up the steps two and three at a time. The only thing that gave him pause was the looming landing. AS he neared it, he slowed his step and waited.

A silver flash of light flickered quickly from the wall a few yards ahead of him. Several stairs beyond where it erupted from where the landing for the second level of seats. Another flash blinked in and out of existence as he tried to figure out what it was and where it came from. A third flash forced him to take a few steps backward and knelt to conceal himself better.

"DO NOT WORRY, OLD FRIEND. I MEAN YOU NO HARM." THE VOICE DANCED FROM THE SHADOWS HE HID IN. "IT'S A CHAIN. TAKE HOLD AND I WILL BRING YOU THROUGH THE SHADOWS AND INTO THE MAIN HALL WITHOUT THE DRAGON

SMELLING YOU. IF YOU CHOOSE NOT TO, THE CREATURE WILL FIND YOU. YOU CANNOT TAKE THE BEAST BY SURPRISE WITH-OUT MY HELP."

"What about the others? Are any of them still alive?" Tipin whispered.

He silently moved toward the flashing light as he spoke. The only noises he could hear, other than his own blood coursing through his veins, was the distant thumping of the sealed door down the stairs. No clangor of metal against stone, like he should have heard from chain dangling in the darkness before him.

"THEY STILL BREATHE, KEEP YOUR FAITH AND YOU SHALL AS WELL," the voice replied as Tipin closed his fingers around the dangling chain.

"I have made a vow to Zelios. I swore to protect the artifacts and only allow those she finds suitable to obtain them." He said as he stared down at Hessa contently.

She could tell the dragon was unsure about her. She could feel its thoughts, no his thoughts. It was aware of her influence over him. Doubt about whether her ability stemmed from the Helm of Durius or if it was some other ability of hers rattled around in the beast's mind.

"Zelios, she is the spirit of the amulet, correct?" Hessa clarified. When she saw him nod his agreement, she smiled. "Then we are fine. You see, I know the man who wears Zelios and I have even heard him speak about her. I am certain she would want me to bring this artifact to her."

Although she was unsure about the whims of the spirit, Hessa knew they both wanted to help Namir in his quest.

"Prove what you say is true," Galadril stated as he shift-ed his weight to find a comfortable position.

Hessa stared at the dragon in disbelief. She knew she had almost bested him, now he called her bluff. Galadril knew she could not prove her story.

"Well, Zelios is dressed in blue and lives in the heart of the pendant on an argent chain," Hessa stated.

"True, but I told you that much. You must tell me more. Tell me about something we have not discussed." He hissed his reply in a whisper as his head lowered to the ground beside her and lightly closed his eyes.

"Well... if I was lying, then I would not have been able to retrieve this Helm in the first place." Hessa's voice was flat and emotionless.

She contemplated why the dragon would be trying to sleep while in the middle of their conversation, but decided against thinking about it too much for fear of getting distracted.

"After all, these memorials have gypsy spells in place to prevent theft." She hoped the dragon would accept this answer.

"That is true as well," Galadril said as it lazily opened the eye nearest to her slightly. "But you could have found a way to beat the spell. You seem to have an unnatural way about you. One that lures others to do as you ask. Maybe this is how you found your way past the curse of the Dekkari."

His deep voice seemed to emanate from all around them as he spoke. Hessa found it a little unnerving. She shrugged as she pondered her dilemma. He refuted everything she said. Her problem was she could not disprove anything it said.

"The only other thing I have is this journal. The problem is only my mother's blood relations can even see it." She said as she pulled her mother's journal from the sack she kept beside her.

The cover of the leather journal pulled what feeble light surrounding them into the dark depths of its surface. Its gilded pages vibrated with life as Hessa twisted it around so the dragon could get a good look at it.

Galadril's eyes widened as it gazed upon the book. "Where did you get that?" He asked. The awe in his voice was universal and unmistakable.

"It was a gift," She said softly as she delicately caressed the smooth cover. Her fingers played along the etched lines of the compass carved into its cover.

Daffer could barely breathe under the pile of rubble. He was pinned face first by the large stones from the council's walls and he could not move. His vision was hampered by both sweat and dirt, neither of which he appreciated. With every breath came another wave of pain and nausea. A new series of hurting to define himself and his life by.

"So this is how it all ends," he muttered to himself in the gathering gloom.

"Not if you care to live, it doesn't," Carness's familiar voice answered Daffer's comment unexpectedly and unasked. "Before I dig you out, you must swear a vow." The edge in Carness's voice was apparent to Daffer.

"Even in death, you seek to manipulate me," Daffer wheezed.

"No, I wish to help redeem you! Vow that you will come clean about your plots with Armani. Help me shine light into the dark underbelly of Ellsted that you helped create," Carness whispered fiercely. "Swear upon Lysanta's last breath that you will devote the rest of your life to bettering Ellsted and her people. Then, and only then, will I allow you to survive this."

Daffer fully understood the threat that Carness posed in the past and was all too aware of what his immediate words meant now. He knew that even if he managed to find a way out from under the debris, he was doomed unless he accepted Carness's offer and he hated not having any other options.

"I swear it. I swear I will be your shadow if needed until

all of the vile deeds I performed have been atoned for." Daffer bellowed as loud as he could.

The world seemed to pulse around them with sounds of stone against metal and Daffer hoped the constable had heard him. The innkeep didn't think he had the strength, or will, to repeat the oath again.

"Good, but don't you dare betray me," Carness warned as he lifted the first of many heavy stones off of the bar owner. "I know most of your schemes never really panned out. The few that did always seemed to come back and bite you. I am sorry for any part I played in your decline. However, as long as you are true to your word, I will not rest until you have recovered everything you have lost." Carness's tone carried through the stones and Daffer knew he meant every word of it.

"We don't have much time," Allair shouted from somewhere to his left.

He knew Saril's dais was in that direction, so he rationalized she had moved over to help the healer. Although he could not see what either Carness or Allair was doing, he figured that it had to be important.

Daffer's eyes widened as the dragon's tail sweep past his face. The monster loomed large through the parting curtain of dust and debris. Its large scaled tail jutted out like a weight and steadied the beast as it searched for prey.

He watched bewildered as the creature went straight toward the little platform where Tipin and Haradine had stood. It was almost as if the dragon knew where the heir apparent should have been and went straight to that spot.

"I know it is distracted for now," Allair reported. "But there is little chance it will stay that way. Once the dragon realizes its target is not among the ruble it created,"

Carness waived his understanding to Allair as he hefted another large rock from the pile Daffer was buried under. "I know you could not hear Allair well, but what little time we have is precious. If you wish to see your inn again, you had better help me dig."

"My inn be damned," Daffer muttered. "I have little interest in seeing that place. If you think the Gathering Place is worth fighting for, then you don't know as much about me as you think."

"If not for your inn, then fight for Jaconis," Carness changed his argument easily as he cleared a few more stones away from his buried colleague. "I know what he did hurt. If you can survive this, you can track him down and figure out why he did it."

Daffer felt his rage build as soon as the constable's words filtered through the haze in his brain. He hated to admit it, but he was sorely hurt when Jaconis decided not to return. His own son walked out on him and there was nothing he could do to stop it.

"I always figured he would take the reins from me and live well here in Ellsted. Where did I go wrong?" Daffer asked himself as he slowly pulled his arms to his side.

"You didn't," Carness assured him as he struggled to move one of the heaviest stones.

Daffer rounded his back and used his massive arms to lift himself off of the ground. His anger at his son fueled his drive to get out and get answers. Daffer closed his eyes and pushed through the crippling pain that erupted across his back and sides. The stones slowly moved and rolled off of his back.

"Good," Carness said as the pile rose in front of him. "Now we need to get somewhere safe to plan our attack if we hope to beat this thing."

The constable took a hold of Daffer's massive arms and dragged him to his feet. Carness pulled the innkeep to the side quickly. The two of them barely dodged the dragon's tail. As soon as they were clear, he led Daffer over to where Allair and Saril huddled against the remains of Saril's podium.

"Saril, can you do your wonders on him?" Carness motioned to Daffer as he asked.

"I can try," Saril offered. "However, if we are in a hurry I recommend we seek safety prior to seeing to the wounded."

"I do not need a healer, not yet at least." Daffer spat in return to Saril's statement. "Let's see about killing this dragon. That is one reptile we didn't face at Watch Keep. Looks like I might get my chance to add it to my list. And here I thought I had finished killing things."

The fire burned and cracked as she listened to the sound of air fill his lungs as he breathed. It was rhythmic and pleasant. She shifted her weight slightly so that she could move her hair from out of the way.

Warmth radiated from his skin and Aves basked in it. She could not help but smile as she thought about everything. The world seemed so much better now than it had been before.

Onas looked so peaceful. The gypsy's face was serene. The way his eyes were closed and the slight smile that pulled at the corners of his mouth were soothing to her.

Aves's hand traced the contours of his well-muscled stomach. Even the dead weight of his arm as it draped over her hips made her feel protected and safe. She snuggled into him grinned deeply. She knew she should be concerned about her sister, but she could not find it in her to be.

"Has she returned?"Onas's deep voice gently disrupted the moment, but Aves did not mind.

"No, but I'm not sure she knows where we are." Aves kissed raised his arm up to her lips and kissed it. "Should we go look for her?"

"That might be a good idea," Onas agreed.

He softly traced the slope of her back with the tips of his fingers. The wolfish grin on the gypsy's lips widened as he heard Aves's breath catch in her throat and shiver into him a little as he did so.

"That is if you feel rested enough to do so," Onas taunted.

Aves slapped his stomach with her hand abruptly. She struggled against the chills he had sent down her back. It was all she could do to not giggle in pleasure. Her lips playfully clamped between her teeth as she looked at him.

"I feel restored to do that and a whole lot more," she teased and looked longingly into his eyes.

"Insatiable," Onas smiled down at her, "I think I may have created a monster," Onas said softly.

His smile broadened as he gently pulled her up to him and gave her a deeply passionate kiss. Aves's world shifted. It was everything she wanted and her heart pounded harder in sync with her need.

When they separated long enough to breathe Onas continued, "Maybe we should take care of a few things first before we begin our search."

"That sounds wonderful," Aves replied as she bit her lower lip harder in anticipation.

Chapter Twelve: Slight Repose

Namir sat completely dumbfounded by what he saw. It was immense. The creature was larger than every building in Ellsted except for the Council Hall and The Gathering Place. It took a few moments for him to regain himself, and when he did he was amazed even more by the sight. He quickly realized that he was not in the safest of places as the creature loomed above his precarious hiding place menacingly.

He studied the debris below him. Carefully he peered into the darkness in an almost futile attempt to see who survived the initial attack. He held his breath as the fanged jaws passed directly above him again. The eerie metallic creek of its neck sent shivers down his spine and the otherworldly whirring noises it made as it searched for its prey made him want to flee. Only his desire to discover who sent the beast kept him still.

Namir spotted Haradine in the wreckage. His mind temporarily reeled as he thought of how the great hall looked mere moments before. He refocused his attention on her.

To his relief, she seemed to be unharmed by the thing's initial attack. He watched as she carefully removed the rubble from her delicate form. Her wherewithal was amazing. The elf strategically placed each piece of rubble she took off her body and created a makeshift shelter to protect herself from the creature's notice. Once Namir was certain Haradine was safe, he continued his search for Tipin and the rest of the council.

The sound of a pebble as it bounced off the wall just to the left of his ear snapped his attention away from his search. Namir froze instantly as he heard a second pebble hit. Moving only his eyes, he looked up to see if he had been discovered. That is when it happened.

With a mind-bending speed and a clangor that forever etched itself into Namir's nightmares, the beast's gaping maw jutted out at his head. Its steaming breath coursed over his face as the beast gnashed its jagged metallic teeth at him in a preparatory attack. Namir instinctively closed his eyes and prayed for his own salvation.

He felt an odd tingle of blood ooze down his arms and legs as it spread from his chest. With a sudden jerk, Namir was lifted from his perch and whipped to and fro several times before feeling the impact of the wall with bone-jarring force.

Namir lay completely still unsure how much longer he had to live. The tingling sensation now completely enveloped him. Namir squinted through his pain. The world swam in front of him. Try as he might, he could not clear his vision. The world was utter chaos.

"How is this happening?" He thought to himself frantically as he tried to make sense of it all.

He knew the dragon had been sent to kill him. But it was a dragon. A beast he had only heard about in stories told by strangers as they drank. Stories from before the last Great War. From a time before he was born. His mind balked at the idea that every fanciful tale he ever heard was actually grounded in reality instead of the ale induced delirium that accompanied drinking too much.

The guttural cry of the dragon pulled Namir forcefully

back from his thoughts. Although a heavy fog of smoke and dust hid the world from his view, Namir saw the shadow of the beast as it passed a few feet from him. Namir could not help but shake in fear at the sight.   It was even scarier through the haze.

"DO NOT WORRY MY LIEGE," the almost too familiar voice from his amulet chimed in his head and reassured him. "I WILL KEEP YOU SAFE." The soft blue glow, that always accompanied her communications with him, leaked a small tendril of light through this shirt and cloak.

The shadow shifted again and made its way back toward him. Namir wasted no time. Now, fully cognizant of his situation, he knew he could not allow this thing kill him. He had far too much to do for Cennicus and for his parents.

"Next time glow softer," Namir thought to his pendant as he quietly slid himself against a pile of debris to hide. "The dragon can see your light." He finished his message with a mental snap and refocused all of his attention to the task at hand. Staying alive.

Haradine barely avoided the Dragon's maw as it lunged at her. It was much smaller than she thought it was at first. Although it was immense, it was a little shorter than the height of the hall.   That is when it stood on its hind legs. When it walked on all fours, it was smaller still.

She steadied her breath as she readied another knife. Haradine glanced around her shelter to see if her last dagger had stayed in its mark and it had. She smiled smugly as she carefully plotted her next throw.

"Assuming I can stay one step ahead of it, I may have found its weakness," she thought to herself.

The elf crouched against the debris and then rolled to a new hiding place. She had to keep it distracted enough to buy Namir some time to get to safety. Haradine just hoped her ploy worked.

Another dagger flew from her hand as she made it to her new spot. Her back pressed firmly against the pile of rubble and she listened for the dagger's impact. The metallic sound of metal on metal let her know it hit's mark.

Instantly she rolled again, this time she moved toward the platform she had once been on. During her roll, Haradine spared a glance at the beast and saw her second dagger lodged itself into the dragon's jaw next to the first one.

"Another dagger on that side of the jaw should stop it from closing its mouth completely," Haradine thought as the creature shook its head.

The dragon's jaw opened and closed several times.

It shook its head as it tried to dislodge her daggers. Haradine smiled at the beast's antics and freed another dagger from her belt. She knew this would be her last chance to really make an impact. After this, she was out of daggers and weapons.

The town was in chaos when Alequa and Valeron entered it. His horse was at a full gallop and the elf clung to his back tightly. Screaming people randomly darted out in front of them and Valeron deftly reined his horse to avoid them. The night had come to life and became a nightmare for the people of this sleepy little town.

"I see it ahead," Alequa shouted to Valeron.

Although the horse moved erratically, the elf knew she was safe with Valeron. At least she was as long as she could hold onto Knight's armor. Something she struggled with.

Valeron nodded and replied, "We can take it from the rear as it hunts for the heir."

"That's fine," she shouted back. The elf had originally nodded her understanding but realized he could not see her.

Alequa emptied her mind and allowed the incantations she would need to fill her mind. Normally she had longer to reflect on these prior to using them, but this was an emergency. A silent prayer to Tumere slipped from between her taut lips as she made her mental selection. The elf steeled herself for what was to come and readied herself for the unknown.

Valeron slowed his horse to a trot as they neared the council hall. In one fluid motion, he pulled his bow from its holster on the side of his saddle and plucked an arrow from beside it. He steadied himself, nocked the arrow, and let it fly. Its white fletching arced through the dark sky and into the rubble. Without hesitation, he nocked a second arrow and sent it on its way as well.

"THE SURVIVORS OF WATCH KEEP ARE REUNITED," Zelios's words fill Namir's mind as he struggled to get into a better place. "THE THREAT OF THE DRAGON IS LESSENED NOW."

"The survivors? What do you mean?" Namir thought irritatedly. "And why would it matter if they were all here?"

"ONLY FIVE WHO FOUGHT THAT DAY SURVIVED. THEY FOUGHT AGAINST ARMIES AND WON, WHAT MAKES YOU THINK A DRAGON WOULD HINDER THEM?" Zelios asked coolly.

Her soft blue glow erupted from the edges of Namir's shirt as she spoke. Its mystical beams easily sliced through the darkness around them. Even the shadows took on a slight blue tint.

"Enough with the glowing!" Namir thought.

He clasped the amulet through his shirt tightly. Namir had to contain the light. He knew he needed to find a way to reduce the amount of light spilling out all around him or the dragon would know where he was.

Namir willed his heart to beat softer. He desperately listened for any sign the dragon might have been alerted by the glow. Only the sound of rubble being pushed aside met his ear. From what he could tell, the sounds came from the far side of the chamber.

He eased his grip on the amulet and let out a silent sigh of relief. The sound of cascading pebbles caught his attention and ruined the slight state of relaxation. There was something odd about the sound. He could not shake the feeling that the pebbles may have been deliberate.

"I wonder if the rest of the building will collapse?" Namir pondered as the new wave of small rocks cascaded down the wall.

"THOSE ARE NOT FROM THE WEAKENING WALLS," Zelios informed him.

"What do you mean?" Namir thought back.

"SOMEONE IS LEADING THE DRAGON TO ITS VICTIMS," the soft blue glow became harsher as the words formed in Namir's mind.

Valeron silently mouthed the words to the ancient spell he had been taught as a child. Although his people were prone to peaceful displays, they needed heat in order to survive the harsh winters of Holo. Memories of the year his dad taught him to make fire out of air danced through his mind in unison with the building waves of heat.

That winter had been harsher than normal and it had come early. What meager crops they managed to plant was threatened by the early frost. His dad swore they would get through it. The families of Holo gathered together at his family's barn one night to ask for their help.

They were Fyrbrig. His family's heritage stretched back to the founding of the area. As a Fyrbrig it was his duty to harness fire from distant lands and set it loose to aid others. During the Great War, he learned of another use for it, killing.

He selected four arrows from his quiver. They were designed for distance. The weight of the narrowly pointed heads matched the balance and lightness of the shafts perfectly.   The white fletching was cut to allow the arrows maximum flight time.

Valeron stared intently at the shaft where it met the head. His words slipped through his lips in a dull drone. He spun the four arrows in his hands.   His gaze shifted from the heads to the fletching. Once he was finished, Valeron quickly placed the arrows head first into the ground by his feet.

Plumes of dust and debris mingled with sounds of something large moving within the structure ahead of him.   He used that to guess where his target should be. The final few words of his spell fell from his taut lips as the Knight nocked the first arrow and fired.

He quickly loosed the second, third and fourth without hesitation. When the fourth had cleared the heft of his bow, Valeron snapped his fingers and all four arrows erupted in flames.

"Are you ready?" Valeron asked Alequa.

He deftly slipped his bow back into its holster as he waited for her response. The stunned look on the elf's face forced him to smile.

"Please tell me that you knew about my heritage." Valeron smiled up at the elf on his horse.

"I did," Alequa said, obviously still stunned by what she had seen. "But I have never witnessed it. Which God grants you power over fire?"

"I pray to no God," Valeron confided.   "My heritage gives me the control. We grew up learning the ways of the flame for survival."

He played off the existence of the spell-like he always had. His dad taught it to him. Valeron was raised to hide his power's true nature. Everyone needed to believe his family's gift came from birth. If not the power their family guarded would become commonplace and abused.

"Amazing," Alequa said as she slid off of the horse and stood beside him. "But you are human, are you not?"

"Aye, through and through." Valeron nodded. "Now we must go. Our friends are expecting to be rescued from this terror and we really should oblige."

"Agreed," Alequa nodded. She barely kept up with the huge man in armor as he sprinted toward the gaping hole in the council chamber's wall.

Aves and Onas pulled themselves slowly away from each other hesitantly. She drank in his well-muscled body as she slowly backed away from him so he could stand. Her hands traced his flank as he turned to gather his clothes. "Hopefully we can continue this after we get back to

Ellsted," Aves said as she playfully nibbled her own lips.

Their recent activities played through her mind and she had to shake them away. Otherwise, she would have been consumed by them. Then she might be tempted to not let the man leave.

"I think we can find some time," Onas said playfully as he pulled his shirt on.

Aves took the opportunity to step closer to him while he was distracted and pull him into a backward hug. She placed her cheek against his back and inhaled his heady masculine scent.

"I hope so," she said a little quieter as she ran her fingers along the base of his stomach.

"We will," he said. He leaned into her embrace and smiled. "But we will never leave this cave if you do not stop that."

"Stop what?" She said innocently. A devious smile tugged at her lips as she spoke. This smile was the only thing that gave away her intentions.

"You know full well," Onas said as he pulled away from her embrace. As he pulled his trousers on he remarked, "While you get yourself ready, I will go and see if I can locate Hessa."

Aves felt his eyes linger on her exposed skin as he spoke. His sardonic smirk broadened into a full smile as she blushed. All the attention he gave her was too much for her to fight against. The redness spread all the way down her chest and only managed to accent her auburn hair and ravishing features.

"Just don't be too long?" Aves said as she cast a heavily seductive glance at him.

She started to pull her skirts on while she assumed he was distracted by what she implied. "This is so much easier with a little help," Aves thought ruefully. Although she could not bring herself to be completely miserable, she tried to appear that way.

Onas cast a longing glance over his shoulder at Aves as he walked toward the mouth of the cave. She watched him shoot at least two more longing glances before she completely lost sight of him. She waved one last time and felt a little elated when she saw him pause one last time at the mouth of the cave.

Arrows fell from the sky around them like a light spring rain as they prepared for their attack. Carness looked across the room at Daffer and motioned for him to move closer.

He was amazed at how well the lumbering brute handled the short blade. Although the blade was no more than a foot long, it was sturdy and could be used to punch through stone if needed. He was pleased to see the innkeep's military training hadn't diminished any over the years.

"Too much happened to drive a rift between us," Carness thought as he waited for Daffer to signal he was ready.

Carness waited for one heartbeat longer before he drew his bow and carefully placed his arrows into the holes by his feet. He recalled the day the dais was built and the arguments he had with the craftsmen in charge. A smile lit his face as he thought about Armani's reaction to them as well.

"Today my modifications prove their usefulness," he

thought as he placed the last of his two dozen arrows into their place.

"Are we ready?" Allair asked as she readied her bow and nocked an arrow.

"We are," Carness whispered. "It looks like Valeron is ready as well." Carness motioned to the fletching of the arrows that skittered about them.

"Then let's give him a target to hit," Allair said just loud enough for Carness to hear her.

"Let's," the constable nodded as he nocked an arrow of his own.

He carefully aimed toward the remains of the stain glass window. Before the dragon attacked it had been attached to the roof of the hall. The scene was a simple one of Ea giving water to a saved young lady.

"So much beauty has been lost today," Carness thought reverently.

Allair let loose her arrows in perfect unison with the constable. He could see her lips move and Carness knew she had whispered a prayer. From what he knew about her, she prayed that Valeron would notice their sign.

Both of them readied another arrow each and let them fly quickly after the first. They repeated this one last time and waited to see if Valeron would respond in kind. Carness reviewed their work. The shape of an arrow pointing downward was precisely cut through what remained of the stained glass.

"Do you think he noticed?"

As if in response, six flaming arrows arced through the opening and lit up the center of the room. The black and red fletching or the flaming arrows caught Carness's eye. This little detail did quite a bit to verify who really was on the other side of the wall.

"He sent us our arrows back," he commented, more to himself than anyone.

"That must be Valeron's response to my question," Allair called out. "I see he still has his usual flair for dramatics," she said with a hint of laughter in her voice.

The dragon was perfectly silhouetted by the flickering lights from the flaming arrows. To the constable's surprise, something else had been revealed by the flames. Haradine could barely be seen as she attacked the dragon and dodged its futile attempts at hitting her.

He marveled at the lethal dance between the dragon and the elven woman. He was amazed at her speed and precision. But the thing that astonished him the most was the weakness Haradine had found in the dragon's armor.

Carness wasted no time. He glanced at Daffer and signaled him to move. Every moment counted if they hoped to survive. He needed the innkeep's attack to be in sync with the dragon's if they hoped to injure the thing.

Daffer did not wait to see if there was anything else he needed to wait for. Carness watched as the innkeep's lumbering form ran toward the dragon. As the constable saw Haradine free from her shelter and brace for the beast's attack. The dragon lunged toward her and Daffer raced at its gaping maw.

In the periphery of his vision, he saw Tipin charge from the other side in perfect step. Carness suppressed memories of Watch Keep from his mind as he watched the two of them in action again.

Daffer drove his blade as far as he could into the middle of the dragon's mouth. The overwhelming combined acidic iron and bile scents filled the air as the creature reeled under their combined assault. It was almost overwhelming.

The innkeep pressed his blade into the beast's tongue and smiled. From the way Daffer's hand jerked, Carness could tell the short blade struck bone inside the beast's mouth. The brute tugged once on his short blade to make sure it held fast and then retreated.

Tipin hefted the blade of his axe into the tender muscles

on the left side of the dragon's mouth. Its acidic blood sprayed over all three of them. He freed his weapon and swung a second time.

Haradine threw herself at the beast and pulled a dagger from its jaw. Carness smiled as he watched the elf take the same blade and drive it into the muscles inside the dragon's mouth.

The three compatriots fell back as Carness and Allair lobbed a volley of arrows to cover them. Without words, the two of them alternately fired arrows as fast as they could.

Carness's eyes narrowed as he saw Tipin motion Daffer. He knew they needed to escape quickly. The smith waived toward the shadows he had come from. Daffer shook his head and waived to the rubble he hid behind prior to the assault.

The innkeep didn't wait for Tipin to respond, he immediately sprinted back behind the pile of rubble that he waved at. Telltale steam hissed off Daffer's clothes as he ran. The blood must have splashed on him when he attacked.

Carness had been taught that dragon blood was supposed to be acidic. Watching this exchange only confirmed it. To the constable's relief, he saw Tipin follow Daffer. He could only hope Haradine had enough sense to hide until they could get over to her.

Chapter Thirteen: Discoveries

The third bead of sweat traced the contours of his cheek as Landolin focused on the flickering flame of the candle. Although the cold winter air blew in through his open window, he felt as if he was one with the fire. The elf fought back the urge to blink as he redoubled his efforts.

"I know you can handle this Karous," his lips moved in unison with his thoughts.

"It just feels wrong to detain her," the hollow sounding voice whispered back. "She is one of us."

"She is. There is something amiss with Farvais and until Doriana can figure out what it is, I need her separated from the rest of the troops." Landolin struggled against the strain of continuing.

"She could have been contained there in the manor easier," Karous offered.

"I know you mean well, but I have things I have to deal with here and cannot afford to keep an eye on her," his tone was shorter than he liked, but his friend was leaving him with little choice.

"As you wish my general," Karous acquiesced.

The tenuous bond faded and Landolin was grateful for its lapse. He took a deep breath before he blew out the candle.

A peaceful combination of darkness and cold air swooped into his chambers and comforted his aching head.

His garnet eyes quickly adapted to the blackness and scanned the room. A sigh of relief escaped the general's lips as his gaze fell onto the meticulously organized bundles on his bed. Although he would rather not have to perform the ceremony, he refused to dishonor those who served under him.

Landolin stood and stretched briefly before he walked over to the edge of his bed. His bare hands fell heavily upon the first pack. Silently he untied the thin silver chord it was held together by.

The black fabric easily fell away from the short sword and crystal sphere wrapped within it. Moonlight played across the orb's surface and shone through it. Deep orange and purple flecks of light danced around Landolin as he carefully lifted the orb. The suspended fractured cloud held within it was equally breathtaking and sombering.

"The time has come to join your brothers," his voice shook as his words slipped past his taut lips.

A tear escaped his resolve and burned its way down his cheek. His muscular frame shook as his fingers reached for the second silver chord. Eight bundles remained and his composure slipped a little as his eyes danced between them.

Haradine lifted her arms heavily as she stepped through another of the deep shadows that flitted and played around her. The elf stepped into the open and waved at the dragon. She wanted to make sure its attention was on her instead of the others as they marshaled their attack.

Every chance she got, she looked for Namir. She worried about her liege. Especially since she could not make out where he was hiding. Another wave of despair threatened to overwhelm her as she failed to spot him again.

"I hope he is alright," she thought to herself. Although she had only known him for a short time, the elf felt as if she had always been a part of his life somehow. Haradine did her best not to reflect on the past, but she could not help it.

Her father took quite a few trips to this small town. Stories about the carnivals and the scents were the things that fueled her imagination as a child. She remembered all of the ties she would beg Aras to tell her about his jaunts to this quaint place. Almost all of his tales revolved around Namir.

Her father would talk about how well the sa'ouvant progressed in his studies or how he was doing in general. Many times Alequa and Aras would discuss their plans for sheltering the boy and eventually inviting him to their manor in Hornshir. There was even talk about bringing him to Esterheim or Style. If only things could have waited for a few more years.

"Now is not the time for these thoughts," Haradine reminded herself.

The soft sounds of pebbles ticked against the wall snapped her mind back into the reality of the moment. She quickly scanned her surroundings for the dragon. The elf quickly realized she had wandered into one of the little nooks designed to house those waiting to approach the council. Her mind reeled as her eyes traced the smooth wall that stretched from the walls on either side of her.

"There's no way out," she thought as she quickly retreated from the room.

Haradine could ignore the sinking feeling that formed in the pit of her stomach. She could even suppress the icy feeling that spread across her skin. Neither of those things stopped her. However, the drop of saliva that slowly lowered itself before her eyes did.

The elf held her breath and froze in mid-step. An eternity exploded between each second as she balefully glanced around the completely empty space that surrounded her. The dragon was close enough to feel the air shift if she moved.

Tick-tack-a-tack-ack. Another pebble bounced off the flagstones directly between her legs. Haradine ever so slowly drew the short blade Tipin tossed her in their last exchange with the dragon. Her breath snaked out of her lips as she did.

All sounds stopped. Everything froze. Nothing except her and the string of drool moved. She braced herself for its attack as the first stream of saliva was joined by a second.

Tack-a-tick-ick. The previous pebble now had a friend that liked bouncing around her just as much as the first one had. It was soon followed by a third and fourth. Each one bounced around her or collided into one part of her body or another. One tapped her knee. Another hit her cheek. Still, another managed to connect with her forehead lightly before it fell into the cleavage of her armor. Haradine started to regret playing the role of bait as she waited tensely.

She would have smiled at the attention of the pebbles. That is if she believed they belonged to an admirer. However, in this case, she did her best not to react. The pebble's velocity and ferocity seemed to slow to as the steamy and rancid smell gathered around her ominously.

All at once Haradine spun to face her attacker. Her sword arced through the air with the practiced skill she worked hard for. Her attack was seamlessly followed by raising the small shield she held in response to an anticipated attack. Unfortunately, fast and fluid as her attack was, she was not fast enough. She chose her moment too late.

Pain erupted from her thighs as the dragon's teeth penetrated the armored scales she wore over them. Haradine anticipated the attack would be a straightforward lunge, but she never expected it to do it from above. Her sword struck a tooth with more force than her grip could take. Although it buried itself in the gums between two of the massive teeth, the impact wrenched her sword out of her hands. The only thing her shield managed to stop was some of the acidic saliva from dripping on her head.

Within heartbeats, Haradine was trapped between the dragon's tongue and the roof of its mouth. Her shield arm was pinioned above her head and the beast's jagged teeth held her legs fast. Pain blossomed all over her body as the dragon raised its head. The beast quickly tossed her into the air to get her into a more edible position.

"Yes, not all dragons are like the silvern. Many hate humans and detest the way you destroyed your surroundings. Be careful when next you meet my kind," its words sent a chill down Hessa's spine as it spoke. The air grew heavier and a little darker. "You know, members of the Dekkari cannot really be trusted," Galadril stated matter-of-factly.

"Is that why you cast a spell on Onas?" Hessa queried and slowly sat up.

"It is. I have yet to meet one of his brethren I could trust." Its deep voice was soothing. "They always look for something to use to their own advantage, some way to advance over others."

The way the dragon offered his advice let Hessa know that it trusted her. Either it was unaware of her heritage or it chose not to cast her in the same group as the Dekkari. No matter what the reason was, she felt honored.

"I will keep that in mind," Hessa whispered. "Is there anything else I should know?

Hessa swallowed a little harder as she adjusted her clothing and stood up slowly. She was still amazed at how the dragon's scales shone star like in the surrounding blackness. The effect was surreal and it felt as if she communed with the nights itself.

"You should be going," Hessa instructed. Her words were quickly followed by the now familiar pull across her forehead.

"I should," Galadril admitted cautiously. "But I also feel the need to warn you. One of my brethren is looking for the man you promised to help."

"We will hurry and see if we can warn him then," Hessa promised.

"Very well," the dragon said.

It glanced backward at the elf then slowly walked away from her. Its gaze lingered for a moment before it turned and arched its head skyward. Majestically, the dragon's wings unfurled. They seemed to pour from its back in the darkness. Galadril's silver wings effortlessly carried it into the air and out of sight.

"That is amazing," Onas's voice startled Hessa and forced her to turn and see who managed to intrude one final moment with Galadril.

"It is and it was," Hessa admitted when she realized who it was. "Is Aves safe?"

"Your sister is fine. We went back to the cave and took shelter there for a while. We waited for you," Onas said as he stepped closer to Hessa. "When you didn't follow, she became nervous. After much discussion, I agreed to look for you."

"Very gallant of you," Hessa replied.

Her hand lightly touched his chest. Onas had stepped in closer than she had expected. He was close enough that his musky scent filled her nostrils. Something was off, but she could not tell what. A different sensation played through the muscles of her forehead as she stared silently into Onas's eyes.

"So is this it? This is the item you came here for?" Onas inquired.

His fingers touched her hand on his chest. His Hazel eyes locked with hers through the slit of the helm. Without hesitation, he traced her arm up to her shoulders softly.

Hessa found it hard to speak. An odd electric buzz vibrated through her skin where his fingers lingered. She tried to keep focused on what happened, but he was more alluring than he had ever been.

"It is," she nodded.

"May I see it?" He asked softly.

The tone of his voice was almost as tantalizing as his touch. His fingers slipped from her shoulder to the middle of her back as he took a small step closer.

He was much closer than Hessa would like, but she felt incapable of moving away from him. The feeling of his fingers as they slid down her spine was intoxicating. Her senses swam as she felt his body lightly press against her.

"Maybe, but I need a little room to get it off," Hessa replied painfully.

Her throat felt raw. She barely managed to say these few words before pain set in. Although she wasn't sure what was happening, she felt compelled to do as he asked. His presence somehow consumed her.

"HE MEANS TO TAKE ME FROM YOU," the voice of the helm erupted in her mind as Onas stepped far enough away from her to take it off. "IS THIS WHAT YOU WANT?"

Hessa shook her head to make the voice stop. Everything blurred around her and she found it hard to think. Although her hands touched the base of the helm, she froze. It sat heavily on her head, too heavy for her to lift. Although her pulse pounded in her neck, she couldn't move.

"What are you doing?" She asked helplessly.

"I'm sorry, you are intoxicating. I can't seem to help myself," he lied.

Onas stepped close to her again. His fingers closed against both of her wrists. Carefully he pulled them from the helm and draped them around his neck. The whole time he kept his eyes locked on hers.

Hessa tried to pull away, but his advances were impossible to resist. She felt like a doll on strings. Her every movement felt manipulated. It was as if her body moved to his desire and not to her own. Nothing she could do seemed to matter. His will was far too strong to resist.

"Aves has feelings for you... this is wrong." Hessa forced the words out of her lips haltingly.

A part of her enjoyed his advances. Hessa hated that part. No matter how hard she tried to deny it, there was something in her soul that yearned for him to do whatever he wanted to her. Whatever it was, she was powerless to suppress it.

A soft moan escaped her lips as she felt his fingers lightly trek down the outside of her bodice. Each stitch he traced only added to the building anticipation as he lowered his hands to her waist.

Hessa closed her eyes and bit her upper lip in an attempt to break the primal effect he had on her. She purposefully thought about Aves and how this could destroy her. Her soul struggled with what she felt was right.

"Do not worry about your sister," his soothing words sent eddies of desire ripple along her spine. "I will let her know about us."

His left hand caressed her back sensually, while his right hand braced against the ground. Slowly Onas lowered her down to the ground underneath him. The grass felt soft against her back.

"I... I do not want this," Hessa said. His hot breath burned her skin through her bodice as she resisted, "This isn't right."

Hatred for herself filled her mind as she felt her body betray her. Lust for him consumed her will. She mentally railed against her hands as they untied the chording holding her cloak in place. Onas's wolfish grin loomed above her as he watched with anticipation.

"Do you want me to stop?" He asked.

The gypsy was careful not to let her eyes stray away from his compelling gaze. His hungry smile broadened as she felt her head slowly shake from side to side against her will. She felt like screaming, but couldn't. A silent tear formed in the corner of her eye as her fingers worked their way up from her cloak to the clasp of the helm.

"Good," he said heavily. "Now take the helm off so we can really have some fun."

Onas leaned forward and hovered near the metal opening in the helm. Her lips parted against her will and her breathing had become ragged. Hessa could tell this only excited him more.

Her inner passions had hijacked her senses and she had no power against them. All she could think of was the heat of his breath and the release he offered her from her pent-up yearnings.

The clasp snapped open and the strap loosened under her frantic fingers. Cold and hard metal resisted her attempted to remove the helm. Perseverance and determination won out and the helm inched slowly upward as she pushed it loose

"LET ME KNOW IF YOU CHOOSE TO KEEP ME. I CAN PROVIDE AID, BUT YOU MUST ASK." The voice sang in her mind.

"I need you," Hessa desperately thought. *"I know,"* the voice replied in her mind.

There was an unexpected edge to it Hessa was unprepared for. It seemed as if the helm held a hidden passion to stay in contact with her. Reality shifted as the helmet slowly slid off. Onas's voice blended with that of the helm the more it slid. The effect was beyond confusing to her.

"Please," Hessa said as her lips were exposed past the bottom ridge of the helm.

Onas's lips felt hot and welcoming as he placed them over hers. Her words caught in her throat as his tongue explored her mouth. She felt her body betray her will and arched against his hungrily.

"Just a little further and we can have some real fun," he

whispered across the skin of her jaw when he finally pulled his lips away.

"Help me," she continued her thought aloud as the helm slid a little farther off.

Just the top of her head lay nestled in the helm. She stared up at Onas's overly muscular form through the slit in the helm. Her eyes were riveted to him and she could not look away. He was so muscular and masculine. Hessa could not imagine anyone looking so perfect.

"I shall," Onas replied as he leaned over her.

His hands moved with a relentless machine-like precision. Cold winter air played across her smooth skin as her clothing loosened enough to gape open. Her mind struggled as bitterly as the wind that raced across them. She was losing the struggle and she could not help herself.

Namir stared in shock as he saw Haradine ripped apart before his eyes. Her body was limp before the beast devoured her. He couldn't look away even though he wanted to.

"This isn't real," he thought to himself.

"It is and it will get worse," Zelios replied.

He really didn't want to hear what the amulet was going to say, but he needed to. Namir wanted to understand the depth of his heritage. What he did not know was what his enemies were capable of and what they might do to stop his ascension.

"I should just let them kill me," he rationalized. "If I die fewer people will be hurt in their attempts to find me."

"If you do that, more will suffer. You are the rightful heir to the throne and Cennicus's last hope for peace," Zelios's words fell heavily on Namir's conscious. "If you let them win, you will have handed the followers of Lotevilar the ability to spread their con-

FLICT TO EVERY CORNER OF THIS LAND. IT WILL GIVE THEM, AND THOSE THEY SERVE, THE CHANCE TO DO WHATEVER THEY PLEASE. NO ONE WILL BE SAFE. A WAR FAR GREATER AND MORE TERRIBLE, THAN ANY THAT HAS EVER BEEN WILL DEVOUR CENNICUS AND DESTROY THE VERY IDEA OF PEACE." The blue glow that accompanied her words was soft, yet the deeper blues were blinding.

"So I am doomed. No matter what I do, people will suffer because of my actions." Namir said aloud. He could not accept what Zelios told him.

"WAKE UP, CHILD. PEOPLE WILL SUFFER REGARDLESS. THE DIFFERENCE IS, YOU CAN CHANGE IT. YOU ARE THE ONLY ONE WITH ANY HOPE OF STOPPING MORE PAIN AND DESTRUC-TION."

"It's not fair!" Namir screamed.

He no longer cared if the dragon killed him. His mind rebelled against his legacy. Nothing had prepared him for this. It was too much and he hated what they all expected of him.

"LIFE IS A STRUGGLE. IT WAS NEVER INTENDED TO BE FAIR." Zelios's glow surrounded Namir in its soft light as more pebbles seemed to ricochet around him.

He wanted her to manifest herself. Somehow her touch calmed his fears and he needed it. If she did, he would die and he knew it. No matter how much he wanted it different-ly, the world needed a hardened ruler. One who could make hard decisions. Someone to decide between life and death of others without hesitation. That was the king Cennicus need-ed and Namir knew he needed to be that king.

Chapter Fourteen:
Tremors

Hessa writhed in pleasure at his touch. Her mind raced. She struggled to differentiate between Onas's voice and the artifact's. The back of her head rubbed against the cooling metal of the helm. It was a strange dichotomy against Onas's hot breath as it danced across her neck.

"Help is on its way," Hessa heard in the back of her head. It was more like a suggestion than a voice and she almost did not hear it.

Onas's fingers slid along the edge of her clothing tantalizingly. His breath played over her neck and ears and she writhed in ecstasy as she felt him fumble with her belt.

Her hands still did not obey her mind. Instead of pushing him away, her nails clawed and tore at his shirt. She hated her lack of control.

A strange hunger pulled at her mind as she felt his hands dip under her blouse briefly. She ran her hands across his torso and up to his face. Hessa desperately pulled his face to hers and kissed him passionately. His lips responded perfectly as her hands pulled him into her. One of her legs wrapped around him of its own volition as their lips locked for a breathless eternity.

Onas slowly pulled away from her and she felt her body

rise with his. He placed one hand firmly on her chest and pushed her back down onto the snowy grass as he rose above her. Although the snow was cold, Hessa barely noticed it. Her focus was centered solely on Onas and the effect he had on her.

Hessa's mind raced as she tried to understand his actions. She grabbed a hold of his legs desperately as she tried to find his free hand. He carefully moved his left hand from her chest and gently grasped her hands in his and slowly pressed them away.

"What are you doing?" She gasped as she finally regained some vestige of control over her voice.

"You will see," Onas said playfully.

A metallic click followed by the sounds of leather against metal let her know he had unlatched the buckle of his belt. He carefully pulled it off and set it on the ground beside her head. She couldn't see where he had set it. Her heart raced as fear set in.

Onas's weight increased against her chest. All she could see was his throat and the top of his chest. Somehow his exposed flesh corrupted her senses and her mind. All Hessa could think about was him.

Onas's handsome features reappeared above her face. Something metal and sharp traced her outer thighs. The sting that accompanied the scratches didn't hurt. It was odd, but she could not find it in her to question his actions.

Onas's eyes shone with an internal fire as she felt the same sensation play across the front of her thigh this time. It slowly traversed from the top of her leg down to her knee. He repeated the motion on her other leg as he licked his lips in anticipation.

He slowly leaned back and let his left hand slide along her skin. Onas's hand followed the contour of her body from her navel to her neck and settled at the base of her neck. The gypsy's hand slowly slid through her hair and gripped it tightly.

A surprised look passed across his face as he tugged painfully on her hair. Surprise abruptly gave way to shock. A frantic look settled in his widening eyes. His lips moved in slow motion. Onas's grin twitched and slipped. She expected to see his tongue dart through his lips as they fluttered open.

Iron and copper filled her nostrils as Onas's blood gurgled from his lips and cascaded on her. The whites of his eyes exposed themselves as they rolled into their sockets. Onas's once vibrant body slowly drained of its vigor and fell onto Hessa.

Hessa screamed and squirmed under his sudden weight. Try as she might, she could not get free. Onas's fingers were wound too tightly in her hair. His weight was oppressive and she struggled to breathe.

Her mind raced as she tried to push him off. She was completely confused and her mind threatened her with the darkness of the abyss. Hessa flailed and writhed to no avail. Her head collided with something metal. Desperation filled her mind as she reached for it. She hoped it was something she could use to make sense of what her senses told her was impossible.

Time came to a halt all around him. Valeron watched the beast devour the young elf in complete disbelief. He screamed and rushed forward. His sword felt heavy in his hand as a blinding rage took over his senses.

The final words of the spell slid past his lips and he swung his sword as hard as he could into the dragon's side. Bright blue and white flames erupted along the length of the blade and buried itself into the belly of the beast.

The creature writhed in pain. He inched the entire length of his long sword into the creature. He sidestepped the dragon's tail twice before he managed to press the cross guard against its scales. A faint blue glow surrounded him and he felt Alequa's hand settle onto his steel pauldron.

"Send the signal now!" Valeron's scream was almost lost in the midst of battle.

Alequa nodded in compliance. She nimbly sidestepped one of the razor-sharp metallic talons as it clawed in their direction feebly. The elven healer dropped into a low squat without hesitation. The palms of her hands slapped the floor of the assembly hall and she closed her eyes.

Her healing sphere ebbed as a new prayer danced from her lips. Instantly she was consumed by the energy of her goddess Tayant. The blinding blue glow erupted from her hands and cascaded all around her before shooting geyser-like toward the ceiling. Alequa's azure blue eyes glowed with a fierce blue flame as the effect quickly engulfed her.

"Tayant guide my daughter's soul to your side if it is her time and keep her safe," she muttered as she gave herself over to her goddess's will.

Before Valeron could blink, Tipin's war cry erupted from the other side of the dragon. A smile played across his tightly pressed lips as he struggled to maintain both the effects of his spell and control over his blade. Although he had designed his gauntlets to lock into its grip, he still struggled under the force the dragon exerted to dislodge Valeron's sword.

"Glad to have your aid," Valeron.

It had been too long since he had seen a Calanari in action, especially this one. Tipin's words flowed through the metal of his helm and forced a wry smile to his lips. His thoughts flitted momentarily to their final night at Watch Keep and the spell of binding they had cast.

All five of them prepaid for their last stand. They were sorely outnumbered and none of them thought they would survive it. Carness had leveled his wolfish stare and forced them to swear a blood oath to one another. That oath not only bound them by honor, it completed a spell Valeron had prepared. With their blood poured into each other's helms, they were all linked. As long as they wore their helms they could hear anything each other said no matter how far apart they were.

"All you needed to do was ask," Tipin's sarcastic reply pulled him back to the fight. "Next time try and leave your playthings at home!" Tipin buried his axe as far as he could into his side of the dragon's belly as he yelled his responses to his old comrade. "Ready on my end," the smith said unnecessarily. Valeron focused on the axe's blade and felt it ignite in the dragon's scaly hide.

The silhouette of a woman appeared above Hessa. She had gained a little traction and managed to pull herself toward the metal thing behind her head. The looming figure held a long knife in her hand and she felt the judgmental look bore through her.

"Who are you?" Hessa asked. Her words tumbled from her lips haltingly.

"Hessa? Is that you? What happened?" The familiar voice echoed softly off of their surroundings.

"He-he attacked me," Hessa lied. She knew something dark inside of her wanted him to do what he did, she just could not understand why.

"I saw his knife and I-I had to help," the woman dropped the knife as she spoke and leaned toward her.

The lady's auburn hair caught in the cold breeze and sent a wave of relief through Hessa. She stared into her sister's hazel eyes in utter disbelief.

"Aves, thank you for saving me," Tears threatened to steal her voice as she choked out her words of gratitude.

Although she was still somewhat pinned underneath Onas's limp body, she knew she was going to be alright.

Her sister was here and that was enough to bolster her spirits.

"Who is he?" Aves asked as she moved closer. "And

have you seen Onas anywhere? He was supposed to find you and bring you back to the cave."

"Oh Aves," Hessa's heart broke. She knew Aves cared for Onas and she knew his death would completely devastate her. "Please don't look."

"Why?" She asked innocently. An awkward silence pressed between them and Aves realized what had happened. "What did you do?" Her accusation bore all of her sister's pain directly at Hessa.

"It wasn't me, it was him!" Hessa yelled. "I didn't do anything!" Her sister's pain was more than she could take and the thought that Aves would blame her for what transpired stung deeply.

"You are holding his shirt in your hands and you expect me to believe he was responsible?" Aves berated Hessa blindly.

"You just said that you his knife. You stabbed him because you thought he was going to kill me. Yet now you think that I did something to him?" Hessa could not believe Aves's blindness. "I know it hurts, but I didn't do this. Onas tried to rape me so that he could take the artifact. You must believe me."

"Must I," Aves's words were icy and harsh.

"You must. Look at his hands. He pulled some of my hair out and there is a knife right beside him." Hessa twisted her hips enough to finally free herself of Onas's dead weight as Aves listened. The cold wind picked up and caused Hessa to shiver as the girls stared at each other.

"I am not sure what to think," Aves said after several awkwardly long moments. "Let's get your cloak and belongings together. We can discuss this later." The sound of defeat was very apparent in her voice. It hurt Hessa as much as her accusations had.

"I'm sorry," Hessa offered as she gathered up her clothes.

"I know," Aves responded as the two of them slowly stood to leave. "Don't forget your precious artifact." She said bitterly as she motioned toward Onas's body.

Hessa stared at the sight. Onas's half-naked body sprawled out before them. Blood stained the snow underneath him and outlined where she had been. The Helm of Durius sat just beyond Onas's outstretched arm. Without another word, Hessa quickly stepped over and picked it up.

"YOU ARE WELCOME," the voice inside the helm said in Hessa's mind.

"I'm sending Daffer in now," Carness yelled as he watched Tipin's assault. "Allair will keep it blinded as I get into my final position."

The constable impressed at how expertly they had all fallen back into their wartime roles. He waved Daffer forward and turned to Allair. He locked gazes with her then looked at her target. A wry grin played across her face as she nocked her first arrow.

Allair nodded and released it on cue. It skittered off the creature's armored eyelids. Another flew and struck less than a moment after the first. She was a machine. For each arrow that she released, another closely followed.

"Just let me know when to stop. I can't see all of you and I won't know if any of you are in danger," she yelled to Carness as she fired incessantly.

"Worry about that after we have killed this beast!" Valeron shouted through his clenched teeth to the others.

While the others coordinated their efforts, Daffer charged at the beast. "By Bela, I swear your death shall be swift!" He muttered as he charged the dragon head on.

Carness studied the dragon carefully as he saw the beast lash out at his companions. He puzzled at how the thing reacted. Instead of using its wings, the beast simply shook its head and swiped at them with its tail and claws.

"What sort of unnatural beast is this?" Carness wondered to himself.

The constable watched Daffer tighten his grip on the cudgel Carness had given to him.   He knew the innkeep would recognize some of the runic markings on it from their youth in Jarstil.

Daffer thundered ahead and braced himself for the impact. Allair's arrows clatter on the stones around him. The din of battle completely drowned out all of the minor sounds and Carness found himself back in the blessed silence of combat.

"Now!" He screamed to Daffer.

He was pleased when the lumbering brute timed his strike. The cudgel stuck the tip of the dragon's nose soundly just as it lowered its head to shield its eyes.

The loud crack of the impact of both Daffer and the cudgel was all but deafening. The innkeeper reeled at the force of the blow. An odd vibration passed through his body from the spot where he had hammered the tip of the cudgel into the beast. Once it passed completely through him, the shock wave reverberated back through him and into the dragon.

The whole ordeal was stupefying to both Daffer and the dragon. It lifted its head in pain and stepped backward clumsily as it tried to escape the brute that had managed to cause it so much pain.

Daffer shook off the odd sensation as fast as he could and threw himself forward at the beast in an attempt to keep it off guard. He raised his left fist and punched the belly of the beast as it raised its head out of his reach. He quickly reversed his grip on the club and drove it into the joints of the scales as hard as he could. A bloodthirsty grin split his features when the metallic scale cracked loudly.

"Daffer try to drive the beast into Alequa's light!" Valeron's scream barely carried over the monstrous growls and moans that escaped the dragon's mouth as it fought them.

Daffer nodded as he attacked the beast again. He alternated between his bloodied fist and the baton. Slowly the dragon reeled backward. Each of his blows caused it to slide a little further toward his goal.

"Ha!" Daffer bellowed his satisfaction as he saw the creature take a few more steps backward. "It might be easier if I had more help getting this critter to move!" Daffer shouted as he narrowly avoided one of the dragon's talons.

"We are working on it," Tipin yelled in response. "Just keep it up!"

Nurn and Jerine entered the elven camp cautiously. There were too many shifting shapes in the snow flurries ahead of them for either to be comfortable. Both were hesitant in case the shapes were created by actual creatures instead of their overly tired minds.

"Not much farther," Jerine muttered quietly to Nurn. They traveled closer to each other than Jerine liked, but he knew it could not be helped.

"Good. Will we seek shelter in one of these hovels then?" Nurn asked quietly as he motioned to the skeletal outlines that seemed to surround them.

"We shall," Jerine agreed. "There is a specific one I want to use. Not only will it offer us the most protection, but it also has the best view of the dwarven entrance we can hope to have."

"I hope we can find it before I freeze," Nurn shivered his response.

The elf knew they needed to find Halin soon. He was just as he had to get his companion out of this snow storm or he would not survive. Nurn's last comment worried Jerine. So far the youth had pushed himself harder than Jerine had seen anyone else do without a single complaint. With this first complaint, Jerine worried that even Nurn's bottomless drive had been taxed to its limits.

"Keep moving forward. I am going ahead to make sure our shelter is not occupied. The rope we've tied to ourselves will be your guide." Jerine instructed.

He waited until he saw Nurn nod his understanding before he left the youth to brave the storm alone. Freezing winds threatened to toss him off his feet. He pulled his cloak tighter and leaned into it. His feet slid backward across the snow each time a new gust caught him from a different direction.

"I hate the snow," Jerine thought to himself.

He pushed through the biting wind and was relieved when he saw the outline of the guard post in ahead. Instinctively the elf quickly ducked around the back side of the structure. The guardian swiftly made his way to the far side and hugged the wall as he did.

Jerine cautiously rounded the corner to make sure nothing tracked him. The loose board he was heading for was almost in his grasp. He recalled the time that Landolin showed it to him.

His general explained to him how the dwarves designed this particular feature. They liked to know if something was amiss before it was too late. The loose board was how they did it. This trick allowed them to quickly see if anything had taken up residence in guard post while no one was around.

Jerine silently pivoted a portion of the board upward and looked through the hole. His breath caught in his throat in anticipation of what he might find. Relief spread through his cold muscles as nothing except emptiness met his probing eyes.

The guardian retraced his steps back to where he had crept around the structure. The loose rope gathered silently in his gloved hand as he followed the rope back to the side of the building he knew Nurn was approaching. He didn't want to force the boy to walk farther than he needed to in the horrific storm.

Jerine slid around the corner and sprinted toward the door. He deftly opened the door and burst into the room. Without slowing down, Jerine tossed a few logs into the fire pit sitting in the center of the room. He then walked over to the set of drawers on the opposite side of the room and pulled the third drawer open.

After a brief moment of sorting, Jerine pulled a piece of oiled canvas out of the drawer and turned back to the fire pit. The guardian twisted the canvas on one end before wadding it up. With one hand he lifted a log and stuffed the wadded canvas beneath it. He quickly pulled his flint from his pouch. With a well-rehearsed motion, he struck the flint against the stones underneath the oiled canvas and watched as the sparks landed on the cloth and started to smolder.

The fire just started to blaze warmly as Nurn staggered in from the relentless storm. He was completely covered in snow and looked more like a beast than the Calanari youth he was. Jerine smiled as he stepped over to the youth and helped him remove his cloak. Within moments the two were warming themselves by the fire and the elf removed several carcasses from his pack.

"When did you have time to hunt?" Nurn asked in wonder. It was obvious to the guardian that the youth had resigned himself to another rough night of poor rations and less food.

"I didn't," Jerine admitted. He hated to reduce the boy's wonder, but he knew Nurn would respect him more if he told the truth. "These birds were caught by the savagery of the storm. I found them where they died. They did not suffer long and were not there long when I happened upon them. Their meat should still be good." Jerine assured the youth as he continued to pluck the bird's feathers off.

Chapter Fifteen: Troubles

The girls walked in silence toward the mouth of the cave. An odd heaviness formed between the two and although neither of them wanted it there, they couldn't bear to talk. Too much had happened between them too fast.

In the still of the night, the only sound they could hear was the powered snow crunch under their feet. Even the whinny of the horses seemed muted as they drew nearer to them.

Pale moonlight silhouetted them as they walked. Since Aves wanted to be left alone, Hessa decided to use her time to look over the helmet. The white light reflected nicely off the snow made for a perfect light to study it by.

The large golden helmet gleamed as she held it up. No matter how she turned it, the light played perfectly across it. Although it was gold, there was an odd black sheen to it. The helmet also looked massive. It easily dwarfed every other helm that she had seen, with the exception of Tipin's.

"I wonder how it fits me so well when I wore it," she thought to herself.

"ALL OF US GIFTS HAVE THE ABILITY TO ADAPT OUR FORM TO THAT OF OUR OWNER," the voice inside of the helmet echoed in her brain.

"You can hear my thoughts?" Hessa asked as she turned her attention from studying the helm to communicating with it.

"AS LONG AS YOU ARE IN CONTACT WITH ME I CAN," the disembodied voice responded softly. Its words still held more of a hollow tone than she remembered hearing before.

"What should I call you?" Hessa wondered.

"I HAVE NO NAME. I AM THE VOICE OF THE GOD DURIUS HIMSELF. I DO HIS BIDDING IN THE LAND OF THE LIVING. I GIVE AID UNTO THOSE HE ALLOWS TO POSSESS HIS HELM," its words echoed in her mind again as she listened intently.

"SO I AM SPEAKING WITH DURIUS DIRECTLY?" Hessa marveled as she turned the helmet to face her.

"NO, BUT I AM HIS VOICE. AS I HAVE ALWAYS BEEN. EVER SINCE HE CREATED THIS HELM AND DECIDED TO LEAVE IT AS A TOOL FOR THE LIVING," the voice explained all of this diligently.

"So that still doesn't answer my question, what do I call you?" Hessa said mentally. She reflexively mouthed her words as she thought them.

"YOU DON'T. I RESPOND AS I FEEL NECESSARY. WHEN I AM NEEDED," the voice responded and then grew silent.

Carness pulled himself into the remains of the uppermost rafters carefully. He felt the wooden beams shift and sway as he eased himself onto them. Once he was certain the beams he had chosen would hold, he tugged the rope loose he had tied to his belt. Carness stretched out along the beam and carefully pulled on the taut line.

The battle rage below him as his weapons made their painfully slow journey up to him. With each pull, the bundle slid another few short spans. Even the noise as they clattered together was drowned out by the roar of the dragons and the sounds of his compatriots.

He scanned the wreckage for any signs of life other than his brethren fighting the dragon. A fresh wave of relief washed over him when he saw Namir crawling through the debris. Carness could not ascertain why the boy was heading toward the battle instead of away from it, but he was certain there was a reason for it.

The constable diverted his attention from Namir and back to his task at hand. He finally managed to hoist his assorted weapons up to the swaying beam. Carness impatiently waited until it steadied itself before he dared to sit upright.

Several long moments passed as he watched his comrades battle the dragon. The constable held his breath as he saw the dragon swipe at Daffer multiple times.

Although he could hear what they screamed to each other, he dared not respond until he was ready to attack the thing.

Carness pulled his pack to him and straddled the wooden beam. He carefully unwrapped his mini arsenal. He smiled when he saw his two prized possessions. One was a javelin and the other was a spear. Both had a solid wood shaft and capped by steel wolf heads on one end and a one-foot blade on the other. The matching wolves were etched into the hafts and the blades looked like the fangs of a wolf.

He deftly strapped the daggers and swords to his back and sides. Then he effortlessly placed his feet on the beam. Grasping both javelin and spear in both hands, Carness straightened himself into a crouching position. He slowly crept along the rafters until he reached its jagged edge. One look straight down at the back of the dragon as they fought below him was all he needed. Another smile broke through his lips as he saw Daffer press his attack and force the dragon another step back toward Alequa.

"I am in place," Carness announced as he readied his

javelin for his initial attack. "Let's end this." His fingers tightened on the spear as he slung the javelin across his back.

All of the muscles in his arms tensed as he waited for the perfect moment. He carefully raised the spear up and brought the point to the utmost periphery of his vision and he waited. He watched as Tipin and Valeron baited the beast back and forth between them.

He tamped down the memories from Watch Keep when he saw the same two pull this trick on the giant lizardfolk that they fought against. Carness could not help but laugh inwardly as Daffer threw himself into the dragon's face when it least expected it. Although the scene seemed some-what comical at best, Carness could not find it in him to enjoy it. The situation was too dire for that.

Daffer had managed to get the beast to back into the river of energy that pooled around Alequa. Tipin and Valeron pulled on their weapons in unison to hold it in place. Al-lair's arrows skittered off the dragon's armored hide and the beast threw its head back in utter frustration. That was his cue.

His spear slipped from his fingers and arced majestically toward the beast. He knew they only needed one solid hit to incapacitate the dragon and, if he was right, he just provided it.

All of his elation sank as the creature brought its head forward and it ended its outcry earlier than it had before. His prized spear hit the hard ridge of the dragon's horns and skittered off into the rubble surrounding his compatriots. Carness could not even be certain if the spear was in one piece or if it shattered by the force of the blow.

The dragon cast a glance in his direction. Carness saw what looked like a smirk play across its scaled features before it turned its attention back to his friends. The consta-ble unslung his javelin and muttered a curse under his breath. He could not afford to miss again and he knew it.

He watched as Tipin and Valeron steadied the beast. Both of the muscular men struggled and fought against its attempts to pull free from Alequa's blue light. Daffer kept pummeling the beast. Even from where Carness sat, he could tell the dragon was bleeding. He watched Daffer line himself up for another attack as the dragon managed to pull itself free from Tipin's axe.

A look of horror crossed Carness's face as he saw wisps of heat build along the gaping wounds from Tipin's axe. It had carved deep enough into the beast's belly that it must have grazed the dragon's heat sack.

The beast swung its tail at the charging innkeep to keep him at bay. At the same time, it tried to grab Tipin. The smith barely dodged the dragon's attempt. A deafening roar slipped from Daffer's mouth as his powerful legs hurtled him at the beast. In response to the yell, it raised its clawed hand and planted it firmly down on the Calanari and pressed him forcefully into the ground.

"Stop!" Carness screamed into his helm. "It's a fire breather!"

He watched anxiously as he saw Valeron dive clear of the dragon's hasty attempt to bury him like it had Tipin. More debris shifted from the force of the beast's attack. The minor tremors shook everything, even the precarious beams he stood on.

"Daffer, do not attack again!" Carness screamed as loud as he could.

The constable knew Daffer could not hear him, but he had to try. Carness could not allow his old friend to literally throw himself to his death. Time slowed to a stop as he looked on helplessly.

Flames flooded from the dragon's mouth like liquid. Each rivulet sprayed forth geyser-like in its ferocity. The constable saw Daffer try to stop as the wall of fire rushed toward him to no avail. The river of fire was too wide for the hulking barkeep to avoid it. Before Carness could blink, the innkeep was completely engulfed.

"This ends now!" Carness's voice ripped from his throat as he threw himself from his perch.

He originally planned on throwing his javelin as soon as there was an opening, but he knew he couldn't wait. His soldier's needed him quickly and he was more than happy to oblige.

Carness knew the dragon could only use its flames in spurts. With its reservoir exhausted it could not manage another blast. The constable let his momentum carry him toward the creature's face. He twisted in the air as he fell. Carness lined up the tip of his javelin with the dragon's eye.

He braced himself for impact. The constable used the combined force of his fall and the power of his muscles as he hit. With one fluid strike, he drove his javelin through the dragon's armored eyelid and deep into its left eye. His impact was heralded by a bellow of pain from the dragon loud enough to temporarily deafen him.

The hauntingly musical sound of pipes and strings followed Landolin up the stairs to the guard tower. Silent sentinels lined his path on both sides. The chill of the dead mingled with the musty scent of rooms rarely used.

He carried Trainor's bundle delicately in his outstretched arms. Gienna's soft footfalls helped to steel his resolve. The general knew she carried candles and water in the same manner he carried his burden.

While a part of him wished she could help him carry the bundles, he was thankful she couldn't. It was his responsibility and his duty. The ceremony also allowed him some form of closure. He just hoped it would help.

Landolin set his package carefully onto the top of the large marble table. Grooves had been carved across the face of the table segmenting it into thirty-six separate sections. Each section was large enough to hold a package with the exact same dimensions as Trainor's bundle.

A tear crept down his face as his fingers slid across the bundle's sides. The elf stifled his pain. His body shook for a moment as he tried to step away from the table. The scent of bee's wax and flames slowly allowed him to regain control over his body.

Shakily, the elf stepped backward a few steps before he turned to leave. Landolin had eight more packages to bring and he needed to make sure he honored them all. He cursed himself silently for his lapse of control and vowed it would not happen again.

The sound of the body as it slid behind their horses was the only thing the two of them could hear. The makeshift sled rattled against the exposed stones along the snowy path. Not even the errant cry from the wolves they had heard on their way to the memorial was present as Aves and Hessa rode side by side.

"You know that I never meant... " Hessa started to say as Aves held up her hand to silence her.

"What should we do with the body?" Aves asked coldly.

"We should take it back to his people," Hessa answered without thinking. The sting of Aves's actions and words hurt more than she had anticipated.

"So I can be brought up on charges of murder? You would like that wouldn't you?" Her sarcasm filled comment hung in the air between them like the first rumblings of an approaching storm.

"It's not like that and you know it," Hessa replied, obviously hurt by Aves's comments. "What happened between you two after I helped you escape from the dragon?"

"Nothing," Aves's lie was obvious. The fact that she blushed at the question did not help make her comment believable.

"I am so sorry," Hessa said as she realized why Aves

was angry. "I had no idea."

The blush on Aves's face deepened. Hessa could read the realization on her face. She wasn't sure if Aves was embarrassed or ashamed. The hue of her sister's face deepened from a rosy hue to almost blood red. Hessa knew Aves understood what had started to transpire between her and Onas.

"Forget about it, please," Aves said as she purposefully looked away from Hessa.

"Let's just bury him here then," Hessa offered as the silence between them deepened.

"The ground will be too hard. I saw a place on our way here that might be better," Aves said quietly.

Her suggestion sounded odd to Hessa. The fact Aves knew exactly where to hide a body was hard to accept.

She nodded her agreement to her sister and the two of them continued their slow trek.

"Too much has happened too fast," Hessa pined to herself mentally. "I wish things could just go back to the way they were." Her mind raced as she turned the helm over and over in her hands.

"THAT CAN NEVER HAPPEN. TIME MOVES IN ONLY ONE DIRECTION FOR YOUR KIND. THINGS WILL NEVER BE THE SAME BETWEEN YOU TWO AGAIN." The helm's voice echoed ominously in Hessa's mind as she glanced at Aves and saw a wicked look in her eyes.

"Today you start on the path of advancement. Each of you survived your initiation into the church of Lotevilar. You all have differing skills and backgrounds. In fact, the only two things any of you have in common is the fact you are here and that you have all decided to walk the Darque road as a traveler," Tali's voice rang out across the entire courtyard as she spoke. "Today is not only your last day on your old path, it is the first day of your new one. Be careful and be wise.   The path of a Darque Traveler is a long one and it is full of perils.

Jaconis swallowed back a wave of fear as he saw his beloved speak.   She was just as charismatic as he recalled her being.   Even after all this time away, he still felt drawn to her.

"What is time to our order," Jaconis scoffed to himself mentally.

He was glad he decided to join the church and become a member of its clergy.   The peace and discipline it offered him was far better than anything he had waiting for him in Ellsted.   That small town was the last place he ever wanted to go again.   This temple was his new home and there was nothing he would do to lose his place in it.

"Unlike your past training, you will not have one deacon assigned to you.   Instead, I will assign them according to your talents and aptitudes.   Do not be fooled.   Lotevilar's goal is to make you a better person.   She will not just focus on the things you do well, She will instruct me to send teachers to also focus on what you need help with," Tali continued speaking from her seat at the altar.

"The challenges and tutelage will be much harder than anything you experienced thus far.   Many of you barely survived the last phase in one piece.   Some of you were irrevocably injured.   Almost all of you know someone the either died or went insane. They were not worthy of being a disciple, but you are," Tali's voice was the most beautiful thing Jaconis had ever heard.   "All of you should feel assured that your soul will be with Her when you leave this world"

No matter what she said, he found himself agreeing with her. His eyes momentarily slipped from her well face down to her well-made robes. She was stunningly gorgeous. Even though she was more than half of the distance across the great hall, he could see every detail of her outfit perfectly.

He always could.   It was part of the bond he shared with

her. He knew when she was hurt or needed something and he was certain she knew the same about him. It was a gift from Lotevilar, or so he had been assured by his last instructor. His knowledge of her came to him in his dreams, that is, aside from the information he already knew about his beloved.

"Look around at each other and see the face of your competition," Tali instructed. She paused long enough to see that everyone did as they were told. "They may surpass you if you are not diligent and careful. Always fight to be better today than you were yesterday. Take the lessons from your masters and learn them with alacrity. Above all else, do not fail. If you do, you will surely die."

Jaconis scanned the room. There were nineteen other petitioners in the large room. All of them sat at small tables and they each wore the black robes of discipleship. There were thirty others in the great hall with them, not counting Tali. Each of these others wore black tight-fitting clothes. Some wore hoods and others had some form of leather armor over their clothing.

"If you only learn one thing about our Goddess today, understand this, Lotevilar does not care what you cannot bear. She only cares how she can shape you to Her needs," Tali rose as she said these last few words and took a few steps away from her chair. "That will be all and good learning to each of you."

"May Lotevilar be praised," everyone in the room joined Jaconis as he said the solemn vow he had grown to love.

His heartbeat skipped as he saw Tali walking toward him. It had been so long since he had been allowed to talk to her. Thoughts and questions about what their next step in thwarting Namir spun around in his mind as she closed the distance between them.

Jaconis could almost smell the jasmine scent of her dark brown hair. He longed to be near her, to touch her. His lungs drew a deep breath as he struggled to maintain his composure. Tali was getting closer and he would not disappoint her by acting brash or out of turn.

"My lady," he all but breathed the words as he knelt. To his dismay, she smiled, then turned and walked toward one of the senior brethren. The man was not much taller than he was, but quite a bit older. From his white robes, Jaconis knew this deacon was a member of the Disciples of the White Rod. He quickly tamped down his ire as he watched the two of them depart the great hall through a side door.

"Jaconis," a gentle voice said from behind him.

The voice was soft and sounded like it belonged to a lady. He paused to gather his emotions before he acknowledged her. The last thing he wanted to do was upset his new teacher on his first day of training.

"Aye," Jaconis said as he turned to face her. He kept his eyes riveted to the floor in case he was wrong about what she wanted from him.

"I am Deacon Myrea," she said and held her hand toward him.

Jaconis lightly grasped her hand politely. His eyes meandered from the floor up to her face. Like so many of the ladies he had met in the temple, she was beautiful. Her long auburn hair was pulled back into a braid and her pale skin had a light dusting of freckles.

He smiled at her as he replied, "I am honored to be placed under your tutelage."

As his words fell from his lips he locked her dazzling pale green eyes with his jade ones. Her reaction was what he expected it to be. Her breath caught until he looked away.

His eyes quickly danced along her robes. Like him, she wore the long black robes of discipleship; however, she also had a sword tied to her hip. This was a little unusual to Jaconis. The last time he had seen anyone wear weapons into the training halls they were flogged for it.

"I am glad that you are such an eager student," deacon Myrea said coyly. "Come with me. I have heard about your ability to see things in your dreams and I am excited to get started on your training right away."

Jaconis nodded and replied, "As you wish."

CHAPTER SIXTEEN: CROSSROADS

The sound of the wood and metal as they clattered against stone drew Namir's attention. He glanced around to see if the pebbles that had followed him had been replaced by knives and daggers. Relief spread through his body when he saw Carness's spear. Namir slowly reached toward the spear, careful not to make any noise that might alert the dragon. Then the world exploded.

Intense heat and light filled the air and threatened to suffocate him in a fiery inferno. It was all Namir could do to hold onto the spear. The sounds of battle were replaced by the white nothingness of the flames. Even Tipin's shouts were consumed by the crackling of intense heat as it scorched the stones around him.

"YOU ARE SAFE," Zelios calmed his fears as she spoke. "ALTHOUGH YOU ARE NOT ITS TARGET YET, YOU DO NEED TO MOVE OR YOU WILL PERISH BY BEING TOO CLOSE TO ITS BREATH."

"What's happening?" Namir asked mentally.

He buried his face into his arms to breathe. The air was too hot to survive much longer. Namir felt his hair singe and his eyes stung in the blistering heat. His whole world to melted as he spoke with Zelios.

"DRAGON FIRE HAS BEEN UNLEASHED UPON THE FIVE AND ONE HAS FALLEN TO IT," Zelios's response, though calm, was filled with sorrow.

"Fallen? Who was it?" Namir's mind raced and started to fill with questions faster than he could dismiss them.

"COUNT AND ACKNOWLEDGE THE DEAD WHEN THE BATTLE IS WON, NOT WHILE IT HAPPENS. NOW MOVE OR YOU WILL DIE AS WELL. NOT EVEN MY POWERS ARE GREAT ENOUGH TO PROTECT YOU FROM THE FIERY DEATH IT BREATHES," Zelios commanded.

Namir nodded his understanding and crept backward. He pulled Carness's spear with him. Its tip slid into debris as he moved. Namir moved slowly at first, but found the strength to move faster the farther he retreated from the flames.

Ear-splitting pops emanated from the cracking stones. It followed his retreat. Only the brightness of the fire diminished as he finally made it free. The blessed coolness the deep shadows that lined the battlefield offered him was a welcome boon.

"I FOUND THE SOURCE OF THE PEBBLES, SA'OUVANT. THEY ARE COMING FROM ARMANI'S CLOISTER, OR AT LEAST WHAT REMAINS OF IT." Deracai's voice pulsed out of the darkness around Namir.

"What is the report from the battle?" Namir whispered back.

"DAFFER WAS ENGULFED BY THE DRAGON'S FLAME. TIPIN FELL UNDER ITS CLAWS. I HAVE ALSO LOST TRACK OF HARADINE. I HAVE TO ASSUME SHE IS DEAD AS WELL. HOWEVER, CARNESS MANAGED TO BLIND THE BEAST'S LEFT EYE WITH HIS LAST ATTACK." Deracai replied succinctly.

The words were no louder than the sound of a light breeze, but it was more than loud enough for Namir. The boy shook his head and sighed at the shadow walker's report. It was all much too fast.

"So all we have left is Allair, Alequa, Saril, Carness and the man in armor?" Namir asked.

"AYE," Deracai agreed. "BUT THREE OF THOSE ARE SUR-VIVORS OF WATCH KEEP. YOU CANNOT DISMISS THEIR ABILI-TIES." The shadow walker's words were accented by the pain filled roar of the dragon.

"I see," Namir said in response as he thought about what needed to be done. "I have a plan, but I need your help." He waited until he was certain he held the shadow walker's complete attention before he continued, "I need you to tell the others to direct the dragon to me."

"YOU WILL DIE. AND WITH YOU, THE HOPE FOR CENNICUS SHALL DIE WITH YOU," Deracai admonished.

"I won't. As long as you are capable of doing what I need you to do I will be fine." Namir assured him. "First let them know I will be the dragon's new target. Once I pro-voke it, I need you to pull me out of the way. I've seen how you walk through shadows. Can you take others with you?" Namir's question fell from his lips with just the right amount of inflection to show Deracai what he had meant to have happen.

"I CAN, AND I WILL BE WAITING FOR YOU. WHERE WILL YOU BE STANDING?" Deracai asked as the shadows deepened around them.

"On Armani's cloister," Namir nodded unnecessarily to the dark shadows to his right as he said this. "If you can, I also need you to take me immediately above its head. I need to be close to it in order to end this."

"YOUR WILL SHALL BE DONE," Deracai agreed.

The shadow walker vanished completely into the shadows and left Namir alone in his thoughts. Namir quickly assessed his position. He quickly calculated the distance to Armani's cloister and plotted the fastest course.

"Why would Armani side against me?" Namir asked himself as he carefully moved across the debris.

"THAT ANSWER IS EASY. HE ALLIED HIMSELF WITH THE FORCES OF DARKNESS." Zelios's response was almost instantaneous and it startled him enough to cause Namir's foot to slip as he moved.

"That much I understand. The mystery is why," Namir thought somewhat perturbed by Zelios's intrusion into his thoughts. "Do you hear everything that passes through my mind?" He asked as he slowed his pace. He wanted to ensure Armani, or whoever was in the cloister, did not hear his approach.

"YES, I CAN AND DO. WE SHARE A SYMBIOTIC RELATIONSHIP, SA'OUVANT. I EXPERIENCE LIFE THROUGH YOU AND YOU GAIN A CONNECTION TO THE UNIVERSE. YOU ALSO GET THE PROTECTION ONLY THE GODS CAN PROVIDE." Zelios replied soothingly.

"You really need to work on your people skills, like your attempt to put my fears at ease," he thought back somewhat lightheartedly.

Namir carefully picked his way through the growing piles of rubble. He paused a few times to inspect larger remains of the wall as he passed. The large scratches and holes seemed unusual, but Namir could not quite figure out why.

"It's interesting Armani's cloister wasn't completely destroyed like the others had been." He thought as he glanced over his shoulder at the fight behind him.

Namir hastened his step. He had to get closer to his position before anyone else died. He crested a pile of rubble as the mystery man in black armor pulled his sword from the dragon's side and then drove it back in a few inches away from where it had been buried before. Even in the brief moments, Namir had seen the sword's blade, he could tell it was blazing hot.

The dragon bellowed in pain and turned toward the man. With a lightning-fast swipe of its claw, the beast launched the soldier into the air effortlessly. Namir gaped as the man spun head over heels and impacted one of the interior walls with a loud and bone-jarring clang.

"THREE OF THE CLOISTERS WERE BUILT BETTER THAN THE OTHERS. DENSER STONES WERE USED TO STRENGTHEN THEM IN CASE OF AN ATTACK. THE MAYOR'S WALL WAS REINFORCED BECAUSE HE IS THE HEAD OF THE COUNCIL. THE HEALER'S BECAUSE HE IS NEEDED TO HELP THE INJURED. THE FINAL ONE WAS THE HEAD MERCHANT TO PROTECT THE ELLSTED'S LIVELIHOOD." Zelios offered as Namir quickly scaled the final pile of debris separating him from the top of Armani's hiding place.

The top of the final heap of stones loomed in front of Namir. Painfully, he half-climbed half-dragged himself to its summit. Thankfully, he found a spot just below it where he could sit and rest.

Clinging to his perch, he glanced around to make sure he had not been seen. Once Namir was certain he was still obscured by the darkness, he reached out and gripped the surface of the stone. Cautiously he ran his hand across the face of the rock and found another place to grab onto.

He carefully moved his foot the same way he had his hand and found a suitable place to dig the toe of his boot into. Little by little Namir managed to move sideways around what had once been one of the huge support pillars of the vaulted ceilings above them.

He swallowed hard as he shot another glance at the fight.

Namir's stomach dropped when he noticed only Carness engaged the dragon. Neither the Shadow Walker nor the strange armored man was visible. The scene was silhouetted by the blue crackling light that cascaded around Alequa. Its soft blue glow acted like a beacon in the darkness.

"I thought you said they could kill this thing," Namir screamed in his mind.

"IT SEEMS I WAS WRONG." The silence that followed her words in Namir's brain was as deafening to him as the dragon's screeches of pain and anger.

The soft sound of arrows against stone jarred him back to the battle. It also made him realize there were more people than just the three he had been focusing on. Allair was still alive somewhere in the darkness.The wave of guilt he felt was crippling when he thought about her plight.

First, her youngest son goes missing and the other one has not returned from his search. Now the man she loves may be dead. All of this happened because of him and his birthright.

Guilt to festered deep in his soul and he hated it. Namir crawled to the perimeter of the council hall. He hoped he could clear his head before he needed to signal to the others.

Namir felt like he was in better control of his emotions. He crept along what was left of the rear wall to Arman's cloister. Smoke and dust cascaded around him. In front of him were the remains of the mayor's chair, perfectly highlighted by Alequa's cascading light.

Soft sounds of fabric as it moved across wood and stones let Namir know someone still sat in it. Every fiber of the boy's being pulsed with rage as he thought about what had happened. He needed to see him, the traitor.

"There is no way Armani betrayed us," Namir thought anxiously.

"THIS IS NOT THE FIRST TIME HE HAS BETRAYED THOSE THAT LOVED HIM. THERE IS MUCH YOU DO NOT KNOW ABOUT

THiS MAN. HE HAS LiEd AND KEPT SECRETS FROM HiS OWN CHiLDREN." Zelios's response was swifter than ever. Its swiftness bothered Namir and he was not sure why.

"He only has one child," Namir fastened onto the part of her statement he understood. The part he knew to be true.

"ANOTHER LiE. I BELiEVE THAT WAS ONE OF THE FiRST ONES HE TOLD YOU." Zelios replied succinctly.

"Is he the one in the chair?" Namir did not want the answer.

"HE iS," Zelios replied evenly. "BUT YOU CAN SEE FOR YOURSELF iF YOU MUST. BUT iF YOU DO, WE LOSE THE ELEMENT OF SURPRiSE."

He turned and glared into the darkness between him and the dragon. "No, I am ready," Namir whispered his answer into the shadows. "Bring the beast to me."

"AS YOU WiSH, MY LiEGE," Deracai's words fell from the air like the fluttering of feathers.

Namir watched as the darkness thickened between him and the battle. The ensuing din muted as it became palpable and congealed. Soon, the only light he could see was Alequa's bright column. Even that shone like the soft flickering flame of a candle instead of the day like brightness.

His spirits rose as Tipin's axe flew through the darkness and embedded itself in the dragon's neck. Less than a moment later the smith launched through the darkness and retrieved it. The gaping hole he left behind was the only sign of where his axe had been.

Another shower of arrows abated momentarily enough for Namir to see him. The armored man, now severely battered, fanned an array of flaming daggers before the dragon. The sneer on his face spoke volumes. He obviously enjoyed the fight, no matter how hard it was to win.

One at a time his daggers flew and buried themselves

into the hole Tipin had created. Both of the men darted back into the darkness before the dragon could attack them, but it was obvious they both fled in Namir's direction. His plan was working. The howling beast slowly turned and diverted its attention from the area surrounding the base of the dais and toward where Namir stood in plain sight.

He stared at the beast and he was afraid. The thing was massive. Much larger than he thought it would be. Although he knew what he had to do, he could barely force his arms to move let alone raise the spear high enough to strike this majestic creature.

Seeing the others doing their part helped him find his resolve. Namir set his jaw and raised the tip of the spear. He knew he could not let them down. They would not fail because of him.

"Over here!" He screamed as loud as he could. "I am your target, not them. Leave them be and come get me!"

He waved the spear at it in diversion. No matter what he needed it to leave the others alone and only focus on him. A smile played across his lips when the dragon turned its head toward him. Even the soft whisper of fabric quickly sliding against the wooden chair in front of him only added to his mirth.

"Now Zelios! Light me up now!" The harsh whisper escaped from his lips.

They tasted bitter and sweet all at once. The reprieve they brought was satisfying. Some small part of him felt like he had just muttered a curse and, for some reason, it felt good.

The all too familiar tingle that accompanied Zelios's power splashed across Namir's skin. A tickling wave pierced his clothed and emanated from the amulet he pulled out of his tunic. The blue light slowly pulsed all around him.

"I just hope it is enough," Namir muttered.

"IT WILL BE," Zelios replied as she directed a blue arcing bolt of light at the dragon's head.

Stunned, the dragon reeled and tossed its head into the side of one the few intact pillars. A shower of dirt and small bricks cascaded down on the beast's face. Its glowing red eyes snapped onto him.

Namir gripped the haft of Carness's spear tightly. He relished the wood's smooth warmth. All the many lessons the constable had given him about how to use a spear flooded back.

The dragon shook off whatever confusion Zelios's attack had caused it. Namir decided to make himself a more tempting target, so he lowered the tip of the spear and rested it on the ground. Then he locked gazes with the dragon and bowed respectfully. Then he raised his hand toward it as a challenge.

"Attack it again," Namir instructed mentally.

Her response was immediate and dazzling. Another bright blue light arced from his extended fingers and shot at the dragon's face. The overall effect felt as if Namir had hurled a bolt of lightning at its head and the dragon reacted in kind.

The blue bolt of energy sparked the air and buzzed toward it true to its mark. In response, the dragon inhaled deeply. As the electricity was about to hit, the dragon unleashed a writhing stream of liquid flames. It reacted exactly as he had hoped it would.

Namir's muscles tensed as the fire melted the shadows in front of him and gush toward him. His first impulse was to run, but he knew he needed the dragon to attack. Instead, Namir crouched and gripped the haft of the spear closer to its head.

Heat rose around him as the deadly fire splashed everywhere. The marble under his feet steamed. The rubble at the beginning of the dais melted in the impossibly hot liquid flames as it splattered across them.

In one fluid motion, Namir threw himself backward into the embrace of the shadows he hoped had gathered behind him. Shock threatened to claim his senses as he fell from sweltering heat into mind-numbing coldness. It was more intense than anything he ever experienced. Namir felt its icy embrace close around his skin as the darkness claimed him utterly.

An eternity of senseless pain passed all around him. He was no longer certain if it was his screams or the occupant of the cloister he heard in his frozen tomb. Either way, he was positive that he did not care. He immediately braced for the impact he hoped the shadow walker arranged.

The sensation of falling slowly sank into Namir's senses and the darkness faded. An overly hot brightness replaced it faster than he wanted it to. The perfect silhouette of the dragon was mesmerizing. Everything was eerily lit by Alequa's geyser and the dragon's fire. The overall effect was spectacular and Namir had to constantly remind himself how deadly his situation was.

He watched as the dragon grew larger. Carness's spear was leveled at the beast's one good eye. Fiery death still spewed from the dragon's mouth where Namir had stood. The liquid fire completely covered every surface of the cloister and pooled in the sunken areas where the dais had sustained the brunt of the attack.

"Your plan is working," Zelios said pleasantly in his mind

"You are distracting me," Namir thought back desperately as he clung to the spear.

He shifted his weight and kept the tip centered on the dragon's red glowing eye. Namir knew the impact was going to be hard. He just hoped he would be able to survive it.

The blue glow still surrounded him. Namir felt the electric buzz along his skin. He took comfort in the gentle reminder that Zelios gave him whatever protection she could.

A bone-jarring thud ran through his body as the tip of the spear penetrated the semi-solid outer membrane of the dragon's eye. His attack was greeted by a spray of acidic blood. As he planned, his weight and momentum buried the spear deep into the dragon's skull. Namir clung to the spear and quickly climbed its length to swing his body as close to the beast's face as he could to drive it as deep as possible.

Namir's feet hit the dragon's skull with a solid thud. All of his weight was still centered on the shaft, which is the only reason he did not slide off. The pooled dragon's blood sizzled across the bottoms of his boots and made the footing slicker than he anticipated. Namir did the best he could to steady himself as the beast started to writhe in agony.

Liquid fire still billowed from its mouth as it reared and twisted. The dragon contorted itself in a variety of ways in an obvious attempt to scrape the spear from its eye. Namir tried to time the beast's undulating movements of the thing. Although he somehow managed to hold onto the spear, he could not dodge one of its clawed hands as it swatted him off his precarious perch.

The wind whipped through Namir's hair and pulled it free from the queue it was tied in. He quickly curled himself into a ball hoping to avoid the jagged stones of the ruined assembly hall. The soft blue glow shifted to a deep azure hue as Namir felt sharp edges of marble cut through his shirt and pierce his skin.

Beads of sweat traced their way down the contours of his face as he slept. Each bead was closely followed by a second and a third. His smooth satiny locks matted themselves against his head as he tossed and turned. The heat of his body slowly evaporated the sweat in tiny waves of steam.

Jaconis awoke from the nightmare of flames and heat in

a panic. A dry and raspy scream barely echoed off his chamber's walls. His eyes scanned his cell frantically as he searched for a way out. Before he even saw the door, his body was in motion. He leaped toward it and closed his hands firmly around the soothingly cold metal handle. As he pressed his thumb down against the wrought iron latch, his mind exploded. This time he was in sensory overload and his world was filled with only fire and ice.

The cool wintry air of Hornshir danced across his exposed flesh forcing him to shudder against it. All at once he was bathed in sweat and freezing. Jaconis looked around him bewildered and confused. His breath escaped in steaming puffs as he righted the robes he slept in. Sweat dripped from his brow and had completely soaked through the thick fabric.

Vestiges of the torment raced through his waking mind. The now muted flames erupted all around him again in his mind's eye. Phantasmal remnants of suffocating heat scorched his lungs and seared the edges of his eyes. Jaconis shook the memory of the impossible event from his thoughts and allowed the refreshingly cold air to fill his lungs.

"What was that about?" Jaconis wondered to himself out loud.

He quickly crossed the room to the pitcher of water that sat on a small table underneath his mirror. Once there, he pulled out the silver goblet he kept in the small drawer under the table top and set it shakily beside the pitcher.

As soon as he was once again in control of his hands, he carefully poured some water into his chalice. Another trembling fit wracked his hands and he waited until they passed before lifting the goblet to his lips. The cold water felt good as it splashed down his arid mouth and throat.

The lessons from the day slowly churned in his mind as he thought about the meaning of his dream. Jaconis recrossed the short distance back to his bed and opened the only drawer in the nightstand. He quickly pulled his study journal, pen, and inkwell from the gaping drawer.

"It felt as if I had to accomplish something. Whatever it was, it felt important. There was also violence. Although I did not want to do it, I knew it was something I had to do." Jaconis spoke the words quietly as he as scrawled them into his journal.

As part of the training, he had been instructed to record his dreams. He also was tasked with pushing the limits of his senses. The deacon in charge provided him the journal, the ink and the pen so he would be well equipped for the task.

"I hope it wasn't prophetic," Jaconis said to himself. He recalled the deacon's warning that some dream working assignments can turn into those.

He used the relaxation steps Deacon Myrea taught him to help force the final vestiges of the dream out of his mind. Powderized salt scattered across the page from his fingers to set the ink. When he was done, he closed the book and placed it back into the drawer along with his pen and ink. The almost imperceptible sound as the drawer slid back into place was the only noise in his cell.

Several long moments passed before Jaconis dared to rest his head on his pillow. Sleep was going to be elusive, but he decided to try to seek the peacefulness he sought in dreams. He quietly swore to himself that he would forego his assignment for the rest of the night.

After all, he did have a great success he could share with the deacon in the morning. As he drifted off into the promising oblivion that spanned in front of his mind's eye, Jaconis felt a wave of depression settle into his heart. Instead of the bliss, he hoped for, the sorrow weighed him down into its dark depths.

CHAPTER SEVENTEEN: CIRCUMSTANCES

Landolin glanced at Gienna before he carefully removed the cloth from the last bundle. She was the only living person in the room with him. The ceremony required only two to be present to give proper respect to the fallen.

The light from all nine orbs cast an eerily pallid glow about him and covered the room in its sheen. Aside from the orbs, the only light in the room was from either the candles or whatever filtered into the rooms through the shuttered windows and walls. A lump lodged itself in his throat as he thought about their sacrifice.

"You will never be forgotten," he whispered to the orbs. "No matter your choice, I will always honor you and yours."

The haunting sounds of elvish pipes mingled with his sister's voice.The song of mourning always brought him close to breaking, this time it was more powerful. He choked back his tears and struggled to regain his composure.

Landolin took a deep breath to help regain his composure. The sweet smell of beeswax mingled with sage and jasmine filled the air. The heady fragrance helped him to center itself.

"Sorrow fills the elves because we outlive time A wall of orbs and swords waits for all

Until they all forget us save in story and rhyme When will you place my own into a wall?"

Gienna's voice carried the melodic refrain of the traditional burial song perfectly.

Since she was an alto, the elf was capable of hitting a variety of notes. From the spine-chilling high notes to the low ones that pocked his flesh with bumps. The overall effect was as amazing as it was sorrowful.

The general looked around the room as he waited for his hands to stop shaking. He wanted this to be perfect. His men deserved at least that much.

"Sorrow fills the elves because all we love dies A wall of orbs and swords waits for all

Time withers around us, but elves it passes by

When will you place my own into a wall?" Her hollow refrain echoed off the walls eerily.

The ghostly sentinels lined the walls of the room. Silent and otherworldly. They cast no shadows and did not move. Nothing about them moved. Not even the slight breeze stirred a single strand of hair.

Although their eyes were riveted on him, it was a reassurance he felt. Landolin took solace in their presence.

Their scrutiny and numbers were what this ceremony was about. The fallen that had come before guard those to follow them.

The general carefully lifted Trainor's orb first. He first raised it up to eye level in his left hand. At the same time, he lifted the short ceremonial blade with his right hand. The orb pulsed with a familiar warmth and the well-balanced blade felt comfortable in his hand.

"Sorrow fills the elves, it robs us of our friends A wall of orbs and swords waits for all

For loving bonds change and we cannot bend

When will you place my own into a wall?" His sister's voice and the words of the song mirrored his feeling perfectly.

"I will miss you, Trainor. If you choose to leave us, I will understand." Landolin whispered.

Without hesitation, he swiveled on his heels. Slowly, purposefully, he stepped over to the long south facing wall of the guard tower. The wall was made of wood-lined stone. Scores of holes were carved into the wall's surface alternating with cold wrought iron hooks. There were three of each aligned in columns covering the entire face.

Each hole was perfectly carved to match the same dimensions of the orb in Landolin's hand. A smaller hole was carved from the back of the hole through the marble wall. Light spilled into the room through these smaller holes adding a unique ambiance.

Landolin walked to the eastern edge of the wall. He stopped briefly at the end and looked over the places that had already been filled. Several of the brilliantly shining orbs were interspersed with metallic grey ones. Blues, oranges, reds, purples, and greens shone brilliantly all around the room. The pattern was as random as the stars. Rusted remains of elven ceremonial blades hung beneath each of the metallic and faded orbs.

The general had always wondered about the patterns. A good portion of his nightly meditations was spent trying to find reason within them. His father and his instructors had all given him the same advice about them. Trying to find a sense of order to them was like trying to scry the divine. Frustrating and pointless, but that never stopped him.

His footsteps rang out solemnly around the room. Their soft and slow staccato kept perfect timing with his sister's singing. Landolin purposefully stepped toward the first hole in the wall without an orb in it. He stopped in front of it ceremoniously.

"Sorrow makes some elves seek another place A wall of swords and jewels waits for all

But some will remain, the sentinels of our race When

will you place my own into a wall?"

Gienna's lyrics had impeccable timing.

He delicately placed Trainor's orb into the hole in the wall. It glowed bright orange as the light of the day shone through it brightly. Without speaking he lifted the blade up into the light and let it bask in his friend's glory. After a few moments, he silently hung the blade under the orb and took one step backward.

An orange glow filled the void in the space he left between himself and the wall. Trainor's armored form slowly materialized in the glowing orange halo. The sword he held in his was a spectral copy of the one the general had hung beneath the orb on the wall.

Landolin cleared his throat before he said the required words, "Trainor, you served our kind honorably in life. You lived by our codes and died by them. Do you wish to stay and be a light in our times of need?" He hoped his friend would accept, but he was prepared for either choice.

His lieutenant stood silently in front of him motionless and solemn. Landolin's heartbeat slowed as he waited for his friend's response. Although he was not sure what to expect, he was certain he would know it when he saw it.

A slight nod was the only response he received. Even that much seemed like he may have imagined it. So the general waited a few moments afterward to make sure Trainor's form did not waiver.

"Those who remain, mourn and count the cost A wall of orbs and swords waits for all

For our brethren fallen and they are all lost

When will you place my own into a wall?" Gienna sang the next verse as Landolin watched Trainor for a response.

Once he was certain, Landolin walked back to the table. He had eight more soldiers to honor. Harvais's glowing blue orb was next on his list. Although he disliked losing soldiers, he was honored to perform it. He just wished he had not lost so many so quickly.

His fingers closed around the blue orb and lifted it to eye level. As the blue light splashed against his face he picked up the blade with his right hand. Gienna's final few words of the verse she sang filled the room in unison with his movements.

Landolin retraced his steps. He walked to the eastern side of the wall and paused. Then he moved over face Trainor again. His lieutenant looked him in the eyes and nodded. He silently stepped to the side to allow the general to place Harvais's orb into the wall.

Like before, Landolin stepped backward immediately after he placed it into the hole. He hung the ceremonial blade on its hook. The orb's deep blue glow signaled the general to step back and he did.

Within moments Harvais's armored form over Landolin. He was tall and brawny. Both traits he received from his woodland upbringing. The general had always marveled at his soldier's physical stature. Even in death, he was impressive.

"Harvais, you served our kind honorably in life. You lived by our codes and died by them," the words rolled off of Landolin's tongue easier this time. Do you wish to stay and be a light in our times of need?"

Landolin waited for a response. Just like with Trainor, the general hoped Harvais would accept. However, he was mentally prepared for the alternative as well.

The glowing blue specter leveled an icy stare. Silent and solemn, just like Trainor. Although his body was rigid, his eyes shifted once. They flickered from Landolin to Gienna and then back. As his gaze rested back on his general, he shook his head.

With his negative reply, his glow faded from blue to grey. His overly large form grew and dissolved all at once.

An odd crackling noise emanated from the blade under

his orb.

Before Landolin's eyes, the orb fractured in place. A liquid grey metallic substance split its way through the orb and consumed it. A dull luster took hold of the curved outer surface. At the same time, the blade grew silent. Small particles of rust-flecked the once shining surface. Even the well-made leather wrap aged under his watchful gaze.

"Fewer now remain to hold lands magic formed A wall of orbs and swords waits for all

Trees, leaves, and rocks your life has warmed

When will you place my own into a wall?" Gienna's voice filled the void of sound left in the aftermath of Harvais's refusal.

Landolin stared at the orb in shock. His sister's song washed over him. He stared dumbfounded at the orb. No matter how ready he thought he had been, nothing could have prepared him for it. The sense of betrayal he felt at Harvais's choice hit him hard.

"Your sorrow now is mine, a wound not to heal A wall of orbs and swords waits for all

Now must I bear your stamp of sorrow's seal

When will you place my own into a wall?" Gienna's final refrain pulled Landolin back from his wandering thoughts.

"I still have seven more soldiers to honor," he thought to himself. "I will not fail them, even if they choose to live with the gods instead of remaining to serve the world." The general steeled his nerves and swiveled to complete the ceremony.

A cool warmth spread across Namir's skin and penetrated the darkness he had blindly slipped into. Voices spoke in the distance and he was unable to make out anything they said. He tried to move, but firm hands stopped him and forced him to lie back down. The brightness hurt, so Namir

decided to keep his eyes closed.

"Are you alright sa'ouvant?" Alequa asked.

It was the first voice he heard and it was soothing. Although he could tell she had asked the same questions a few times by the tone of her voice, he could not recall how he had answered. It was all he could do to nod his answer.

He tried to open his eyes again. A dark blue light framed Alequa's body perfectly. The glow added an otherworldly, almost angelic, quality to the elf's lithe build.

Namir attempted to speak. He tried to let her know he was ok, but he failed to find his voice. The frantic suppressed feeling cleared as his vision did. More of the wreckage around him faded into view, as did his worried companions.

"Don't worry my liege," Alequa said softly. "I see you are recovering. A few more moments and Tayant will have you restored enough to move."

She paused as she assessed his reaction to the healing process. Fleeting looks of fear and dread crossed the elven healer's face. Namir knew she could see his furtive glances enough to hint at what troubled him the most.

"The dragon is dead, you managed to slay it." Her voice was calming. We are still searching the wreckage to assess the needs of the survivors as well as the identity of those not as fortunate."

Namir nodded his understanding. The unique sensation of Alequa's healing washed over him uninhibited and with it came an unbridled euphoria. He allowed himself to ride the waves of energy subconsciously as they bathed his psyche in their healing powers.

Aves watched Onas's face vanish into the darkness. His body slid off of the ledge at the edge of the road. She closed her eyes so Hessa would not see the pain that filled them.

"How is this possible?" she thought to herself.

The last thing she saw was his arm as it followed the rest of his body. Memories of their tryst in the cave filled her mind.

Aves felt Hessa's eyes on her in silence. She knew her sister was aware Onas had somehow stolen her heart. Now all she had left of him had was pain. The bitterness of her love dying inside of her mingled with the guilt she felt about killed him.

Several more long moments passed as the two of them stared into the darkness. Aves stood stoically beside Onas's horse while Hessa sat on her horse in silence. She knew her sister was quiet out of respect, but that did not change the anger she felt build in her because of it.

Without a word, Hessa slid off her horse. She immediately set to reconstructing the berm Onas's body had destroyed when it went over the edge. Her sister avoided eye contact with Aves and this only added to her rage.

"That should dissuade anyone from thinking he was disposed of here," Hessa said softly as she finished her task. Aves avoided making eye contact with her as she replied, "Good work, now let's get back to Ellsted. I need to be around familiar people and activities. There have been far too many adventures for me I'm afraid."Her own voice sounded hollow and broken. "Of course," Hessa agreed.

As she replied Hessa checked on both horses. Once it was apparent she was content with their arrangements, her sister mounted her horse and said, "If we head straight to town from here, we should be able to make it home by tomorrow afternoon."

"Only if we follow the roads," Aves interjected. Hessa's confused look compelled her to say more.   "When Onas escorted me to your mother's house, he took me another path. It was much shorter. If we use that route, we should be able to make it back to Ellsted in a few hours."

"Do you think you can find it?" Hessa asked.

"Aye," Aves nodded. "I think I can. Did you pay attention to the path here?"

"I did," Hessa said.

Her sister's eyes widened a little as she replied. Aves realized the distant and take-charge tone that took residence in her own voice must have startled her. She knew Hessa's discomfort should matter, but she felt nothing. Nothing except a painful numbness.

"We need to head over the crest of this hill. The road leads down to a little path beside some boulders. It will lead us to my mother's house."

"Then let's be off," Aves said as she clicked her horse into motion and left Hessa to stare in disbelief at her back.

"Is he awake yet?" The unfamiliar and gruff voice was the first thing Namir could fully focus on.

"Not yet, but he should be soon," Alequa's soothing voice crooned back.

"Please let us know the moment he rises," Carness said urgently.

Namir tested his sore muscles and was pleasantly surprised. He could move. There was pain, but it was minimal.

"I have recovered enough to talk," he cleared his throat before he called out to anyone that waited for his recovery. "Please let them in."

Namir pulled himself into a sitting position and nodded to the healer. Alequa reluctantly pulled open the curtain that separated his cot from the rest of the world. The devastation that met his eyes was immense and far worse than he thought it would be.

"The dragon did all this?" Namir's voice, though cracked, held enough power in it to be heard over the sounds of the search.

"Aye," the man in armor responded.

"But there are some things we need to attend to before we discuss the wreckage," Carness stated plainly. "Many good people died in the fight last night. More may die of exposure if we fail to get things set in place for them immediately. Recovering from something like this is hard."

"What can I do to help?" Namir asked calmly.

He could tell the two men wanted to ask something, but neither offered a hint about what. Namir was sore, tired and frustrated. None of which made him want to guess at what it was they needed from him.

Several long moments passed before Namir spoke again, this time out of frustration, "I know you both have something to ask me, so we might as well get to it."

"I think it's safe to say the dragon was sent for you," Carness started cautiously. "I only say this because there have never been any sightings of dragons in the nearby shires." The constable paused long enough to make sure Namir understood what he just said before he continued. "I believe the fires in the square were somehow a part of this.

"Fires in the square?" The armored man asked. "Can you elaborate?" His voice quavered a little and Namir saw his right eyebrow arch as he spoke.

Carness sighed deeply as he cast glances at each of them. Dark lines appeared across his forehead as he did so. Something bothered him and it weighed deeply on his heart. "Before you tell us anything," Namir said as he looked at Carness. "I don't believe we've been introduced." He turned his attention to the mysterious man in armor as he spoke.

A smile appeared on the roguish man's face. "I am terribly sorry," he said as he bowed deeply. "I thought you knew. My name is Sir Valeron, Knight of the realm."

"A Knight of the Realm, here in Ellsted?" Namir knew his confusion was not just from his injuries. "What brings you to this town of all places?"

"You," Valeron said succinctly.

"Valeron was at the battle of Watch Keep," Carness

interjected. "His unit was sent from the Crown to support us."

"Thank you for that, but it still doesn't really give me an answer."

"It does, but not a detailed one," Valeron agreed. There was a hint of laughter in his voice and it rankled Namir. "I came to see if there was any truth to the whispers I had heard."

"Sorry for my naivety, but you came from where and about what?" Namir asked bluntly.

"I came here from Drandear. I decided to come here because the man sitting on the throne is nervous and danger-ous." Valeron explained. "I overheard him speaking with someone about a possible heir in Hornshir."

"Ellsted is not Hornshir," Namir commented. "So you came here instead of there to what? Ease the acting king's mind?"

The look in Valeron's eyes hardened. The easy stance evaporated as his stance widened. He was uneasy and Namir knew it. There was something the Knight was not saying.

"No. I came to Ellsted because I knew Carness was here." The Knight replied succinctly.

The Knight held Namir's steely gaze as he spoke. His dark eyes gave away nothing, neither did his demeanor. Namir glanced at Carness and took solace in the constable's stance.

His hand rested lightly on his club and he watched Valeron's movements closely. His mentor waited patiently for the discussion to be over so he could get on with his report. Namir could tell it bothered him.

"Go on," Carness added.

"Things at Watch Keep were strained when my troops and I arrived. There were three people he could not account for and his reports to the Crown seemed a little incomplete.

All of those years ago I had a feeling he had hidden something important." Valeron's gaze drifted from Namir to Carness as he spoke. "When I heard they thought an heir may be in Hornshir I figured out Carness's secret.

"As it turns out, you were right. I just wasn't aware of it at the time." Carness agreed. "I knew a baby had been found. I also knew we were outnumbered and our chance for success was a slim one. There was no way to guarantee the infant would survive if he stayed. So I did the only thing I could, I sent it away." His voice bore no hint of emotion as he spoke. "That is why I had three fewer soldiers to fight with us. It is also what I never placed in my reports to the Crown."

"At the risk of repeating myself," Namir cut in, "you still haven't mentioned why you came. At least not fully," Namir said calmly, "so let me be direct. Are you here to kill me?"

Valeron's eyes widened as he sucked in his breath. "No, I'm here to atone."

Namir was confused and he knew the Knight could read it on his face. There was more to this. He waived for Valeron to continue.

"Ever since the last queen died, I have been serving the wrong people. Like now, I knew things were not right, but I was sworn to protect the realm. Part of that protection is keeping the peace." Valeron continued. "When the usurper took the throne, his first order was to send me and my men to Watch Keep. We had been instructed to spread the news of the new regime as we did. I now understand that I have forsaken my oath."

As the last words fell from his lips, the Knight knelt. He gripped his sword's hilt tightly. Amazingly the large man managed to reverse his grip on the blade in the process. His brown hair hung over his face, but Namir could tell the Knight stared at the ground and not him.

Namir was taken aback by Valeron's actions and words.

He had never imagined this sort of thing would happen to him. Even after he found out his true lineage, the reality of his position never fully sank in. Not like this. This man literally was putting his life into Namir's hands. It was too much for him to process all at once.

It was obvious to Namir the Knight waited for him to respond, so he obliged. "Please make yourself comfortable. I fear we have much to discuss later," Namir said quietly to Valeron. "But for now we need to focus on current issues. Carness, I know you are hesitant to continue with Valeron present, but I think its best."

"Very well," Carness agreed reluctantly. He waited until Valeron had settled himself into a more comfortable position before he started. "There have been a couple recent events that seem interconnected. Some of them are also tied to some guards that came from Hornshir with Faris."

"Wait a moment. Faris? The traitor of Watch Keep?" Valeron interjected.

"The same," Carness agreed and continued. "Evidently, since the betrayal, he became Hornshir's constable. Faris and his men escorted the newly negotiated supplies back to Ellsted. Ever since then we have had nothing but issues in our fair town."

"So you believe all of this is tied together?" Namir asked hesitantly. "Why would they go through that much trouble?"

"That much is easy. They are trying to get to you through others," Carness replied. "I know there have been plots against you since you have come home. That much is indisputable. What I do not know is who all of the players are," the constable said the last few words a little slower than he had.

"I think what my old commander is asking is if you know who is involved in these attacks?" Valeron asked as he cleared his throat.

"No, I do not. Last night I was just as surprised as everyone else when the dragon attacked. Once I realized someone in the hall helped it select its targets, I was livid." Namir confided.

The moment he was able to suss out where the person with the pebbles hid replayed through his mind as they spoke. He recalled how much that realization had churned his stomach. Namir was still abhorred by the implications of it.

"How many of the council members survived?" Namir asked. He desperately wanted to change the subject and gather more information at the same time.

For Aves's sake, Namir hoped Armani was not the one throwing the pebbles. He entertained the idea someone could have snuck in and tossed the pebbles after Armani was thrown clear of the wreckage.

"Only three of us lived. Saril, Allair and myself," Carness reported solemnly.

"What happened Daffer and Armani?" Namir asked incredulously.

"Both were claimed by the dragon's flames," Valeron replied.

His voice carried respect and admiration in it. The last time Namir heard anything like it was when Arras had mentioned the fallen heroes from his own lineage. The Knight's reverence showed Namir more about himself than anything he had said.

"How long was I unconscious for?" Namir asked as he realized, for the first time, his sanctuary was well lit.

"Several hours," Alequa chimed in as she passed through the flap.

She handed each of the men cups filled with water. Alequa cleared away some of the rubble to Namir's right and then sat. The elf took the time, while they all drank, to check on Namir's bandages.

Namir could tell by the lines in her face that the elf was

exhausted. Nevertheless, she saw to his needs instead of getting the rest she needed. The level of dedication she always has shown him always astonished him.

"Thank you," Namir whispered to the elf. He took another long drink before he faced Carness. "This is going to be hard on Aves and Jaconis. Has anyone seen her at all?"

"I have not checked, but I don't believe so," Carness replied.

"We also need to get a message to the church Jaconis has joined. Which church was it again?" Namir asked everyone.

"The church of Lotevilar," Alequa answered before anyone else had a chance.

"Lotevilar, really?" Valeron asked. "Yes, why?" Alequa wondered aloud.

"I find it interesting because Drandmir, regent of the Crown, has a heavy involvement with that church," Valeron answered.

"This is all interesting, but it's not helpful right now," Carness interjected. "We need to come up with a plan of action for right now. These are things we can discuss after that." The sound of stress in his voice was heavy.

"Agreed," Namir conceded. "But I did need to know where to send news of Daffer's death to Jaconis. Alequa, with your knowledge of religious channels, is this something you can do for me?" The disdain in his voice was plain.

"I can," Alequa agreed. "I will have the message drafted for your review by midday."

"Good. Is Saril badly wounded?" Namir directed his question to Alequa.

"No. He was shaken up, but that is all." The elf replied easily.

"I'm glad to hear it. Carness, we will have Saril head up the plans for recovery for now. I have something else that you need to see to." Namir's tone brokered no questions. His own voice sounded odd to him, but taking charge of the situation felt right.

"What is more important than taking care of the townsfolk?" Carness asked.

"Ellsted needs to be safe. I think we all can agree to that. I feel it is in the town's best interest to have both walls like Hornshir's and a standing guard. That way this sort of thing can be avoided in the future." Namir watched Carness's expressions as he stated his decision.

"Absolutely not!" Carness slammed down his cup and glared at the youth. "If we had walls, we would need more than just a handful of guards. Those guards would have to be armed and, in my experience, guards tend to cause more problems than they solve. I prefer to be the only armed person inside this town's borders. If there is only one person with weapons, it is far easier to negotiate disputes."

"How well did that work? Did it help prevent any of the recent events you briefly alluded to?" Valeron asked his old commander with a hint of mirth in his voice. The only response Carness offered back was a hurtful glare.

"Carness, I understand your position. I have seen the slovenly conduct of lesser men in Hornshir, but Valeron is right. Your way did not prevent anything that has happened in the last few days." Namir stated bluntly.

Namir turned and looked at Alequa. "Can you please go and ask the rest of the remaining council to join us. If I know Saril, since he wasn't injured badly, he is tending to the wounded. I need you take over for him while we discuss the future of Ellsted."

Relief spread through Namir when she nodded her acquiescence. All three of them watched Alequa go in silence. Silence took a hold of the room as they waited for the other two council members.

Chapter Eighteen:
Passages

"How much longer until we are there?" Aves asked Hessa for at felt like the fiftieth time.

"We are almost at my mother's house," Hessa answered. "It should be just up ahead."

The night had grown colder as they rode. A stifling silence had accompanied them ever since they disposed of Onas's body. Only Aves's incessant question broke the monotony of their ride.

Hessa felt drained. She was exhausted from everything that had happened and she knew Aves was as well. She could hear it in her sister's voice. A slight whine had taken root in her voice. Even her words were a little more drawn out and slower.

The trek from the monument to her mother's place seemed much longer this time. Without the feeling of excitement that had fueled them, everything seemed much more monotonous. Hessa had not realized how much more enjoyable Onas had made the trip the first time.

"We should stay there for the night. We can ride back to Ellsted once the sun has risen." Hessa said over her shoulder.

"I'd rather not," Aves replied. "I miss our father. I

didn't tell him I was going to find you. I can only imagine how worried he has been since I left."

"Even so, it would be better to finish our trip after the sun has come up. There are wolves and worse in these woods," Hessa unconsciously ran her fingers across the surface of the helm as she spoke. "We are in no shape to defend ourselves from whatever might lie ahead. Not to mention that we cannot see in this blasted darkness."

"I just want to be home already," Aves said sorrowfully. "I regret coming to find you. Everything that has happened since then has been a nightmare."

Hessa heard despair well up in her sister's voice as she spoke. It hurt her to think that Aves held anything against her, but she understood. Ever since she found out the truth about Armani, she felt the exact same way.

"Nothing we do can ever be undone," Hessa replied softly. "All we can do is learn from our choices."

"Aren't you just the sage all of a sudden," Aves retorted bitterly.

"Please sister," Hessa replied somewhat hurt. "Let's not fight. We are almost to my mother's house. Once we can get some sleep, and get refreshed, things will seem better."

Her hand now fully rested on the helm as she spoke. A now familiar tugging sensation played across her forehead as her words fell from her lips. Hessa's eyes widened as she felt it and she immediately realized what she had done.

"Fine," Aves replied more obediently. "But I want us to leave as soon as we can get ourselves ready in the morning."

"Agreed," Hessa replied sadly. "I just wanted to make sure."

"I thought I had to wear this thing to use its powers," she thought frantically to herself.

"NO. ALL YOU NEED TO DO IS TOUCH ME. THE MORE CONTACT WE HAVE THE BETTER I CAN HELP," she heard the words as they materialized in her head. Although they were faint, they were loud enough for Hessa to understand them.

"Now I understand why my mother got rid of you," she thought back at the helm.

"WHY?" the question carried with it a sense of confusion. "I HAVE BEEN SENT TO BE A BLESSING TO YOUR KIND. WHY WOULD ANYONE REFUSE ME?"

"Because, while I have you, I will never be certain if people are just doing my bidding because of your gifts or if they want to." Hessa thought back.

"DOES IT REALLY MATTER IN THE END? AS LONG AS THEY COOPERATE WITH YOU, THEIR MOTIVES ARE MOOT." The response was swifter and stronger than the previous ones.

"It matters to me," she replied aloud.

"I have already agreed to stay the night. Please, leave it be," Aves replied.

The confusion in her sister's voice helped snap Hessa's mind free from the conversation she had with the helm. Without hesitation, she lifted her hand from its comforting surface.

Hessa frantically looked around her for anything she could use to cover the helm. A sigh of relief escaped her lips the edge of her cloak whipped past her. It had been caught is in a sudden breeze and she was happy that it had.

She quickly unclasped her cloak. As soon as she did she regretted it. The freezing air around her was harsh and uncaring. It forced the girl to breathe in its bitter wintery crispness. She shivered as she hurriedly wrapped the helm up in her cloak.

"That should take care of it," Hessa thought to herself triumphantly.

"WE ARE NOT DONE," its response was almost too faint for her to hear, but it was still there. Somewhere in the back of her head, she felt it waiting to pounce.

"We are for now," she thought back.

"Why are we staying out here?" Nurn asked. "We need to wait out the storm," Jerine replied.

"That is what I don't understand. Aren't we going into a cave? Why would it matter if there is a storm?" Nurn asked abruptly.

Nurn felt his aggravation level rise. He spun Séregon impatiently in his hand as he hunkered close to the meager fire. Although it was bitterly cold, the overriding need to find his brother weighed heavily on his thoughts.

"This elf made less and less sense the longer we are here," Nurn thought to himself as he waited for Jerine's reply.

"We are safe here," Jerine explained. "There is no way of knowing what awaits us in the cavern, or hiding in the storm."

"We won't know what is in there until we go in," Nurn cut off the elf's explanation bitterly.

"There may be nassarid waiting for us," Jerine said softly.

"Nassarid, like Morcant, here?" Nurnasked incredulously. "Why?"

"Aye, like Morcant, but hopefully not." Jerine's words held a calming tone to them.

Nurn knew the elf did not want him to panic, but it was too late. His youthful mind whirled at the thought of the possibility. Morcant was more than formidable when he saved Jerine from him in the alleys of Hornshir. He was certain the only thing that allowed him to drive the beast off was the element of surprise. Even then he had not finished it. Instead, the nightmarish beast had managed to escape.

He felt the elf's eyes watching him. Nurn knew Jerine was trying to suss out his state of mind. He found some comfort in the elf's concern. He just wished the guardian was more forthcoming with his thoughts about what they might be facing.

"Why do you think we might face nassarid?" Nurn asked reluctantly.

Jerine took a long pull on his pipe as he studied the boy before he responded, "The last time I was here we faced them. Although Landolin's men had managed to kill most of them, some fled. Morcant was one who managed to escape. From what we could tell by their tracks, about a dozen escaped."

"Were you hunting them then?" Nurn asked.

"No, we were rescuing our own from them," Jerine replied.

"So these tents are from the elves. Was this an outpost?" Nurn continued to pry.

"Not exactly," Jerine answered as he breathed in another draw of smoke.

"Then why, exactly, were the elves here?" Nurn's frustration with the non-answers Jerine provided dripped from each word.

"Landolin had given a small contingent of elves to Aras for protection. From my understanding, Aras has been working on finding the true heir to the throne. Most of his travels have involved not only finding the heir but to secure support for whoever can pick up the mantle," Jerine explained.

"But why was Aras here?" Nurn asked somewhat confused.

"As I mentioned before, this cavern was built by the dwarves. At least it had started to be built by them. For some reason they departed prior to finishing it," Jerine explained evenly. Smoke from his pipe flowed out of his mouth as he continued, "Aras told Landolin he needed to come here to find a clue to where they went. He hoped to find the dwarves and get their support for Namir to claim the throne.”

“Alright,” Nurn nodded his understanding. “But where did the nassarid come into this?”

“That, sa’trandon, is a great question.” Jerine took another puff from his pipe then added, “Aras said they tracked him there. I fear the only one who truly knows why is Aras and that information is something he took to the grave with him.”

“Unless he told someone other than Landolin,” Nurn said his thoughts aloud as they tumbled through his head. “Who might he have trusted this information with? Did he have a family?”

“He did. He was married to Alequa. And they had a daughter. I think Haradine was that girl.” Jerine confided. “But he thought of Namir, Halin and yourself as if you were his children.”

Nurn blinked a little confused at Jerine’s last words. He stopped fidgeting with his axe and set it onto the nearby table. It struck him as such an odd thing to say.

“Why would he think of us that way? I can’t recall ever meeting him,” Nurn pondered aloud.

“I’m not sure,” Jerine replied. “I know he was close to your parents, more so with your father than with Allair. He also knew Kalta and Cerona very well, so that might explain it.”

“It might,” Nurn agreed skeptically. “Do you know if Aras might have sent any messages to my parents with Namir?”

“I do not,” the elf replied solemnly.

For some reason, Nurn felt less agitated. He wasn’t sure if it was the elf’s calming presence or the sweet aroma from whatever it was he had in his pipe. Either way, he was more relaxed and willing to stay in the tent until the blizzard passed.

His hurried footsteps echoed through the empty halls as he walked through them. Jaconis was late and he knew it. The fact the halls were void of activity was the first thing that tipped him off. The almost deafening silence was the other.

The air stung his back under his robes. He knew he should have wrapped his wounds better, he just ran out of time. A novice mistake, Jaconis only hoped it was one his new teacher would overlook.

Jaconis ignored the feeling of blood running down his back. Only one more hallway to go and he would be in the courtyard where he would start another phase of his training. Almost imperceptible footfalls met his ears as he rounded the corner.

"Excuse me, may I have a word?" The words came from behind him and the voice that propelled them was lovely.

"How may I help a devotee?" Jaconis asked as he turned toward the lady's voice.

The last thing he expected as her fist as it struck his face. He tried to turn with the blow. Another hit, this time to his ribs, stopped him. Whoever she was, she was fast. Much faster than he thought possible.

"Who are you? What do you want?" He shouted as he rolled away from, his attacker.

Her boot against his chin was the only answer she offered him. He had just managed to get into a crouched position when she struck. Jaconis resisted the urge to roll with the blow this time. He figured she would expect it of him. Whoever she was, she knew how the brethren trained him.

Jaconis pushed as hard as he could against the ground and threw himself backward. His right hand frantically grabbed at his robes. He kept a small knife in the seam of his left sleeve, just as he was trained to. His other hand quickly tugged off the rope he was using for a belt.

The whole time he moved closer, Jaconis did his best to get a look at his assailant. From what he could see, she was gorgeous as her voice sounded. Her dark hair hovered around her head as she moved. With each graceful advance, her hair whipped around her and concealed her features. She also wore black robes, just like his.

A small knife hurtled at his face and confirmed his suspicions. She was part of the church. He quickly spun his belt in front of him defensively. Somehow he managed to catch her blade in it. Jaconis's mind reeled as fast as his rope did.

Before he had a chance to ready his weapon she was on him. Another well-placed kick laid him on his back. Pain washed over him as his back hit the ground. He writhed in pain.

Without any warning, she dropped onto his chest. Her weight forced him down onto the floor again. Another wave of pain shot through him. The sharp edge of a blade against his throat brought him back to his senses. Jaconis could not see the blade, but she made its presence known.

Her golden brown eyes bore holes into his soul. Most of her face was concealed under some sort of mask. Something about it looked familiar. Like something he had seen when he was younger. Jaconis could not place where he had seen it.

"I was told you showed promise. Too bad they were wrong." She rocked her weight onto his stomach and pressed her shins against his wrists as she spoke.

"You still haven't given me your name," Jaconis spit through his teeth.

"My name is Keeta. I am your new instructor and mentor. Needless to say, you have twice disappointed me today." She looked down at him one last time before she slid off of him.

Jaconis laid there for a moment and collected himself. He rubbed his throat where she had pressed the blade. Relief spread through him when he saw there wasn't any blood on his hand.

"I promise to obey your commands," Jaconis said as he stood back up.

"I know you will," Keeta said mirthfully. "You have no choice. It's either that or death."

The house's silhouette was almost indiscernible from the trees as they approached. Hessa was exhausted and so was her horse. Its gait faltered every few steps just to maintain a walk. Her steed did its best in the darkness, but a few of the loose rocks along the trail made the horse falter enough they could not keep a decent trot.

As soon as they neared the stables, Hessa dismounted. Without sparing a thought for her sister, she took a hold of the reigns and led her horse into one of the three empty stalls. She spared a quick glance at Aves to make sure did the same. A small smile played across her lips as she saw her sister lead her mount into the stall beside hers.

"It's best to loosen the front cinch a little before you take the saddle off." Hessa offered. "Like this," she took the time to show her sister when she saw the perplexed look in her widened eyes.

"Thank you," Aves muttered. "I have never done this part. How do you know what to do?"

"It was one of the things our father made sure I was trained to do," Hessa offered. "I'm not sure why it mattered though."

"Oh?" Aves asked.

"Armani didn't own any horses. I know he had the carriage, but hitching a horse is different than saddling one." She explained to her sister as she started unclipping the breast collar.

She was happy to see Aves mimic her actions. Her sister seemed to have an aptitude for handling horses. Hessa meticulously rolled the latigo and fastened it. Then she stowed the cinches to make it easier to ready the horses in the morning. Once she was done she hefted both the saddle and the pad off and carried it over to the beam close by.

"Let me know if you need help with the saddle," she offered.

"How far do I have to carry it?" Aves asked.

It was obvious to Hessa that her sister was worried about dropping it. It reminded her about her first time handling a saddle. She dropped her saddle three or four times before she learned how to move the saddle correctly.

"Not far," she replied, "only a few yards. Don't worry about dropping it though. It happens."

"I don't plan on dropping Onas's saddle," Aves replied. Her voice was strained from trying to carry the saddle's weight. "It is the least I can do to respect his memory."

Hessa moved out of Aves's way as she watched her sister approach. The look of determination on her sister's face melted Hessa's resolve a little. She knew Onas was not who he seemed to be, but she also understood her sister's feelings for him.

Without another word, Hessa collected a couple brushes. Once Aves had finally wrangled the saddle into the open space beside hers. Then she handed her sister a brush. The two of them walked back to the horses in silence.

"Try to use large circular strokes," Hessa instructed. "It gives the horse a slight massage and helps them relax after a hard ride. Once we are done, we will take their bridles off. Then we need to check their shoes for stones."

"Can't we do these things in the morning?" Aves asked.

The sound of exhaustion in Aves's voice was apparent to Hessa. Even if it hadn't been, the way her arms hung at her side was all she would have needed to see how tired she was. Her own tiredness sapped her reserves as well.

She felt a little sorry for her sister. Hessa knew she wasn't used to this kind of life. Not that working was below

Aves, she just didn't have to do it much. Hessa's heart broke in a different way. She finally realized that by trying to get free from a life of servitude, she was forcing her sister into a life she never asked for or wanted.

"It needs to be done," Hessa said wearily, "or we will be delayed." The pained look in Aves's eyes ate away at her. "But we can wait a little bit. Let's go inside and rest for a bit. I'll draw you a bath. Once we get you settled, I can finish up the rest. Are you hungry?" She asked Aves as she collected the brushes and set them aside.

"I'm famished," Aves confided. "Thank you."

Chapter Nineteen: Returns

"Three days," Nurn growled at Jerine. "It has been three days since the storm hit. When is it going to end?"

"It will blow over soon," Jerine replied easily. "The flakes are lessening and getting larger."

"When it does, what is the plan?" Nurn growled again.

His patience was wearing thin. Halin had been missing for far too long and even his vast amount of faith had been tested sorely. Every chance he had, he prayed to Tumere for his brother's safety.

"First we need to search the other tents to make sure we are indeed alone. Then we will enter the cavern. We are not going to progress through it swiftly. Please understand, if we move too quickly we might miss something or walk into a trap." Jerine spoke slowly with a sense of purpose.

"I know," Nurn replied. 'The waiting is just hard for me. Halin has been missing for such a long time and I worry about him."

"He has been," Jerine agreed, "but there is a good chance he is still alive.

"Don't patronize me," Nurn rumbled at the elf. "I know that if we find my brother alive it is only because of

Tumere's will. He has been lost too long with no food or shelter from the cold."

"I never thought I would have to say this to you," Jerine confided. The subtle inflection in his voice let Nurn know he was shocked by what he had just said. "You should not sell your brother's skills short. Halin's skills with the bow were improving before he vanished."

Nurn bowed his head as the elf spoke. A very real part of him was embarrassed for losing his faith in his brother. Another part hated himself for it. Halin wouldn't have lost faith and Nurn knew it.

"It's time we get going," Jerine's words brought Nurn back from his reverie. "The flakes are stopping. The storm has passed."

"Then let's go," Nurn said as he opened his eyes once more.

The world spun for a few moments before he took to his feet. Séregon's weight in his hand helped tether him in reality. Halin needed him and he was not going to let his brother down.

"I'm going to scout ahead while you make your way to the fire pit in the center of the camp," Jerine said over his shoulder as he stepped out into the snow.

The disorienting effect as the elf vanished was almost too much. Nurn looked away for only a moment. But it was long enough. When he looked back to where Jerine had been, he was gone.

He quickly strode out into the snow. The elf left no footprints in the snow and no indication to which direction he went. Nurn muttered under his breath as he waded out of their tent toward the center of the encampment.

Nurn ignored the bitter coldness of the snow as he pressed through it. Three days of blizzard had deposited more snow than he had expected. His breath froze against his lips as he waded deeper in. He would not let his brother down, especially not now that they were so close.

"This one is clear," Jerine called out.

The elf's voice erupted from the first tent to his left. Nurn glanced over at the guardian as he faded from sight again. The effect did not hit him nearly as hard as it had in the past. A smile creased his chapping lips as she made it to the fire pit. He was finally getting used to the elf's magic.

"I'm going to build a fire. I think it will help," Nurn called out.

He knew Jerine would hear him. Nurn also knew the heat would help against the cold. The wood was wet and would smoke if he managed to lite a fire.

"The smoke might help us drive out anything in the tents," he thought numbly.

Nurn quickly surveyed the fire pit itself. There were several large logs stacked in the middle. They had been placed in a pyramid position. This helped the snow to settle along the base of the wood instead of along the whole length of the logs. That allowed them to be dryer and more or less ready to burn. All he needed to do was scoop out the snow and find enough kindling to get it going.

The latter was easy. He kept small balls of separated wool in a pouch in case he needed to build a fire quickly. Nurn thumbed out two of the small balls and pulled them a little farther apart.

He easily reached into the stacked logs and scooped out a fist full of snow. Nurn repeated this two more times before he was sure it was dry enough to attempt a smoky fire. The two wool balls slid between the logs and nestled into place.

The sound of Séregon's blade against the fire stick twice filled the muted clearing as the sparks hungrily took to the woolen fibers. All it took was a few well-placed puffs and the fire leaped from the wool to the awaiting logs.

"This one is clear as well," Jerine's voice floated over to Nurn on the breeze. "There are only two left to check. Then we can make our way into the cavern entrance."

Nurn nodded as he took off his cloak. It flipped easily in his hands and directed the newly formed smoke toward the tent to his furthest right. The guardian should have been in the other tent, so he felt this was the best option. It also happened to be the closest one to their own.

The growl that emanated from the inside of the tent was not the response Nurn expected. With a quick flourish, he flung his cape back around his shoulders and readied his axe. There was no sign of Jerine. A large knot formed in his throat and stomach as he saw two sets of glowing eyes in the billowing smoke. He hoped he had not just made a grave error in judgment.

"We have company!" Nurn yelled.

He hoped Jerine heard him. Nurn chose his words carefully. While he hoped to alert the elf to his predicament, he also did not want the nassarid to think there were only two of them. That way the might buy some time before they attacked.

His ploy did not work. As his words rang out over the snow-covered terrain, one of the things leaped. The glowing yellow eyes moved through the smoky haze straight at him. He lost sight of them momentarily as it neared the fire.

Then, without warning, it was upon him. Like a nightmare, the wolfish being flew through the growing flames hurtling right at him. Without thinking Nurn sung Séregon upwards to meet the beast. He instinctively pivoted as the shining blade sliced the smoke. Nurn was surprised with the ease of his own attack. Although he felt the impact as his axe clove through the monster's fur and bones.

In an instant, the initial attack was over. A small rivulet of warm blood washed over him as he finished his attack. Two muted thuds accented the finality of his actions.

Nurn spared a brief glance at the bisected beast before he turned to find the other one. Although he had managed to separate the torso from its legs, the thing clawed at the snow in agony. The scent of burning fur caught Nurn's attention about the same time he felt his skin getting hotter. His eyes widened in fear and wonder.

At first, he thought the beast must have caught ablaze when it leaped through the fire at him, but it was not igniting fast enough for that. Instead, he watched as the blood along the snow slowly combusted. The flaming trail burned towards the two halves of the beast's body slowly. When it finally made its way to the creature, it howled in pain and erupted in flames.

That is when he felt it, the indistinguishable searing pain. His skin sizzled where the blood had splashed across his arms and face. Tendrils of smoke slowly spun off Séregon's blade and haft just as it did from his cloak. He was burning and he knew it.

Numbness and fear wrestled for control of his thoughts. The mental haze it created was almost as thick as the smoke from the fire he had built. Instinctively Nurn knew he needed to put the flames out. He struggled with his thoughts as he desperately swatted at the flames on his right hand.

Then it struck him, the snow. The very thing he had been complaining about was his key to survival. Without thinking he unfastened his broach and let his cloak fall. As the flaming cloth cascaded to the ground, he dove into the largest snowbank he could see. Blessed coldness instantly doused the flames. A bone-chilling wave of coldness quickly replaced the searing heat he had felt just moments before and he was thankful for it.

"Tumere, thank you for saving my life. I know you have a plan for everything, so please let Jerine be able to handle the second nassarid," his teeth chattered as he mouthed his prayer.

He felt the melted snow soak into his leggings and shirt and he knew that he had to move. It was either that or freeze. Nurn also knew that if he did move, the second monster would be upon him faster than he could react. But he had no choice.

Air filled his massive lungs as he launched himself out of the snow in a roll. Within moments he was on his feet and back near the bittersweet heat of the bonfire. He frantically scanned the dwindling smoke for the glowing yellow eyes of his attacker. Nothing. There was no sign of the other beast.

A deep sigh of relief escaped his lips. He was grateful for the opportunity to relax a little. Without thinking, he turned his attention to the burning body a few feet away from him. He neared it cautiously in case the beast held any other surprises.

Stabbing pain erupted across the middle of his back and he realized his mistake. Savagely his attacker snarled and tore through what little protection he had left. Carness's training took over. Although the beast was on him, Nurn somehow managed to turn and throw the thing off.

The few seconds of freedom his maneuver secured evaporated quickly. It was all Nurn could do to lift the haft of his axe up enough to block against the snapping jaws the nassarid tried to devour him with. This one was much larger than the last one. Each of its maniacal thrusts forced Nurn to use more and more of his strength just to stay alive.

Nurn struggled under the weight of the nassarid. Its teeth gnashed together inches from his face. The stench of the thing's breath mingled with burning smell of fur and flesh to create a gut-wrenching mixture.

"Jerine!" Nurn cried as loud as he could.

He desperately hoped the elf was still alive and could help. His feet flailed against the beast's legs in a vain attempt to dislodge it. The sheer force of will was all he had. Even with his great strength, this thing seemed to be able to keep him pinned.

Then it happened. Adrenaline coursed through his veins as the creature lifted up to try and get a claw past his axe. He took the opening and hammered his first into the side of the thing's face as hard as he could. Without hesitation, he twisted the axe and drove the spike on the back of Séregon deep into the nassarid's chest.

An iron-like flavor filled his senses with each hit. Another heavy blow to the beast's jaw allowed him enough room to get his feet under him and he pushed as hard as he could. His axe freed itself from the thing's torso so he spun it and swung as hard as he could. He repeated his attacks again and again. Over and over. Nothing was going to stop him from stopping this thing.

A bone-chilling sensation washed over him and slowly brought him back to his senses. Flames licked at his fingers and arms from the nassarid's battered and desiccated corpse. Blood pooled around him and soaked into his pants where he knelt, half buried in the beast's body.

"It is dead," Jerine's words were softly spoken, yet held an edge of approval. "You will need to wash all of its blood off unless you want to burn.

Nurn nodded his understanding as he slowly stood. Waves of pain slowly replaced the fury-filled numbness that had consumed him. With each movement, he felt his muscles resist the cramps that threatened to stop him.

"There were two in the last tent," Nurn unnecessarily reported.

"There were another two in the tent beside it," Jerine advised. "The fire was a good idea. It allowed me to surprise them."

"Next time I think we may need to coordinate our actions a little better," Nurn replied somberly. "I don't think I can survive another attack like that."

"Hopefully you won't have to," the elf said sagely. "Before we go into the cavern, it might be best if we rested for a bit.

"Agreed," Nurn nodded.

He looked over to where the elf stood and was amazed that he could see him. The elf's cloak was thrown over one shoulder and revealed a few gaping wounds across his torso. Although Nurn recalled seeing Jerine fight Morcant in Hornshir, he hadn't recalled seeing him this battered.

"Too bad you elves are so small," Nurn attempted to make a little light of the situation, "otherwise I would ask if there was any armor lying around in the tents.

Jerine snickered at the jest. He knew the guardian had been right to want to search the area before they blindly entered the cavern. The only thing Nurn really regretted was resisting the guardian's plans so vehemently.

The final bridal swayed on its hook as Hessa finished brushing Onas's horse. It was peaceful, more so than the rest of the evening had been. Although she loved Aves, her sister needed so much attention. Hessa really worried about how her sister was going to survive without her.

"I see you both made it home safely," the voice sliced through the silence.

Hessa's eyes widened when she heard the voice. Small bumps played across her skin. It followed them. She wasn't sure how, but it some managed it. Her mind raced in blind panic. The helm sat on her bed inside the house.

"Galadril, I hadn't expected to see you again," Hessa called out into the darkness.

"I had to make sure you were safe," the dragon replied softly.

"I am now," Hessa admitted. "But I was attacked by Onas. I was a fool for thinking that he was a friend."

"I warned you about the deviousness of the Dekkari. They are good at gaining trust and just as skillful at breaking it." Galadril agreed.

Hessa relaxed a little as their conversation progressed. She still felt in complete control of her actions, unlike the last time they met. Although she wasn't sure why the dragon was not trying to control her, she was happy it wasn't.

"What about dragons?" Hessa asked a little hesitantly. "The last time we met, you weren't exactly friendly toward us. But when we parted, I felt there was some sort of bond. To me, it seemed almost as if we had started to become friends."

"Dragons are unique. Like humans, each of us is different, but in general, we are cautious. Once a silvern dragon gives a pledge, we honor it. No matter the circumstances leading up to giving it. Other types are different, depending on their race and what they experienced throughout their lifetimes"

"Ok, but I don't recall any pledges being exchanged," Hessa added conspiratorially.

She walked cautiously to the doorway of the stables. Her feet tingled in anticipation. Hessa wanted to see the dragon again, but she was afraid to let it know she didn't have the helm with her.

"Between us there was none," its deep voice rumbled lightly, "but that does not mean I am not bound to a pledge I made with another."

"May I ask about this pledge you made on my behalf?" Her heart beat rapidly as she asked.

Hessa felt the need to lean against the door frame for stability. She pivoted slightly and pressed her weight against it. The aged timbers felt good through her cloak. Their strength made her feel safer as they spoke.

"What would you like to know?" Galadril replied smoothly. "I may answer, that is if I fell it is something you need to know."

"Fair enough," Hessa nodded. "Who did you make the pledge to and how does it apply to me?"

"Good questions," the dragon said. She could tell by the light tone that the dragon weighed its words before it spoke. "It seems that I have made a few pledges that involve you, one more recently than the others. How they apply is simple, I have been asked to watch over your safety and the Helm of Durius."

"By whom?" Hessa cut in impatiently.

"A few different people, most recently it was a shadow walker." There was a hint of mirth in its voice as it spoke and this confused Hessa a little. "The promises I made in the past were made to those that have passed this world's veil. Those I will not reveal."

"When you say that you will 'watch over my safety,' what do you mean exactly? Are you going to follow me around?" Hessa felt a degree of paranoia awaken in the back of her head.

"How am I going to explain this dragon to Namir and the others? More importantly, how am I going to survive it? This thing might not understand a tryst or a look exchanged in a moment of passion. Is it going to kill anyone I argue with?" These thoughts flew through her head faster than she could ask them.

"Wh-why me? H-how did I become so important?" She stammered.

"Relax child," Galadril replied. "I will not be invasive. However, I will check on you from time to time. As far as why you are so important, that one is easy. You matter to the shadow walker. You also have stumbled into the greater skein of things and are now in possession of one of the great artifacts of power. These items were given to the Gods by the Lafor to create and maintain this realm."

"The helm I found is one of these?" Hessa asked in awe.

"It is, as is Zelios. Both of which I have vowed to keep from the hands of those who would use them unjustly," the dragon informed. "That is one of the reasons I will watch over you. If you choose to use the helm wisely I will not try and strip it from you. However, should you decide to subvert its power, we will be at odds."

"I wouldn't," Hessa replied quickly. "I mean, from what

little I know of it, I can understand the temptation. But I would never do that, I couldn't"

"I know," Galadril said softly in another attempt to ease Hessa's fears. "I discovered as much in our last encounter."

"What did you promise Deracai?" Hessa hoped the dragon would tell her.

She knew what she felt for the shadow walker, but she was unsure of his feelings for her. Deep down she wanted him to be as attracted to her as she was for him. He was too hard to read and, although this frustrated her, it also added to his allure.

"So you know his name," Galadril said mirthfully. "He asked me to keep watch over you and to keep you as safe as possible. He seems to know about your propensity for getting involved in dangerous situations."

"Did he say why he thinks I need to be looked after?" Hessa asked a little hurt. Although she was glad he thought about her, she could take care of herself without his help.

"He did not," Galadril replied. "But he has never asked me to look after a person, even when they have one of these artifacts."

A warm sensation spread through Hessa. "He cares for me," she thought to herself. "He really does." The warm glow spread across her face and hands as she basked in it.

"Is there a way I can contact you when I need help instead of making you follow me everywhere?" Hessa asked.

She wasn't even sure if her request was possible, but she felt like she had to ask. After all, if Deracai could seemingly travel through shadows, maybe Galadril had some other unimaginable abilities.

"There is," Galadril answered. "I am leaving you with a gift. Since you feel safer staying in the stable, I have hung it on a hook outside. Guard it with your life and only use it when there are no other options left."

"I shall," Hessa agreed.

Hessa waited until she was certain the dragon had left. Although she understood Galadril meant her no harm, she still felt uneasy around the dragon without the power of the helm to protect her. Something about how he had manipulated them all the first time she met it did not sit well with her.

After a few long moments, and her body's insistence on sleep, she ventured through the stable's open door. She glanced around the open snow-covered yard between the house and the stable, just to make sure the dragon had not tried to fool her. Once she was certain it was clear, Hessa made her way to the hook Galadril had mentioned.

Her gift was not hard to find. A fine golden chain sparkled in the moonlight. It was looped over a hook her mother must have used for a gardening tool of some sort.

At the end of the chain was a pendant. Hessa's hand trembled as she carefully scooped it up in her hand. The silver dragon faced pendant glittered in the pale light and its gleaming sapphire eyes stared back at her.

Without thinking, she unclasped the chain and placed it around her neck. It felt unusually warm in the night's chilled air, but she didn't mind. It was comforting and beautiful. Hessa stared down at the pendant one last time before she decided to go into the house and find her bed.

Chapter Twenty:
Displays

"Is that a dragon?" Faris asked over his shoulder to Skara.

He was completely taken off guard by the distant rumble. Nothing made much sense to him concerning this assignment he had agreed to take. Everything from their targets to the ways they were asked to deal with them seemed to conform to anything the veteran soldier new.

"A dragon of darqueness to be exact," Skara confirmed as she darted through the trees.

"If she had a dragon, why did she send us?" Faris asked incredulously.

"We prefer to do thing a little more discreetly and with finesse when we can," she advised. "When that fails, we have other, less subtle, options available to us."

The felinoid was lithe and this made her much more suited to this mode of transportation than he was. Faris panted as he struggled to keep up with her. He wished he could have taken a horse at least. If they were on horseback, the trip wouldn't be so hard.

"I thought you said you know a faster route. So far this seems to be the same as the way we came." He shouted to her fleeing form.

"There is a faster way," Skara called back, "and we are almost there."

"I hope so. I can't keep this pace up the whole way back to Hornshir." Faris grumbled to himself.

"You won't have to," Skara confirmed.

There was a sense of mirth in her voice that Faris hated. She was always too smug and aloof for his liking. Not to mention the fact that she seemed to hear almost everything he said.

"Just another one of her more annoying traits," Faris snickered to himself silently.

Keeping an eye on the nassarid became an increasingly difficult task. Especially since the trees blocked most of the moon's light. The thickening undergrowth and deepening drifts of snow forced him to stumble more than once as they progressed.

Faris's breath caught in his throat as he followed Skara into a thicket. It was beautiful. She stood statuesque in the middle of a small clearing. Everything was snow covered and, in the moonlight, had a silvery blue sheen to it. It was pristine and untouched, even the snow that separated them.

"Are you planning on standing there gaping all night, or will you join me so we can get back to Hornshir?" Skara admonished him.

The annoying playful lilt was still in her smug voice. Even so, her rebuke stung his pride. He would be so much happier when he no longer had to work with her.

Faris watched Skara kneel down and dig into the snow. He couldn't quite see what she was doing, but he was certain it was nothing he had ever seen before. Faris needed to make sure it wasn't a trap of some sort meant to kill him, so he waited until she was finished. When she started to rise back to her feet, he carefully made his way over to her.

"Are you ready?" Skara asked bluntly. "Ready for what?" Faris replied.

He was still unsure of her motives and intent. Something just did not feel right about this. It was the same feeling he ignored all those years ago when he first met Skara at the road to Watch Keep. Back then he had made a terrible choice and a part of him hoped he wasn't about to do the same thing again.

"For the quick way back to your room in Hornshir," her beguiling voice had a soothing effect that he hated.

"Let's be done with this. I hate your riddles now just as much as I have in the past." Faris spat out.

"Make sure to stand close to me," she purred as she stepped closer to him.

He felt her body press close against him. Her hot breath scorched its way across his neck. Faris was certain that some men may have found this alluring, but he hated it.

The thought of copulating with an animal like Skara turned his stomach.

"Alda torathu riktem eglimach!" Skara said once in a soft, yet commanding tone.

As she spoke, she quickly extended her left hand above them. Skara had concealed a small vial filled with some sort of silvery powder. He noticed the powder glowed as it spilled from the vial.

Faris stared in wonder when a small breeze picked up and whipped this fine glowing dust in a spiral around them. Even some of the snow was caught in the sudden wind and flew up from their feet.

Then it grew brighter. So bright that Faris felt he was going to go blind because of the intense white light. A slight tingle slipped through his clothes from where Skara pressed tightly against him. It pervaded his thoughts and every inch of his being.

Just as quickly as it started, the light was gone. It didn't fade. The brightness just was not there anymore. With it went the tingling sensation and the bitter coldness of the forest.

Slowly the details of his chambers faded into view. Everything was as he had left them. The small table sat undisturbed beside his bed. His spare weapons hung in their proper place on his wall. Even the stack of papers he had left on top of the flat-topped chest at the foot of the bed looked like no one had touched them.

The only difference was it was quiet, far too quiet for the barracks at this hour at least. Normally he could hear his men as they ate. The guards usually swapped stories about their day at the gate or some belligerent drunk they had to straighten out at one of the many taverns.

Faris stepped over to his window and stuck his head out. Nothing seemed wrong. The city sprawled out below him, brightly lit and extravagant just as it always was. Some of the now familiar sounds of raucous drinking and the usual parties floated up to his ears, but nothing came from the guard towers.

"So we are home then," Faris said as he pulled himself back into his quarters.

"We are," Skara agreed. "But I can tell that something's bothering you."

"It's nothing," Faris lied.

"You are right. The unease you are feeling is just the remnants of the spell I cast. It will pass."

Faris simply nodded his response. He wasn't sure how to tell her that something felt off. For that matter, he did not know if he even wanted to. She had too many secrets. Besides, this had nothing to do with her. He would look into it on his own.

"I'll have to call an all-hands tomorrow," Faris muttered to himself.

"Feeling a little threatened?" Skara asked playfully. "No, the lack of comradery is just odd. Don't you have somewhere you need to be?" He asked.

"I do," Skara admitted. "I wanted to make sure you will have your report ready for our mistress tomorrow. You know how she hates to be left waiting for things."

"Worry about your own report. Mine will be made on time." Faris snapped at the felinoid.

He stared at her long enough to make them both feel a little awkward. Faris could tell his ploy worked when she started to fidget with her armor. After a few moments, she walked over to his window and crawled through it.

Faris watched as Skara slipped out his window. He moved closer to it so he could keep her in his sights for as long as possible. Her lithe form was no more than a shadow as she slipped across the rooftops far below him.

"Now I need to check on my men," he thought to himself.

Although a part of him longed to crawl into his bed for the night, he knew he couldn't. Instead, he had to figure out why his men were being so quiet. Something was wrong and he knew it. He refused to rest until he could get to the bottom of it.

Faris quickly stripped out of his armor and clothing. He removed the ceramic basin form his shelf and walked over to the water pump installed along the outside wall to his room. Two swift pumps on the handle sent just enough water spilling into the basin for him to shave and clean the most important parts.

Once he finished, Faris crossed over to his armoire and pulled out his standard uniform. He slipped into it and grabbed his spare set of leather armor. After a few moments, he strapped on his spare sword and daggers. He knew he would have to have someone clean his primary set in the morning, but he could not wait until then to make his presence known.

The door to his room opened begrudgingly. To his surprise the hallway was dark. The faint sounds of the city were muted by the thick walls of the guard rooms. Even so, the guards were usually noisy enough to fill the void. Tonight was an exception.

Faris crept down the empty hallway uneasily. He cautiously entered the darkened guard room. This was where his men typically sat and shared storied and mead. Tonight, however, the room was dark. No one sat at the tables and even the fire that usually burned in the hearth was out.

He glanced around the room. Faris hoped to spot something that would give him a hint about what had changed in his absence. Without a thought to his safety, he knelt at the fireplace and restacked the logs. Two solid strikes against his flint allowed the fire to blaze back to life.

"Excuse me, but what do you think you are doing?" The voice was gruff and unfamiliar to Faris. He could easily tell the person was used to being listened to by the air of authority it held.

"I was about to ask you the same thing," Faris said as she stood. "Why is this fire out and where are the men?" He snapped as he turned and faced the person who had addressed him.

"Why should I tell you?" The man in a guard's armor asked, obviously disgusted at being questioned.

"While I do not know your name, you should at least recognize the uniform of your commanding officer," Faris's voice grew threatening as she spoke. He took two steps toward the guard in the far entrance to the room as he continued, "Don't worry. I promise I will learn your name and I promise to make sure you never forget me."

The threat was a real one and he sensed the guard realized it. The fact that he physically shrank under Faris's withering stare only confirmed what he had already determined. This was one of the newer recruits hired after Faris left for Ellsted.

"Now, where are my men and why is this room abandoned?" Faris snapped at the guard before he could say another word.

"They are on patrol," the guard replied quickly.

"Is that how you were taught to report to your superior?" Faris asked angrily.

He stalked closer to the guard. With each step, he took he allowed a little more of his wrath seep into his words.

"No sir," the guard replied visibly shaken. His voice cracked as Faris approached, but he stood his ground resolutely.

"That is better. What about the men that are not patrolling? Where are they?" Faris barked, now only a few feet away from the cowering soldier.

"Asleep sir. Everyone who had a shift during the day was instructed to get enough rest for tomorrow." The response was quavering, yet swift.

"By whose authority?" Faris demanded.

"The mayor sent an elven representative. I think his name was Landolin, sir." Now the guard looked at Faris in complete unbridled fear.

Faris knew the guard could see the anger burning in his brown eyes and smiled. "So now we are taking orders from elves. I won't have it! Go and have the acting chief meet me in my room. Once you have finished your rounds, I expect you to be there as well. I want to have your full report, then you can see to cleaning my gear. Do you understand?"

"Aye, sir!" The guard replied.

He had practically yelled his response as he tried to run backward away from Faris. It was comical to see the man practically fall over himself in his haste to get away. While Faris was tempted to chuckle, he knew this was serious. If Landolin had seen the mayor while he was gone, he may have to support his right to maintain his guard the way he wanted.

"Damn you Skara," he muttered under his breath as he watched the guard stumble away into the dark hallway.

"We have to take his saddle and horseback to the Dekkari!" Aves protested. "They don't belong to us. If we keep them, it's theft."

"I know, but I also don't want them seeking revenge for killing Onas," Hessa explained carefully.

"We didn't have a choice though," Aves said shakily. "I didn't want to kill him, but I didn't want you to die either."

"They might not see it that way. Neither of us knows how Dekkari law works. I think it would be best if we use the spare saddle my mother has here and take his saddle with us. Then, instead of talking to them when we get to Ellsted, we go to Armani and ask him what we should do." Hessa said softly. "Surely as a previous Dekkari he would know what the best course of action should be."

"But they know Onas left Ellsted with me. We were in their encampment outside of town and we went together into the forest on his horse. When the Dekkari see me in Ellsted without him they will know something is wrong."

"That can't be helped, so let's not worry too much about it." Hessa soothed. "Before we go, we need to eat and pack something for the road, just in case we get lost."

"Now you doubt my ability to find our way home via Onas's path," Aves said a little indignantly.

"No, I'm just trying to make sure we are over prepared. Father once told me, 'it is best to be over prepared than under.' I admit that I had no idea what he meant back then, but I get it now." Hessa admitted as she deftly changed the topic. "It's winter. We have no idea what might happen. What if a blizzard starts and we get turned around? Or if we take shelter or even hide from wolves? We might need the extra provisions. There is no telling what might happen on the way home."

"Okay, okay. I agree. Let's just not waste too much time. It is already heading toward midday. Why don't you cook us some breakfast and ready something for lunch? I'll go up to our rooms and get us some extra clothing. I think I saw a couple leather satchels in the room I slept in last night. Those should work for the clothing and the extra provisions." The old authoritative tone in Aves's voice once had resurfaced.

"That sounds good. I should have the food ready in about an hour. Do you think you will have the necessary clothing picked out and packed by then?" Hessa asked demurely.

"I will, I promise," Aves said as she quickly left the room and headed for the stairs.

"Has anyone checked on the prisoners?" Tipin asked Carness over the large stack of debris that separated them.

"Not yet. We need to get the hatch cleared of rubble before we can," Carness called back.

"We should make that a priority," Tipin replied as he lowered the last piece of rock he had pulled from a walkway to clear it out.

"Agreed," Carness said as he too set down a large rock.

Both of them slowly walked toward the main entryway. Although most of the Council Hall had collapsed, somehow it remained standing. Like the resilient nature of Ellsted's spirit and will to survive.

"We thought we would find you two here," Namir's voice carried across the debris.

"We?" Carness asked.

He turned to look at Namir. His eyes narrowed a little as he saw Valeron behind the boy. Both in the same stride and both had the same look on their faces. Their determination was easy to understand, especially given the circumstances.

"I see the two of you have had a chance to talk," Carness said once the two of them were close.

"We have," Namir confided. "That is one of the reasons we are here."

"Can we talk while we walk?" Tipin asked. "We are trying to check on the prisoners survived."

"We can," Namir agreed. "In fact, I would rather we discuss our matter once we are away from the earshot of others."

"Good. Please feel free to join us," Carness said quietly.

He turned toward the sloping hallway leading to where petitioners addressed the council. Carness heard their footsteps behind him and it was reassuring. The constable slowly led them to the end of the hall. Once there he placed his right hand on the wall. He pressed firmly against it and waited for it to open.

"It might need a more sturdy push after the attack," Tipin offered.

"By all means, my friend," Carness replied. He stepped away from the section of wall and motioned for the smith to try his luck as he completed his sentence, "feel free and try."

Tipin grinned a little at his old friend and then moved forward. He placed his right hand on the wall, just as the constable had, and he pushed. His massive arm rippled with the effort. Once finished he lowered his arm and waited.

A deep vibrational groan came from the wall less than a second after Tipin's attempt. A metallic grinding noise started to rumble as well then stopped. The wall shuddered a little as the noises started, but even these slight movements stopped in unison with the sounds.

"It looks like it's stuck," Valeron said with a hint of laughter in his voice.

"It is," Carness agreed.

"What now?" Namir asked hesitantly.

"Now it's time to use a little force. It looks like we will have to rebuild this wall as well Carness," Tipin said as he glanced over his shoulder at the others.

"You might want to move back, sire," Valeron stated bluntly to Namir. "I've seen this before, although it was many years ago." His final few words were clearly meant as a jab at Tipin's age.

"Calanari are longer lived than humans," Tipin replied back mirthfully. "And sa'ouvant, he is right. It is best that you move back a little. This is going to be a bit messy."

Tipin obviously waited for the rest of his companions to give him a little more room. Once he was satisfied they were far enough away, he slid his axe off his back. He closed his eyes for a few moments and mouthed something Carness could not see.

Then, without warning, he spun his axe in his hand and swung the long butt spike at the wall. Tipin let it sink in halfway before pulling up on the handle. As he did, he yanked it out of the wall and spun. This time the spike impacted in an upward swing. Deftly the Calanari pushed down on the haft and pulled it free from the mortar that held the stone in place.

Small pieces of rock and dirt rained down as the smith made short work of the wall. Each strike was precise and embedded in the mortar connecting each of the large stones. As each stone was freed, Tipin managed to slide it out and powdered them in one smooth motion.

Carness spared a look at Namir and saw the look of wonder on his face. The constable smiled and realized he must have worn the same look when he first saw Tipin in action. The Calanari was just as impressive back then. He had helped them excavate a secret tunnel at Watch Keep, the tunnel that had wound up saving their lives.

Within a matter of moments, Tipin had the passage cleared. The smith carefully wiped off his axe with his cloak and closed his eyes. The Calanari's lips moved again in what Carness figured was a silent prayer of some kind. Tipin had always been highly religious, a trait the constable both admired and envied.

"That was amazing," Namir said quietly.

"Yes, it was. I would say a once in a lifetime event, but

this is my second time seeing it," Valeron replied unbidden.

"Now that the way is cleared," Carness cut in, "I think it is best that we check in on the prisoners. Tipin will be down in a few minutes. He needs to finish his ritual." The constable said before he disappeared down the tunnel.

"Very well, after you," Namir motioned to the Knight as he spoke.

"If you insist," the Knight replied.

Carness heard the exchange and smiled a wolfish grin. "The boy really knows what he is doing," the constable thought to himself.

He walked around the room and lit the torches before the others made it down the stairs. The constable easily freed a torch from its sconce. Carness decided to check on the prisoners while the others made their way down the stairs.

"Wait in the main chamber, I will check on the prisoners," Carness called over his shoulder.

The Constable studied the walls and ceiling as he hurried down the corridor. From what he could tell the structure seemed to be solid. Nothing seemed damaged in any way.

When he came to the first cell, he paused and opened the small window in the door. He held the torch above the gaping hole so he could see into the darkened room. Carness was shocked at what he saw.

He sprinted to the next door down and threw the window open. Horror filled his veins as he peered into the cell. It was just like the last one. Part of him feared the other four would be the same. But he had to make sure.

The next door was just across the hall. And Carness slowly opened the portal. His heart sank as he looked at the burning remains, just like the other two. The constable continued down the hall to the final two doors. He paused before he opened the little windows. Carness knew what he was going to find.

"Ea, guide their souls to Your side," Carness whispered

as he turned and retraced his steps back to the main chamber.

Carness's footsteps fell heavily on the flagstones under his feet as he entered the chamber. He saw Tipin enter from the stairs across from him. The constable scanned the room and saw Namir and Valeron each standing opposite each other as well.

The king-to-be looked like he was just meandering around the room, but Carness knew otherwise. He saw Namir glance ever-so-slightly at Valeron as if to keep an eye on him. There was something about the Knight that the boy did not trust and Carness was glad of it.

The constable cleared his throat to get everyone's attention, "We are away from the ears of others, how may I be of service my liege?"

"I just have one quick question," Namir stated bluntly. "Now that Armani is dead, who is the acting mayor of Ellsted? Does the job fall on your shoulders Saril's or Allair's?"

"Normally Allair would become the acting mayor. However, since Armani died due to an invasion, I become acting mayor until we can get things under control and back to some semblance of order." Carness explained.

"In that case, mister mayor, the Crown has a request," Namir said coolly. "I request we get to the bottom of the attacks immediately. No more wasting time clearing rubble, instead, we need to find those responsible for this and bring them to justice."

"We already know Armani was behind the attack," Tipin replied from the stairway.

"No," Valeron interjected, "we know he was responsible for helping the thing find its prey. However, I doubt we know who actually sent the dragon here."

"True," Carness cut in. "And I agree, my liege," the constable turned and faced Namir as he continued. "So I ask that we start with us here in the room. As the leaders of this community, and the country, as well as those who would protect the populace from harm, we need to be certain we are all cleared of any wrongdoing."

"Agreed," Namir nodded. "Sir Valeron, please sit in the chair." He motioned toward the only chair in the room as he spoke. "I ask that you answer all of the questions asked honestly and completely. Free from malice or deception. You may speak freely about all matters, even those of the Crown past and present."

Valeron nodded and took a seat. As he did Carness and Nurn both took a step forward to block any perceived exit the Knight may have. Namir kept his eyes riveted on the Knight as he paced around him.

"Sir Valeron, do you agree to the requests made by the Crown?" Carness asked diligently.

"I do," Valeron acquiesced.

"Then I will leave you three to this. I have things I must see to," Namir looked at Carness as he spoke. "I expect a full report of your findings. I am also going to call an emergency council meeting at the Gathering Place this evening."

Carness nodded his understanding to Namir and waited until the boy left before he turned his attention to the Knight. "Then let's start with a simple question. Why did you kill all five of my prisoners?" Carness leveled a wolfish glare at the Knight and locked gazes with him as he asked.

Namir's eyes burned as he stepped back into the light of the day. He waited until his eyes adjusted before he stepped free from the passage and into the debris field that was once the Council Hall.

A bitter wind caught Namir's hood as he surveyed the hectic scene. Most of the townsfolk had been engaged in sorting through the debris in their search for survivors. He hated what had happened because of him, but Namir knew he could not do much about it.

"Allair? Alequa? Saril?" Namir called out as he walked through the remains of the Council Hall.

"Over here," Saril's frail-sounding voice echoed back to Namir.

Namir noted the direction and headed for it. Even the surrounding streets looked unfamiliar to him in the aftermath. Namir thought the devastation had been contained to the Council Hall, but now he realized the full extent of it.

Although the dragon had attacked the council, it originally landed in the square. The beast destroyed the two buildings on either side of the square. To Namir, it was as if the beast had to search for its prey before deciding to attack the Council Hall.

"You wanted to speak with us sa'ouvant?" Alequa's voice pulled Namir from his observations and back to more immediate matters.

"Is Allair with you two?" Namir asked as he looked at the makeshift infirmary.

Three large sheets of white canvas had been secured to the top of what was left of the fountain. Several cots and blankets were scattered underneath them. All of which was occupied by wounded people.

"No, she went to find Aves and Hessa," Saril answered as he adjusted the bandages on one of the wounded townsfolk.

"Thank you. I am going to call an emergency council meeting. I think we should hold it at the Gathering Place since the Council Hall has been destroyed." Namir said. "I will find Allair and let her know. Alequa, is there any way you can heal the wounded faster?"

"My gifts are from Tayant. I can only heal as She allows," the elf answered carefully.

"I am sure you are doing as best you can," Saril interceded.

"Thank you for your service," Namir said a little rebuked. "In case Allair returns before I find her, please let her know I went to search Armani's house."

"I will tell her," Alequa replied.

Namir nodded and turned toward the road to Armani's house. Memories of running through the streets played through his mind. He remembered what it was like last year. Nothing could go wrong. Life was an adventure just waiting to be had. Nothing like it is now.

He fought the urge to leave the streets and climb onto the rooftops. Namir knew it would be much more dangerous with all this debris. Besides, he was not sure if he could even get there using it. Too many buildings had been either damaged or destroyed.

Namir was lost in thought as his feet retraced the path he had taken so many times. A route he once claimed he could do blindfolded. As he rounded the final corner to Armani's house he tripped.

His arms flailed as he struggled to catch himself. The world momentarily spun and shifted under his feet. To Namir's relief, he felt something soft break his fall.

"Are you taking lessons from the smithy boys?" Aves's shrill voice erupted out from underneath Namir's body.

A warm feeling spread across Namir's cheeks as he scrambled to get off of her. "I'm sorry," Namir stammered his apology.

"Let me help," Hessa offered.

Namir grabbed her outstretched hand and used it for leverage as he stood. Once he was sure of his footing, he reached down and helped Aves to her feet. He quickly brushed snow off of his cloak and pants as his friend did the same.

"So, Allair said you were looking for us," Aves said as she finished dusting the snow off the front of her bodice.

"I have been," Namir admitted. "I wanted to make sure you were both safe."

"What happened?"Hessa asked as she looked toward the town square.

"You guys didn't hear it last night?" Namir asked incredulously.

"We weren't in town," Aves offered hesitantly. "Aves and I were at my mother's house," Hessa said

quickly.

"I didn't know your mother had a house," Namir said somewhat confused.

"We didn't know either," Hessa replied. "So, what happened?"

"I think it would be best to talk about it in your house," Namir said as he turned to Aves. "There is too much to discuss and sometimes having familiar surroundings makes things easier to hear."

He hated not just telling them, but he had to make sure no one overheard them. Namir knew he would have hated to learn about his parent's death in the open like this. Besides, he had a feeling there was something the girls were not telling him. He hoped if they were at their place they might be more willing to open up to him.

"Fine," Aves said a little perturbed. "We can go back home, again."

The three of them walked in silence. The sounds of stones being moved were muffled by the large drifts of snow. For a moment all of Namir's problems seemed distant, almost like a surreal and demented dream.

Wood scraping against wood pulled Namir back from his thoughts. The warm rush of air pulled a sweet aroma from the interior of the house with it. He watched as both girls entered the house.

Namir waited for a brief moment before he entered. He had to plan how he was going to tell them about Armani's death and the charges against him. Their father had been a mentor for him and he hated the implications that surrounded the mayor's death. He needed to spare them as much pain as he could, he mulled over his thoughts as he stepped into the house.

Hessa stood waiting inside and took his cloak from him. She had slipped back into her role as a maid so seamlessly that it took Namir a moment to realize she what she had done.

"Thank you," he said to Hessa as he followed her into the mayor's living room.

"Think nothing of it sa'ouvant," Hessa said as she curtseyed.

"Please, when we are in private you do not need to address me like that," he said somewhat embarrassed.

He noticed that Aves was already sitting in one of the four chairs, so he sat in the one closest to the hearth. He could tell something was bothering her. Namir glanced at Hessa and motioned to one of the other chairs.

She shook her head as she said, "I will be right back."

With no other explanation, she disappeared up the stairs. Namir took a deep breath and mentally rehearsed what he was going to say to the girls. He was certain Hessa would take the news better than Aves, but it would still be difficult to for him to say.

"Did Allair say where she was going?" Namir asked to break the building silence.

"I think she said there were things she needed form the smithy," Aves answered quietly. "What is going on Namir? Why are things changing so much?"

Namir looked closely at his friend. Almost imperceptible tremors shook her randomly. "There is more wrong than I thought," Namir thought as Aves shivered again.

"What do you mean?" Namir asked as innocently as he could.

"Ever since we returned from Hornshir things have been different," Aves blurted out. "I'm not just saying this because Nurn, Halin, and Jaconis are not here. Everything has changed."

"You mean like Hessa's mother having a house?" Namir asked.

"Yes," she sighed as she continued, "but there is more to it. We found things there, bad things. Things Armani had given her. My father is not a good man, Namir." Tears streamed down her face and her body shook as she spoke.

"What do you mean Armani was not a good man?" Namir asked. He had been taken off guard by Aves's comment.

"He tried to kill Natlia. He gave her something as a gift, a mirror," her eyes widened as she spoke and her tone shifted to a conspiratorial one. "The mirror is evil and he gave it her knowing what it could do."

Namir felt it difficult to follow his friend's thoughts. Aves had never been this scared or scattered in all of the years he had known her. Whatever she saw had frightened her and he desperately wanted to know what it was.

"Go on," he said soothingly. Namir hoped to ease her fears so she would elaborate more.

"It was magical and held some sort of thing in it," Hessa said as she walked in the room. "He had given it to her as a wedding present."

"So he knew your father?" Namir asked Hessa. "You might say that," Hessa admitted. She walked over to the long table in the middle of the room and set a helm on it. "It seems that Armani was supposed to marry Natlia."

"Armani was your father?" Namir said in complete and utter disbelief.

"He was," this time it was Aves who spoke. "He admitted to me that he loved both Natlia and Shara deeply."

"Wow," Namir said amazed. "So you two really are

related."

Hessa smiled at the thought. "Yes, we are sisters. Now before, when I was on my way back down the stairs, you said, 'Armani was.' What do you mean was?"

"There is no easy way to say this," Namir said softly, "He is dead."

"What?" Aves practically screamed. "How?"

"A dragon attacked the council last night. Daffer and Armani both were killed by its flames."

"Why did it attack?" Hessa asked in disbelief.

"It was after me," Namir admitted. "But someone helped it find its victims. They were not the only ones who died. Haradine was eaten by the monster." Namir took a moment to let his words sink in before he continued. "We believe Armani was the one that helped it."

"Why? That does not sound like my father," Aves erupted.

"But it was. I baited the dragon to breathe at where the person was. He was on Armani's dais. It could only have been him," Namir explained.

"He has done quite a bit he never told us about," Hessa said quietly. "But to have a dragon attack the town. It is too hard to believe. He left his people for the chance to be mayor of this town."

"He left his people? I thought Armani was from Ellsted," Namir asked.

"He was one of the Iohai Dek Kir," Hessa confided. When she realized Namir had no idea what she was saying she added, "a gypsy lord. It seems my parents were both Dekkari and Aves is a half-blood.

"Dekkari?" Namir asked. He felt like he was missing something.

"The Dekkari are the race others call gypsies," Aves said sullenly. "So you are certain about my father's involvement?"

"I am," Namir said bluntly. "But the rest of Ellsted does not need to know. I plan on speaking for him at the funeral and I am not going to mention anything about his role in the attack." It was a promise he felt strongly about. "There is no need to make things any harder for the two of you."

"Thank you," Aves all but muttered.

"If that is all you needed to tell us, I have something you should know," Hessa confided.

"Go ahead," Namir replied as he settled into the chair a little more.

"We also encountered a dragon. His name is Galadril. He is the silvern dragon tasked with protecting the Artifacts of Power." She saw Namir's worried look cross his face, so she continued before he could interrupt her. "That helmet is the Helm of Durius. My mother wrote about it in her journal. Like Arras, Natlia inscribed the locations of where some of them are hidden in her journal."

"She wrote it in that journal there?" Namir asked a little shocked.

"Wait, you can see the journal?" Hessa asked. The lingering sound of disbelief clung heavily to her words as she spoke.

"I can. Why, am I not supposed to see it?" Namir asked pointedly.

"I can't see it," Aves's words dripped with an odd sort of melancholy.

"The shadow walker told me that only those related to my mother and Aras can see it," Hessa said in wonder.

"Maybe I can see it because of Zelios," Namir said as he motioned to his amulet. "But tell me more about the helm. What can it do?"

"It is easier if I show you," Hessa said as she reached over and lifted the helm off of the table.

Chapter Twenty-One: Plagues

The cold air stung Namir's lungs as he stood in the bitter solitude. There was no discernable breeze, yet small flakes of frost danced in an unknowable current. His grey eyes followed a few of them as they fell in their mesmerizing dance. His thoughts shifted about in his head. They darted from bitter memories to remorse for past deeds and unspoken sentiments.

"How can they both be dead?" His words hung in a cloud of steam as he spoke them softly.

The scenes from two days ago careened through his mind unbidden. The walls of the Council Hall erupted again in his mind. The battle raged anew every time he closed his eyelids. With each blink, he heard the sounds in flashes and could not stop them. His senses reeled from the acrid scent of blood and mortar stirred up in the flood of memories.

The deafening sounds of stone and glass exploded over and over in his mind. The citizen's screams echoed in Namir's mind as well. Those souls unfortunate enough to be caught under the debris from the dragon's entrance at least.

"How many of them were there?" Namir pondered silently.

Phantasmal shouts mingled with screams as he thought

about what had happened. Steel against steel haunted his mind as he watched his friends fight against the nightmarish beast helplessly. The softer noises of stones and pebbles buried themselves under the intense heat of dragon fire.

"Only twelve died, although quite a few more were injured," Zelios offered.

Namir took solace in the soft blue light that accompanied her response. Its paleness reflected across the snow's surface and momentarily turned his work blue. Just like during the battle. His mind slid unchecked to the fight and the pain it had brought him. All of the plans he had made in haste, more out of desperation than anything, haunted him.

"Make it stop, please," Namir begged aloud.

"If that is what you desire," the gentleness of her voice in his mind surprised Namir. "However, I do not recommend it. Many have died to give you a chance to declare your heritage. Much more will do the same. Would you dishonor their memory? Or, instead, would you rather remember their names and deeds so their deaths can serve a higher purpose?" Zelios asked softly.

"Of course I do," Namir thought back to the amulet bitterly. "I don't know if I'm strong enough."

He purposely forced himself to look at the trees instead of the snow. Namir knew Zelios's blue glow would reflect across its white surface and he did not want to slip back into the battle. Although he saw the needles of the tree turn blue, his plan worked. He remained in control.

"Strength is gained through trial and experience. You will get stronger and grow into what you need to become," Zelios offered.

"How do I function until then?" Namir shouted.

"By taking the time needed to grieve," the melodic voice

said from behind him.

"Easy to say," Namir muttered as he turned to see who had spoken.

To his surprise, he saw two cloaked ladies stood just a few feet behind him. Somehow the pair had managed to approach him completely silently. His eyes flashed between each of them. Their burgundy cloaks were almost identical. Both were thick and velvety. Both covered each of the lady's diminutive forms completely.

"And who do I owe the honor of this advice?" Namir asked helplessly.

There was something familiar about the voice, but he couldn't place it, at least not now. Too much had happened too quickly. His mind spun through all of the possibilities and he came up blank.

To Namir's relief, both ladies removed their hoods in unison. Their beauty was breathtaking. Namir found his eyes moving from Allair's brown eyes and tanned features to the pale skin and azure blue ones of Alequa. Although he had seen both of them many times, he had never seen them like this.

They looked almost like sisters. Both of them had their hair pulled back and tied back with burgundy ribbons that matched their cloaks. Each of them wore matching white gowns. The combination of fabric and fur framed their exquisite features perfectly. They were both stunning examples of the best both of their races had to offer.

"It is easy to say," Allair replied calmly. "Especially since it is also the truth."

His friends' mother's voice was soft and gentle. It also held a musical quality he had never heard in her voice before. The sing-song pattern, though similar to the phrase spoken a moment before, held a slightly different tone to it.

"Alequa was the one that offered the first bit of advice," Namir deduced to himself.

"Namir, you need not grieve alone. But you do need to move through it. You also need to sort out your emotions," Alequa chimed in. "Normally this takes time. However, time is not a luxury for the Crown. You must work through this succinctly. As heir to the throne, everyone will expect you to say something at the funerals."

"Does the Crown always speak for the fallen?" Namir asked a little confused.

"If they are present at the time of death, they may," Allair offered. "They also are present for leaders of communities."

"And heroes of the Crown," Alequa interceded. "Daffer was one of the survivors of Watch Keep."

"That wasn't the man I knew," Namir objected. "How am I supposed to speak to something I know nothing about?"

"We can help. I can tell you of his heroism and his deeds," Allair said softly.

She glanced at the falling snow as she spoke. Namir knew there was something she was not saying, but he knew better than to pry. He never really noticed how beautiful she was. It was odd to think of his friends' mother that way, but it was true.

"You were there then?" Namir asked shocked. "Aye. Carness, Valeron, Daffer, Tipin and I all served there. We are the last of our unit and the final defense of the Crown." Her answer was curt and swift.

There was an edge to her voice Namir had never heard before. She was colder than she had ever been, colder and more distant. He was glad Tipin had survived the attack. If he too had fallen, he wasn't sure Allair would have survived it.

"Thank you, I will need to hear it," Namir acquiesced. "But it may be best if I had all the remaining heroes tell it to me at once. It will be faster and easier on you all."

"I appreciate it, my liege," Allair said with a slight bow.

"There is also the matter of Armani," Alequa added.

"He directed the dragon's attacks."

Sounds of pebbles tapping against the stones around him haunted Namir's mind. Slight sounds, soft sounds. No matter where he went they followed him. The clattering erupted from wooden beams and stone columns. Everything that could make a noise did. Nothing was safe and everything seemed to be a target for the incessant rain of pebbles.

"Namir," Allair said softly pulling him back from his thoughts.

"Agreed," Namir whispered his response. "I know what he did, I just can't begin to understand it."

He looked at each of the ladies in turn. Alequa's eyes were stunningly blue. They reminded Namir of Zelios. Both glowed with an almost otherworldly light, as had Haradine's.

"It must be the magical quality of the elves," he thought to himself.

"I fear no one can," Allair offered as solace. "And no one has to," Namir said solemnly. "What do you mean?" Alequa asked.

"I mean that I am not going to say anything about it. It wasn't the Armani I knew. It wasn't the Armani any of us knew." He could tell by the looks in their eyes they were confused by what he said, so he continued. "He has already paid for his crime. There is no sense in causing his loved ones more pain. I want my first acts as heir to help remove pain, not bring it."

"He was responsible for your uncle's death," Allair's voice held an unusual edge. It seemed different than the pained tone she had earlier. "Armani made an attempt on your life. We cannot cover this up. He needs to be buried as a criminal."

"I have made my decision," Namir answered.

"Armani killed Haradine," Alequa's voice was unusually tight. Her limbs practically shook as she glared at Namir. "He killed my daughter and you are going to let him get away with it?"

A fresh wave of disbelief washed over Namir. He had no idea his guard was the healer's daughter. Her anger was more than justified. Her daughter was dead because of him. That thought was bittersweet since she had lost her husband to his cause as well.

"Haradine was your daughter?" Namir said in disbelief. "Why wasn't I informed of this?"

"She had to prove herself to the elves on her own," Alequa said quietly.

"What do you mean that she needed to prove herself?" Namir asked.

"It's hard to explain," Alequa said demurely. "Please try," Namir suggested coolly. "I need to

understand why I was deceived. All of you, the elves, your

husband, even those close to me say I am the sa'ouvant. Yet you purposefully kept this information from me."

He knew his anger showed, but he didn't care. Namir felt betrayed. Although it seemed a little childish, he could not help it. They either lied to him or did not tell him every-thing, either way, it felt bad. Namir needed to understand why.

"It's about our heritage. You see, elves never truly pass. It is one of the gifts the Gods have given us. We were the Gods' second attempt at mortal life. Not as hardy as dragons, yet not as frail as humans. As such, we were given the blessing of choice." Alequa explained. "When we grow world-weary we may pass into the realm Aeternais or serve forever at a safe house for the living. Even when slain. The guards at your manor in Hornshir chose the latter. Their souls were added to the wall. Once assigned, they cannot leave and will not perish until the end of all things comes to pass.”

Alequa's voice held an odd sadness to it Namir had never heard before. Her voice bore the sound of despair centuries old instead of the normal veneration for the dead. It struck him deeply.

“It still doesn’t explain why she had to prove herself,” Namir said somewhat more docilely.

“She was a half-breed,” Alequa’s azure eyes welled with tears as she said these words. “As such, she was graced with many abilities, including long life, but they must earn the final gift the Gods’ granted us.” She took a tenuous pause before she continued, “All half-blooded elves can attempt to claim their birthright if they choose to. According to the doctrines, they are only allowed three tries. If they succeed, they are given the boon. If they fail, they are bound to the cycle of life all newer races were given.”

“How many times had Haradine tried?” Allair asked sheepishly.

“Her assignment to Landolin’s garrison was her final attempt,” Alequa confessed as she looked down at the snow. “The laws forbade us to treat her as our own until she suc-ceeded. We couldn’t tell you or she would forfeit everything she was trying to achieve.”

Tears streamed down her face as she spoke. Her body shook from stifled tears and Namir felt horrible for it.

Although he understood that he needed to know, he hated to put her through this.

“How do you know if she succeeded?” Namir asked softly. He wanted to spare her as much pain as he could.

“The main temple would have been notified. However, now that she is gone, Landolin would know first. He would receive her orb and sword.” Alequa said as she struggled to keep control of herself.

“Orb and sword?” Namir asked even more confused than

he had been.

"Elves souls are split in twain upon our deaths. Half is in an orb of crystal and half is in our blade. It represents Gods' plans for why we were created. Elves were tasked with helping shape the seed of nature and defend it with our lives. That is what these are for."

"I think we need to get a message to the general then," Namir decided swiftly.

"So, will you please rethink your decision about Armani?" Allair asked for her friend.

"No," Namir said resolutely. "My decision remains. I am not going to disparage a dead man. I will still try and find out why Armani did what he did. I also promise to bring every living person who is involved with Haradine's death to justice." His tone was as firm as the promise he swore.

Namir turned away from the two ladies and put his hand on Zelios. He took a deep breath and focused on the trees again before he continued. He knew he needed to steel himself against the possibility of the flashes. The last thing he wanted to burden either Allair or Alequa with was seeing this weakness in him.

"Did she succeed?" Namir thought to his amulet. "Was she able to pass her final test?"

"SHE WAS. THE GODS HAVE GRANTED HER THE CHOICE OF THE ELVES. LANDOLIN SHOULD ALREADY HAVE HER SOUL AS WELL AS HER CHOICE." Zelios's response eased Namir's burden a little.

"Allair, please ask the other heroes to meet me in the Gathering Place," Namir instructed over his shoulder. "I think we should give Alequa some time to contact Landolin and see if her daughter passed her final test."

His tone betrayed none of his knowledge. He needed to have his distance for now. The sting of not knowing how much of an aid Haradine could have been was too much for

him to handle. Besides, he believed this was something the elf needed to find out on her own.

Halin fumbled around in the darkness. From what he could tell, the cavern was filled with stalagmites. These monstrous growths of rock made traversing the cavern more difficult than any of the others had been. Although he could easily stand up, finding an even and flat surface to walk on proved exceedingly difficult.

He felt drawn into the cavern, by what he had no idea. A small part of him hoped it was by the almost musical voice he had heard before. But another part believed his need to search was all in his head. Either way, he was determined to find a way out of this cavern and back to his friends.

Halin stumbled in the darkness. His arms flailed wildly as he fell. It was all he could do to catch himself. Unfortunately, it was not enough. The rugged ground rushed up to meet him and knocked his breath away.

Darkness enveloped him. As he lay there Halin could not tell whether the inky blackness was blinding him or if he had finally lost his sight. He decided to roll onto is back and rested for a few moments until he could catch his breath.

Tiny movements of his hands let him know this part of the cave was different. The wall just a few feet beyond his head felt carved and smooth, unlike the cavernous passages he had been crawling through. Although the ground underneath him was pocked with baby stalagmites, he was certain he had found some signs of civilization.

Once he was certain he had found his breath, Halin rolled into a familiar crawling position. His hands darted around him to make sure there were no unexpected pitfalls. Absently he plucked at a wooden shaft that protruded from the ground less than a foot away from him.

"It must have fallen from my quiver," he muttered to himself.

Deftly he freed the arrow shaft from the rock and slid it

with his other arrows. While he put it away, he ran his fingers over the rest of fletching. He needed to take an assessment of how many other arrows he may have lost.

"Wait, I only had twelve arrows. This one makes thirteen," He said genuinely surprised. "I need to see this area better."

As his words fell from his lips he pulled out the new arrow and drug its tip across the ground. Tiny sparks flickered to life and briefly illuminated the floor. Halin's eyes widened as they did.

Bones and arrow shafts littered the floor around him. He struck the arrow against the floor again. This time a monstrous inhuman skull jeered back at him from the all-consuming darkness.

Halin quickly pushed himself along the floor backward until he could feel the wall. He pressed his back against it firmly. He wanted to make sure that whatever had killed that thing would not get him too. He decided to forgo the sparks and explored his immediate vicinity with just his hands.

Each arrow shaft he found, he pulled and placed in a pile next to him. Several long silent moments passed. His little pile of arrows quickly grew to thirteen.

"There is no end to these," he thought to himself miserably. His teeth chattered unbidden as he pulled yet another arrow free from a rock. "I need to get warm and see where I am," Halin decided.

"Tumere thank you for providing me something to burn," he said under his breath.

Halin stacked the arrows in a small pile. Once he was certain they would not fall, he quickly struck another arrow against the floor toward it. After three more attempts, he was successful. Small wisps of flame licked hungrily at the fletching he had placed on the bottom as kindling. He gently blew on the little fire and coaxed it into life.

"It's not much, but a little warmth is better than none," he said quietly to himself.

He allowed his eyes to grow accustomed to the meager light before he looked around. Another surprise met his gaze just a few feet away, torches. At least ten of them were strewn across the ground and look as if someone had dropped them.

"I'm not sure why anyone would lose these, but I am grateful for their loss," Halin said a little happier.

It took him less than a second to grab the first one and toss it into his fire. The sweet scent of oil-filled his nostrils as the whole torch burst into flames. Greedily he tossed the second one into the fire. The warmth it created was nothing short of heavenly.

Halin foraged in one of his pouches and pulled out a dead rat. He spared no time in gutting and spitting the thing yet another arrow he found next to him. Four more arrows made for a quick rack and before he could blink, the rat was roasting.

"Now, let's have a look to see what else we can find. Whatever happened here, it was violent," he commented as he glanced around the large cave. "I think I can spare a few moments while dinner cooks, or is it lunch. I guess it doesn't really matter. Food is food no matter the time of day."

A smirk played across his youthful lips as he stood and stretched by the fire. The warmth was the best thing he had felt in quite some time. He had almost forgotten what it felt like.

Once he had stretched, Halin collected a dozen more arrows and stacked them beside his fire. Most of them looked like they had either missed whatever they had been shot at or scorched by something hot. Either way, they would work just fine for their new intended use, burning.

Halin knew he should not wander too far from the fire. So he decided to only go as far as he could feel its heat. The last thing he needed was for the thing to go out. Then he would lose both his meal and the light it was providing.

He glanced back toward the roasting meat and held his stomach. It growled incessantly, but more now that he was actually cooking something. The delicious searing aroma was almost too much for him. He found his feet shuffling edging their way back to the fire unbidden.

"I guess I can explore a bit after I've eaten," He said as if he was trying to convince himself.

A slight glint from the base of the wall caught his attention as he neared the fire. Whatever it was, it had been pressed under the large flagstone. Halin knelt over and tried to get a better look, but all he managed to get was a face full of smoke.

"I guess there's no other choice," he muttered to himself. "If I want to know what someone thought was so important about this thing to hide it, I'll have to try and pull it out."

Dripping juices from the rat sizzled in the flames tantalizingly. He licked his lips hungrily and eyed his dinner. Once he was certain it was not ready, he laid down beside the wall and squeezed his hand into the crack.

Cold metal brushed against the tips of his fingers. It was smooth and impossible to grab. Halin shifted his weight and slid his hand to a different angle. His fingers traced their way around the rounded surface as he tried to discover what it was.

Whatever it was, it was larger than he had first thought. He managed to close two fingers around the ball-like end and wiggled it toward him. After he moved it a little, he slid his hand up further. Firm well-wrapped leather met his probing fingers and he smiled. From what he recalled of his father's forge, this had to be a weapon of some sort.

"I hope it's a sword," Halin thought absently to himself as he carefully worked the object out of its hiding place.

His eyes widened in awe when he finally pulled the

sword free from the base of the wall. He cradled it as he stood. It was beautiful. Although he had seen some of the blades Tipin had made, this weapon was far superior to any of them.

Its finely blade all but gleamed in the meager light. Halin marveled at its perfect weight and balance. Even the hilt was shaped to fit his hand perfectly.

He took a couple practice swings and was even more amazed. Somehow the way the steel wire was woven into the leather grip enhanced his control over the blade's movements. In a way, it felt as if the sword was an extension of his arm.

"I knew I would find you here Aras!" Morcant snapped from behind Halin in the darkness.

The beast's steel-shod feet slid across the rough floor a few feet behind him as it spoke. Halin winced at the thought of being caught off guard. Not only had he forgotten about his food, he had been so wrapped up in this sword he failed to listen for trouble.

"Aras?" Halin replied with as much conviction as he could muster.

Fear swelled in his soul as he turned to face the beast. He tried to inch away from Morcant. No matter where he looked all he could see was his dwindling fire and the monster's hulking form blacker than the darkness itself.

"Do not FEAR." The voice startled Halin as it erupted in his head.

His hand tingled where the sword rested in it as the voice spoke. It was an uncomfortable feeling. I did not hurt, it just buzzed oddly and Halin almost dropped it in response.

"Yes Aras, I know it is you." Morcant's rancid breathe accosted Halin's senses as it moved closer to Halin's position. "You can drop this charade. Although I don't know how you managed to turn back the hand of time, I do know you have nowhere to escape to this time." Morcant snorted derisively as he continued, "None of your precious elves are close enough to protect you. You have finally run out of options!" Morcant spat as he lunged at Halin.

The sword pulled him to his left abruptly and he struggled to keep his feet under him. A barrage of pebbles freed themselves from the flagstone. More stones showered down on him as he felt Morcant's claws sliced the air where his throat had been. Each time he regained his balance, the sword tugged him in another direction. It was as if the sword knew where the beast was about to attack.

"I WILL NOT LET YOU DIE." The sword's voice echoed in Halin's head again.

"I am not Aras!" Halin screamed as he darted blindly through the darkness. "My name is Halin!"

Morcant recovered his footing and grinned. The exaggerated malicious smile on the beast's face was terrifying. But it also made Halin think about the look Daffer would get when he discovered the missing part of a puzzle.

"So, Halin and Aras are one and the same! I should have realized it earlier," Morcant chided himself aloud.

Halin heard the strain in Morcant's voice. It was apparent the beast fought to keep his rage in check. He hoped he could find a way to use the beast's mind control against him.

"The most fearsome warrior to ever walk the face of Cennicus and the keeper of the Faeselian Blade are one and the same." Morcant's laughter peeled off the narrow walls of the cavern eerily as the creature hunted through the darkness for a sign of his prey.

"What?" Halin's confusion was apparent in his voice as he tried to work through the beast's logic.

"You do realize that if I had known this before, the great wars would never have happened." Morcant continued as if he had not heard Halin's outburst. "Not only would thousands have lived, but my freedom would have been easier to obtain!" Morcant's voice filled with rage with each word uttered and Halin could feel the creature's grip against his anger slip.

"No," Halin replied timidly.

Morcant quickly made his way around the stalagmite Halin hid behind. His glowing red gaze cast horrific shadows on the walls all around him. Even the fire's meager light could not compete against it.

The thing's eyes felt heavy to Halin when it finally looked at him as he spoke, "I have waged wars across the breadth of this continent. My only goal was to flush you out of hiding. I have destroyed entire civilizations in order to kill you and obtain my freedom!" Morcant continued as he pressed his momentary advantage.

Halin could not move. His arms felt like lead and he struggled to lift them. He remembered this feeling from the alley in Hornshir, the first time he met this beast.

"Your people would still be alive today if I had known the two of you were one and the same."

"Wha-wha-what?" Halin stammered. "What do you mean my people?" The second question had more conviction to it than Halin thought he could possibly muster.

"The Calanari," Morcant's matter of fact tone slapped Halin's mind sharply. "I killed the great Calanari warriors by destroying the very thing that gave them their strength. I obliterated their forest. After the blight I introduced took the last of Tumere's great trees, the Calanari withered and died. They just let the sands come and claim them." Morcant drove each word home as if it were an arrow. "It was a pity really, the once feared nation just laid down and accepted their fate without even so much as a fight. To think, their savior didn't even care enough to help them in their final hour of need."

"What are you talking about? Who is the Calanari's savior?" Halin asked, a little afraid of Morcant's answer.

"You," Morcant said evilly.

An odd look of confusion spread across the beast's face as it looked at him. Halin struggled to keep his emotions in check, but he knew the thing could tell he was shocked by its rant. He felt his eyes widen unbidden and his mouth had fallen open. He felt as if he had lost all control over his muscles.

"You really had no idea they were dead?" Morcant enjoyed the turmoil of emotion he visibly read on Halin's features. The creature leered at him mirthfully. "To think I knew something my old advisory didn't." Morcant broke into a masochistic laugh as he spat his final few words at Halin.

"STRIKE!" the voice screamed in Halin's head as he shouted. All at once his whole body tingled and Halin felt Morcant's hold on him slip away.

"No!" Halin screamed at Morcant as he blindly swung the sword as hard as he could.

The darkness between them separated into two halves as the blade sliced through it. Halin saw a glowing red line form along its edge as the blade hungrily absorbed the glow from Morcant's eyes. A rage deeper than anything he had ever felt consumed him. He wanted the beast dead. An alien sensation pulsed from the sword. The energy danced across his skin and filled his soul with fire.

Morcant barely avoided the tip of the blade as if he had sensed Halin's onslaught. Halin could tell his speed and accuracy astounded the nassarid by its widened eyes. Yet the beast still managed to dodge behind a stalagmite and into the awaiting darkness.

"Yes!" Morcant hissed. Somehow the nassarid's technique caused his voice to reverberate throughout the room. "Don't act like you had no part in it. You chose to attend to the royal family instead of living amongst your own kind!" Morcant spat.

"I don't understand!" Halin screamed as he fell to his

knees.

"GET UP!" The sword's words stripped Halin of his will and he crumpled.

"Finally," Morcant said as he crept.

Halin knew the beast was moving toward him, but he could not move. His legs felt rubbery and his arms, though tingling, seemed like they belonged to someone else. On top of it all, he felt helpless against the information the creature was sharing.

"Give me the blade and I will let you live." Morcant's voice dripped with hatred combined the odd sound of desire.

The nassarid's words erupted from behind Halin. The blade in his hands forced him to turn and face the creature from his nightmares once more. All of his strength had left him again and now he felt weaker than ever.

"What makes you think I would let you have it?" Halin replied with more courage than he possessed. An odd warming sensation spread through his muscles as he took to his feet once more.

"Because I know you value your life." Morcant smiled a toothy grin.

"I don't believe you will honor your word." Halin did his best not to look into the beast's eyes.

He vividly recalled the last time he made that mistake. If Jerine had not of interceded, he would have already been dead at the monster's hands. Even the thought of it caused him to shudder involuntarily.

Halin forced himself to look at the sword in his hand to ground his mind to the present. Morcant's glowing red eyes cast an eerie glow along the blade as Halin looked at it. Other than the odd glow which played along its surface, the blade now looked plain and blunt.

"Why does this creature want this sword?" Halin puzzled.

"Give it to me!" Morcant growled as he lunged once

more from the shadows at him.

Reflexively Halin stepped aside and let Morcant leap past. A little puzzled by his own movements, he looked at Morcant as his foe turned to face him again. He could tell by the stunned look on the beast's face that it was as shocked as he was at his narrow escape.

"Why is this blade so special to you?" Halin asked as he held the blade aggressively between them.

Morcant growled in frustration as he spit his answer, "You know the answer to that, now give the sword to me!"

The monster leaped at him again and somehow Halin once more evaded it. His mind flooded with images of their fight. Each time Morcant moved, Halin felt some small part of his mind find the right sequence and moved along it perfectly. He could tell the nassarid barely held its frustration in check, just as he could tell what the beast would do next. All of it played out in his mind like a macabre dance.

Morcant turned slowly to face him once more as he said flatly, "You think because my armies are not here that I cannot take this blade from your cold dead hands? How easily you forget about our last encounter. The difference is that this time you are alone. You have no guards and the guardian is nowhere to be seen. Give me the sword now or I swear I will gut you!"

The nassarid's glowing eyes narrowed as it spoke. Something about it forced little fingers of fear into Halin's mind. He could not help but look. The seizing effects it had on his muscles took hold once more. Horrifically Halin watched the look of anger on the beast's face shift to more of a leering grin.

The sword bobbed and swayed involuntarily in front of him as he felt his muscles shake. What little strength he had ebbed as his gaze remained locked on Morcant's fiery red eyes. He stood frozen and helpless once again as the crea-ture approached him slowly, one agonizing step at a time. Halin flinched inwardly as the beast's putrid breath wafted across his face.

Somewhere inside him, something stirred. The electric vibrations from the sword moved deeper and kindled a fire. Halin felt as if his insides were burning and the heat needed a vent.

Morcant's clawed hands meticulously reached for his hands. No matter what Halin tried, he felt unable to move. He closed his eyes as he waited for the inevitable pain he knew would come when the claws sank into his hands.

"ΠOШ!" His mind was consumed by the nassarid's words and the sword's command felt like it vented the internally building flames.

Halin's body suddenly moved of its own accord. He reflexively swung the blade as hard as he could. Somehow the sword had managed to take control of his paralyzed body. Burning pain shot through all of his nerves and it was all he could do to focus on the sensation. Halin felt like a passenger in his own body, completely out of control. He felt the fire dance from deep in his soul and play along the blade's edge as he struck at Morcant.

"NO!" Morcant screamed.

The tip of the blade sliced through the nassarid's chest plate easily. Halin could not feel any resistance as the sword turned in his hands. He felt his feet plant with each step as his legs stepped forward and closed the gap. The blade hungrily sliced through the air. Morcant barely rolled away from it before it could bury itself in his neck.

Chapter Twenty-Two: Consequences

The light fragrance of cooking potatoes and stewing meat filled the air. The normal bustle of the Gathering Place was gone. The only perceptible sounds came from the fire crackling in the hearth and the chairs as the five of them shifted in their seats.

"How much longer do you think it will take for Carness to join us?" Tipin asked.

The Calanari was unusually restless. Namir could not recall ever seeing him like this. He pried his eyes off Tipin and glanced at the others to see if the smith was the only overly anxious person.

Valeron was the epitome of patience. He sat perfectly still directly across from him. The only time he moved was to take an occasional draught of ale as they waited. He had no idea how the Knight did it, but his stillness was unnerving.

Allair seemed perfectly calm. Although she shifted in her seat beside her husband occasionally, she did not have the same unease Tipin wore like a shroud. Her brown eyes glanced around the room as his did, perceptive and wary.

Alequa also was relaxed and calm. Namir had grown accustomed to the elf's demeanor. Her golden locks flowed freely in the slight breeze of the room and her dazzling blue eyes were fixed on the table in front of her. She seemed just as distant as usual. While this bothered Namir a little, he finally understood why. Elves cannot get too attached to the living. There is too much risk of pain for them to form deep bonds with their allies.

"I am sure he won't be much longer," Alequa replied before Namir could.

"While we wait, I'll have the cook bring us out some of the food," Namir said as he stood up.

"No, please my liege, sit. I will go talk to the cook," Allair said.

She rose and left the room before Namir could even take a step. He hated how much Allair had changed toward him since he had returned. She was his best friend's mother, not a servant. She did not have to wait on him.

He sat back down sullenly and said, "Tipin, do you think you can find him?"

"I do," Tipin's deep voice answered without any hint of hesitation.

"Please do. There is so much more that needs to be done before the funerals. I would like to get this over with as soon as possible." Namir said as he rested his head in the palm of his right hand.

"I will not fail you," Tipin said as he rose.

Namir listened as the large man's steps moved away from him. Tipin was an odd man. He could be as loud as any other person he knew, but he could also be deathly silent.

He felt the elf's hand touch his left hand lightly. It was soothing. Namir knew he could always reply on Alequa to keep grounded in the present. He refocused his thoughts to the task at hand and turned to face her.

"Once Carness and Tipin return, please leave us. There are injured that need seeing to and I want to make sure the townsfolk are well cared for." Namir whispered to her. He leaned over just enough to make sure the others understood his words were meant for the elf alone.

Namir waited until she nodded her understanding before he continued, "Until then, please update me on the status of the wounded."

Alequa's azure blue eyes closed for a moment as she listened. When she was ready to speak she opened them and looked only at Namir. She stared into his steel grey eyes as she adjusted her dress slightly. Her actions reminded him of a soldier preparing to speak to their commander.

"Of the remaining injured we still have in the courtyard, I feel almost all will survive. There are a few that were too far gone for either Saril's or my Goddess's magic to heal," she reported succinctly.

"I had hoped all of the deaths were behind us," Namir said wearily.

"For the most part, we are. These last three are remnants who have held on longer than expected. Aside from them, all others will recover in time." The elf elaborated.

Namir nodded and sighed deeply. He rubbed his temples and silently mourned the additional losses. So many catastrophes had happened because of him. It was far too much for him to think about now.

"So the death toll will be at fifteen in the next few days then?" He asked although he was sure he knew what the answer was going to be.

"No, it will be at twelve," Alequa replied quickly. "I did not know you had been keeping track of the deaths."

There was a hint of surprise in her voice and on her face. Namir looked at her pale features and wide eyes. The way her lips pulled at their edges let him know her surprise was genuine.

"I have been," he nodded. "But thankfully it seems my count was off," he added a little relieved.

The smell of stewed meat and cooked potatoes filled the room as Allair entered it again. Several waitresses followed close behind her. Each held bowels and plates filled with food. Once each member of the gathering had been served, Namir motioned for them to leave settings for Tipin and Carness.

"Alequa, please lead us in our blessings," Namir nodded toward the food.

"My Goddess, please bless this food and my brethren. Allow it to nourish our bodies and well as our souls. Give us the strength we need to survive the coming tribulations and allow us to serve Your calling in all things." Her musical voice was captivating.

"Thank you," Namir said as he raised his head. "Eating without us?" Tipin's deep voice entered the

room before the door even opened.

"Would we forget about you?" Namir replied with a slight hint of mirth in his voice. "We have settings for you if the two of you would get in here."

As the last few words escaped from Namir's lips, the door opened. Tipin stepped quickly into the room. His hulking form completely blocked the view through the door. He quickly removed his cloak and shook off the snow that clung to it.

Carness stepped in with a bit less spectacle than the smith had. Although he did remove his cloak and gave it a good shake before he hung it on a hook near the door. Once he was fully in the room he faced Namir and knelt.

"I am sorry for my tardiness, my liege. I needed to check on a few things before I could free myself for this meeting," the constable remained kneeling as he spoke.

"Please rise and find your seat. Eat, the food will get cold. You were not here when I told the others there is no need for this formality when it is just us." Namir reiterated loud enough for everyone to hear him, in case any others held any doubt of his words before.

Carness quickly took to his feet and crossed the short distance to his seat. Namir had never really noticed how fluid the constable moved. The way he stalked his way to his seat was almost animalistic.

"I assume you can report to the overall safety to what's left of Ellsted," Namir said bluntly.

"It is as safe as can be expected," Carness replied around a piece of meat he had shoved into his mouth. He dipped a fresh roll into the soupy broth the potatoes floated in and said, "The only thing left to decide on is what we are going to do about the dragon's carcass."

"If I may be excused, sa'ouvant," Alequa said as she stood. "There are some tasks I need to see to. Since I am neither a part of this town's council nor a survivor of Watch-keep, I think this is a good time to see to them."

Namir liked how well the elf handled the subject of her leaving. Not only did she acknowledge his request, she set up the topic of conversation perfectly. A slight smile tugged at his lips as he nodded his consent.

As she made her way toward the door, Namir said, "Please take some food for the wounded and Saril. Once he has eaten please send him here."

The elf nodded and turned toward the kitchen. Namir noticed that she still held her bowl of food in her hand. He was glad Alequa was looking out for her own health as well. He needed people who could shoulder some of the smaller details and he was glad he had found it in her.

"Madam Mayor," Namir said as he turned his attention to Allair. "What are your plans for rebuilding Ellsted?" His tone was plain, but he knew she had not expected him to ask.

"I have reached out to our craftsman. They think they can rebuild all but the Council Hall in a week or so. Due to the vast amount of damage it sustained in the dragon's attack, the hall needs to be the last thing we look at. It will take months, if not years, to completely rebuild it." Her answer was on point and succinct.

"I want to add a wall to the discussion," Namir said. He held up a hand to quell any objections. He knew Carness's thoughts and did not want to have the conversation about it again. "I would prefer it get built first. Once it is finished the rest of the reconstruction can be started."

"Where do you propose we get the material to build it with?" Carness asked obviously aggravated by Namir's demand.

Namir stared into the constable's golden wolf-like eyes as he replied, "Use the stones from the Council Hall. If you need more, then tear down the rest of it. The safety of the populace is my primary concern. They need to know I hold their needs above that of governance. Besides, I need them to be able to survive without any of you."

"What?" Carness roared. "What do you mean without us?"

"I have given quite a bit of thought to this," Namir said as he looked at each of them in turn. "You are all more than just survivors, you are heroes. The kingdom needs you to be that. They need symbols of hope, something larger than themselves to believe in. They need heroes to look up to and to guide them to a better future. One free of the tyranny they have grown accustomed to." He paused to let his words sink in. Namir took a long sip of his ale before he continued, "It's more than that. I need you. In order to reclaim the throne, I need to show the populace that my way will be different. That it will be a better path to the glory and peace we once had."

"So we don't have a say in this?" Carness said as he looked at the others.

"Of course you do," Namir said quietly. "I am not demanding that you follow me, I am asking. Each of you has already told me that you think I am the rightful ruler, either by your words or your actions. I am just taking those declarations to their next step, binding you to my cause to claim the throne and strip the usurper of his stolen power."

Once glance at Valeron reaffirmed his thoughts. Namir knew by the Knight's look of resignation he was correct in his decision. He glanced at Nurn and Allair as well. Both of them had the same look. The only one who did not share their resolve was Carness.

"I, for one, agree," Valeron said loudly. "Who else is of the same mind?"

"I am," Tipin said as he nodded. But I will not speak for my wife."

Namir watched as Allair looked from him to Tipin and back. He could tell she was amused by her husband's words and touched. She slowly tucked a stray lock of brown hair behind her ear as she stood.

"Well, husband," she said to Tipin. 'If you are committed to our liege, I cannot see why I would not be as well. Besides, with our children gone, there is nothing left holding me here except my role as Chancellor and acting Mayor. Both of which I would gladly relinquish to do my part in the coming days."

"That leaves only you, Carness," Namir said pointedly. "Are you with us or would you rather stay and see to the safety of Ellsted. Either way, you will be seen as a hero."

"It does," Carness acquiesced. "If I agree to leave, this town will be helpless. There is no one trained to take over for me. The people of Ellsted are farmers, not soldiers. None of them would have the slightest idea how to defend themselves if another dragon attacks."

Namir felt the sting of truth to his words. He was right. Not even a wall would stop another attack like the one they just faced. The constable's words tumbled in his mind as he pondered them.

"That is true," he admitted. "But would they really have to worry about that. Once we leave Ellsted most of the danger will follow us. All they need is time to learn how to defend themselves. Aside from Tipin, Daffer and yourself, have you trained anyone else to help you if you needed it?"

"Aye," Carness nodded. "There are a couple youths I trained, aside from Nurn, Halina and yourself that is. One of them shows promise."

"Good. You can recommend him for the role of Constable. Then you could leave him instructions on how to train others. That way we can assure Ellsted won't be threatened by your presence as well."

"By my presence?" Carness asked hesitantly. "Aye," Valeron answered. "As soon as people hear

that the Heroes of Watchkeep have banded together behind

Namir's claim to the Crown, we all will become targets."

Carness nodded his understanding. "So, although you are giving us a choice, we really do not have one."

The resignation in his voice stung Namir. He wanted them to follow him of their own will. But he also knew he needed their help. He was deeply torn. Namir hated to force their hands and he had not expected to need to.

"That was never my intention," Namir confessed. "But I will do whatever I need to in order to ensure my people are safe. Without a new vision, I cannot guarantee it."

"I understand," Carness conceded. "I do not like it, but I can see why it is needed."

"So all we have left to do is make sure the town gets as much help as we can offer to it while it rebuilds. Part of that is finding new council members for the populace to vote from," Namir stated stoically.

"We also need to appoint a new Head Merchant," Allair added.

"Why do we need to do that?" Saril's voice surprised all of them.

The healer stood in the entryway covered in snow. He

almost looked like a ghost. As he brushed the snow from his slight shoulders, his too pale blue eyes darted about the room.

"With Daffer dead the position is open," Carness interjected. "Since we have to replace the Head Merchant, we should hold a new election for the other positions."

"Only if more of you are planning on leaving," Saril said calmly.

"Thank you for joining us at such short notice," Namir said in an attempt to derail the conversation. "Did you have a chance to eat?"

"I did," Saril replied. "Alequa brought the food you sent. For some reason, I feel like I missed out a large part of the discussion though."

Namir smiled at the healer's astuteness. Saril always had a knack of keying in on the heart of any situation. It was something Namir had hoped to learn from him.

"That is because you did, my friend," Carness admitted. "There were other things that needed to be discussed while we waited for you."

"I asked the remaining heroes of Watchkeep to join me in my quest to bring peace back to Cennicus," Namir said bluntly. "And they agreed."

"I see. Now I understand the urgency for a new election. We should at least come up with a few choices for each of the positions, otherwise, the election could turn into chaos," the healer said sagely.

"That is one of the reasons I asked Alequa to send you up to us," Namir agreed. "The other reason is to ask a favor of the current council. I need you all to bear witness."

"Witness to what?" Carness and Saril asked the same time.

"Valeron, please rise and step forward," Namir said evenly.

Valeron nodded and stood obediently. When he was a

few paces away from Namir, he bowed and dropped to one knee. The large man kept his gaze on the floor and waited for Namir to give him further instructions. The movement was precise and seemed well rehearsed.

"This morning I collected Valeron's sword, chain, belt, and spurs," Namir informed the others. "You see, he had informed me that he had betrayed his original vows of Knighthood to my family. I have given his plight some thought and I believe he should be allowed to redeem his honor."

Namir's words echoed oddly in the Gathering Place's main room. He looked at each of the faces in the room and noticed the shocked looks. None of them expected this from him and he found some comfort in the fact.

"I know that I am new to all of this, but Zelios has informed me of the details I need to know. Normally this sort of thing is performed by two Knights. Currently, I have none to serve in this, or any other, capacity." Namir paused for a second before he continued, "As the current council I ask all of you to bear witness that I have stripped him of his previous rank. We all know he has more than proved himself in the battle against the dragon. And after our long discussion, I fell that I can also vouch for his motives."

A lump formed in his throat as he spoke. Namir swallowed hard to dislodge it. He needed his voice to be firm and resolute.

"Carness, Tipin, and Allair please come forward and join Valeron," Namir said as he motioned for the three of them to approach him.

He watched all three of them rise individually. All of them had a peculiar look on their faces. Namir knew none of them were aware of what he wanted them to do, but none of them spoke.

Out of the three of them, Tipin was the only one to move without hesitation. The Calanari moved swiftly and smoothly. Before Namir even had a chance to direct him, the smith took a knee beside Valeron silently.

Allair followed her husband's lead, but her movements were stiffer. Her steps faltered a little as she navigated around her chair. She glanced at Tipin and Valeron, then up at Namir. Her nervousness was more than apparent. Slowly she curtseyed to him and then knelt beside her husband and lowered her head.

Carness was the last to rise. Before he left the table, he took off his belt and laid it on the table. He also removed several daggers hidden in his boots and tunic. Then he turned and faced Namir. His wolfish golden eyes darted from person to person and he hesitantly closed the distance to the other three. Once he was to Valeron's left he bowed and took a knee.

"Saril I know you cannot see well, but I need you to bear witness as best you can." Namir intoned.

"I shall," Saril nodded.

"Carness, Valeron, Tipin, and Allair, in an attempt to create an order of chivalry I ask you four to be the cornerstones of this venture. Although only one of you has ever had any experience, or desire, to become a Knight, I ask all of you to consider this honor and what it would mean to you and the entirety of Cennicus.

"In days gone by, there existed many orders of Knighthood which recognized the skill and honor of their members. In the service of their King, and in the defense of the noble and lofty ideals of chivalry, did these orders achieve their exalted rank of Peer to the Crown. The vows of Knighthood are not to be entered lightly and so I strive to ensure all of you are willing to consider what the bonds will bring.

"To wear the belt and chain of a Knight is to hold a sacred trust. This trust will bring obligations and demands that will require you all to make sacrifices every moment for the rest of your lives.

"A Knight must be respectful of all religions and never offend the faith of another. They must also defend any who cannot defend themselves, whether it is due to age, infirmity, poverty, or vows made. They must be dependable beyond doubt or question. A Knight will never flee from the face of a foe and must be generous to all in need. And, as always and everywhere, must be the champion of the right and good.

"Above all else, a Knight is representative of justice for the Crown. You will be expected to portray and represent the kingdom when I am not available. Your confidence and advice will be expected and listened to at all times.

"The laws and customs of Cennicus require that a Knight demonstrate prowess on the field of battle. All of you have done that much and more. They also require that a Knight be selfless toward others. Another quality I have seen in the four of you. The final requirement is that a Knight is loyal to their King, but more importantly to the populace of Cennicus. This last part I believe has already been tested and proved, but I leave that decision to each of you to determine for yourselves.

"Do any, or all, of you desire to accept the burden of Knighthood? If you accept it, please remain where you are and state your acceptance. If not, you are free to rise and take your seat at the table."

Namir held his breath as he finished speaking. He wanted all of them to accept the honor, but he was willing to let them decline. Zelios's soft glow leaked out of his tunic as he waited for them to decide. The beating of his heart filled his chest as if it were caged when Carness shifted a little.

"I accept the burden, my liege," Valeron was the first to respond.

"I accept, sa'ouvant," Tipin replied after a few more moments.

"While the normal custom reserves this right for men alone, I accept the honor," Allair said softly.

Namir sighed a little easier when he saw Carness nod his acceptance. He dared not move in case the constable decided to rise instead. The verbal acceptance was needed and Namir did not want to unduly affect his choice.

"I too accept this great honor and even greater burden," Carness finally stated ruggedly.

Namir breathed a sigh of relief as Carness voice his acceptance. Now all he needed to do was have their tokens made. He shook these thoughts out of his head and refocused on what Zelios had taught him earlier.

"Saril please meet with them tomorrow and pray for them. The Knighting ceremony will be held after the wakes for the dead. Each of you will need to stand a vigil separately the night before. During that time any of the townsfolk who wish to hold council with you will be encouraged to do so. Listen to their concerns and wisdom. Glean their will for the future of Cennicus and bring back to me what you have learned. Do any of you have any questions?" Namir asked although he knew they would not voice them if they had.

"I shall pray for them and get them prepared for their vigils," Saril agreed.

Namir waited a few moments in case any of them had a question. Once he was certain they did not, he said, "Please rise and take your seats. We still have much to do before the night is over."

Alequa closed her eyes and let the sounds from the wounded wash over her. Most of them slept fitfully. Although there was a large fire lit, the bitter coldness in the air increased their pain. She wished there was more she could do, but she was drained.

"Landolin," she whispered into the breeze as she focused her mind on his.

The tendrils of her mind reached out across an unknowable distance as she attempted to make contact. The elven healer needed to know what her daughter's fate was. She desperately hoped she could find out before Saril returned.

"Aye," Landolin's reply was softer than it was the last time they spoke this way.

"I need to know, have you received Haradine's sword and orb?" Her question hung in the air as she whispered it.

A small part of her did not want to know. She was afraid Haradine had failed her final test. If she had, then Alequa would have lost any hopes of seeing her daughter again.

"You can rest easy," Landolin's voice danced around in her mind. "I received them and placed the orb in the wall along with her sword."

"Did she... did she decide to stay or leave?" Alequa fought hard to keep her anxiety in check.

"She chose to stay," Landolin replied.

The hint of pride in his voice was exactly what Alequa needed to hear. Her daughter had not only passed her test, she had chosen to stay and help. A tear crept down the elf's cheek unbidden.

"Thank you," she said to her friend.

"You sound tired. You should rest. We can talk again in the morning," Landolin's final words shared a feeling of comradery before the link faded.

Chapter Twenty-Three: Lights

The smell of burning fur filled the air around them. Jerine glanced at the three bodies that blazed behind them. Even in death, the nassarid were deadly.

"Why do nassarid burst into flames when they die?" Nurn asked.

Jerine turned to look at the Calanari youth. Shadows danced and flew all around them. The well-built stone walls of the tunnels echoed the crackling flames ominously.

"They burn because of the shadow walker. They fear him so much they cast spells on their abominations. These spells were designed to kill the shadow walker if he even gets a single drop of their blood on him."

"The shadow walker is real?" Nurn asked somewhat confused. "I mean, Hessa told us about how he saved her in the forest, but I thought she imagined how the man appeared."

Jerine smiled at the boy's confusion. "He is quite real, I assure you. He has been an ally to everyone who kept Namir's secret, and him, safe."

"From what I have heard, the shadow walker is formidable. But to purposely make their blood ignite? Is he really that much of a threat?" The incredulity in the youth's voice was more than apparent to the elf.

"He can be. That is if you are on the wrong side of his intentions," Jerine said quietly. "But enough about this, we need to focus on the task at hand, finding your brother."

"Agreed," Nurn said as he caught up to the elf.

Jerine needed to stay ahead of the youth. Nurn carried a torch and if he let him take the lead, his keen elven sight would be of little use. With all the nassarid they had faced so far, the elf wanted to make use of all the advantages they had at their disposal.

"There are odd markings on the wall," Nurn called out quietly. "Did you see these?

The elf turned and looked where the youth was pointing. His eyes narrowed as he studied the marks. The deep grooves seemed to have been etched by a sword being dragged against the flat face of the wall.

The guardian quickly pulled a dagger from his belt and mimicked the motion below the existing mark. To both of their surprise, an excessive amount of sparks flowed down the wall and partially lit up the darkness. Although the light faded quickly, Jerine could make out enough of the passage to navigate through it easily.

"It looks like we have found a way to track your brother. That is if he was the one who created these indentions," Jerine whispered.

"Some of these marks are too deep for his knife to create," Nurn added skeptically.

"True, but I think we should see where they lead us. If we don't find your brother at the end of them, we can come back and search the passages that were not scored in the same way."

"I can live with that," Nurn said quietly.

Once he heard Nurn's response, Jerine followed the markings. Although he still scanned his surrounds, he picked up his pace. The elf nearly sprinted around the next corner. An odd tingling sensation played across his skin and he felt his spirits rise for the first time since they had started searching for Halin.

"We are close," Jerine thought to himself. "We should find the boy soon."

Feeling energized, he only paused long enough to find the markings. Jerine listened to make sure he still heard Nurn's faint footfalls before he moved again. He only waited until the boy was around the corner before he dashed around the next one.

A low snarl emanated from all around him as he paused to find the next set of marks. Jerine instantly recognized it as Morcant's. The deep throaty growl was quickly followed by the sounds of battle. Steel against stone reverberated from farther down the tunnel ahead of him.

"Morcant has found him," Jerine yelled over his shoulder to Nurn.

"Then we need to move faster!" Nurn replied.

He heard Nurn's rapid approach and he braced himself. Jerine deftly flung his cloak open so the youth would see him. The elf pivoted with the force of the young Calanari's impact. His ploy worked. Not only did he keep his feet, he managed to stop Nurn before he barreled down the hallway.

"While I agree we need to make haste, I do not think we should throw all caution to the wind," Jerine's reprimand was not said harshly, but he knew Nurn might take it that way.

"Why not?" Nurn spat back.

"What if Morcant left a few more nassarid on guard? I want to save your brother, but running headlong into a trap is not the right way to do it," he instructed firmly.

Seeing Nurn's nod, Jerine resettled his cloak on his shoulder and ducked around the corner. His steps quickened the further he went. Halin's voice rang off the stones, but it was harder to hear than Morcant's bellowing voice.

He knew Nurn was running just as fast as he was. They both were awash with a newfound sense of urgency. His keen elven eyes darted from wall to wall in search of any new signs of Halin's passage.

The small pile of discarded torches caught his eye before any new divots in the walls did. Their location made no sense. They were scattered in the middle of the hallway, not at an intersecting tunnel. He slowed his pace quickly and held up a hand as a signal to Nurn.

A small sigh escaped his lips as the elf heard the large boy slow down. He stooped to examine one of the torches. It looked old, at least as old as the supplies they had found in the elven encampment outside of the cave.

"What is wrong?" Nurn asked quietly.

Jerine motioned toward the torches as he replied, "It makes no sense. Why would anyone drop their torches here?"

Nurn moved closer and waved his torch over the extinguished ones. The fire wavered and flared toward the right-hand wall as he did so. Jerine glanced at the opposite wall. The combination of the sputtering torch's light and the natural darkness in the passage made it impossible for him to get a good look at it.

"Take your torch over to the other wall," Jerine said softly.

Nurn nodded and did as he was told. Both of their eyes widened in surprise. A small hole gaped back at them. The draft that forced the torch's flame to flicker emanated from it.

"They are through there," Jerine whispered.

"Then why are we waiting?" Nurn growled his irritation at the elf.

"Because there is no floor," Jerine pointed out. "From what Alequa told me, this is the cavern they found Aras in after Morcant tried to kill him."

"So?" Nurn's irritation was apparent in his voice and it grated on the elf's nerves.

"If I am right, it is quite a drop. We need to use some rope." Jerine stuck his head through the hole as Nurn pulled the torch back. "Please tell me that you brought it with you."

"I did," Nurn grumbled."

Jerine heard the boy set his torch on the floor and rummage in his pack. The faint glow of a small fire filtered through the darkness below him. That was the sign he was looking for.

"I have it out," Nurn said quietly to him.

"Good," Jerine replied as he pulled himself away from the hole. "We just need to secure it."

The elf picked up a small iron hook as he studied the opposite wall. He frowned when he noticed there was nothing to fasten it to. Jerine refocused his attention back to the mouth of the hole.

The base of the opening started less than a foot off the floor. He carefully tested the largest part with his hands. It did not budge.

Without another word, Jerine grabbed the rope. He quickly threaded an end through the loop made in the hook. Skillfully he spun the rope into a girth hitch and slid the other end through it. The, he tossed the rest of the rope into the hole. As it fell, Jerine fastened the hook as best he could to the base of the wall.

"Are you ready?" Jerine asked Nurn. "I am," the boy replied.

"I will go first. When I get to the bottom I will yank on the rope to let you know it is safe," the elf said quickly and quietly.

He did not wait for a response. As soon as his words slipped from his lips, the elf darted through the hole.

He gripped the rope tightly with his gloved hands. His

foot spun around the rope and flipped it around his leg.

Jerine quickly descended into the blackness. Although it was a large drop, it did not take him long to reach the bottom. Once there, he quickly tugged the rope as hard as he could. His keen elven eyes pierced the darkness around him as he struggled to see either Morcant or Halin.

The sound of Nurn's boots hitting the ground was his cue to move. Thankfully the youth had decided to abandon his torch in the hall before he descended. This allowed him to use the other nearby light sources to get an idea of where they needed to go.

"NO!" Morcant's scream reverberated loudly off the stalagmites that surrounded them.

The beast's bellow was closely followed by the distinct ring of a sword as it sliced through steel. Jerine and Nurn shared a frantic glance. Halin and Morcant were close, possibly just around one of the massive natural columns.

Jerine motioned to Nurn to circle the stalagmite to the right while he traced its base left. As soon as the boy nodded, the elf quickly adjusted his cloak and pulled his hood over his head as far as he could.

A blinding light was the first thing Jerine saw as he stepped away from the column. His hands flew up to his eyes defensively. Pain seared his senses. Elven sight was useful in the dark, but it made him susceptible to bright flashes of light.

His knees buckled and he threw himself against the base of a small stalagmite. Jerine cursed soundlessly. He hoped Nurn would wait to attack Morcant until his eyes had readjusted.

"Where did you go?" Morcant bellowed.

The bright circles slowly faded from Jerine's view as he huddled against the rough stone. The soft glow of the fire mingled eerily with the blazing red light cast by Morcant's eyes. With each blink the pain that stabbed through his eyes slowly dissipated.

Although Morcant frantically searched the chamber, he was not far from him. He tugged his hood over his face tighter and scanned the area himself.

Only Morcant stood near the fire. As he cast his search a little wider, he saw Nurn huddled against a small stalagmite just as he had. Even after seeing the large both, something bothered him. Not only was Halin nowhere to be seen, the elf could not pinpoint what had caused the blinding flash.

"I will find you!" Morcant growled.

"There is nothing for it. We will have to search for Halin after we subdue our adversary," Jerine thought to himself.

The cool hilt of his sword felt refreshing to the elf as he dropped his hand down to it. Silently Jerine drew his sword. He tilted it so only Nurn would see the dim light flash along its reflective surface.

A smile crested his lips when he saw Nurn freed his axe from his belt. All of the training had paid off. The youth was learning the art of subtly. Hopefully, Halin would stay hidden as they attacked the beast.

He waited until Morcant turned and faced toward the fire before he moved. As soon as the beast turned,

Jerine lunged at him. Uncannily the beast moved as Jerine's blade sliced through his cloak.

"Where is he?" Morcant growled as he caught Jerine by the throat.

"I do not know," the elf struggled against the beast's grip in order to get enough air to speak.

He felt the heat from Morcant's glowing eyes play across his skin. Jerine knew better than to look at the creature. As he kicked his legs in a futile attempt to free himself, the elf clamped his eyes shut tightly.

An abrupt jolt passed through Morcant's hand and the elf felt the beast's fingers open. Jerine quickly rolled as soon as he felt his feet touch the ground. He made sure his cloak settled around him enough so he could blend into the rocks before he even dared to open his eyes.

"That is the question I want you to answer," Nurn's voice filled the cavern.

The sound of an axe as it clove into the beast's armor forced Jerine to open his eyes. Morcant was now facing Nurn and growling. The nassarid crouched and looked ready to pounce at the first opening the youth gave him. Blood dripped from the war axe Nurn gripped tightly in his hands.

Before Morcant had a chance to look for him, Jerine lunged at him again, this time from his side. He wanted to let his sword slip out from under his cloak until he was certain he was going to hit. The satisfying feeling as his blade bit into the nassarid's triceps only broadened the elf's grin. With a quick flick of his wrist, Jerine pulled his sword free form its arm.

"Guardian," Morcant sneered. "I see you brought a friend this time. Another of the lost race I see. No matter. I will kill the two of you and then find my prey."

"Lost race?" Nurn asked.

Jerine heard the confusion in the boy's voice. He could not let the nassarid undermine Nurn's resolve. Hatred boiled in his blood for all of the atrocities Morcant had committed over the years.

"This ends now, Morcant," Jerine said through his clenched teeth. "I promise you that I will be one to end you."

"You might have to share that vow," Nurn said as he threw himself at the nassarid.

Morcant sidestepped the youth and sprang backward. It was obvious to Jerine the beast was trying to put more distance between them. He lunged at where he figured Morcant was heading. This time his blade thrust into the darkness ahead of him. Then, with a slight twist to his waist, he sliced the sword through the air toward Morcant's torso.

The ringing sound of Nienna Nénharma as it sliced through the part of Morcant's breastplate that protected his stomach was music to his ears. Blood flooded down the length of his blade and pooled in the small creases of his leather gloves.

"You are finished!" Nurn screamed as he threw his axe.

The head of the axe embedded itself into the center of Morcant's breastplate. He had not noticed that the youth had fastened a thin silver chain onto the haft of his axe.

Jerine had little time to ponder about it before Nurn revealed its purpose.

With a hard yank, the boy pulled Morcant, axe and all, toward him. Although the nassarid squirmed, he seemed unable to resist the young Calanari's strength. Jerine did not wait either.

He threw himself at Morcant's flailing form as Nurn dragged him in front of the elf. The nassarid raised his hand just in time to stop Jerine's sword from slicing into his head. With a flourish, the guardian freed his blade from the beast's forearm.

"I will not die today," Morcant screamed.

His left hand finally found the axe. In a desperate attempt to get free, the nassarid managed to pull the axe free from his armor. The beast's blood gushed out of the gaping hole left by Nurn's attack.

Before either Jerine or Nurn could react, Morcant leaped backward again. Within seconds the nassarid was completely enveloped in the darkness. A deafening silence replaced the harsh clangor of their brief battle.

"Is he gone?" Nurn asked quietly.

His axe spun in the boy's hand as he spoke. Jerine watched as Nurn glanced around them. His eyes flitted from one deeply shadowed area to the next.

"He is. Now, all we have to do is find your brother,"

Jerine confided.

"Was he even here?" The lack of hope in Nurn's voice was disturbing.

"He was," Jerine assured his friend. "I heard him and Morcant talking as they fought."

"Then what are we waiting for?" Nurn asked. "Halin, where are you? Come out if you are here!"

"Sa'trandon, we are here to rescue you!" Jerine shouted as loud as he could.

He kept an eye out for Morcant in case he was still lurking around somewhere. An odd feeling tugged at the back of his mind. Somehow he sensed that the blinding light had something to do with Halin, he just wished he knew how.

Halin, the game is over! Show yourself!" Nurn yelled desperately.

A bitterly cold wind tore at his cloak. His breath steamed out of his mouth. Namir's eyes darted over the twelve burial prams. His gaze lingered on the ornately carved transoms of Armani's pram.

"Even in death the mayor has to outclass everyone else," Namir thought mirthfully.

He knew the mayor had no say in the design of his funeral boat. Just as he understood the shipwright decided to hand carve the stem of Armani's and Daffer's prams.

"They were council members, after all. They are the closest thing to royalty Ellsted has," Zelios informed him unbidden.

"I know. It was just an observation," Namir thought back.

He stood silently on the top of his favorite hill.

Although the snow was deep, it was peaceful. His eyes lingered on the blue sheen Zelios cast on the snow. Somehow the unnatural light made everything seem more tranquil. For once Namir was glad he had been given the amulet.

A sense of unease settled around him as his eyes scanned over the town. Although there was quite a bit of wreckage, most of the town was intact. His spirits fell father when he saw the gaping hole where the Council Hall once stood. The only thing that brought him any hope was the sight of the gathering throng of people.

It seemed like the whole town turned out for the occasion. Namir smiled inwardly at this. Although he was not close to his uncle, Daffer deserved at least this much respect. He fought to remember him for the good deeds he did while he lived instead of the man Namir had grown up knowing.

"I guess it is time to get this over with," Namir thought to himself as he turned toward the trail that led to the heart of Ellsted.

Aves looked out her window. The town was different, nothing like she had ever expected. People milled about all dressed in black with no sense of purpose. This would never have happened when her father was in charge.

Armani had a way of getting people to do what was right for the town, not just for themselves. Aves knew she was going to miss her father, she just did not realize this would be one of those things. She knew Armani had held secrets, some darker than others.

"He has to have a record of how he managed to keep everything straight somewhere," Aves thought. "Maybe Hessa would know where he might have kept something like that."

"You miss him, don't you," Hessa's voice echoed across her room.

"You know, when we were younger, I thought were a mind reader. You had a knack of always knowing when I needed something," Aves confided as she turned away from the window and faced her sister. "Is this one of those times?"

Hessa stood in the doorway. She looked radiant. Although she wore on of Aves's funeral dresses, it seemed less dark on her. There was an internal light that shone in her sister that Aves could only hope was inside her somewhere as well.

"It does not take a mind reader to know that you are in pain," Hessa replied softly.

Aves heard the pinch of sorrow in her sister's voice as she spoke. Hearing it affect Hessa did little to relieve it in herself. Somethings just are not meant to share, grief may be one of those things.

"You always have been perceptive," Aves said thoughtfully. "Hopefully, in spite of everything that has happened, that will never change."

"I would like to think so," Hessa said reassuringly. "It is almost time to leave. Have you thought about what you are going to say?"

"I have, although I am not sure that I want to. Some things are just too hard to say. That is especially true about the important stuff," Aves confessed.

"That is so true," Hessa agreed. "I am just glad that I will not be expected to share my thoughts. I loved him too. I just do not care for some of the choices he made. Armani was a complicated man, but I am sure he made his choices for what he thought were the best reasons."

"Thank you, dear sister. I know we have not seen things the same recently, but I am glad you are here for me now." Aves said solemnly.

"I will always be here for you," Hessa assured her. "But we need to go if we are to be in our places before the ceremony starts."

"I am ready, we can leave anytime," Aves said as she walked toward Hessa. "I would hate to be late to my father's funeral."

"Tipin would have been proud of you last night," Jerine said to Nurn as they huddled in the tent.

"If I had found my brother maybe," Nurn said dejectedly. "Are you certain you heard him in the cavern with Morcant?"

"Aye," Jerine nodded. "His voice is not an easy one to miss. Besides, we found the rat he was cooking and his fire, remember?"

"I do," Nurn shook his head as he spoke.

A pit had formed in his stomach ever since their encounter with Morcant. Nothing could dislodge it, not even knowing that they had finally figured out where his brother had gotten off to. Nurn feared that without actually finding his brother, he would never be able to rest again.

"It proves that Halin can take care of himself. That has to relieve some of your fears," Jerine explained. "We also know he found a sword."

"No, we think he did. The only way we can be certain of it is if we find him." Nurn said still somewhat disheartened.

"Halin had to have been the one to make the marks on the walls. Most of the nassarid can either see in the dark or smell things well enough they don't need to. It just makes no sense to think Morcant or his brood would have done that." Jerine reasoned aloud.

"Fine! He knows how to burn rats, make extremely small fires, and he found a sword that he can barely use. Which one of these things is supposed to make him feel better about the fact that we still have no idea where he went to?" Nurn spat.

"What is supposed to make you feel better is that he escaped. It is obvious that your brother still had enough strength to climb our rope. As well as the wherewithal to know he needed to flee from Morcant while we fought him.

It means he is a survivor. Halin somehow has the needed skills as well as the will to live." Jerine said a little quieter. "Since we killed the nassarid that would have prevented his escape, we also know he was able to make it out safely."

"Now what?" Nurn asked hopelessly. "We have not found any other signs that he left the cave."

"Unfortunately more snow fell while we searched for him inside the cavern. Even our own tracks were buried by it." Jerine admitted.

"You know that does not answer my question," Nurn snapped.

"Now we go back to Hornshir. You need to tell Namir what happened and I need to report to Landolin with an update," Jerine replied. "With any luck, we will come across him on our way to the manor."

"Daffer was a great man." Namir's tone was somber and filled with respect.

His new black cloak was lined with white fur and it managed to keep the cold at bay. He knew the cold would not be a problem for long. Once the fires were lit, the makeshift docks would be warmer than he would like. At least until the pyres are launched.

The boards shifted noisily under his feet each time the wind picked up. It was unnerving the way it moved. The little motion did not seem to affect any of the others and he wondered silently to himself why.

"Many of us know him as the keeper of our inn, to a few here he was a friend and to others, family. But above all, he was a hero. Not only did he risk everything to save the lives of those who call Ellsted home, he also saved countless others as a Sargent in the Queen's army."

Namir glanced at Carness appreciatively. The town's constable stood iron straight and unwavering in his resolve. Even though he seemed emotionally as distant as Namir's uncertain future, there was a sense of solidarity he exuded.

"Those of us that knew him well still understood very little about this complicated man. Although he had a temper, Daffer was a pillar of Ellsted. In his own way, he was as much a sculptor as Armani or the other members of the council. In the end, he was just the man we needed to make sure Ellsted was well guarded and cared for. In the end, whether or not we agreed with his methods or actions, he died doing the right thing. He proved to everyone he was still a hero."

Namir looked across the sea of faces that stared up at him. He knew each and everyone. Sorrow and hatred mingled bitterly in their eyes. Their thoughts were laid bare to anyone skilled enough to read them. Most of them were afraid the world was over and they were right, at least partially. The world as they knew it was definitely over, no matter who wound up claiming the throne.

His gaze fell on Aves and Hessa as he spoke. The two girls looked stunning in their black velvet dresses. They looked more like the sisters they were than he had ever seen them in the past. It felt as if he was finally seeing them for who they were. All thoughts he had held about them were gone.

"Another one of our leaders that fell during the dragon's attack was our beloved Mayor, Armani. While he had not served in the military, he did serve our community. All of us know him. He was the person we all turned to when we needed advice. Whether it was something personal or official it did not matter. He was always available and never wavering.

Namir felt a tear creep down his cheek as he spoke. No matter how hard he tried, he could not stop them from coming. He paused long enough to take a few deep breaths and reinforced his resolve before he continued to speak.

"He was a surrogate father to many of us. Armani was a mystery of a man, really. One many of us will not be able to unravel. I knew him as a fair man. One who would sacrifice everything he knew in an attempt to create a better future. In the end, I believe that is what he did. It will be hard to carry on without him. And, I fear, it will be impossible to replace him." He finished his sentence with a ragged breath.

He let a few more tears roll down his cheeks. The Mayor deserved this much. While he knew the man had betrayed them, he felt responsible in a way. Armani was one of the few people in Ellsted that had always believed the best in him and Namir could do no less for him.

The stinging tears lessened slowly as he waited in silence. Namir knew that soon the fires would have to be lit. Until then, he planned on making sure the worst thing to have ever befallen this quiet town was remembered. Atrocities were powerful and they needed to be ingrained in the public's mind. Otherwise, the chance to learn from them is lost.

"Ten other lives in Ellsted were snuffed that night and ten other families lost an integral part of them. While it is hard to move on, that is what we must all do. Each of the fallen died for a reason. A cause, if you will. That reason is a simple one, hope. Whether they believed in the cause or not, they all passed on so that we could make something better out of the world we live in.

"For far too long darkness has devoured our lives and taken those we hold dearest. I know that I cannot promise it will never happen again. Instead, I promise not to let it stop me from doing what is needed, what is right.

"We may never know who was responsible for sending the dragon of darqueness. Is it important to know?

I do not believe so. What is important to decide what we are going to do about the attack and that is simple. We mourn for our loses and we learn. Without these important steps, we can never heal. If we do not heal we cannot survive. And that is what life is about, surviving. Ellsted can weather anything this world can throw at us because we are a community of survivors." Namir said as he raised his hands into the air.

Several hours ago, he had worked with the torchbearers. This was supposed to be their signal to light the fires. Instead, the only response he received was a shocked silence.

Namir glanced at Carness, Tipin, Allair, and Valeron for support. All four of them stood with their heads bowed in silent prayer. Even Saril had his head down and seemed transfixed in the moment.

"Let us all remember this day as Founder's Feast. It will be a day of remembrance in Ellsted. We will make it a day for solidarity and compassion. A time to reconnect with loved ones as well as helping those in need. With this," Namir reached for Valeron's bow and took an arrow with it, "I will commemorate our fallen and help send them on their way to a more peaceful place."

Without hesitation, Namir thrust the tip of the arrow into a nearby torch. Once he was certain the shaft was on fire, he nocked the arrow and let it fly. He had aimed for Daffer's pram.

Namir was relieved when he hit his target. He was even more at ease when the entire pram erupted in flames. It would have been more embarrassing if he had either missed or the boat did not catch fire.

A satisfied smile played across his lips. The members of the fire brigade snapped out of their initial bout of shock. Within moments they were igniting the other prams. After all of them were lit, each of the pyres was sent off into the water.

Morcant packed more snow into the gash in his armor. Red stained snow completely surrounded him. His eyes followed it back to the rugged crack he had crawled out of.

"All these years later and I still had to escape the same way I did before. Damnable elves," he cursed to himself.

The bittersweet smell of electricity mingled with his own blood as he lay in the snow. He did not need to hear the soft sound of leather as it sank in the snow for him to know what was happening. Blood flecked his lips as he coughed. The pain he felt sapped all of his strength.

"I wondered how long it would take our mistress to send you," Morcant said in shallow puffs.

"She knew you were in need," Skara purred her reply back to him.

"Can't you just let me die?" Morcant coughed. "You know she will not let you out of her service so easily. Besides, she has things only you can oversee," Skara cooed.

He watched as the feline witch knelt over him. The pain was almost too much for him. His vision swam with each beat of his heart. If Skara had not shown up, Morcant knew he would be dead.

"Like what, killing you?" He knew she could see through his bravado, but Morcant did not care.

"You know, things like babysitting her favorite humans," she grinned playfully down at him. "Besides, I would get bored without you."

"Too bad," Morcant replied.

Part of him hoped to keep her distracted. If he could manage it long enough he could die and finally be free of his mistress's clutches. He knew it was a futile hope, but he held onto it as another cough freed itself from his lungs.

"Where are the others?" Skara asked curiously. "They are probably dead," Morcant said.

"How many did you have with you?" She said as he saw her eyes dance across his exposed wounds.

"Six," Morcant tried to turn as he spoke so she would not be able to see how bad off he really was.

"All of them are dead. Our mistress will not be pleased. You have a bad tendency to lose too many of our brethren when you go on missions." Although there was an unusual softness to her voice, Morcant knew she was reprimanding him.

"Damn witch, out with it!" He writhed in pain with each word. "I know you have a question you want to ask."

"Did you at least succeed in retrieving the sword?" A look of pity pulled at the corner of the felinoid's eyes and he hated it.

"No, the boy got away," Morcant admitted.

"I see. Well then, it is time to go home," Skara said as she slipped a small vial filled with a silvery powder from one of her pouches.

Chapter Twenty-Four: Assemblies

Dark oppressive clouds blotted out what little sun attempted to shine through them. The growing sense of foreboding that had been building over the last sorrowful week had not eased in the slightest. Namir hated the feeling. It had crept in unbidden and formed a ball in the pit of his stomach.

He walked away from the window he was looking out and moved back to his place at the head of the table. Daffer's favorite chair had been placed at the head of the table and several others had been moved around it as well. Namir glanced at the faces of people he had met but did not know overly well.

"Thank you all for coming on short notice. As you know there is no longer any one place large enough for everyone to attend a mass wake." Namir said clearly. "I have opened the inn up to as many that can fit into it to remember the fallen. Aside from that, I expect people will want to be with their loved ones."

"That is very gracious of you," Mistress Clara said demurely.

"It was the right thing to do," Tipin replied. "That it was," Saril agreed.

"But that is not why I have asked all of you here," Namir said solemnly. "I want to make sure the town is prepared for tomorrow."

"What happens tomorrow?" The deep baritone voice of the town crier asked somewhat confused.

"Tomorrow I plan on leaving Ellsted, Namir confided. "As most of you are aware, I am laying my claim to the throne of Cennicus. To do that I need to be surrounded by people I can trust, all of which need to have a better understanding of how things work than I do. I can think of no better people than the current Council of Ellsted."

Namir could see the panic written on the faces of those that did not know what was happening. He raised his hand to retain control of the conversation. Although this settled them down a little, he knew that he needed to fill them in or they would quickly descend into protests.

"Saril has agreed to stay behind and remain the resident healer. However, I need to take both Allair and Carness with me. Carness was initially opposed to this, but as a Hero of Watch Keep I need him." Namir said softly.

He saw the looks of despair mingled with outrage on several of the prominent townsfolk's faces as he spoke, "Before you ask, yes I have considered what this will do to Ellsted. That is why I have asked you all here. Each of you either has been a prominent member of the town or will be in the upcoming months. You are the people the rest of the citizens are going to turn to for help after we leave. As such I am going to declare an emergency proclamation and place several of you onto the council until proper elections can be held. This will give each of you a chance to determine if you would like to run for office and allow the town to understand that their needs have been thought about."

Namir took a deep breath to let his words settle in before he said anything else. While the small crowd thought about what he had said, Namir waved to one of the barmaids and motioned for drinks to be brought out. If nothing else they might be sated with some wine while they decide their level of participation.

"Mistress Clara, I would ask that you consider the appointment of Mayor. I know that you are well versed in running a business and are reliant upon the rest of the town for your prosperity. From my understanding, the role of Mayor is comparable to that.

"Thank you, I will definitely consider it. However, may I ask why I was not appointed as the Head Merchant?" Her words were well chosen and Namir saw where she was going with her thoughts.

"The Head Merchant, though important to the businesses in Ellsted, does not have as much say in managing the town's needs," Namir said coolly. "Ellsted needs a strong thinker and negotiator at the helm. That is why both Allair and myself thought you would be the best choice."

"I appreciate the explanation, thank you. And it clears up my questions perfectly," Mistress Clara replied smiling. "I accept the title as well as the role."

"Braythe," Namir said to the Gathering Place's cook. We have decided to ask you to be the Head Merchant and the new owner of the inn."

The look of shock that played across the older lady's haggard face was nothing less than comical. She opened and closed her mouth a few times as she tried to decide how she should reply. The flush of crimson that consumed her pale and freckled features only added to the comical effect.

When she could finally speak, she stammered, "Thank-thank you my-my liege."

"You are more than welcome. Jaconis has made it more than clear that he will never return to this town. As King, I will have little use for an inn, even as successful as this place is. I will gather a few of my uncle's things tomorrow before I leave. Everything I leave behind is yours."

"Than-Thank you again," Braythe replied humbly.

"Tegau, you have been the town crier for many years. Allair told me that she has cherished working with you. More importantly, she feels that you are ready for the next step, to become the Envoy of the council. What do you say, will you accept the responsibility?" Namir asked as he eyed the man.

Tegau was someone he had never really noticed. Although he remembered hearing the latest decree or update the Council passed down, he never really had taken any time to get to know him. Likewise, he had never really seen the man in the Gathering Place.

"I am honored to be considered. Of course, I will accept it," the middle-aged man bowed as his crisp voice boomed throughout the inn.

"That leaves the final role of Constable. From what Carness says, you are the best one to replace him," Namir said as he turned his attention to the only other person in the room his own age.

The boy had flame red hair and pale skin. His brilliant green eyes flashed as he met Namir's steely gaze. Although he was not nearly as stout as Nurn, he was well built with a brad chest and thick arms.

"What say you Aneiri? Will you accept the mantle of Constable?" Namir asked proudly. He was glad that Carness had chosen someone as young as he was. It bolstered Namir to think that there were others his age destined for greatness in their own community.

"If Carness says I am fit for the job, who am I to disagree?" Aneiri replied evenly. His voice was deeper than Namir's but nowhere as deep as Tipin's. There was also an odd edge to it that reminded Namir of Carness.

Namir nodded to each as the barmaid refilled their glasses. As soon as they were all filled, Namir rose. He waited for everyone else to take to their feet before he raised his glass high.

"What is done can never be undone, to the health of you and yours. May your time in office be for the betterment of Ellsted," he toasted.

After they all had a drink, Namir motioned for each of them to take a seat. As they did Namir pointed to both Carness and Allair and beckoned them to him.

"Please make sure that everyone is briefed about what they need to know for their appropriate offices tonight before the wakes. I want to give them as much time as they might need to comprehend what they may need to understand." Namir said quietly.

After the two of them nodded and went back to their seats, Namir looked over the small gathering. He raised his glass one more time and said, "These announcements were not the only reason I asked you all here."

A hush fell over the room as everyone looked at him. Namir smiled broadly as he pulled Zelios out from under his shirt. The amulet was warm to his touch and its weight was soothing.

"There are several among you that I would like to honor tonight. Not only are they well known for their deeds and service, but they have all agreed to be the first of my Knights of the Realm," Namir said solemnly. "As your first act as the newly formed Council of Ellsted, I ask that you bear witness to their vows and elevation."

He reveled in the looks of shock that washed over everyone's faces. He knew none of them expected this now, but he did not want to wait any longer. He wanted everyone at the various wakes to know about their Knighthood. That way the townsfolk might take the news of their leaving better.

"Saril, were you able to acquire their Knightly tokens?" Namir asked loud enough for everyone to hear him.

"I have. I have also blessed and consecrated them in

Ea's name," Saril replied dutifully.

"Very well," Namir nodded. "Clara and Aneiri, please collect these items from Saril and have them ready to be given to the new Knights," Namir instructed in his best official sounding voice.

He stepped away from the table and walked over to the hearth. The heat from the blazing fire felt good across his back as he stopped in front of it. Namir waited for the new Mayor and Constable to rise and collect the items from Saril. As soon as they had them, he motioned them to stand a little behind him and to his right. At the same time, Saril crossed over and stood to Namir's left.

"Tegau, would you please honor us by calling my prospective Knights up to receive their tokens and give their vows?" Namir looked at the new Envoy and smiled at his confusion. "You should have a list in front of you. Please rise and call them forth."

Tegau rose and brushed a stray lock of brown hair away from his face. He cleared his throat and took a quick drink of wine before lifting the folded piece of paper off of the table. He quickly unfolded it and shakily raised it up so he could see the names.

"Valeron, Carness, Tipin, and Allair, please rise and approach your King," although his demeanor betrayed his nervousness, his voice did not.

Namir was glad he had taken the time to let Braythe know in advance. He watched as she slipped away from the table as the four rose and crossed the room. While each of them knelt in turn, she opened the door and ushered the townsfolk into the room. She skillfully directed them to available seats and managed to finish just as Allair took her knee.

"As some of you know, we have gathered to invest these four heroes with their tokens and trappings of Knighthood. I implore all of you to take heed and understand that these four will be the first of my Knights and shall hereby have the title of Knight of the Realm." Namir said clearly.

"Master Saril, do we have the first trapping of Knighthood so we can invest them with it, the chain?" Namir asked the healer in as clear of a tone as he could.

"Yes, my liege, in the safekeeping of your servant, Master Aneiri," Saril replied.

Aneiri nodded and carried four stunning gold chains looped over his left wrist. He stepped between Namir and the prospective Knights so they could be examined.

They were amazing. Each link was designed to intertwine and was stamped with the official seal of Cennicus, a dragon's head facing to the right with a circle of roses in its mouth. When Namir nodded his approval, Aneiri turned and faced the four people kneeling in front of them.

"This chain of gold, the purest of metals, signifies the purity of the chain of fealty which binds the Knight and his King to one another." The young constable said as he placed the first chain around Valeron's neck.

"This chain is heavy to symbolize and remind the Knight of the heavy responsibility he bears," the second chain was looped around Carness's neck as the boy continued.

"This chain is strong and runs around the neck of the Knight signifying obedience to the commands of his sovereign and the order of Knighthood," Aneiri said just loud enough to be heard as he placed it around Tipin's massive neck.

"This chain is the unique symbol of the Knights of the Realm," the constable finished as he placed the final chain around Allair's neck.

"I pray that you let your behavior and deeds charge this symbol with as great a reverence and respect as you would any of the symbols of our forbearers," Saril instructed them.

"Now that we have bestowed the first trapping of Knighthood, do we have the second trapping? Master Saril, do we have the cloak with the Coat of Arms?" Namir asked as soon as the healer was done speaking.

"Yes, my liege, in the safekeeping of your servant, Mistress Clara," Saril replied.

Clara smiled and curtsied to Namir before she retrieved the items. When she returned she had four thick leather cloaks folded over her left arm. Like Aneiri had, she stepped between Namir and the prospective Knights. She easily unfurled the first one with a flick of her wrist for inspection.

The deep burgundy cloak looked almost black in the light of the fire.The dragon's head was embroidered in silver with a golden circle of roses clutched in its teeth. To Namir, it looked as if they were made of actual metal instead of thread.Namir nodded his approval and Clara turned and faced the four people who knelt in front of them. "Shamefastness or fear of shame," Clara said as she draped the displayed cloak over Valeron's shoulders and fastened it to the chain.

"These arms ensure that all might know this Knight from afar, and judge him fair or foul, to ensure obedience to the order of Knighthood," she opened the cloak with a flourish and let its own weight guide it down onto Carness's shoulders. With exquisite skill, she quickly fastened it in place with the chain of Knighthood.

"It symbolizes the hardships and travail that a Knight will suffer foremost in battle and always placing his body between his Kingdom and her foes," Clara smiled as she draped the cloak over Tipin's massive shoulders. Although she probably did not need to fasten it in place, she did just as deftly as she had the other two.

"Just as the cloak receives any blows, rain, or insult before the armor and body of the Knight, let the Knight be the barrier betwixt us and our enemies," she concluded as the final cloak settled into place over Allair's delicate shoulders. Clara looked at Allair with overt admiration she fastened the cloak into place with the chain.

"Master Saril, do we have the belt to bestow upon our goodly Knights?" Namir asked.

"Yes, my liege, in the safekeeping of your servant, Mistress Clara," Saril replied.

Clara had just managed to make it back to her spot when she heard Saril say her name. She giggled silently as she spun around and faced Namir. She quickly looped the four white leather belts over her wrist and curtsied once more. She stepped between Namir and the prospective Knights and held up the first belt for inspection.

Even in the yellowish orange light of the fire, the belts look pure white. Unlike the other vestments, the belts were only stamped with the circle of roses along its entire length, while the buckle was designed to be a silver dragon's head. Just like the rest, these were a pure work of art. Namir could not see any imperfection in its construction. He quickly nodded his approval and Clara turned and faced the four people who knelt in front of them again.

"The Knight's white belt symbolizes purity and chastity," Clara said as she slipped the first belt around Valeron's waist loosely and clasped it in place.

"A Knight must reign in his body steadfastly," the second belt slid around Carness's waist and clasped it in place as she spoke evenly.

"Constantly avoiding the scandals of the body: gluttony, sloth, and lechery," Tipin's massive waist proved a slight challenge for the seamstress as she fastened it too in place.

"Purity of purpose and a new beginning or rebirth to begin again in the steps of the Path of Chivalry," Clara finished as she easily fastened Allair's belt in place.

Namir waited for Clara to take her place this time. He was a little embarrassed that he had not given her enough time between the last two trappings. Once she was in place he nodded and continued.

He took a small breath and said, "Master Saril, do we

have the spurs for our gallant Knights?"

"Yes, my liege, in the safekeeping of your servant, Master Aneiri," Saril replied.

Aneiri bowed to Namir and carried four sets of gleaming spurs in his left hand. He stepped between Namir and the prospective Knights. Then he offered them one set up so Namir could visually examine it.

The shining bronze had been crafted into a scaled loop that ended in a dragon's head. In its teeth, the steel spur was designed to look like a circle of sharpened roses. The overall effect was stunning. When Namir nodded his approval, Aneiri turned and faced the four people kneeling in front of them.

"As Knight's spurs goad the warhorse, so should they goad the Knight to Valor, Service, Diligence, and Swiftness," his words flowed easily from his mouth as he fastened one of the spurs onto Valeron's left foot. The other spur he placed on the ground next to the Knight.

"Let the spurs hasten the Knight to his duty that he might maintain his order in the high honor that belongs to it," Aneiri repeated the process with Carness and only affixed the left spur to the man's outstretched boot.

"By precious spurs near his feet, displays disdain for worldly things," he paused slightly to adjust the loop before he attached the spur to Tipin's left foot.

"They should be worn with honor and discretion lest they are hacked from your heels in shame and disgrace," Aneiri finished. Since Allair knelt with both knees pressed to the floor, he fastened her spurs to both boots before he stood and took his place beside Clara.

Namir allowed himself to smile as he watched Aneiri finish his task smoothly. "Master Saril, do we have the next to last trapping, the Annulet?"

"Yes, my liege, it is in my safekeeping," Saril replied evenly.

Saril reached his left hand into his pouch and pulled out four golden rings. Each one gleamed majestically in the stark light of the fire. Namir could easily see the royal device etched into the ring's center. It had been fashioned like a signet ring.

"This gold Annulet signifies the marriage of the Candidate to the Order of Knighthood, and as such is bound to its values, duties, and obligations," Saril said as he handed each of the Knights a ring.

"That leaves the final token of Knighthood, the weapon. While a sword is customarily the symbol of a Knight, I have decided to change this. Each of you four has proven your abilities with the weapons of your choosing. Although I am aware that you all know how to use any weapon available to you, you have developed specialized skills in a particular one. With that in mind, Master Saril, do we have the weapons which these four will offer in service to the Crown?"

"Yes, my liege, in the safekeeping of your servants, Mistress Clara and Master Aneiri," Saril replied perfectly.

In unison, both Clara and Aneiri stepped forward. Each of them carried two weapons, one in each hand. Clara held a spear and a bow while Aneiri carried a sword and axe. Namir instantly recognized each of the favorite weapons of his new knights, so he nodded his approval to the council members as they stepped between him and his four Knights.

"One edge to cut to the truth, one edge to administer justice and a scabbard to counsel mercy," they both said in unison as they placed the weapons on the ground in front of the four.

"We are not yet finished," Namir said to the gathered masses. He could feel their excitement and understood why they were growing restless. Nothing like this had ever happened in Ellsted. He was glad he could give them this glimpse of merriment on the same day they mourned their fallen friends.

"Zelios, please grant me the use of the Sword of the Realm so I may officially grant them the rank and standing of Knight of the Realm," his words echoed off the walls as the gem glowed brightly.

Gasps of shock and amazement filled the room as Zelios materialized kneeling between him and the four Knights. Her arms were outstretched in supplication. Lying across both of her palms glowed an ethereal sword. The blade cast a blue light, but everyone could plainly see the burgundy leather that wrapped the hilt. The crossbar was a dragon's mouth opened wide enough for the blade to protrude like a snaking tongue. A golden rosebud formed the perfectly sculpted pommel.

Namir lifted the blade hesitantly. Although she had told him what to expect, the reality of it was completely different than what he had imagined. It felt warm to the touch and lighter than any other sword he had ever lifted. As he picked up the blade, Zelios rose and waited for him to move forward. When he did, she took his place in front of the fire.

Namir slowly walked over to Valeron first and lowered the sword to his left shoulder and said, "In remembrance of oaths given and received." He raised the sword and then lowered it to the Knight's right shoulder, while saying, "In remembrance of your lineage and obligations." He raised the blade once more and let it rest on the man's head as he uttered the final part, "Be a Knight of Honor in both deed and word. Rise, Sir Valeron."

A loud cheer filled the room as Valeron stood and sheathed his sword. Namir smiled and shook his hand. With a quick motion, he made sure Valeron knew he needed to stay where he was before Namir moved on to Carness.

Namir slowly stepped over to Carness first and lowered the sword to his left shoulder and said, "In remembrance of oaths given and received." He raised the sword and then lowered it to the ex-constable's right shoulder, while saying, "In remembrance of your lineage and obligations." He raised the blade once more and let it rest on his friend's head as he uttered the final part, "Be a Knight of Valor in both deed and word. Rise, Sir Carness."

The room erupted once more as Carness stood and held his spear with pride. Namir's grin widened as he shook his hand. Then he communicated his desire to Carness just as he had with Valeron.

Namir settled himself in front of Tipin and lowered the sword to his left shoulder and said, "In remembrance of oaths given and received." He raised the sword and then lowered it to the Knight's right shoulder, while saying, "In remembrance of your lineage and obligations." He raised the blade once more and let it rest on the man's head as he uttered the final part, "Be a Knight of Faith in both deed and word. Rise, Sir Tipin and be the first of the Calanari to be Knighted."

This time the room fell silent as the smith stood and secured his axe. Namir knew that none of the previous rulers had ever made any other race a Knight, save the elves. He was proud that he was the first to share this honor with another race.

His pride increased when Carness cast a sharp glance at those closest to him. The result was a deafening cheer. Several toasts were spontaneously made as Namir shook Tipin's hand. He knew the Calanari needed no instruction, so he just smiled up at him broadly.

Namir ended his small walk at Allair. He smiled at his best friend's mother before he lowered the sword to her left shoulder and said, "In remembrance of oaths given and received." He raised the sword and then lowered it to the lady's right shoulder, while saying, "In remembrance of your lineage and obligations." He raised the blade once more and let it rest on the top of her head as he uttered the final part, "Be a Knight of Courtesy in both deed and word. Rise, Dame Allair and be the first woman to serve as a Knight in our fair Kingdom."

A final cheer emanated from all around him as Allair rose and slung her bow across her chest. He smiled at her happily as he shook her hand. Emotionally Namir was bursting at the seams. It was all he could do to just stand there for a moment.

Once the cheers died down a little, and he regained his ability to move, he turned to Zelios. She quietly knelt in front of him again. This time he held the sword aloft and placed it delicately in her hands.

As he did he said, "Thank you for allowing me to use the steel of the Gods to imbue honor and righteousness to these Knights of the Realm.

Zelios simply nodded and faded once more from view. The amulet around his neck glowed brilliantly and bathed all four of his new Knights in its blue sheen. As the light faded back into a glow, Namir stepped to the middle of the four.

Namir cleared his throat to get the room's attention before he said, "We now see four Knights gathered before us. Each one of them hales from a different part of these lands. While I would love to say that this was done on purpose to unify our Kingdom, I cannot. Instead, I want you all to know it was their deeds that brought them this honor. It is a testament to how they lived and what they have done with their lives. This honor is one that I can promise to all of you in attendance. If you choose to live your life in such a way, then no matter your standing, you can become a Knight as well."

Namir turned to Tipin and said, "As the only Calanari Knight, I would like to honor your people by borrowing a custom from your homeland. I was once told that the Calanari charge new warriors with a task and I would like to do the same for all of you."

He did his best to hide the tear that crept from the corner of his eye as he looked at each of them in turn. Namir took a deep breath and said, "Know, that now you are each made Knights. You must now, and forevermore, succor the defenseless, seek justice for those of every station, and maintain the honor of Knighthood. Let this blow remind you that Knighthood shall bring you pain as well as honor. This blow will also be the last unanswered attack on you for the rest of your life."

Without warning, Namir swiftly hit each of them in the center of their chest. Although he did not hit them hard, the responses he received were perfect. Each one of them took a defensive stance before they realized why he had hit them. Once they understood, each of them hit each other in response.

"Now let's turn the inn over to the mourners and honor our dead," Namir said loud enough to elicit another cheer.

The sounds of the mourning floated into Aves's window as she brushed her hair. Somehow they brought back the revelry she had heard during the festival and it bothered her. Her father was dead and people were cheering and partying. It was not right.

"Are you planning on joining the mourners at the Gathering Place this evening?" Hessa asked from her sister's doorway.

"I'd rather not," Aves said bitterly. "I'm in no mood to celebrate."

"Neither am I," Hessa replied. "Too much has happened. I just want to crawl into my bed and hide."

"We should really pack our belongings and whatever we want of Armani's," Aves said as she turned and faced her sister. "Mistress Clara is bound to want to move in as soon as she can. After all, this is the Mayor's house and Namir was going to appoint that position to her sometime this evening."

"I am sure she will give us time to do that, she has a place of her own," Hessa said softly. "Besides, there are many more pressing matters she will need to attend to first."

"Like what?" Aves asked incredulously. "The acting Mayor will need access to Armani's notes and journals if she is going to follow up on anything he had in the works. All of that is in his study, at least what remains of them."

"We should go through the things in Armani's study tonight. That way if she needs something we can tell her take what she wants from there," Hessa offered. "I will let her know that everything else is off limits. If she doesn't like that, then I will get someone to move everything from here into my mother's cottage where we can go through it at our leisure."

"That would be great. Are you sure you can take care of all that?" Aves asked. "There is just so much to do and I know Namir was planning on going back to Hornshir tomorrow."

"Even if he does, I can leave after that if I need to. Namir will certainly leave us a note at the manor if he leaves before we can get there." Hessa rationalized. "I honestly think it will take him a few days to leave. He needs to make sure the new council has everything they need to succeed and Tipin will want to make sure his best remaining apprentice has what he needs to work the forge in his absence."

"You are right," Aves said a little happier. "He will be lucky to be able to get out of town in a week."

"Well then, we should get started," Hessa motioned for her sister to come with her.

"The first thing I want to find is our father's personal journals," Aves said as she rose and joined Hessa in the hall. "Do you think he would have those in his room or his study?"

"Why not split up and check both?" Hessa replied. I will check the study and you can check his room. If I find it I will bring it to you."

"That sounds like a plan," Aves said. She tried to hide her building enthusiasm from Hessa. The last thing she wanted was for her sister to know why she wanted the journals.

She carefully made her way down the hallway toward her father's room. Although she could have taken a lantern with her, Aves preferred the darkness. It was somehow soothing to her.

It did not take her long to get to her father's room. After walking to the end of the hall, she steadily climbed the flight of stairs to the top. Getting through his door was another matter entirely.

She carefully pressed down on the handle as she tried to open the door. It was locked and she could not budge it. Part of her wondered if Hessa had found their father's spare key, but she did not want to admit defeat. Not now, not when she was so close to finding his journals and learning about his secrets.

Aves retraced her steps back to her room. She knew her father's balcony was above hers. There had been many mornings she awoke to the sound of him eating breakfast on it. Getting to it from hers should not be too difficult. Once she was on it, getting into his room should be easy.

A freezing gust of bitterly cold air stole her breath as she opened the door to her balcony. She shivered involuntarily as she pulled her cloak tightly around her. Aves struggled against the urge to close the door and retreat back into the warmth she knew her room offered. Although she knew she could wait until morning, she did not want to give Hessa a chance to find their father's secrets first.

This was Aves's chance to finally know about something that her sister did not. Unlike Hessa, she did not have a network of friends willing to be her eyes and ears all around town. Aves resented having to rely on Hessa for information.

Until recently she had not thought anything about it. Then, when Hessa left them with almost no notice, Aves understood her dependency better. She had to do this without Hessa's help if she ever wanted to prove to herself she was able to survive on her own.

Aves stepped out onto her snow-filled balcony carefully. The snow quickly seeped into her boots and froze her skin. Her dress, though warm, offered little protection against the almost two feet of snow she waded through.

She stretched her neck awkwardly in an attempt to gauge the distance from her balcony to her father's. Although she had only taken a couple steps onto her balcony, she did not want to go any further because of the depth of the snow. An exacerbated sigh escaped her lips as she stood and silently debated her options.

There was no real choice. Aves stepped back into her room and closed the balcony door. She stood next to the fire in her room as her skin thawed. A change of clothes was in order, but she needed more than that. She needed a rope.

Her mind buzzed with options. She could twist a sheet up and tie t to her blanket or she could take her curtains down and use those. Both ideas seemed viable, but she was not sure if she could do it. She had never really tied a knot before. While it looked easy when she saw Namir tie one, it seemed like it might be harder than it looked.

Aves slipped off her dress as she mulled over her options. Her fingers picked their way through her wardrobe with a mind of their own. She knew she was missing something, but she just could not place what it was. Instinctively she pulled a pair of riding breeches Hessa had given her from Natlia's place, and a warm jacket from her wardrobe before she closed the door.

She mechanically worked over her options as she pulled the dark blue riding breeches on under her dress. Each thought she had seemed to be off or missing something vital. She tried to recall where Armani might have kept some rope as she tugged her boots onto each foot and then pulled her jacket on.

Then she saw it. The rope went from her wall up to the ceiling and over to the chandelier in the middle of her room.

She knew it would be more than long enough for what she needed to use it for.

Without another thought, Aves walked over the wall and examined the knot Hessa had used to hold the chandelier in place. She meticulously untied it and kept track of how the rope had been looped over itself. Once she was certain she could retie it, she quietly lowered the chandelier to the floor.

She easily pulled the rope from the moorings that held it in place before she crossed over to the middle of her room. Quietly she twisted the centerpiece out of its place. Aves was pleased to see that she could remove the metal hook from the rest of the contraption and still leave it attached to the rope. That would make it much easier to throw it over her father's balcony and attach it.

Before she decided to open her balcony door again, Aves crossed her room to her doorway. She quickly closed the door and latched it. That way Hessa would not just stumble in and see what she had been up to.

Aves smiled to herself at her ingenuity as she walked back over to her balcony door. As an afterthought, she grabbed her cloak and threw it around her shoulders. The added warmth would be nice in case it took her longer than she had planned for. The last thing she needed was gloves. Thankfully she still had the pair she had borrowed from her sister from their jaunt to the memorial.

Pulling her gloves on as she opened the door, Aves stepped back out onto her balcony. This time the bitter air was more tolerable to her as she waded out into the snow. Even the snow seemed less formidable to her as she walked deeper into it.

She glanced at her father's balcony again. She could see quite a few places where she would be able to attach the rope. None of them were too far from where she stood, but she chose the one closest to the wall in case she needed to use it to climb.

Aves tested the weight f the hook by tossing it up in the

air a couple times. It seemed about the same weight as the rocks Namir and her used to throw into the river when he was shirking his chores at the Gathering Place. Although those rocks were not attached to a rope, she figured it would be just as easy to throw it.

Her first attempt ended in utter failure. She tossed it just like she had the rocks, but the rope dragged heavily through the snow and forced it to fall short. Her second and third attempt ended the same way. Again she felt like she was missing something.

There had to be a way to get the rope across the short distance. Aves mused about the problem as she played with the rope. It twisted and turned in her hands as she thought the problem through. The hook swung easily from one side to the next as she turned her ideas over and over in her mind.

"If only I could just swing over there," she thought bitterly.

An idea quickly formed in her head as the rope swung a little further from one side of her balcony to the next. She suddenly knew what she had to do. Aves shook her head at her own stupidity. Both Nurn and Namir swung ropes over tree branches countless times when they were younger. It was something she had not thought about in such a long time, but it was also so very obvious.

Aves grabbed the loose end of the rope and tied it around her left wrist. She used the knot she had found the rope originally tied with. She did not dare lose it once she threw the other end. As an added precaution, she also decided to hold it tightly in her left hand. After she was certain it was secure, Aves carefully walked over to the outer edge of her balcony. She slowly lowered the hook end a little over the side so it could swing freely without hitting the house. Gradually she swung the rope in a circle. With each revolution she allowed it to pick up a little more speed. Once she was certain there was enough force to get it to where she needed it, she let go.

To her surprise, it worked. The hook arched upward toward the balcony and wrapped around the railing her father had built in case he needed to steady himself. She tugged on the end she still held tightly in her left hand to make sure the rope was secure and thankfully it was.

The only thing she had left to do was jump. Aves glanced down at the large snow drifts that had accumulated against the house beneath her. A lump formed in the pit of her stomach as she walked over and climbed up onto the railing of her own balcony.

"At least the drifts will give me a soft landing if I fall," she thought ruefully to herself.

Without another thought, she tugged the rope tight and swung over to the wall beneath Armani's balcony. The feeling was both exhilarating and terrifying. Before she knew what was happening, her boots struck the wall. All of the times she spent with Namir and the smithy boys played through her head. Climbing was one of the things she could do better than any of them. Now it was time to see if she still had it in her.

Her arms moved of their own volition as Aves concentrated on moving her feet up the wall one step at a time. In less time than it had taken her to lower the chandelier, she was within reach of the metal railing. She easily grabbed it and pulled herself onto it.

Before she knew it, her hand was on the latch of the door. Aves pressed down on the handle and the door swung easily open. The door opened quieter than her balcony door did and she wondered if it was designed that way for a reason.

The bitter chill of the night air followed her into Armani's room. Although she was inside, it was just as cold as it had been while she was on the balcony. Her eyes darted over to the unused fireplace and realized that neither Hessa nor herself had been here for the past few days. Obviously, her father was not one to light his own fire.

Even with her cloak and jacket on, she was cold. Her teeth rattled against themselves as Aves stooped to light the fire. After she took care of this, she was free to search his room for something she could use to find out more about her father's secrets.

"Where should I start," she asked herself as she fumbled with the fire kit.

Thankfully Hessa had already stacked some logs in his fireplace before they left. Aves quickly removed some cotton wadding from the kit and stuffed it between the logs. In less than a heartbeat, she had managed to strike a spark and coax the fire into life.

Her hazel eyes danced around the room as she warmed herself by the fire. Everything was so organized. It was even better kept than either his office in the house or the one he had in the Council Hall. Although she never thought of Armani as a slob, this meticulous level of neatness was more than unusual for him.

"His nightstand, I think," Aves said to herself out loud. "That is where I keep mine after all."

Visions of the mirror Armani gave to Natlia played through her head as Aves walked to her father's bed Reflexively she pulled at her gloves. She was not going to fall for any of his traps. The last thing she needed was to touch the wrong thing and be trapped by it or worse.

Aves shook the haunting images of the creature from her mind. Her finger slipped through the brass ring handle of the drawer and she tugged on it delicately. A silent prayer to Ea ran through her head as the drawer slid silently open.

Even in the slight light of the fire, she could see the drawer was empty. She let her eyes wander over the room again as she slid it closed. Although her father had lavish tastes, his room was minimally decorated.

Like in her room, there was a chandelier hanging above the center of the room. He had a large feather bed complete with a four post frame and a nightstand. Two dressers and a wardrobe lined the wall opposite to the bed. A single desk was placed under the window and two comfortable looking chairs sat near the middle of the room facing the fire with a small table between them.

As she looked around the room again, her eyes kept being drawn back to the small table nestled neatly between the chairs. Although it was round, there was something odd about the dull grey wood. It seemed as if she saw something that was not there, but when she looked at it directly the image vanished.

She walked over to it and stood a pace away from it and stared. The firelight cast her shadow over it in an odd rhythmic dance. It was mesmerizing and tranquil. Her eyes followed the captivating movements of light and dark as they played across the smooth grey surface. Sometimes they seemed to pause, in the middle of the space. It seemed almost like they were trapped for a second, before finally being released.

Aves blinked heavily as she watched the trapped shadows again and again. Just like before, she only saw it when she was not looking. As soon as she reused on the spot, the effect vanished.

"This must be it," she thought to herself. "Maybe he has a book like Hessa's. That might explain it."

Without thinking, Aves lowered her hand toward the center of the effect. To make sure she was on track, she looked once at the table and then immediately shifted her gaze to her father's favorite chair. Carefully she pressed her hand down to where the thing should be.

Disappointment wracked her brain as her fingers met the hardwood of the table. There was nothing there, not even any resistance. She slid her hand along the table's surface in all directions with the vain hope of finding something.

Angrily Aves threw herself into the chair she assumed was her father's favorite one. Although it was comfortable, it looked to be much more worn down than the other one.

The leather-wrapped cushion groaned as she pushed herself into it.

"I will figure this out," Aves promised herself.

From this angle, she could not see anything out of the ordinary. Nothing was unusual and nothing froze or was distorted, not even when she looked through the edge of her eyes. The flickering light played over the table's surface unobstructed. Even the dark grey rings seemed to blend into the tabletop.

After a few moments, she stood back up and paced the room. Each lap brought her back to the table. No matter how far she went, she always wound up right in front of it. With every glance, she saw the same effect. It felt like the table was taunting her and she did not like it one bit.

Aves glared at the table as she walked around it one more time. This time she decided to view it from near the other chair. It was her last hope to solve it.

"There is only one place I have not tried looking at it from," Aves muttered to herself.

She abruptly decided to sit in the newer of the two chairs. Carefully her body slid along the leather-wrapped cushion. The chair groaned as she pressed herself deeper into its softness. She did her best not to look at the table as she situated herself. Aves did not want to ruin the moment.

Once she was settled, she reached toward the distortion. Her eyes widened when she felt her fingers brush something leather. Without looking at it, she lowered her left hand onto whatever it was. She gently closed her fingers around what felt like the spine of a book and she lifted it up.

The firelight seemed to be absorbed by the books deep black cover. She delicately placed it on her lap and half expected it to vanish. Her heart beat loudly in her ears as she stared intently at it.

When the book did not vanish, she let out a breath she had not realized she held. Her trembling fingers slowly opened the cover. Milky white pages with her father's writing in a deep blue ink met her gaze. She shivered inwardly as she flipped through the pages one at a time.

"He did keep one," she thought to herself.

The weight of the book warmed her lap as she read a passage on each page before she turned it. The entries dated back to when she was a child. Although most of them were cryptically written, several plainly outlined some of the things he hoped to accomplish in the coming years.

Every page contained both secrets and events. Some of them she had heard about, while others she could not comprehend. After a few moments, Aves gingerly flipped through to his more recent entries.

She needed to know how her father was involved with the recent attacks. Why he would sacrifice the one thing he had struggled so hard to create and keep safe. His actions made no sense and she hoped this journal would help her sort it all out.

Aves's lips moved as she silently read each entry Armani had written over the last few days. Her eyes widened a bit more with each word. Although she could not quite decipher all of it, she was able to understand enough.

"I know why Armani betrayed the town," Aves practically screamed, "and I need to warn Namir."

Epilogue

The roughly hewn stairs seemed to go on forever. At least that is the way it felt to him. After the blinding light as he fought Morcant and the immediate darkness that followed it, nothing seemed to make any sense. Even the sword felt odd on his side as he collapsed onto the top stair.

"Giants must have made those monstrous things," he thought to himself in dismay.

"No they were made by the dwarves," the voice of the sword corrected him.

"Awfully tall dwarves," Halin muttered back into the darkness.

The sound of the sword laughing in his mind did little for Halin's composure. He winced at the malicious sounding laugh. If something was funny, he sure did not see what it was.

"They would have to be in order to create such huge steps," Halin thought defensively.

"What you call stairs are large excavation sites. They discover and dig up the stones they need to build the rest of the passage. They mine as they go, not the other way around," the sword clarified.

"So those weren't stairs," Halin said as he finally understood the sword's meaning.

"CORRECT," its amusement was still evident in the thing's voice.

"Why didn't you say that, to begin with?" Halin muttered again. "Next time just tell me what it is instead of letting me think it is something completely different."

"I will do my best to remember," it said somewhat more obediently.

"What should I call you, by the way?" Halin asked as he struck a dagger against the wall to get a little light.

"I AM THE FAESELIAN BLADE, THE SHARPEST THING EVER CREATED. I WAS GIVEN TO THE WORLD BY THE GOD FAESIN," the sword replied.

"Okay," Halin said slowly. "I guess that lets me know what you are, but that was not my question. I asked what I should call you. Other than Fay-sel-eean Blade, what would you like to go by?" Halin asked as he sounded out the things name slowly to emphasize his point. "You know, for a sharp sword you are not too bright."

"MY PREVIOUS OWNER CALLED ME BY MANY NAMES, BUT HIS FAVORITE WAS LUGANDIHAR," the blade replied. "I BELIEVE IT IS CALANARI FOR LIGHTENING."

Halin blinked in confusion as he heard the name. "Are you saying that my namesake was your previous owner? I thought Morcant said Aras was the one he had been tracking to find you."

"THAT IS IT EXACTLY. THE TWO WERE ONE AND THE SAME," the sword revealed. "IN FACT, YOU ARE ONE OF THE FEW PEOPLE TO HAVE EVER WIELDED ME, ASIDE FROM FAESIN HIMSELF."

"That doesn't make sense," Halin admitted.

"IT WILL IN TIME," Lugandihar replied.

"If you are the sharpest thing ever made, what can you

cut through?" Halin asked as he tried to change the conversation to something he might be able to understand.

"I was made as a tool for the God himself. Faesin needed to be able to sculpt and shape the lands of this world. To do that he needed a blade that could cut through anything. I am that blade," the sword said in his mind.

"Correct me if I am wrong, but you are saying that you can cut through anything, right?" Halin asked incredulously.

"Yes, there is nothing that I cannot cleave through," Lugandihar replied.

Halin scratched his head as he thought about what the sword had just said. "I can see what Morcant wants to get his paws on you."

A light warm breeze slowly stirred the fine pebbles around him. With it came the savory aroma of cooking meat and vegetables. Halin's stomach growled loudly.

"There is time for these discussions later," the sword prompted. "You need to eat or you will surely starve to death."

"Agreed, but what makes you think whoever is cooking will give me some of their food?" Halin asked as he stood up carefully.

"I know a great many things, all of which I will eventually share with you," Lugandihar replied. "For now, just trust me. I already promised that I will not let you die."

"Fine," Halin said grudgingly, "but I will keep you to your promise."

The passageway wound on and on as he half walked and half stumbled his way through it. At each turn, he thought he was about to finally be free from the eternal darkness that had been his home for the last few months. Every step seemed to bring him both the promise of warmth and certainty of food.

"Where am I?" Halin asked the blade mentally as he wandered through the darkness.

"You are still in the same cave you found me in, but not for long," the sword replied cryptically.

Several turns and a few dead ends later, Halin stumbled out of the cave's entrance. The light was blinding and forced him to cover his eyes. His legs threatened to give out, but he was finally free.

Clean air filled his lungs as he leaned against the mouth of the cave for support. The trilling sounds of birds filled his ears and he basked in an unbelievable warmth. Something was not right, the last thing he remembered the season of dread had just started. It should not be over this quickly.

"Where did you come from?" A young elf called over to him.

Halin slowly lowered his hand from his face and let his eyes adjust to the sun's relentless light. Green trees and lush grass was the first thing he noticed. Several long moments passed before he could make out where the person was that spoke to him. A few more moments and he could finally see the amazed look on the elf's face.

"Originally, a town called Ellsted," Halin replied as his mouth struggled to form the words. "But more recently, I came from an elven encampment not far from Hornshir."

The elf scoffed and asked, "Why would we have an encampment outside of that dung heap?"

"I don't know. I was told that the general in charge of it had made arrangements to keep travelers safe on their way to the city."

"The only city near here is Kaut," Halin did not need to see the elf's features to know he did not believe him. The disbelief in his tone was more than enough for him to tell.

"Kaut is leagues away from Hornshir," Halin admonished the elf with his indignant tone.

"You are obviously quite lost and delirious," the elf scoffed. "Let's get you back to my camp so you can eat and rest. We can discuss where you are from after that. Besides, we need to leave before the dwarves see you and refuse to finish our stronghold."

ACKNOWLEDGEMENTS

In writing this book I have come to know many people very well, many of which I never caught their names. So I'm going to start off by thanking them first. I believe you know who you are and if you have a doubt, then it is definitely you whom I am referring to. Yes you, right there, the one reading this bit and hoping to see an honorable mention.

Some of the others I did get names for. And while the list is not too terribly long, I would like to get it over with next. A gracious and heartfelt thank you goes out to the following: Poncie Rodriguez, Paul Britton, Trevor Hall, Mel Johnson, and, of course, Victoria Salinas.

Poncie, you are a great artist and I would never have been able to make it through the last gambit of public appearances without you. Your perfect rendering of Tipin attracted so many new readers that I know I will never be able to properly repay you.

Paul Britton, you are probably correct when you say that you are "my number one fan." The little discussions we have about the story as it unfolds for you have been inspiring for me. Our little "1-of-1" endeavors are just as fun for me as they are for you. I feel honored that you were inspired to write possibly my first piece of "fan fiction" and I look forward to reading it.

The obligatory shout out to Liana Serrano and Arley Smith for the idea to separate Shadow Play from Shadow Flight. Without you two, the book would have been a cumbersome failure. Thank you for the initial push to split it. Without this voice of logic, I never would have ever thought about the separation and the series would still be stuck spinning its wheels.

The next group, like the last few times, is the Savage Clan: Derek, Tabitha, Kai, and Keeley. I admit that the bulk was written far away from your home, however, your kindness and collaboration are always needed and provide me a way to reconnect with my muse. My brief retreat to Cassa de Savage this summer really allowed me to recharge by being around good people.

Savages, thank you for the long nights and longer allowances for me to visit. Your support is instrumental. Especially the sanctuary your house represents for me. I also have to thank you for the inspiration of Deracai and Keeta. It is just my way of writing your names into the stories and forever into the hearts of my readers.

John Williams, although still missing in action, your work is visible on the maps and I doubt it will ever change. Look me up. I'd love to work on special projects relating to this series and others.

I know without your blood sweat and tears, I would have had to use the map I created as a kid. Although nostalgic, it wouldn't have been anywhere as nice as yours nor would it have been as cool looking.

The next group of people I need to mention are my beta readers. Sorida Gallegos, Marc Tucker, Derek Savage, and David Camden-Britton. All of you helped in your own special ways to flesh out the story.

Derek, what can I say that hasn't already been said. I'm glad my writing still proves to be an inspiration for you and your family. I hope you fully realize how much I have come to rely on your keen mind and creative input. The fact that we can chat about either your stories or mine and feel more bolstered. Our joint resolve is only a testament to your abilities as a fellow writer and friend.

David, or should I say Groovy, congrats on the new job at the University of Idaho. I can only hope you can still be available for future projects of mine. As always your grammar requirements are a godsend to me and I am forever indebted to you for it. Your desire to better my writing through technique and description are always on my mind, even as I pen these acknowledgments.

There are a few others that I need to mention. They are the wonderfully creative folks I met at Modesto Con this last July. Victoria Salinas thank you for putting me in touch with Douggary Grant, Perry Louis, Camille Wright, and Ashley Fee.

Douggary and Perry, you guys are a team for an author to know. Between Douggary's connections with the cosplay community for possible cover models and Perry's unique skills with a camera, I don't think the cover redesign would have happened.

Ashley, thank you for letting me use your costume design and unique patch for Keeta. It perfectly matched what I had in mind for her and the fact you already had it made was priceless.

Camille, you were a pleasure to work with. Because of your ability to get into character and your zeal for modeling, I was able to get two, three if you count the coloring shift, out of our photoshoot.

The final group that I want to thank is a rather large one. My loyal fans that have helped push me to have more releases and further development of the characters and their stories. Thank you for your continued support.

Thank you all.

About the Author

A Reiki Master and internationally-acclaimed author, John Harrison lives in central California and enjoys spending time with his family when he is not trying his hand at literary endeavors.

His current projects include: *Shadow Guard* (the fourth novel in the Shadow Saga), *Sebanik*, and *Bella Rouge* (a standalone novel based on "Unholy Trinity"— a short story published in Michael Moorcock's New Worlds Magazine).

John has been writing since he was in elementary school. His family and friends all love his imagination and his ability to weave a good story in a very short time. His professional writing has ranged from business processes to short stories and now novels.

For more information about John, or to find other works released by him, check him out on the web:

www.amazon.com/author/johnaharrison

http://jalbertharrison.wix.com/author-page

www.ingramcontent.com/pod-product-compliance
Lightning Source LLC
Chambersburg PA
CBHW070826190726
48292CB00006B/2125